Queen to Ashes

Black Dawn Series

Book II

Mallory McCartney

HEIR OF LIES

Copyright © Mallory McCartney 2020

All rights reserved.
No part of this publication may be reproduced, stored in a retrieval system, or transmitted, in any form or by any means, electronic, mechanical, photocopying, recording or otherwise, nor translated into a machine language, without the written permission of the publisher.

Condition of sale
This book was sold subject to the condition that it shall not, by way of trade or otherwise, be lent, re-sold, hired out or otherwise circulated in any form of binding or cover other than that in which it was published and without a similar condition including this condition being imposed on the subsequent purchaser.

ISBN: 978-1-9992547-5-9

The moral right of the author had been asserted.
This was a work of fiction. Any resemblance to actual persons, living or dead, events and organizations was purely coincidental.

Cover Art by Cora Graphics
Shutterstock.com
Formatted by Rebecca Garcia at Dark Wish Designs
Map art by Lizard Ink Maps

MM BOOKS

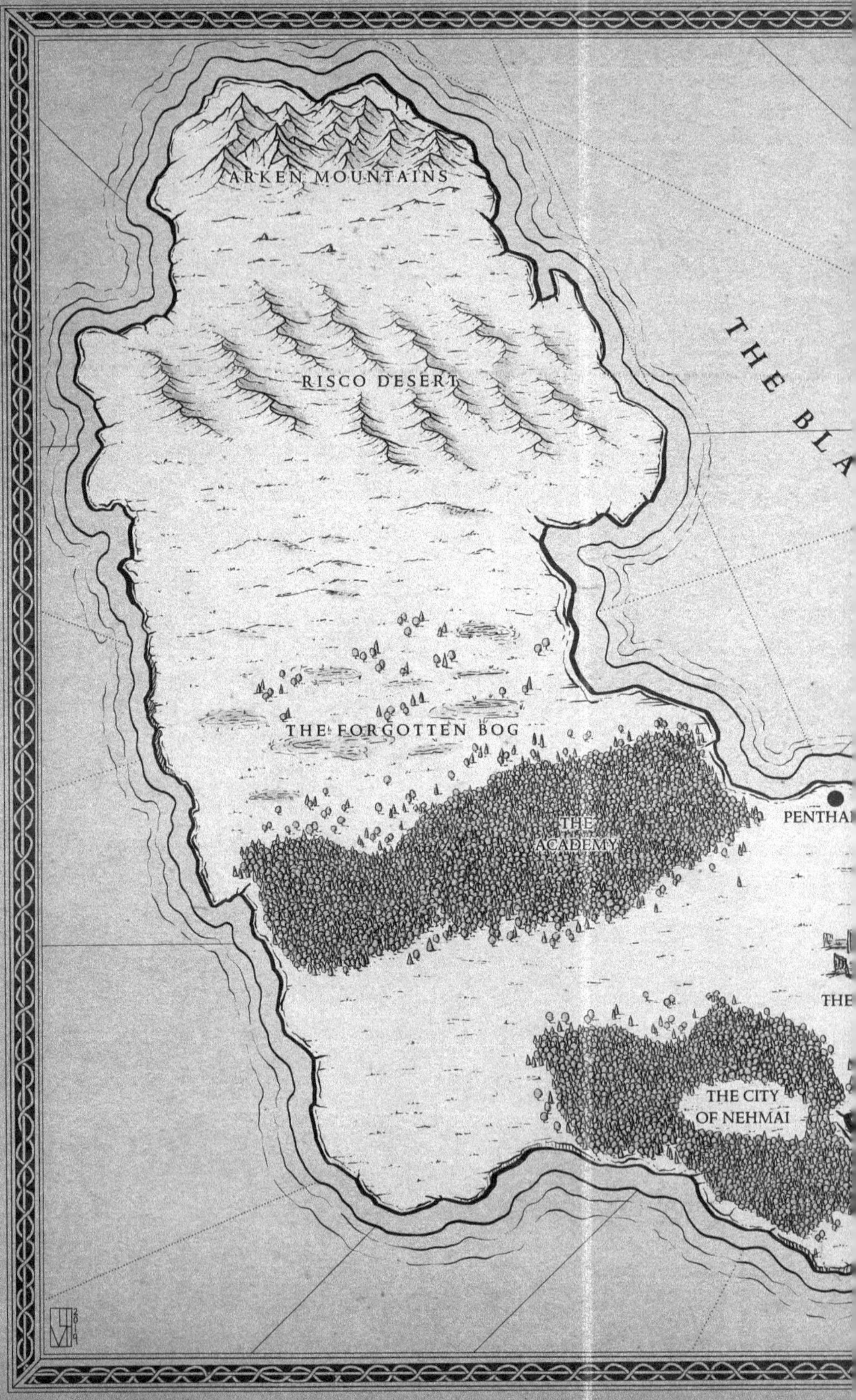
ARKEN MOUNTAINS
RISCO DESERT
THE FORGOTTEN BOG
THE ACADEMY
THE CITY OF NEHMAI

KIERO

THE SHATTERED ISLES

1. HARBOUR OF NEWSOLL
2. TERDES HARBOUR DISTRICT
3. HRISTE
4. OAKLAND WHARF DISTRICT
5. DURDOVER PORT

Table of Contents

Prologue 1
Chapter One 4
Chapter Two 9
Chapter Three 15
Chapter Four 25
Chapter Five 29
Chapter Six 49
Chapter Seven 57
Chapter Eight 67
Chapter Nine 76
Chapter Ten 80
Chapter Eleven 95
Chapter Twelve 106
Chapter Thirteen 124
Chapter Fourteen 136
Chapter Fifteen 150
Chapter Sixteen 180
Chapter Seventeen 187
Chapter Eighteen 203
Chapter Nineteen 210

Chapter Twenty	227
Chapter Twenty-One	239
Chapter Twenty-Two	254
Chapter Twenty-Three	269
Chapter Twenty-Four	281
Chapter Twenty-Five	293
Chapter Twenty-Six	307
Chapter Twenty-Seven	310
Chapter Twenty-Eight	312
Chapter Twenty-Nine	314
Chapter Thirty	317
Chapter Thirty-One	325
Chapter Thirty-Two	334
Acknowledgements	337
About the Author	338

Queen to Ashes

Black Dawn Series
Book II

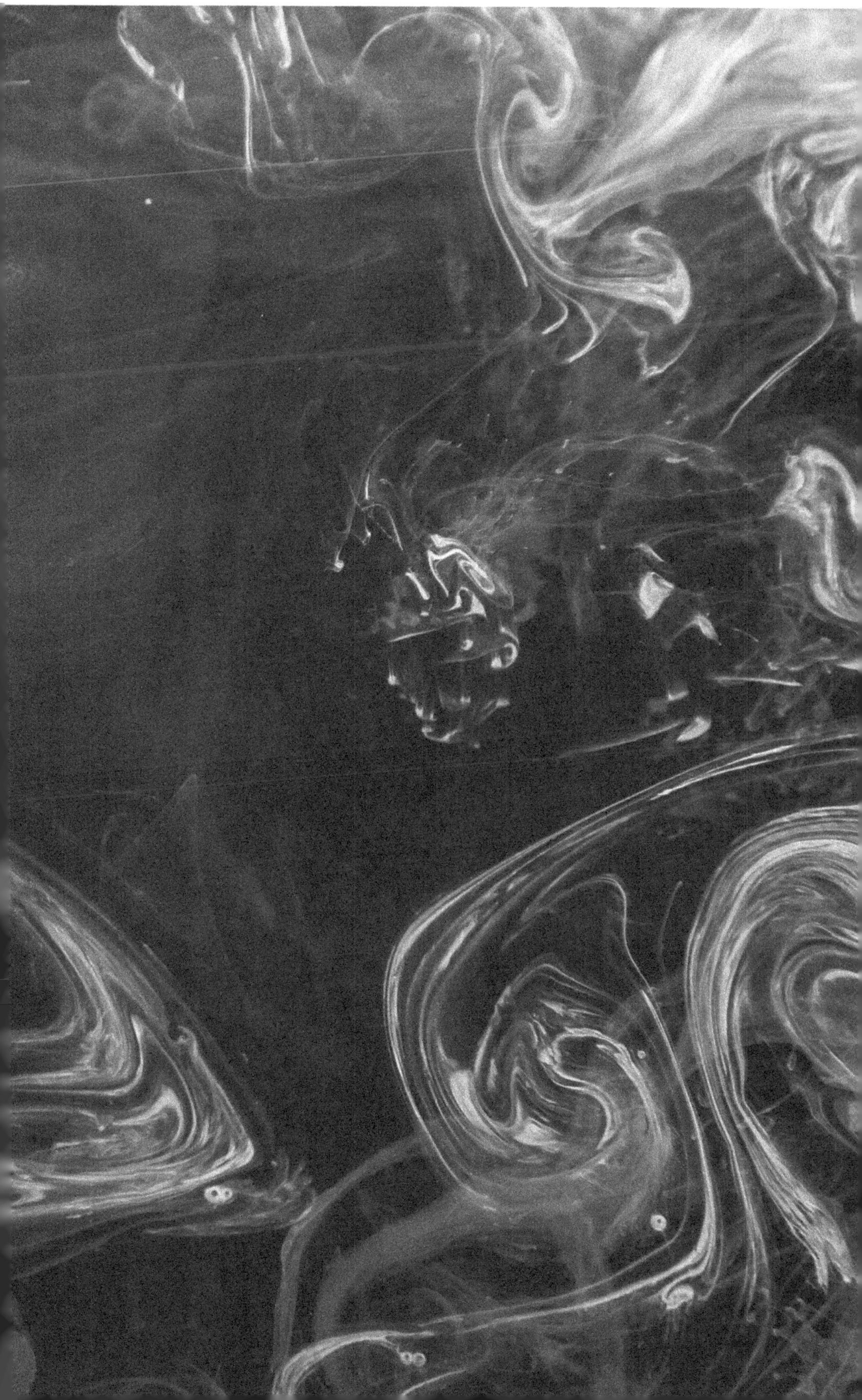

*For everyone who is following their heart and fueling their passions.
This is for you.*

Part One

Naithe Warrior

PROLOGUE

The Oilean

The sisters knew their world, Daer, had been born from the marrow of nightmares: A flicker of shadows and a drumming of lust was the first sluggish recognition of a memory they had. Their rage was cultivated from the echoes of screams, a private orchestra just for them, building a woven masterpiece—crashing, consuming, inspiring, haunting.

It stirred within them, in this in-between place, and like a vessel, existence and sustenance carried them on. For years, they waited, feeding and growing. The shadows grew, and their minds and bodies did as well. The fear of the world waged, igniting them. Then, in fractured, splintering light, it all changed.

They had been *found*. No longer just a pulse of darkness. No longer caged. And as that man grinned viciously at them, they knew everything from then on would be different.

The sister that had been once called Lasair tilted her head, ripping herself out of the memory. She inhaled the scents on the wind, a web of stories that she sifted through, searching for the one they sought. Her bloodlust was a wild, burning thing, and she quelled it. They couldn't win this world if their king made rash decisions. No, they had to play this game of lies and betrayal until they moved their pawns exactly where they needed them, leaving their path clear... Then nothing could stop them.

Hissing in pleasure, her magic flared, burning and consuming: destroying worlds had always been an exchange of energy; even in Daer. The sisters killed and stole the magic of the fey for their master until Daer was nothing but an empty shell and their king had been made invincible.

After the world lay barren, the sisters were sent searching for another world to feed their king and ensure his immortal reign.

Rolling her neck, Lasair's bones cracked as she walked toward the other Oilean. The wind now hinted at the change of seasons, and she knew they were running out of time, that their king was running out of time.

She stopped, about to snap at the other Oilean that they needed to decide on how they would end Brokk Foster when she felt it. They all froze as they felt the chord snap; the dark magic that had made up Brokk Foster's living doppelganger was gone. They had carved him, shaped him, broke him... Lasair had banked on the fact that they had never failed before.

Tilting their heads in unison, they felt the dark magic bleed out from Brokk's doppelganger like a dying star: Strange. For the first time, someone had defeated one of their servants. The sisters shivered against that fading light, growling as the emptiness replaced it. Their beautiful, dangerous creation had been destroyed.

"The girl is stronger than we thought," the sister to the far left hissed, looking behind them to where the false king's city lay. "But not strong enough to face us. She wouldn't stand a chance."

They paced, ashes softly floating around them as the ground became scorched. But one sister stalled, looking to the horizon as if seeing past the trees, past the flickering shadows in the forest, to where the demons that resided within their land grew and flourished.

"We must do this ourselves, sisssters." They stopped, looking to her as she rolled her neck, bones popping and cracking, her pale skin drawn. "Emory Fae must be stopped. They *all* must be stopped. Our King left us with the task of preparing this world for him. We have wasted time—no more spells. No more hiding. Not while they can still find out the truth."

Whispers cut through the wind, and Lasiar tilted her head, breathing it in. This world would be theirs. This world, its power, would be harnessed.

The three sisters started to giggle—first a hiccup of a laugh here and there—until soon the forest was filled with their madness; and in cracking bones and ripping of sinew, their limbs elongated and grew. The Oilean all looked toward the Draken Mountains and the sinister force that had seeded there: They shot off, loping through the fading light, sparks chasing at their heels. Lasiar led the way.

In the fading daylight, she hissed in pleasure as night started to sweep in. The woods blurred around her, and she started to count down the seconds, the minutes, the hours until she sank her teeth into their necks. Until she would kill Emory Fae and Brokk Foster.

CHAPTER ONE

Adair

Adair Stratton tugged his button-down jacket tighter around him, trying to block the wind from his lookout post. The vastness of the sky was consuming, a strange energy clinging on the night air. The churning dark clouds cast a purplish hue, bleeding with the softness created from the moon. The stars shone between the pockets, obscuring the scene and making it beautiful.

Far below him, the Ruined City lay in its grave, quiet and still, the broken buildings reminding him of splintered bones. The once thriving capital of Kiero—Sarthaven—was nothing more than a whispered memory to him now. His gaze wandered to the edge of the Draken Mountain range, the wildness of the Noctis woods flourishing, the purple hues of the trees pulsing like gems.

It had taken *years* to build his kingdom, shackling Kiero in fear. The people that now lived in the Draken Mountains valued their lives and were loyal to him.

Sighing, the darkness in his veins was smothered ever so slightly as he breathed in the crisp air. In this brief and flickering moment of clarity, his mind wandered to the girl who was locked in the cells of his kingdom, waiting for him: Emory Fae, the Princess of Kiero.

Popping his collar up, he scowled. Under the blanket of night, he could trace back to the man he used to be when Emory had known him-an echo of his humanity. Thinking of her, he could see the splaying of memories come back to life all around him, of his friends, of the Academy. And it was in these sparse moments of lucidity, he allowed himself to remember, relishing it, pushing back that yearning for destruction, pushing back the voices, trying to lock *them* away.

And like every other night, he lost.

The wind howled, making the edges of his coat and pants tug upward, his hair standing on end from the sudden chill. His heart raced as the smooth voices filled his consciousness.

"Adair, this kingdom is yours. Make her bow, make her bleed... make her pay for what she has done."

He closed his eyes for a beat, digging his fingernails into his palms.

"Why do you wait? You know what you want. What you have always wanted."

Images were thrown at him; so quick and enthralling, they swept his breath away: The inky crown, embedded with roses and thorns, lay delicately on top of Emory's ebony hair. Memphis Carter, the once commander of the Black Dawn Rebellion, bowed, pleading for his life as Adair smirked above him. His darkness had whisked away any trace of rebellion and Emory was by his side as they watched the world continue to burn until it was only them.

Always for *them*.

Adair snarled, then said, "Leave me alone."

Their snickers bounced around him, their whispers tugging at his heart.

"*Do not falter now, our Mad King. You have come so far, achieved so much. The binds your father tried to keep you in, you broke. The ones the Academy kept you in, you turned to ash.*

"*We are a team. We know the desires of your soul, how you revel in watching the world shudder in your reign. You have always been more. A reckoning force that no one can stop. Can never stop.*"

He became still, his muscles taut. Opening his eyes, his gaze fell a thousand miles away, to where the Academy had stood. Where a boy that once wanted to explore the world and not shackle it had lived.

He knew both were dead.

Ice coursed through his body, spreading through his core faster than he could register. His pulse slowed, the roaring emotions he felt slowing as well. Darkness encased him, pulling him down, down, *down*. Locking him away, roaring, snarling, and clawing at him.

A slow exhale escaped from between his dry lips, and as he stood, every movement was precise, a predatory grace. Flicking his gaze below him once more, instead of the dark beauty that he was met with earlier, the world around him was bleeding. Dark, black blood gushed from the mountainside, thickly caking the field and the Ruined City. Echoes of screams filled the air, and Adair was reminded of his bloodshed, of his control and power.

"*Do not disappoint us, our King.*"

The corners of his lips tugged upward as he whispered to the wind, "I won't."

Inside, he screamed, ripping at his mind, battering against the iron wall, only to be drowned entirely by it.

He turned, walking back into his world, each step anchoring him to his intentions: *Make them bow and make them pay. Make her pay.*

He didn't look as he stepped off the side of the cliff, freefalling. He plummeted, the wind howling, the cool night air stinging his skin. He laughed, relishing in the exhilaration of adrenaline before he was wrenched up, his body breaking down into particles of smoke and darkness.

Cutting through the sky, he didn't think, he just reacted to the power inside of him, and everything else bled away.

Arching, he sliced through the clouds, moisture collecting around him like glinting crystals before they exploded, and he shifted down, racing toward the mountain range. The moon bathed his path in luminescent light, and it was mere seconds before he glided through the wall, through stone and marble. The smoothness of the throne room's granite muffling his footfalls and causing the guards on their rotation to jump at his arrival.

"You all seem uneasy," Adair taunted.

They bowed their heads, their low murmurs cutting over one another.

"My King, we weren't expecting you."

"We have never suffered losses like the ones the rebels inflicted in the stadium last week. We should spill the heir's blood now—in retaliation, my King."

"What is our course of action?"

"Enough!" he snapped, his cold voice bouncing off the walls and silencing them instantly. He looked towards his throne, smooth, each curve carved precisely, the bones of monsters and humans long forgotten inlaid to rest in it.

Taking a steadying breath, he studied each guard, before stating, "You will do your duties and leave the Rebellion to me. As for the girl, bring her tomorrow, along with the other prisoner. Each decision I make has a purpose. Never forget that."

Shifting uneasily, the guards paled in the soft light, swallowing nervously. Their silence was answer enough.

Beginning to pace, he snapped, "Now, leave me. Return to your stations."

Bowing low to him, Adair watched them leave, each footfall a distant tick against his mind until the stillness of the night filled him, and he was alone once more.

Striding forward, he threw himself on his throne made of bones, legs hanging over the edges, hands interlaced behind his head. Far above him, the stars glinted down, the sky showing him the thousands of uncharted miles in between space and time.

And he thought of the girl who had defied it all.

Chewing his lip, he started to count down the seconds, the minutes, and the hours until he was alone with Emory. And they would both see what side of him would decide her fate.

CHAPTER TWO
Emory

All she could hear was buzzing. Tight, unrelenting buzzing. The world dipped, and she was a ghost amongst the living.

Her mind screamed that she was going into shock as the color drained from her skin, as her limbs trembled harder. Her body betrayed her for the briefest of seconds as Adair looked at her hungrily, his dark gaze ravaging her.

The room seemed to tilt, and her mind felt thick and constricted. The bloodied sword was still in her hand, and Brokk's body splayed out lifelessly between them: Life and Death. Love and Loss. Light and Dark. This is the divide her life had taken, and one that she was completely and utterly lost in. Suffocated in.

What had she done?

What. Had. She. Done?

Before Emory could take another look, to convince herself that it wasn't him—it couldn't have been—a strong hand gripped her arm and Adair said something she didn't register. Then, she was ushered out with the promise of tomorrow on his gaunt lips, and the burly guard led her away from the king.

The door shut, sealing away the gory scene.

Breath lodging in her throat, Emory tried to adjust to the world around her. It was numbing, her senses overloaded, the bustle of Adair's world seeming too sharp and loud as they moved through it. Her pulse roared, and beneath the grime and blood she held on, trying not to give in to the panic tearing through her.

Walk. Breathe. Survive. Make him believe you want him. Then end him. Walk. Breathe. Survive. Survive.

The guard was silent as he pulled her down the twisting hallways, past the prying eyes and chasing whispers.

She could barely register what had happened. And again, that mind-numbing ringing droned out her surroundings.

In the arena, her adrenaline had smeared his edges, and he was just a deranged king on a broken throne. But in those few moments in his chamber, during their charged verbal dance, she had been so overwhelmed because his presence had unravelled a part of her long forgotten. That out of anyone else, he had brought snippets of blurry memories to surface: The feeling of recognition, of friendship. Of betrayal, of loyalty, of confusion and pain.

Swallowing hard, she walked onward, pushing the king from her mind; allowing that heavy nothingness to blanket her, to numb her further.

The bath water poured into the clawed tub and churned, making several eddies in the water. Standing rigidly, Emory watched the spout gush. Too fast. Too loud. The frothy surface reflected the paint flecking the gold and red of the walls. She blinked, turning slowly.

In her chambers, a fire blazed in its hearth, bookcases lined the stone wall, and a huge four-poster bed waited for her. Flush to the sidewall, a closet full of clothing beckoned to her as well. It was lavish, a place fit for someone the Mad King potentially *wanted* to keep alive. Not for a prisoner. She shook with adrenaline.

For the time being, *he had believed her.*

Clenching her hands, Emory looked down to see they were caked with blood. Clawing at her skin, she tried to scrub it off, only making it smear. All Emory could see was the flash of steel, the spattering of red, and the crunch of bone. Brokk's golden eyes, echoing of memories and loyalty before everything distorted and twisted.

A strangled sound bubbled from her lips as she slid to the floor, not caring about holding her broken pieces together anymore.

They had brought *Brokk* in. The same curve of his lips, same flecked golden eyes. At first glance, it had been, without a doubt, him. All it took was one second: His golden hair turned black; his eyes bled into nothingness, and his edges blurred. Her instinct had screamed imposter. Anger had filled her, and she remembered seeing red. How dare someone try to use the illusion of Brokk against her!

But doubt now lay thickly on her mind and heart. Was she one hundred percent certain that it hadn't been Brokk? She was living in a world where magic and deception intertwined, and Emory knew she was vulnerable. Closing her eyes, she took in a deep breath.

The sword had felt like lead in her hands, and with a flash of steel glinting in the firelight, she had *killed him.*

Standing to turn the water off, her vision twisted and churned. Nausea swept over Emory as she barely made it to the toilet before her stomach emptied. Cold sweat coated her body as she retched and retched.

Gasping after she stopped and wiping her mouth with the back of her hand, hot tears streaked down her face. Biting her shaking knuckles, Emory screamed: The sharp, metallic taste of blood filled her mouth, and she ripped her hand away, her breath coming in ragged gulps.

She was in a lethal dance between her past and the truth; between love and loyalty. Closing her eyes for a moment, she willed herself to see all their faces: Memphis. Brokk. Alby. Azarius. Even Nyx. She hoped they were safe and had found time to grieve for the Rebellion. And as for Nyx, Emory hoped that she had time to explain her actions, that she didn't lose her only family.

Standing, she shook as she took off her bloodied and grim covered clothes then slipped into the steamy waters. It instantly turned pink from the blood. Taking the creamy bar of soap, Emory scrubbed herself until her skin was raw. Her mind spun in the harsh play-by-play: The real Brokk coming to Adair's doorstep would warrant his death. Would Brokk follow in Emory's footsteps in being dangerously reckless?

Inhaling and closing her eyes, she dunked underwater, allowing herself to free float. The water was steaming hot, loosening the knots in her muscles, unravelling her tension, but those whispers that had chased her finally caught up.

Emory Fae, liar, betrayer. She wouldn't have been able to go through with her plan if the Rebellion had known; Memphis would have tried to stop her. Her heart gave a painful clench, and her lungs were on fire as she burst upward, gasping for oxygen, splashing water everywhere, before slipping back under.

Those final days and nights in the cell were filled with terror. Darkness had seeped from every angle, and her mind was the main target. Memory after memory had come to her in her sleep, in the prison of Adair's kingdom.

And she remembered the frigid air circling around her as she pled with Memphis and Brokk to come with her. And how Memphis had taken away her memories of Kiero, of her life right before she was plunged into the unknown world. She had been *so* wrong about her mysterious shifter. Brokk had been twisted by a best friend's jealousy, and she had complied, not allowing him to prove what he had been to her—what he *meant* to her.

Busting through the surface of the water again, her lungs screamed for mercy. Rubbing her eyes, Emory sighed deeply. A shiver ran down her spine at the thought of Adair somewhere nearby-the snippets of her life slowly being pieced together.

She would play her part flawlessly. She would pass these trials, and then as Queen, she would free Kiero, liberate the Rebellion, and destroy *Adair*.

If she survived.

If she believed she had a running chance to overcome Adair and find a way to get to the Rebellion.

If. If. *If.*

Standing, she got out of the tub when she heard the clattering in her room. Wrapping herself in a soft towel, Emory poked her head around the corner, seeing the back of a woman fleeing her room, shutting the door firmly behind her.

Stalking toward her bed, Emory eyed where a small tray of sliced meats, cheeses, and fruits now lay on her nightstand. Her mouth dropped opened and she lunged toward the tray, shoveling it in. She couldn't remember the last time she had eaten.

"Holy shit, this is good," she mumbled to herself knowing she wouldn't be any use half-starved.

Finishing the tray, Emory sighed, flopping on the bed. The whispers of her mind lured her into a restless sleep filled with dreams of dark eyes and steel cages that tried to keep her locked away.

And then there was herself, never fast enough to outrun any of them.

Chapter Three

Brokk

He was a lot of things: time manipulator, soldier, shapeshifter. But as he skidded to a stop, his fur matted and sides heaving, Brokk realized, in this moment, he was just a broken man.

The scene was splayed before him, slashing into his core and devouring any hope he had clung to. Ash coated the once rolling hill, and where the Academy once stood, all that was left was the skeletal frame of his home, laid bare for the world to see. The air tasted of blood-stale, old blood.

Panting, he licked his maws and lowered his muzzle to sniff the crusted ground. Scents assaulted him, Adair's men and Nyx's scent the most prominent, and he allowed the sorrow to flood in.

The Academy, its empty windows now exposed, brick and metal scattered amongst the ruin and ash. Flashes, ghosts of the past, tugged on his consciousness, and growling, he shook his head, pleading with them to leave him alone. But as he numbly forced his paws forward, his nails digging into the scorched ground, they struck him anyways.

Moving slowly and deliberately, his thoughts were relentless. These woods, ancient and unyielding, had been his fascination and safe hold. Flashbacks of the last time he had seen Emory as she remembered him and not as Memphis portrayed him, came to him next-of a time before Memphis had placed a hand gingerly on her temple and erased her memories: Of her parents, of Memphis, of *him*. And he had allowed her a taste of another life, of freedom.

Shuddering, he stalled. Were they all lost to him now, after everything he had fought for, had sacrificed? It had killed him to give Emory distance, to be a shadow of her actions.

Brokk snarled under his breath, his frustration building. At the time lost, at not taking the chance to find his way back to her. His fur bristled as he threw back his head, his howl lamenting and resonating up to the dying light of the day. He had been too late.

Numbly, he entered the front door of the Academy, wires and cords exposed in the fading light, the frame barely standing. His hackles rose against at the scent that greeted him: Death. He continued into the hallway, growling lowly. Everything was destroyed; everything was *burnt*.

Red smears covered the cement walls, Adair's signature mark. He stopped, staring at the jagged slash. It was red, like the blood on his hands: His lies, his passion, his shadows, his heart. He sometimes forgot that this madness was born from a broken boy who had dreamt of a different life.

Shaking his head, he loped toward the empty elevator then skidded to a halt and looked down the shaft. The darkness prevented him from seeing anything, and with a deep breath, he threw himself forward, freefalling. The wind howled, and everything was disorientating. Landing hard, several bones cracked and broke; white hot pain flared through him, and he lay panting as the bones healed, and his eyes adjusted.

He stepped forward and froze.

Decay and destruction surrounded him, suffocating him. He gagged on the scent that overwhelmed him as he took in what was left of the Black Dawn Rebellion. Destroyed. His friends. His *family*, lost in the darkness, mixed in with Adair's soldiers.

Dead, their ashes and bones remaining.

His heart throbbed with each loss: *Jaxson. Wyatt. Bryd.* He moved silently, a demon amongst them. *I should have been here. To help them, to fight with them. And to die with them.*

Brokk's whine echoed off the stone walls, lost in the hallways.

Stalking toward Memphis's room next, he feared the worse. He had caught his friend's scent and *hers*. It was only a matter of minutes before he stood outside the broken frame, trying to make sense of what he smelled.

Nudging the door, it slowly cracked open, bits of it breaking off in ash: The bunker had been upturned, and the bookshelf violently moved over to the side, exposing steps leading down into a tunnel. *A secret tunnel. An escape.* His heart pounded, and he quickly shifted back to his human form, breathing raggedly. Catching his reflection in a broken mirror beside the bookshelf Brokk frowned, steadying himself. His wounds from the Oilean had healed, leaving scars that roped around his biceps, shoulders, and neck. A constant reminder of the torture they had inflicted, his terror never truly leaving him.

Grimly ripping his gaze from his reflection, Brokk set his resolve. For the first time since bringing Emory back, he dove deep into the pool of power that raged to escape him; ice ran through his veins. His head pounded as the world spun, and he was spiraling, shadows and whispers circling him.

Suddenly, he was back in the past, and he opened his eyes to see his best friend, Memphis, standing before him dressed in formal wear, pushing Emory down the staircase, frantically urging her to go. Her eyes were wide, her face flushed, fear and defiance oozing from her. Brokk turned his head toward the screams of his dying friends lost in time then watched as the bookcase slid shut, Emory frozen, her heart breaking in her eyes.

Memphis turned around, running through him, and opened the doors, rushing back toward the fight. He looked lethal, a deadliness in his eyes Brokk had never seen before. He roared for Nyx, and the memories blurred, Brokk's heart breaking entirely. He had to hold on.

He saw Memphis and Nyx. Shaking, the same amulet hung around her neck the night Nyx had stabbed him.

Nyx cried, "Memphis, I never thought...."

Memphis's silence was icy as he launched attack after attack—an uncaged beast—and threw himself at Nyx, rage moving him with one purpose. To kill. They danced around each other, lunging, growling, Nyx parrying each blow, her muscles trembling as sparks flew. He watched Jaxson fight for his life in the background.

Memory slid into memory, and he could do nothing as Jaxson died, as Memphis and Nyx were captured. It wasn't until the screams died down that the remaining soldiers flooded the hallway, binding the two of them. Memphis was unconscious by this point. The soldiers split up as his friends were dragged away. Two stayed behind, casually lighting a fire in the dining hall.

Walking back toward Memphis's room, Adair's soldiers stopped and looked, commenting, "Where do you think she went? Couldn't have gotten too far..."

Brokk stood in horror as he watched them search the room, flames growing larger and moving faster, smoke billowing down the hallway and engulfing the Academy. They found the secret tunnel in a matter of minutes, following Emory into the darkness as the edges of his vision flickered, and he was brought back in the present, into his world of ashes.

Choking on his breath, bile rose in his throat. He held his stomach as he retched. They had been butchered, unaware as Nyx led Adair straight into their rebellion. But they had survived- some had survived. An inhuman growl ripped from him as he ran toward the tunnel, shifting mid-flight into his wolf form, barrelling down into the passage.

He left his past behind in that moment, leaving the Academy, leaving his friends, leaving his soul. A spark had lit up within him; fire consuming him with each pounding step as he promised to himself he would kill Adair. He would tear his throat out with his bare teeth, and that would be a merciful end for what he had done.

The emptiness resonated through him, each loss making a hole in his heart until it was shattered, and he was lost.

Blindly, he ran faster, further into the depths of the world. Dampness surrounded him, and he couldn't focus on where he was going, couldn't focus on the scents, couldn't focus on anything but the burn throughout his body as he pushed himself. Dull colors blurred around him as he soared, curving with each turn.

His thoughts flickered with each movement: Emory, Memphis, Alby, and Nyx. They were alive. His fears reared to life, every worst-case scenario burning images into his mind. He snapped at the thought. Nyx had brought this upon them, but she wasn't stupid enough to not know how destructive Adair was. He had wiped out their world, their families. Nyx's motive was love—the thought of losing Memphis. She had sold out everything, *their cause*, to have Memphis to herself.

Maybe Brokk would kill her first.

The dampness of the tunnel encompassed him as he galloped faster. The torture he endured with the Oilean was nothing compared to this. Skidding to a stop, he panted when he realized he had come to a sloping incline that met with a ladder popping out into the grassy land overhead. His grief gripped at him, latching on, threatening to drag him down. *Take a breath.*

He inhaled weeks-old scents trying to figure out what had happened. She wasn't wounded, but the soldiers' scents were still strong. There had been a fight until... He growled deeply. Pacing back and forth, he inhaled again, trying desperately to make sense of what he smelled. Another human he did not recognize was mixed in. The stranger's ability oozed onto everything, marking it with its strong scent. Whoever it was had saved her.

Throwing his weight back onto his haunches, Brokk propelled himself upward, scaling the ladder with ease in his wolf form, then landing onto the grass outside. Lowering his nose, he followed the scents once more, painting a picture for him. Emory had been flung onto the ground. The stranger, a human male, had caused a distraction. He stopped and followed the deep grooved indents into the earth until he stumbled onto the decayed bodies of the soldiers.

Galloping back to the edge of the forest Brokk looked longingly toward it. Emory had trusted him enough in that moment to follow him, to allow him to help her. *Others had survived.* His heart raced at an uneven pace. Adair had *not* put out Kiero's light. Not yet.

Stepping forward, to the edge of the woods, his hair stood on end, his body freezing. The world was bathed in golden hues with red-tinged edges, and the sun quickly moved lower in the sky. Shifting back to his human form, he sat on the sloping earth.

For the first time in years, he watched the sun glow in brilliance, reflecting its crimson hues on everything it touched. His breath came in ragged heaves, and dropping, he hugged his knees, caving into himself. Tears blurred his vision as he allowed the utter hollow feeling to overtake him: Being trained as a soldier, he would pick himself up and keep going.

He would not fail to save the people that made up his world.

He couldn't lose Emory again.

He would not let their spark sputter and die.

Above all, he would not let his friends' deaths be in vain. If after all these years he gave into defeat now, it would have been all for nothing.

Swiping his bloodied hands across his cheeks, he watched the horizon as the last of the sunlight burned over the horizon, casting shadows over the Draken Mountains and the Ruined City before darkness tinged the edges of their world.

Standing on shaking legs, he turned to look at the scorched remains of The Academy one last time.

Bowing his head, he whispered into the air, "It was our home. I loved and lost there. We all did. I hope you all find peace beyond this world." Taking a steadying breath, his voice cracked when he added, "I'm so sorry. I should have been there with you." The words tasted heavy and like ash as they rolled over his tongue.

He placed a scarred hand over his heart, and then lurched forward, every human aspect of him shattering as he gave in to his beast. His paws soon thundered over the ground, and he inhaled deeply, catching Emory's scent and allowing it to overtake everything he was. He would track her first and bring her back.

The sun dipped further into the horizon as he ran, brilliant highlights blending the hues. He allowed the thought to propel him forward, always toward her. No matter what stood in-between them.

Their world was changing; he could taste it in the air, feel it beneath his paws. The night air was heavy as Brokk wove in between the trees. He didn't know how many hours had passed, but he pushed himself harder and *harder*, relishing in the burn of his muscles, in the ragged catch in his breath. He had followed the stranger's relentless pace.

Snarling, he soared over a fallen tree, the ground thundering from his force. *You could have helped them.* Brokk pinned his ears back, baring his teeth. *The Academy has fallen.* He ran faster, his golden fur a streaking comet in the night. *Your family is dead.* He was consumed by the beating of his heart, by the forest and his blurred surroundings. His demons and guilt chased at his heels, but he would always be faster.

The ground sloped upward as he scaled the hill, grinding to a stop for a moment. The forest was thinning, and he could see the skeletal remains of the Ruined City. But his gaze fixated on one thing, the Draken Mountains behind them—and *Adair*.

A sharp whine escaped him, then he was flying, following their scents straight toward The Mad King's realm, his hopes melting away into the night, flaring for a fleeting second before they were stripped away, one by one.

QUEEN TO ASHES

Hitting the Ruined City limits, he didn't stop, couldn't look too closely at the life and culture that had been stripped of Sarthaven. Once upon a time, it was the heart of Kiero. He wove through the crumbling buildings, the streets a blur as he made sharp turns, their journey flashing before his eyes.

Until he stopped.

Shifting back, sweat plastering his skin, golden hair slicking to his forehead, his wild gaze hungrily consumed the empty space before him. A stream of harsh curses flowed from him as he sat on his heels, cupping his head in his hands. It didn't make sense. Peeking through his fingers, he willed the bloodstains in the abandoned building to disappear or to erase the scents he had catalogued in his mind and the story they told.

The blatant truth stared him in the face. The truth he couldn't believe.

Baring his teeth, he slammed a fist into the concrete, all his knuckles breaking in a fluid moment, pain momentarily freezing him.

He knew he could dip into that well of power, to trace back through the memories in time. To see it play out before his very eyes. But he couldn't bring himself to. Feeling his broken bones pop and heal themselves, Brokk allowed himself one second and a harsh breath cut through his lungs. His limbs shook, and he cast a look back at the Draken Mountain Range, willing it not to be true.

His anger lashed out then, igniting him, and every aspect of his core yearned for a fight, especially with Adair and his doppelganger that had also ventured past this city into the heart of darkness. But this man and Emory had gone willingly. Fear mixed in with determination drenched their scents, and one scent that had left the city cut into him. And it wasn't Emory's.

Chewing his lower lip, he looked at the stain and back at the mountain range. Then, he was sprinting, his boots pounding against the ground, leaving the city of ghosts behind him. With a howl, he shifted mid-run, his wolf form pushing him forward again, racing toward Memphis and Nyx. Toward the stranger and the other scents of *people* he led.

If Emory had chosen to go to Adair, he couldn't follow her. He could never beat Adair alone. The decision to find the rest of the Rebellion weighed heavily, as he left Emory in the clutches of their enemy, along with his heart.

CHAPTER FOUR

Azarius

The moonlight kissed her skin, bathing Lana in its silver light as it poured through the window. Azarius had no idea what time it was, and frankly, he didn't care. He wished to be locked in this moment forever, spending endless nights with the woman he loved. Smiling, he watched as she stirred in her sleep, murmuring at things unseen to him. He brought his lips to her shoulder, gently and slowly covering her body with a trail of kisses.

She sighed, waking and cracking an eye open, groaning. "Do you know what sleep is?"

He grinned at her in the darkness. "Not with you around," he murmured.

She gently brought her hand to rest against his chest, stopping him. "Are you finally going to tell me what happened?" Lana, his love, his other half, could read him like an open book.

He ran a hand through his fiery red hair. "Lana, you know *exactly—*"

"No, Azarius, I want to hear it from you." She waited, her caramel eyes blazing in the night. Pinning him with that stare, he knew he didn't have a choice.

Sighing, he leaned back, propping himself up with his elbows as he searched for the right words. "I made a mistake."

Her eyes ignited him like a thousand suns, flashing in the darkness. She of all people understood better than most.

They survived as refugees for six years in Azarius's old village, Pentharrow. Morgan found them in time, before Adair's soldiers advanced. It was timely on her part; Azarius shivered in the night. Without Morgan and her dark magic, they would have all died.

He would never forget that night, how she had advanced from the night, a demon bathed in red. She had locked eyes with him, and he knew from that one look that everything would change. As a stranger, he had advanced upon her at once. He was the only security in their small town. He was a fighter, a survivor, and he would protect his people. *She had known.* He had demanded where she had come from. Her retort had been, *"Your savior."*

"Azarius?"

He shook his head, coming out of the memory and taking Lana in. Since that night, Morgan had proclaimed that unless she was made leader, they would meet their end. She was trained in magic, in witchcraft. She could protect them. It made his blood boil, but he had bowed to her every wish.

And to this day, he knew *nothing* about their leader. How she had known about their fate and what her intentions were. As her second in command, he had pushed for answers to only get punished in return. It was always done publicly too. Every time he stepped outside of the line, he greeted the whipping post like an old lover. The leather would snap and bite into his skin, and he *always* said nothing. He took it and walked away, swearing to all gods above that he would get revenge and would free his people from her.

Lana had always had her suspicions, but neither of them ever said anything aloud. Morgan always *knew*. Lana wouldn't risk him getting hurt further—enough scars ridged his back as it was. That was until tonight.

"Azarius..." Her voice caressed him, a thousand unsaid things flying between them in that moment.

He pushed on, crumbling. "I brought Memphis Carter and my twin brother, Alby, to her. To assess for trial. I was so angry that my brother was part of this *rebellion* that hid for years. That I almost died helping a princess that came back from the dead.

"You are my world, Lana, and they all almost ripped the chance to see you again from me. I knew what would happen. I knew Morgan would never see reason or be fair. But I didn't care. All I could think about was that while we were living in this world of darkness, a group more powerful than you and I could ever imagine was slumbering while thousands of people died. We could have *died*.

"I wanted them punished. Lana, because I almost dared to hope that they would make a difference."

Rebellion. The word, the meaning, the thought behind it was an ember softly pulsing in his darkness. It was greater than he would have ever hoped. But now his brother and the rebellion were just as broken as he was. Just as lost.

Lana leaned in close, kissing his jawline softly. "This is far from over yet. Come with me. I need to show you something that I should have shown you long ago."

He took her in. Her lips curved sadly in the night as she held out her hand to him, beckoning him to come with her down a road filled with mystery and question. His fingers met hers, warm and reassuring.

His heart pounded against his ribcage, and he was too tired. Too confused. Too scared about the forces circling their world and the leaders that had broken it, leaving them in ruin. He had survived in Adair's darkness for so long. Under Morgan's tyranny, Azarius had become a shadow of himself.

He always had picked up the pieces, and like every other day, he followed the only thing that made sense to him in this life- Lana. Pulling away, she draped the robe around her, her dark hair tumbling. Quickly, he dressed, his alertness bleeding into his panic with each second. Her eyes were luminous as they devoured him.

Swallowing hard, her words broke down the last of his sanity, his hope. "Azarius, I have not been honest with you."

A cold wind spun around him, churning the contents of their room. His breath stilled, ice running though his veins. Silently, she nodded for him to follow, and he did the only thing that he could: Trying to keep his ability steady, he followed her out of their room, weaving through the darkness toward the kitchen.

He grappled to get back to their suspended moment, in the safety of each other's arms, in the blanket of the night. His heart dropped, and in his gut, he knew he was already chasing after a lost memory. His reality held a different story to be told, and the cracks of darkness fused within him, holding him steady as he prepared himself for what he was about to hear.

CHAPTER FIVE
Emory

The darkness kissed her, embraced her. Squinting, Emory tried to make sense of where she was but was met with a black, dense wall. Sweat pooled at the base of her neck, warmth flaring through her body. Fear choked her then as she gulped down stale air. She knew she wasn't alone because she felt them before they said anything.

"Emory, you need to wake up." Memphis's voice, just barely a whisper, caressed her.

Right beside her left ear, another voice sounded. "Em, wake up." Brokk's rough voice was harsh and clear, but she felt her body still being pulled, pulled down into the black abyss.

A third voice then sounded; one she could only recognize from her dreams. "Emory, darling, wake up." Her mother. Her voice danced all around her, and she clawed blindly, trying to connect with her lost friends and family. Trying to find them.

Silence landed heavy, and a putrid smell enveloped her senses. It smelled of rotting meat. Bile rose in her throat as a she felt a slimy, boney hand wrap hard around her wrists, pulling her toward it. She couldn't scream; she couldn't move.

Sweat drenched every inch of her body as the creature she couldn't make out leaned closer, whispering right in front of her, "Emory, I have found you." Swivelling around, she was met with darkness until the monster pulled her closer, its breath tickling her ear. "And you belong to me."

The knife slid in between her ribs, pain blossoming, and cackles spun around her. Then, she was dragged down into the darkness.

Screams tore from her chest as she shot up. Drenched in a cold sweat, it took her several minutes to register where she was and the guard standing at the foot of her bed, arms crossed and eyebrows raised. She screamed again, pulling her blankets around her, her nightdress clinging to her curves.

"Who gave you permission to be in here?" she demanded.

Smirking arrogantly, he said, "I did."

Blinking, she recognized the man as the same one that guarded her down in the cells. Rubbing her eyes, she tried to shake the feeling of that damp death-like hold of the creature in her dream.

She pointed to the door. "Get the hell out."

He scoffed, rolling his eyes. "It's time to start your day. The king awaits." Throwing a bundle at the bottom of her bed, he turned his back, briskly stating, "You have five minutes to get ready. I'll wait outside."

Shutting the door, he left her in stark silence.

It was time.

Panic clutched her heart, squeezing it, threatening to break it. She couldn't breathe. The walls seemed stretched too thin.

She could do this—she *had to* do this. Emory would grant the rebels the time they needed, the time *she* needed. Dying wasn't an option. Besides, she was already dead to the people who had believed in her.

Leaning forward with shaking hands, she opened the parcel. Several stacks of light black clothes spilled out, including shirts, pants, and undergarments. A blood red sash sat atop them all. *Lovely.* Sitting on top all of this, though, was a light, sheer, gold chest plate. Squinting, she leaned closer to inspect it. Markings she didn't recognize adorned all the edges, and its sheerness was unearthly. She was so close, her breath was fogging it, her reflection lost. Strong leather buckles joined at the shoulders; its back plate just as impressive. She shimmied out of bed, quickly dropping the armor.

Emory went through the motions of getting dressed numbly. Braiding her long ebony hair back, she looked in the mirror behind her. She didn't recognize the woman standing before her, the stark cheekbones, emptiness in her eyes, bruised skin underneath them. Tying her sash tightly, she set her resolve.

Emory Fae of Earth was dead.

Everything had led up to this moment.

Her parents shaped their world, defying the paths they were told to go down: A warrior from the Shattered Isles and a Prince of Kiero were never supposed to break away and build a refuge— The Academy—for peace. In her heart, Emory knew they had made mistakes, but their life's dream was to fight and to ensure everyone, no matter their ability, would have a place to call home.

Emory loosened a breath. She would not let her parents' dream die. If Adair wanted a challenge, he would get one. She would make him pay. For her family. Her friends. For herself.

Grabbing the chest plate, she stepped outside her room, meeting the guard. He dipped his head at her, eyeing the armor curiously but not saying a word. Leading her down the spiraling staircase into the hallway below them, she fell into step with him.

This world was bleak, consisting of cold stone and regimented life; they traveled in silence. Curious now, she inspected the guard out of the corner of her eye. He was around her age with dark brown hair and kind eyes. What had happened to him, to get him *here?* She clenched her jaw, controlling the anger that was bubbling inside.

Kiero had bled, the open wound festering, until all that was left was an infection that still spread. Entire lives had been compromised, and she should have been here to change that course. Adrenaline poured through her, heating her core: *Good. Good.* She would use this; she would not be afraid.

They stepped into the activity of the main hallway, soldiers throwing curious glances their way.

"This way," the guard barked at her, and they veered left into a smaller, narrower hallway, causing them to walk in single file.

The temperature dropped several degrees, and goosebumps erupted over her body. Several more minutes of walking in silence passed, and Emory couldn't handle it anymore.

"Do I get the name of my valiant watchdog?" she purred at his back, feigning courage.

He rolled his shoulders once, and she could sense his tension. "No."

Fair enough. She had no retort to that, and instead settled with drinking in her surroundings. Deep green moss speckled the cavern walls, visible moisture making them slick. They must be heading into the bellows of this hive, even lower than the cells. Light from the lanterns danced at them as they passed, causing shadows and her mind to run with their mystery.

She recalled everything Memphis had taught her, clenching and unclenching her hands. Breathing in, she felt that deep well of power within her lift its head, acknowledging that it was *there*. She wasn't alone. Over the months that had passed, ever since she had stepped foot back into Kiero, her ability had grown. The power collecting in her core, pumping through her veins, echoing her thoughts. *My lifeline.*

It grew every day, and she had banked her entire plan on that. Risked her life on it. She would be trained and turned into the weapon Adair wanted, but she would use her skills on him, to kill and take back her throne. With that thought, a cool resolve settled over her as they approached the ancient door before them, the king smirking sickly beside it.

After a quick nod to the guard, Adair's eyes appraised her as he took her in, practically purring, "Good morning, Emory. I see my parcel has found you well."

His voice was liquid fire, and it ignited her. She stood as silent as the stone walls around her, studying him. He wore nearly identical clothes as yesterday except a loose belt hung from his waist that was adorned with different sizes of vials and daggers. *So, it begins.*

Adair chuckled at her lack of reply and swung the door open, motioning for her to walk inside. Just her. She didn't look back at the guard as she followed.

They entered a cavern the size of a small gym, different posts with a strange glass bowl hanging from each. Except for this, the room was weaponless and silent.

She tried to still her racing heart as he spoke. "You wish to join my forces, but I am very selective about my soldiers. Only the quickest, smartest, and most *powerful* succeed here. Usually, I have scouts watch the potential subject to decide his or her worth. Loyalty lies with safety, and in my world, you are safe with me."

A spark lit in his eyes as he stared her down hungrily. "You have succeeded in not only disappearing for the last six years without a trace but have gained the rebels' trust, and dare I say, *love*, only to break all of that to finally reunite with me, desiring your title as Queen. A title that you will have to work for, seeing as you are my most potential and dangerous subject ever. But I must admit, Emory, that I am intrigued by your alliances. Maybe my efforts all those years ago weren't in vain."

Snapping his fingers, an electric blue flame ignited, blazing against each glass bowl, casting the room with their glow.

The retort broke through her lips before she could think twice. "Been learning some new tricks, I see?"

His smirk was as sharp as a sword's edge. "You can't even begin to imagine." His gaze trailed down her arm to where she still clung to the armor. Mouth quirking, his dark eyes shone as he breathed, "Ah yes. This brings me to my next thought. I have had this specially made for you. Its metal is very rare and only found in the Draken Mountains. Feather light, it will mold itself to your body, and I have made some slight adjustments from there." His lips curled up, and the pit in her stomach grew deeper, every fiber in her body telling her this was bad.

"During these trials, this armor not only will measure your body's strength and stamina, but your *ability's* strength and stamina, for my own personal records. If I should catch a hint that you are here to inflict harm on me and my court, then with my control, a poison trigger system will activate and inject into your blood, killing you within seconds." Adair spoke low, looking at her with malice in his eyes, waiting for her to react.

Dread pooled in her stomach, but she gritted her teeth and bowed her head in acknowledgement. *She had to make him believe, to trust her.*

"Well then, the choice is easy. You should have nothing to fear." Again, he studied her with those calculating eyes, weighing her reaction as he nonchalantly toyed with her life.

With surprisingly steady hands, Emory lifted the gleaming piece over her head and slipped it on over her clothes. It reminded her of every horror movie she had ever watched. Like a live organism, the metal moved and shrunk, slinking underneath her clothes until it expanded over her skin, covering her chest, breasts, upper back, and just stopping before her lower back. Gasping, her pulsed raced, trying not to panic as she felt the chest plate bite into her bare skin, latching on.

As she felt the warm trickles of blood running down her stomach and lower back, it was with all her self-control that she didn't rip his throat out then and there. She had to bow and beat him at his own game. And he was radiating, like this was the best day of his life. If she died, it would be. It was torture to know that at one touch, her ability would cause Adair's power to be at her disposal. She could so easily flip the coin if given the opportunity. *Buy the Rebellion the time they need to act,* she reminded herself.

He circled her, popping the black collar of his jacket up. "Now, the rules are simple. You will drink this vial, and it will initiate a series of events that you will undergo. I will be on the defensive side of each simulation. Defeat me, and the blue flame will turn gold, triggering the next test. You pass this, and then I will reward you with a training session. This will continue until you have earned my trust. From there, we can talk about your proposal."

She took in this Dark King, a thousand emotions charging through her. Half of her felt lost, longing for the Rebellion, for her friends that were dead because of *him*: For Memphis, for his familiarity. For Brokk, and guilt pushed at the thought of him. She should have given Brokk more of a chance, should have been more open with him about how she felt returning to Kiero. How she only remembered him as a nightmare—thanks to Memphis.

Anger, steady and consuming, ate away at her thoughts. She believed in the Black Dawn Rebellion. She believed in the Academy, and even if she didn't remember all the details of her past, one thing she knew for certain, Adair had slaughtered her parents. Had burned their dreams, the gains, and peace in Kiero. His madness had corrupted the minds of his kingdom and had incinerated the idea of a democratic society. He was a fearmonger, preying and thriving off the bloodshed and destruction he had caused. He was a tyrant who had been unchained for far too long.

Meeting his dark eyes straight on, she felt the corners of her mouth tug up slowly. She wouldn't become his weapon. Emory would become his nightmare, feeding and draining him until there was nothing left.

He placed the vial in her outstretched palm. It was cool against her skin and no bigger than her thumb. A pristine, clear liquid swirled within, and popping open the small latch, she raised it toward Adair in a toast. "To your good health."

Smirking, she tipped her head back as she felt the icy substance crawl down her throat, spiraling into her stomach, spreading within her. Then she was falling.

Falling.

Falling.

Falling.

QUEEN TO ASHES

Emory was surrounded by particles of the earth: wind, fire, water. She still felt as if she was plummeting, but dark earthy moss lay under her leather boots on solid ground. *Focus.* Snapping her attention to her surroundings, she took in the rawness of the forest around her. Everything was so still.

Taking a step, she released a breath. The trees burst with life around her, the green leaves vibrant and pristine. Taking another step, she raised her eyes to the tree line. It was with a snap of a twig and a slash of broken light that all chaos broke loose. Shouts and fire surrounded her as darkness fell heavy on the land, the only light being the flames and a pulsing light from beneath her shirt. Scrambling, she realized it was her *armor*. It pulsed as if it had a heartbeat—alive and gripping her. Her entire being screamed *magic. Ancient magic.*

She ran, trying to escape the wall of flames, her skin burning and blistering from the heat, trying to make out who surrounded her. In that moment, a snarl and snap of jaws sounded from behind her as she slowly turned around. A creature born from eternal darkness loomed before her, skin dripping off its body in a slow, decaying way. Its eyes were as red as the flames that circled them, and it locked on to her, baring its teeth, which were gray and bloodstained.

Whispers exploded in her mind, an ancient language, a long-lost story that beckoned only to her, that wove and played only to her heart. Her body quaked as she scrambled to think, to react. The monster's nostril's flared, and a low growl tore from its chest, as it tasted her fear; was challenging her.

Frantically, she dropped to a low crouch, looking for any weapon in sight. The creature stalked toward her; its muscles tensed, readying itself to lunge at her. Its talons sliced into the soft earth, and the smell that rolled off it reminded her of scorched and rotting flesh.

Gagging, she could have sworn the *thing* was mocking her, already victorious. *No. No.* She would not curl up and die. The heat was blistering her skin as a thrumming so strong started in her mind, and she had to clench her teeth to ground herself. The demon hissed, spittle flying from its maw.

Voices dark and fierce erupted in her mind, yelling instructions at her. It clicked, and the song turned into a language she recognized. Her heart viciously thrummed against her ribcage when she looked down to her boots. She had no other choice: *Make your move, Emory Fae.* Those alluring voices crooned to her, and it was as if she were a puppet on strings.

Charging the creature, she swiftly rolled onto her side. Roaring, the demon sprung over the top of her, landing where she had been standing, the flames twisting to both their wills. Her arm connected with an upturned knotted root, and hot blood spilled from the wound almost instantly onto the ground around her.

The demon froze, tilting its head to the side, calculating, confused that the prey had just switched to predator. Panting, she felt the ground move underneath her. Breaking the creature's gaze, she looked down and had to blink hard to make sure she was seeing correctly. Bubbling from the dirt, a sword was forming, materializing from her blood. Not waiting, she grabbed the now solid hilt and watched the blade form in front of her. The steel shone, glinting a deep ruby red.

The world erupted into mayhem once again as the ring of fire that had been surrounding them jumped and twisted, alive, spiraling toward the end of the sword, wrapping around it, absorbing its light, its *power*. It didn't stop there. Flames tore into her world, Emory was consumed in the fiery dance of golds, reds, and oranges. The flames coolly kissed her skin, her body, but they did not hurt her. Instead, she felt her ability roar to life, consuming every ounce of the magic, of the flames.

Bursts of power screamed through her limbs, her bones, shaking her very core. She was a whirlwind—she was the *fire*. It raged around her, smoke twisting up like a tornado. As fast as it consumed her, the fire stopped, embers glowing all around her feet, ashes floating in the air as she opened her eyes. Exhaling, Emory snarled at the monster.

Her blade seemed to move with life, reflecting the flames it had consumed. She flicked her loose hair back, noting the ends were now dip-dyed dark red. Looking across at the growling creature in front of her, she took a deep breath in and steadied herself: The creature roared at her, the power of it jarring her bones. Emory narrowed her eyes. *For the Rebellion.*

She charged full tilt as she distantly heard the whimper behind her, as if she was swimming through water. *By fire and flame. He knew exactly where her scars lay.* She stopped in her tracks, knowing what she would see behind her. She would know that sound anywhere. Fear licked at her heart, but Emory turned anyway. Memphis bloodied and broken knelt on the scorched ground. Brokk was beside him. Within seconds, she was lost in the sea of their pain, and it destroyed her.

They whimpered, "Please, Em. Help us."

At their pleas, the demon stopped, head tilting as it took in Memphis and Brokk, salvia dripping from its maws. Dread pooled in her gut as the demon changed his course, flinging himself toward his new prey. She knew what Adair expected her to do, what he so desperately *wanted* her to do. Her legs flexed and burned, and she plunged toward them. She would beat the creature. She had to.

Her surroundings were a blur, and her two best friends' features lit up as they saw her. Swinging her sword, the creature roared behind her. Time had no meaning as a strangled cry tore from her throat, and the steel found its mark. Memphis crumpled first, then Brokk, and she looked away from the blood-stained dirt.

The demon was sitting on its haunches as it started to melt away, its skin oozing into nothing but a pool of blackness around it. She couldn't focus. Bile tore up her throat as the world spun.

It's not real, not real, not real, not real, not real.

The voices encased her again, their whispers just a wall of noise. Gravity pulled her down, and she fell, the wind howling around her. Landing hard on the edge of a cliff, her core burned. She was a wall of flame, despair, and anger, and she was relentless. This was who her people had been left with, what the rebels were trying to overthrow.

Emory stood there at the edge of a cliff, her blade crackling as flames jumped from it, lighting up the night. "Every good sword has a name, right?" Emory asked herself.

Anithe.

The name came to her, but fear collided into her as she took in the scene around her.

Dozens of eyes stared back at her, glowing yellow and green. Their snickers sounded, and she gripped the pommel harder. Stepping forward, small hooded figures with pointed, sickly green teeth surrounded her. Thick venom oozed from their mouths as they cooed at her edging closer, closer.

"Enough!" Her yell cut through the silence, and flames roared from Anithe's steel as if it was an extension of her and her emotions. Cutting and twirling in a lethal dance, the creatures screamed around her, still trying to claw their way toward her body. Emory didn't think—just reacted. Running, she prayed she would live long enough to find a way out of this.

The wind howled through the night, the screams growing louder behind her as she staggered to a sudden stop, barely catching herself at the cliff's edge. Looking down, she could see nothing but darkness. Exhaling hard, she looked at the advancing figures and with no visible way out, jumped off the edge. Wind engulfed her as she plummeted down into the darkness, sparks flying behind her in a brilliant trail. The horizon tilted once more as she squeezed her eyes shut, waiting for her body to collide with the ground.

The impact never came.

Opening her eyes, she blinked hard, momentarily blinded. Disoriented, Emory realized she was in a small cottage filled with bottles and vials of various sizes. Her legs quaked, getting used to being on solid ground as she waited. No one came. Seconds turned to minutes, and she took even breaths as she searched the room. There were no windows, and the stale air was suffocating.

Then, finally, a soft voice spoke, "You betrayed us. You betrayed *me. And you will pay.*"

Moving into her line of sight, Memphis was shaking, there was a menacing glint shining in his eyes when he threw a dark hood over her head. Disoriented in the sudden darkness, her knee-jerk reaction screamed at her to fight back, to scream, to bite. Quietly reminding herself Adair was on the other side, weighing and watching, she used every ounce of her control to remain still as faceless people slammed her down onto a chair.

Memphis leaned in; his breath hot against the fabric. "Tell us everything, or else we will torture you until you are praying for death."

Sweat collected at the base of her neck, her pulse throbbing against her skin. Her mouth ran dry as punch after punch slammed into her body. Her ribs snapped, and she felt a bone puncture into her lung, causing her to scream. He asked again and when she answered with silence, pain flared as heat surged from her limbs, from *every part of her.*

"What is Adair planning, Emory? How did he use you?" Spit hit the hood as Memphis bellowed, and Emory grunted as her neck snapped back from the next blow, blood oozing from her broken lip. She became numb, a silent wall. Pain laced through her body, silently begging for him to stop. Couldn't he understand *why?* Didn't he see?

No. She couldn't go there. She wouldn't.

Wildfire rushed through her in a course of adrenaline. Diving deep into that well, her body, motivated by hurt and anger, screamed as everything rushed through her, magic singing in her veins. An icy wind sent her kidnappers staggering back, and Emory, with inhuman strength, snapped her restraints and pulled the hood off, spitting blood out onto the floor. Five men, including Memphis, stood frozen around her as she surged for her sword lying on the ground. Upon her touch, embers swirled amongst the steel, the blade's edge igniting into flame.

Steeling herself for their attack, Emory memorized Memphis's face with every second that passed. That moment, the scene dissolved in front of her as if it was nothing more than a faded memory. Completely unhinged, she realized she was back in that cavernous room. A slow clapping sounded from behind her, making her jump.

She turned around, chest heaving. The King's eyes gleamed with excitement. She quickly found herself back in her reality, three glass bowls shimmering from the brilliant gold flame that

QUEEN TO ASHES

they contained. She had passed. Relief flooded through her as Emory stared at the Dark King, lost for words. Her body begged to curl up in a ball and scream, and this was only a taste of Adair's wrath. Of the inhumane king planting madness in all their minds.

Her nails dug into her palms as she slowly walked up to him, not a flicker of the boy she had once known or had believed in was present in the king that stood before her now. Adair just stared at her, then he took in the sword she clutched like a lifeline.

His smooth voice bounced off the walls in a disarraying echo. "That was most enlightening. You did *much* better than I could have ever hoped. What I find strange, though, is how you knew how to achieve this."

He motioned to all of her: The blood-red tips in her hair, the brilliant sword, how she had fought so well. She was lost in that question, in how to answer, but when Emory cleared her throat, he cut her off, still pacing around the cold room.

"Now, I could have believed you had the ability to read my thoughts, but I highly doubt that is how you knew, since *no one* can do that." He stopped in front of her, his eyes an emotionless void. "The magic spoke to you."

It wasn't a question and she kept her face a mask as he stared at her, with a look as close to wonder as she had seen him so far make. Her heart pounded at an even pace. To be kissed by the darkness, marked by it. She turned cold.

His voice was just barely a whisper when he mused, "How did you survive?"

Sweat dripped into her eyes. Her chest plate tightened at his question as if warning her, waiting for a detection of a lie. Her palms turned slick with nervous sweat. He stood, waiting to see how willingly Emory would prove her devotion to him. *Like she had a choice with the bloody contraption on her.*

Licking her lips, she choked out, "On a different planet."

He froze. Standing there, trembling, Emory waited for poison darts to shoot into her bloodstream. Waiting for Adair not to believe her. Silence pressed down hard between them, and she tried not to squirm while pinned under his stare.

Tilting his head curiously, he breathed. "How?" She gritted her teeth, and never breaking his gaze, the truth tore from her, her resolve nearly with it.

"The Academy had fallen." She was transported to the memory, the tang of winter, of Bresslin's madness. She could still feel the chains. Her desperation and despair. "I knew Brokk had been lying to me. He was hiding something from all of us." How her heart had pounded, as she remembered the last time she had looked at him. "I knew he could help me. Help keep me safe from you." She had been lost in her loyalty, too blind to recognize Memphis had been lost in his jealousy.

Adair stepped forward, ghosts playing behind his dark eyes. "Brokk Foster placed you in another world?"

They were face-to-face as she breathed, "He traveled there. Manipulated time and bent it to his will."

His eyes sparked. "Let me get this right. Brokk hid you in another world after I destroyed the Academy and killed your parents and my own. I rose to be the Mad King, finally wiping Kiero of its infection, teaching the entire world that their one true king was me. And all this time, you and the rebellion eluded me... And Memphis? What part did he play?"

Tears stung her eyes. *Six lonely years. Not knowing my world was burning because of you. And I never remembered it because of Memphis.* It came out in snarl, her frustration and rage piled up into a tangible beast, and she didn't care about the Mad King standing in front of her. "He ensured I never remembered any of it. This world. My past. Or you."

A pause. A flicker of shadow across his features. There was a hunger in his eyes she wanted to run away from, to take all her words back. But she just stood there, waiting for his reaction: Adair didn't say anything more as he stalked out of the room, slamming the door behind him. Leaving Emory alone with the gold dancing flames and her consuming fear of the truth she had just shared.

Body shaking, a strangled noise escaped from her. The walls were closing in, time slipping away with every second. And already, she was a partner in his chaotic dance filled with madness. She didn't know which way to turn without those shadows filing into her heart, without Adair controlling her every movement. When the time came to end Adair, would she be enough? Cursing, she glanced down at Anithe in her right hand.

She made her way to the door, leaving her doubts and ghosts behind. The door felt like iron as she pulled, heaving it open. Setting her shoulders back, she jutted her chin out, barely glancing as the guard followed her. The echo of their footfalls rang out in the corridor as she clenched her teeth tightly together. She blended in, with their dark garb and bloodied sashes blurring into a streamline of bodies, unrecognizable and nameless. Yet, each soldier, each woman and child lingered, their gazes cutting like knives into her back, into her heart.

Her guard snapped at her suddenly, making her jump. "Move." Scowling, she stalked ahead, not realizing she had stopped, her thoughts darkening as she stared at his back.

"And where do I have the pleasure of going now?" Emory asked the guard, looking behind her.

Mallory McCartney

The guard's eyebrows arched, the corners of his lips turning up. "It's time for your first training session." Emory desperately tried not to blanch but knew she had failed as the guard chuckled. "We are to meet the king in ten minutes. Most of the morning has already passed with your trial. So, keep up."

Knees quaking, her stomach rolled. The guard moved to lead, picking up his pace as they weaved back through the twisting hallways, the flush stone mocking her as they climbed up. Every second, her surroundings became clearer: a turn she recognized, a doorway that she had passed before. Like a spider web, lines started to connect.

Chewing the inside of her lip, one thought clawed up against the rest: This hidden kingdom, nestled in the depths of the earth, housing a bloodthirsty king was achingly beautiful. Structured, but still, the enormity of it was breathtaking. She had dreamed of the kingdom that lay above her while she was in her cell for a week, her imagination running wild with bloodstained hallways and the tortured screams of his people.

Shaking her head and picking up her pace, she pushed all thoughts down as the hallway started to widen and the mouth of the room opened before them-it was cavernous, exploding with life. Twisting up alongside of the walls, stacked staircases and homes were embedded into the stone, the happy clatter of families going about their day-to-day business erupting around her. Carts filled with fruits, vegetables, and wine cut through the throngs of people, businessmen trying to pull their clients in with smooth words and promised prices. Across the expanse, the steady clang of metal on metal pulled her in, the blacksmith's rhythm providing the pulse, exploding the energy around him. Clothes, exotic and exquisite, hung on lines on the surrounding shops, and she stood there, mouth hanging open, taking it all in.

"You're causing a scene." The guard's callused hands gripped her arm, too hard, as he dragged her along with him. He muttered underneath his breath, "It would seem you haven't seen a market before."

Emory allowed him to lead her, as her mind drank it all in. It was explosive, a stunning array, and the coursing lightness around her led her gaze up, toward the carved-out ceiling, pouring in natural light, to the clouds dancing far above them. Emory imagined what the room would look like at night, when the moonlight transformed the cavernous walls in a glowing silver backdrop, the stars twinkling.

Walking numbly, she tried to even her breathing and steel her heart. But that did nothing against the crashing voices in her mind, memories from long ago slicing through her.

"Don't you ever wonder what it would be like, living in Sarthaven? In a city where you could be anyone? A place filled with culture. With adventure?"

She rolled her eyes, looking out from their perch on the rock wall outside the Academy, the rolling forests stretching out in front of them.

"What? Being a part of one of the most influential families in Kiero isn't enough for you then?"

Adair looked at her, smiling lopsidedly. "Not even close."

Her pulse picked up as she dissected every detail, her blood running cold at the memory. Adair had been her best friend, understanding better than most the dream to break away from the pressures of the Academy. The dream of what life would look like when they were adults.

And now, he was a Mad King, and she was the martyr who would end him. Beneath her anger and fear, a tiny sliver of hope bloomed. What maniac king would build this for his world?

What king so overpowered by his destruction would nourish vibrancy and culture?

Each step brought her closer to Adair, as she absorbed the families, the homes that made up the kingdom in the mountain. The sweeping arcs of the architecture, of the towering staircases that made up this splendor. Each step brought a sliver of doubt, wedging into her that maybe the boy she knew was still in there. The boy who was a dreamer, misunderstood, and uncaged. Who just wanted a taste of being lost, to find exactly who he was.

Exhaling hard, Emory looked forward. They passed underneath a carved archway, and the guard pushed open another oak door. The howling wind met them, and as the door shut behind them, she stopped. The ledge was small, the wind tearing at their clothes as she looked out at the expanse of Kiero- or the skeletons that were left of it. Panic froze her, and she ripped her arm out of the guard's hold, flushing her back against the mountain. Heights were one of her worst fears.

The guard smirked. "The king should be here shortly." And with that, he left, locking the door behind him.

CHAPTER SIX

Adair

His mind was spinning. Reeling with the possibilities, with his mistakes; his surroundings a blur. The voices were quiet, like the calm before the storm; always looking to drag him back down in their grasp. Quickly finding his way back to his room, he threw the door open and strode across the space.

Adair took the old weathered book from his cloak and slammed it on his desk. The room dropped several degrees, and it took all his restraint to not scream as he snapped, "Explain. This. Now."

With an unseen wind, the cover flipped open, flying back and forth as thick blackness oozed from the yellow pages, voices cackling from within. Shadows encircled him, semi-visible in the half light as the tang of magic filled his soul.

"Our King, what could there possibly be to explain?"

He hissed through his teeth. "This changes *everything*. You swore that if I fulfilled what you wanted, I would conquer this world. Now..." *I lost my soul. I lost everything.* "Now the Fae girl saunters in and casually tells me not only that she escaped me six years ago, but escaped to another world? And the man who was the key to this is dead!" He was yelling now as he continued, "Were you aware of this information?"

A hushed silence followed before the silky voices cooed, "You are following your destiny as you should. Train Emory. Make her suffer and then make her yield. The Rebellion will show their hand for that. We cannot answer what you wish, but you are playing your role beautifully, Adair."

Treacherous lying creatures. Before they could say anything more, he tossed the book across the room, their presence disappearing as fast as they came.

Riddles, always riddles.

Even as a teenager, their voices had called to him, promising him a life he could have never imagined. They told him beautiful and terrible things, and he wanted it all: So he took it. Their poison flooded in his bloodstream, clouding his heart. His mind. Making him hardly human.

Six years following their instructions, death and destruction was all that was left in his wake on the climb to be King. He had built an almost indestructible army, including hundreds of dabarnes, and had allowed these demons to play him for their pawn. Adair never questioned the lust for power overshadowing everything else. He had unlocked that part of himself as well, and he loved it.

Running his hand over the smooth edge of the desk, he tried desperately to sort out his thoughts. But all he could think about was *her.*

Pacing now, each step fueled his rage. He should have known, should have seen it years ago. Of course, Carter would try to manipulate Emory. Try to cage her. As for Brokk... Through a thousand possibilities, he had never foreseen that an orphan mutt would possess such raw power, that Brokk would be the one to stand in between him having Emory.

In his indignation, Adair threw open his desk drawer, shoved the Book of Old in it, and slammed it shut. With a flick of his wrist, it locked. And he gave himself one second. Breathing unevenly, he clenched his fists, and then he was gone, dissolved into smoke and ash.

Cutting through his kingdom, propelling himself faster, he sliced through time and space. The wind hit him, fierce and refreshing, and it was only a second before he materialized before Emory, her features stretched in fear, her already pale skin white, emerald eyes blazing.

His voice was too calm as he held his hand out to her. "Your first lesson begins now." Tilting her head, she didn't move. Another silent battle of unsaid words and his fingers shook, the beast inside of him trying to overtake him. Her eyes flicked down as he tried to steady his hand.

Raking her gaze up to his, he could taste the fear rolling off her as she croaked, "My sword?" The tang of magic surged through him, and smoke enveloped around her, the leather materializing in seconds in a sheath. Her eyebrows flicked up, as she secured the sword in the sheath.

His patience bled into nothingness as he snapped, "Now, are you with me?"

She stepped forward, her muscles trembling. The wind ripped at her hair, the red ends catching in the light, radiating. Her hand met his, and he wove their fingers together. Heat surged up his arm as he pulled backward, and they freefell. Her screams ripped through him as her body slammed into his. He wrapped his arms around her as they soared up, his magic blanketing them.

It was freedom and ecstasy, and Adair lost himself in it. Her nails dug into his arms. And when he looked down, he saw fresh tears spilling from her eyes. He smirked before then dropping like a comet being pulled into their orbit. Again all he could hear was Emory's screams as they picked up speed, and his mind became clear, sharpened by her fear and his wrath.

In an explosion of smoke, they landed into the heart of the Noctis woods, the deep purple hues reflecting around them. She dropped from his grasp, emptying the contents of her stomach.

"Get up. Now."

"You are out of your mind," Emory said breathlessly as she stood.

He stalked up to her. "So, I've been told. It's your choice whether you stand by your decision."

Her features darkened, sweat slicking her skin. She unsheathed her sword, arms shaking as she asked, "Where are we?"

Prowling around her, his sword materialized, its double-edged side blade a mammoth beside hers. The stillness pressed around them as he murmured, "The Noctis Woods. Better known as the Heart of Midnight. I only dare pass through, the residents here can be ... not very understanding."

Circling around, he came face-to-face with her. "Now, it's time to forget everything you think you know. Whatever Carter *taught* you is child's play. You claim you want to stand by my side? You claim you want to be one of us? Then you have to earn it."

He shivered in pleasure as ice encrusted his blade, the air around them dropping several degrees. *Destroy her.* That electrified rush ran through his veins as she furrowed her brows, setting her jaw. He smirked, whispering, "Now, show me what you are made of."

Emory charged, roaring. Running to meet her, ice raced around them as flames erupted from her blade, and they met in the middle. Water hissed, sparks flew, and Adair twisted, becoming smoke before materializing behind her. She cursed, twisting around as he landed a blow, slicing with aim at her neck. Their blades clashed together, her arms shaking.

He was relentless, not stopping, each blow filled with fury as she parried, stumbling over her feet. Again, he spun, appearing at her back as she ducked down just in time. Adair pressed his lips in a thin line, slicing at her calves as she rolled out of his reach. She was fast, he would give her that.

The metal tang of magic filled him as his ability exploded forward, pinning her in place. Ice cracked beneath his boots as he prowled toward her. Her eyes started rolling back, and she quivered beneath his claws.

"Always know your opponent. Always know when it is a lost battle. Always think one step ahead. Always weigh your strengths and weaknesses." Adair brushed a finger against her cheek, her wide eyes, taking him in as he whispered in her ear, "And always remember, that you will *never* beat me."

Letting her go, Emory dropped to her knees, gasping. "Your ability is budding, but it is weak. We will start there. You must work at it every day, a muscle you train and strengthen. Fighting with your heart is never enough. You must fight with your mind, you must plot and plan, and execute with a lethal grace. Fighting isn't a reaction. It is an essential part of you, like breathing. Always with you but not overthought."

Stopping, he tapped his blade underneath her chin, bringing her gaze to his. "Again." Her lip trembled, but she stood, leveling her sword in front of her. He sighed, "Now, let's break it down, starting with our feet first. If you don't work on your swordsmanship, then your ability is just a fraction of your advantage."

His words poured from him, and in a slow tempo, they arced their swords, bowing against one another. Sweat plastered her forehead, matted her hair, as time after time, she failed. Her feet stumbled, her movements clumsy and always too late. Adair shook his head. "Without the swords. Emory, focus."

Frustrated, she drove her blade into the ground, chest heaving. He mimicked her and strode up to her, speaking softly, "You have to find that place within yourself. Where everything goes quiet, except you and your intention. Where you find that peace and that endless rage, and it feeds your soul, ignites your purpose."

"I'm not a soldier!" Emory seethed.

He stalked around her. "Not yet, but that's what you want to become. So, you will achieve it. Or has everything you claimed been a lie?"

She shook her head. "No, it's not."

He nodded. "Then do not throw it away." Grasping her wrist, he brought it up to eye level. Placing another hand on her hip, he breathed deeply. "Your body is slow. Also, clumsy." Stepping forward, he pushed her back, then smiling, he raked his gaze up to hers. "See?"

Slowly, he started the dance, his hand never wavering from her hip, his other leading her hand, arching slowly, sweeping wide and far. Pushing her back, her body naturally reacted: Back, forth, side to side. Parry and react. Parry and react.

Nodding, he said, "Now I'm going to break away, but continue this. We will add our blades."

Pulling back, his gaze never wavered as he flicked his hand, her blade appeared in her grip and his in his own. Her held his, raking over his face, but he didn't break their focus. His body responded, turning in to the fake blow, and her body met his, coming face-to-face. "Good." He lightly pushed his blade down, making her back bow, and she swiftly twisted out, her feet carrying her.

He twisted with her. Twist. Parry. Block. Twist. Parry. Block. Continuing in silence, their bodies responded to one another, and he lost himself in the rhythm of it. Minutes slipped into hours until dusk splayed across the sky, the leaves surrounding them becoming luminescent, flickering like hundreds of lanterns. Stopping, he held up his hand.

"Enough. That's a good start. We will continue this every afternoon, but once you get the basics down, then we will incorporate your ability."

Sheathing her blade, she wiped sweat out of her eyes, her silence absolute. What was she thinking? Did she feel it? That deep down, he had always been here, always would be. Instead, he held out his hand to her. "That's all for tonight."

Emory's eyes flashed in the twilight. "And what waits for tomorrow?"

Adair's words were soft when he answered with, "Another trial."

Before she could say anything more, he took her hand, and in a moment, they were nothing more than ash and smoke, leaving the unnerving woods far below them. Her screams echoed around him, sharp and piercing, but in seconds, they flew through the mountain range, through levels, weaving through doors and stone. He could feel her body tense, waiting for the impact she was so sure was coming. He exhaled, and they appeared outside of her chambers, solid ground underneath them once more.

Stepping back, Adair swept his gaze over her before he turned, stalking down the hallway without a word, smirking as he heard the steady stream of curses behind him.

CHAPTER SEVEN

Azarius

The last trace of moonlight bathed their cottage in enough light that they could easily maneuver around the various bookshelves and jars of herbs that made up most of their home. Looking out the window, Azarius could see the trace of dawn breaking the horizon. The promise of another day.

"Azarius." It wasn't a question, or a command, Lana said his name like it was her conviction, every lingering hope apparent in her voice.

Clearing the table in front of her, she moved with a feline grace. He stood frozen, lost in the fire in her eyes, completely transfixed by her.

"Our paths didn't cross by accident. Six years ago, when Adair came in to power and this world was cast into his shackles, Kiero wasn't the only world that was affected."

Only world.

At those two words, his world slowed, time suspended in air between them. Lana stepped closer to him, taking a deep breath and, with trembling fingers, reached for his hand.

"My true name is Lana Steethea, and I am heir to the world of Langther. The world of windwalkers. I have stayed here, hidden, to help right the wrongs of the past."

Windwalkers. Another World.

His mouth was dry, and he watched as she rubbed her hands together, a soft white light pulsing from her skin, inky tattoos stretching and winding up along her arms. Images of ancient worlds and creatures filled her skin with eerie details, as if they were watching him.

Her voice sounded husky and far away as she continued, "Many years ago, a group was formed to achieve balance and prosperity across the lands and, in so, across worlds. They were a hidden organization. Nei Fae wasn't wrong when she stated that the magic wasn't only born into people but into the channels as well and has a ripple-effect reaching out to every world surrounding Kiero. Nei married Roque to ease the tensions building in Kiero for political reasons, and in building their government, they formed the Original Six: A member from Kiero, Langther, and Daer. And from the world of windwalkers, the fey, and here."

He couldn't breathe. She held his gaze as she placed her hands onto the table, and the light pulsed beneath them as a map of Kiero started to form before Azarius's eyes, spilling like smoke.

"The group was built to make sure that the magic was always distributed equally and that they pooled their knowledge together to log and cherish each culture of each world. They called it the Book of Old. They could travel from one world to another with Damien Foster, who was a time manipulator."

Azarius scoffed. "Time travel?"

Lana whispered, "Yes."

He couldn't utter a single word in reply.

"But things went wrong," Lana continued. "You must understand the magnitude of the secrets written in this book, and the utmost trust that was put into the group to protect them. In the wrong hands, it would be horrific. There were secrets of magical spells and covens from every culture. A group called the Oilean from Daer infiltrated the group, trying to steal the Book of Old away for themselves. They succeeded.

"Their magic bled into the Book of Old like a poison, corrupting its power. Transforming it from a book into something more. My mother's sacrifice trapped them in an in-between state where they could not follow us." Her eyes hardened as she became lost in the memory.

"I went into hiding. I was young and scared of what the future held for me. Lana, the healer, could blend in, and that's exactly what I did. I stayed alive. But now, the tides of the world are changing again, and we cannot hide anymore. Too many whispers, too many lies have circulated around Adair, but I believe he had achieved this through the means of the book. And we must destroy it." She took a shuddering breath, her eyes never leaving his.

He didn't realize that throughout her tale he had been gripping the table, his ability giving away his emotions as a cold wind cut through the room. He tried to digest the information, but questions battered against him.

Choking out a harsh laugh, he asked, "Why wait until now? Why wait for *hundreds of people to die?*"

His own personal losses clutched against his heart as he stared at Lana; the quiet healer he once knew was gone. The woman who stood before him surged with power, and he didn't recognize her. In a few minutes, the person he thought he knew was ripped away from him. Knowing she kept such a big secret from him, he found himself torn between anger and denial.

"I couldn't risk drawing attention to myself. Before my mother died, she left me one mission. Above all else, wait for the one who can manipulate the channels. Before the Faes were murdered, my mother told me a secret, one that has made me comply all these years.

"That the one who can help us will resurface, and they will be our only hope. We open the channels and build an army not seen by their world. We start by bringing down our own tyrant. Before Morgan or Adair can hurt anyone else."

His world spun as he processed the information. He was white knuckled as the seconds passed by, the light of dawn starting to wash the room.

"Azarius, are you with me?" She sauntered over to him, cupping his face, gently tracing circles. He felt like he was drowning. He snapped his teeth together, trying to find focus through his roaring emotions.

A light clapping sounded behind him, making him jump as he turned around to meet the gaunt looking Nyx. Her purple hair was tied back messily, a bandage peeking out from her light shirt. Lana immediately stepped in front of him.

"You, my *dear*, are supposed to be very knocked out right now."

Nyx gave Lana a cocky grin. "I didn't feel like missing out on the fun. You give a very inspiring speech. Is it true, Lana *Steethea*, everything you just told him?" Despite her arrogance, a trace of hope lingered behind her words. Azarius realized Nyx was looking for something to hold on to as much as he was.

Lana narrowed her eyes. "As true as you or me."

Plopping down in the nearest chair, groaning, Nyx sweetly said, "Well then, what's the course of action, because the *gods above* know I need a good fight before Adair's cronies kill me."

"Absolutely not." Both women froze at his tone. Shaking his head, he stared at Lana. "Years, Lana. You lied to me for *years*."

Nyx's lips pulled up into a grimace. "Welcome to the club."

He jabbed a finger in her direction, wind spinning jars in the kitchen. "Not another word from you. I mean it."

She grinned viciously but crossed her arms over her chest, complying as she watched.

Lana stepped forward. "It was the only way. Before you, I didn't know who I could trust. My mom had just died for the Faes. And they did *nothing*."

"Just like you have done until now."

Her face crumpled as if he had slapped her. "Azarius, please, I'm begging you."

He laughed darkly. "What, just to understand? Just to raise arms, to enter a war? For w*hat?*"

Lana crossed the space between them. "Don't you dare say I have done nothing. I have lost my home, my family, just like you. I gave up everything I am to go into hiding. I didn't know that Morgan was alive. I didn't understand the forces that were playing against us.

"All I do know is that if you and I are lost to one another, then that's it. It will have been all for nothing. I lied. I wanted to tell you a thousand moments, a thousand days and nights. But I fell in love with Lana the healer. A simple life, filled with a thousand moments together, with you. I was scared to lose that."

His hands shook, tears burning his eyes. He swallowed hard, the walls feeling like they were pressing together, cutting off his oxygen.

"If not for me, then at least to kill Morgan," Lana said.

Nyx froze at her words, and Lana pressed on, "Azarius, I'm not asking you to understand everything this second. I'm not asking you to forgive me. I'm asking you to help me kill the one person who has taken too much from you."

He looked at her, the curves and angles of her features too familiar. "I will help with Morgan. But the rest... I need time."

Her hurt reflected in her eyes, but she curtly nodded once.

Sighing, he started to pace. "First off, how do we trust *her*, when to the best of my knowledge, she is the reason half her rebellion was destroyed and taken by Adair in the first place? How do we know she won't take the first chance to kill us all?"

A heavy silence fell between them, and Nyx was as still as stone, assessing him to see if he was going to start something further. Lana also stared curiously.

He didn't move.

Nyx suddenly jabbed a finger in his direction. "Let me clear this up for you *now*." Her voice was a deadly calm. "Yes, I sought out Adair to bargain with him for our freedom. Yes, I gave him the one thing he wanted: Emory Fae.

"What would you have done differently if for the past six years you were lied to, been with a man who was in love with the long-lost heir, which he not only brought back to bring Adair down, but kept *safe* while our world burned.

"You don't think that the weight of the deaths doesn't stay with me every day? You don't think that I tried to think of every other possible option before going to him? If Memphis would have followed through with his original plan, we all would have died. I didn't know your group existed since you were just as well hidden as we were.

"It was a last desperate act to protect my family, and the price was Emory. I made a mistake and trusted that Adair would keep his word. If you want to kill me for that, then so be it. But know this, I am prepared to go to any lengths to stop him, and for the first time since being a part of this doomed rebellion, I think we have a chance if what she says is true." She took a shaky breath and didn't break her stare.

Lana was smirking from ear to ear as she said to Nyx, "You and I are going to get along, I think."

Nyx dipped her head toward Lana and then asked him, "So, Azarius, will you have *me*? I'm a trained, lethal woman with nothing more to lose."

What would you have done? Her words struck home, as he had thought of every option to protect his home, *his family*. He took lashes every day for protecting his people, his back a map of scars as proof. If he was in her position, going to Adair would be the last feasible option, but if he believed he had a chance, he would do it to save the ones he loved.

The battered woman before him had given up everything, the hard glint in her eye a hollowness of a life she had to bury, due to the Faes, due to the Academy, due to Emory, due to this *world*. *Maybe he could do right by her.*

He had allowed himself to hope Emory was the edge of the rebellion. In helping her, letting her in, Azarius had wished that despite hiding all these years, she would be the key to stop Kiero's madness instead of adding to it. Nothing was black and white; they were on the brink of a looming storm, and it was their choices that would dictate it all. No more dealing with long lost princesses or promises from the past.

It came down to moments.

Running a hand through his flaming hair, he nodded. "Don't let me regret keeping you alive." He kept pacing, his mind spinning. Tendrils shot forward, connecting as a plan formed, and he asked Lana, "This Book of Old. What exactly do you know?"

How could you lie to me for so long? About what you are—who you are? is what he really wanted to say, but he bit his tongue.

Sighing, Lana nodded down at the map still illustrated on the table. "Many years ago, when the group was still being formed, my mother and my people's leader took me to one of the meetings in Kiero. I was her second-in-command. We emerged here—" she pointed to the borders of the Risco desert "—from our channel and had to travel many weeks to reach the Academy.

"During this time, my mother told me everything she knew about the group that was being built in Kiero and why. I didn't understand then, but she was preparing me for the worst-case scenario, being this." Sadness pooled in her eyes.

"She brought me to as many gatherings as she could. In those days, peace was on the horizon between all the worlds, a promising future. Each meeting, one world representative would write something in the book, collaborating a log of sorts for the next generation of heirs to follow in their footsteps and be gifted with the knowledge of their ancestors. It was never supposed to generate evil.

"I remember the day like it was yesterday, when the Oilean came. Those fey, if you can call them that, are much closer to demons, and they can appear as any form and have such a lust for blood being spilt. They came in the form of Daer's heir and got as far as to condemn the Book of Old before Roque knew something was off. I don't know exactly how, but they put a spell over it, to ensure whoever had it in their possession would follow its will, and only that."

An icy silence fell between them and Nyx did a double take of Lana. "Wait. Exactly how *old* are you for you to have been there in the beginning? You don't look a day over twenty. Also, are you saying that potentially, if Adair didn't have the book, that maybe he wouldn't have destroyed everyone we loved?"

Lana nodded. "Power seeks power—of any kind. If the book didn't exist, maybe it would have been different, maybe not. But even then, only he knows what truly happened."

Azarius sighed in frustration. "To kill Adair, we have a chance of survival, to end this Book of Old and its dark magic. We have a shot at a normal life."

"Exactly. And to answer your first question," Lana said, raising her eyebrows at Nyx, "I'm immortal. I have lived a hundred generations... Besides, age is just a number."

His mouth hung slightly ajar, which only sent Nyx into a fit of laughter.

Lana blushed and murmured, "We have our entire lifetime to learn about each other, Azarius, if we live through this. If the channels are opened, and we can go back to Langther, I have my kingdom waiting for me. My people's abilities exceed Adair's soldiers, and he won't see us coming. We bring them back, and we have a chance. We can build an army and march on Adair. We fight for our freedom, for this world and every other one that has been cast in the darkness. We fight for our life together and for every life that has been lost."

Her eyes hardened. "But first, we have to start with Morgan."

They were insane and most likely were going to die. But even as these thoughts floated through his mind, an adrenaline he hadn't felt in a long time coursed through him. His voice was gruff. "We kill Morgan and save my brother."

"And Memphis," Nyx added.

Lana agreed. "And Memphis. Then we find the person who can open the channels."

"And I know exactly who he is."

Nyx yawned as she said this, and both he and Lana froze.

Tension sparked in the room as Lana said, "You just thought to mention this now?"

"In my defense, I had to make sure you weren't going to kill me first. The man you mentioned before, Damien Foster. In Black Dawn, our second-in-command was a shapeshifter named Brokk Foster. He is the one who brought Emory back. He opened the channel to Earth; I think the place was called. Though last time I saw him, I might have stabbed him."

"What?!" Lana and Azarius exclaimed in unison.

She shrugged. "It's a long story, but I had to make sure he didn't follow me. I haven't seen him since. He has healing abilities. I assure you it didn't kill him."

Lana started to pace, her excitement contagious. "We will find him. We must. But first Morgan."

Settling, Azarius pulled a chair out, sitting down as Lana launched into how she thought they should bring down their leader, Nyx watching her every movement. Their plan formed, and as sunlight poured in through the windows, he tried to tame his anger, dulling it, instead of letting it consume him and incinerate what little trust he had left for the people he loved.

CHAPTER EIGHT

Brokk

He needed to stop. The pounding of his heart and burning in his lungs seared through him.

Soaring over a fallen tree, the scent of the forest filled his nose. Brokk was consumed by his rage. By his disbelief. By his grief. The ground thundered beneath him, and his ears pinned flat against his head. *Stop.* Shuddering against the thought, he shifted back into his human form in a single motion.

The night was fleeting, the traces of dawn now tingeing the sky. The Ruined City was long behind him as he had transitioned through empty towns, forests, and grassy plains, all a blur as he followed their scents. Sweat slicked every inch of his body, and he paced, agitated. *Emory is in Adair's kingdom.*

The thought he was running from, the thought he couldn't even begin to wrap his mind around had caught up to him. In the Ruined City, the scents he tracked didn't lie. Emory had gone into Adair's kingdom and had not come back. It was like being back with the Oilean, having his body dissected inch by inch, torn slowly apart, only to be put back together.

How could he keep moving forward when all he wanted to do was turn back? To see her, to hear her side of the story. Why, after everything they had gone through, that her parents had done, would she throw it all away? Would douse their hope? How could he turn back? Brokk pulled back to his reality, only to hear the nocking of an arrow.

Ducking, he contorted his body so fast it winded him. The arrow sliced through the air with a *hiss* before it lodged its sharpened end in the tree behind him. Four sets of eyes peered at him from the coverage of the trees, and he only had time to take in the midnight-black paint that smeared underneath their eyes before arrows rained down on him. *Raiders*. Shifting back, his adrenaline kicked in, and he snapped. Roaring, he charged forward, unhinged.

He could smell their fear; it coated the air, thick and instantaneous. A low growl of approval ripped through his chest. He was exhausted, defeated. But rage bubbled within him, fueling his movements, and like a thousand times before, Brokk lost himself in the feral part of his soul.

Barreling forward, his nails dug into the ground, flicking his gaze up to see the sharpened ends of the arrows glinting, hurtling at him. Muscles tensing, he pushed off with his back haunches and flew. Ten arrows thudded wetly, slicing through fur and skin. He snapped three mid-flight, splinters flying from his maws. He landed heavily, crashing into the tree line, right into the raiders. They scattered, curses flying from them.

Moving lithely, Brokk charged with his sharpened claws and his teeth slicing through their clothes, their flesh. They were faceless men to him through his rage and empty heart: It exhilarated and scared him. The attack was over before it had begun, the young raiders full of life but inexperienced. Shifting back, his shirt shredded, blood slicking his skin, the injuries made his movements jagged.

Vaguely, he remembered the gentle sounds of water bubbling over rocks and sifting through dirt, a river not too far from here. *Move.* The pain anchored him to his human form, each bloodied step through the forest reminding him that he wasn't invincible. He could bleed just as easily. The ends of the arrows were imbedded deeply in his muscle, and he cringed as he felt his body try to heal, moving around the arrows' sharpened ends. He was going to have to pull them out. Moving slowly and silently as a shadow, he concentrated on his breath, his lungs wheezing.

But as he walked, Brokk couldn't escape his demons, and he silently repeated their names aloud, his voice cracking on each one. "Memphis. Alby."

They were alive. And they needed him. As much as he wanted to curl into himself and let himself be defeated, he forced himself to keep walking.

The landscape was rugged, the branches creating sharp corners and edges in his vision. Each time he passed a towering tree, he flinched, his imagination warping it to a slim figure with pitiless eyes, just waiting for him to let his guard down. *Not real. They are dead. The Oilean are dead.*

Rubbing his eyes, his heavy lids constantly reminded him he needed to sleep. Pushing the thought down, Brokk took a steadying breath, his fear clawing away at him. He hadn't slept properly in weeks, not since those nightmarish demons had chased away any sense of his life. He could still imagine those giggles in the dark, those sneering faces. The prick of the edge of the knife, slicing down and then up, whittling him away.

The pain, the blood.

"Enough!" His voice was hoarse as he yelled to the empty forest. He clutched his head, shutting his eyes as he steadied his tilting world. "*Enough.*"

Trembling, his body begged him to shift back, to run, to get *away*. Lurching, the woods spun on its axis, but he held on. The heavy scent of rain filled his senses, and Brokk looked to the oncoming grey sky, starting to eat away at any sunlight. A low rumble sounded in the distance, and he shifted uneasily, the hair on the back of his neck standing on end. He had nothing to worry about; nothing would come that he couldn't handle.

He trudged deeper in the woods, losing track of time. He followed his heightened sense of smell, trusting it would lead him true, and he allowed the deep ache in his shoulder blades to remind him he couldn't stop, even though he was so tired. His legs gave out as he stumbled, feeling the mud underneath him as his reality bent and blurred together.

"*Brokk.*" It was just a whisper on the wind, soft and delicate. Emory's voice, calling out to him.

"Em!" He walked faster. "I'm coming."

The scene before him dipped and changed, the soft forest floor shifting to a hard concrete. He took it in with uncertainty, and the temperature dropped to an icy state, his breath coming out in misty puffs.

"*Brokk, you need to stop.*" Her voice dipped and echoed around him, and he paused as he looked at the floor caving in to reveal a small pond. The water was still, its smooth surface like a mirror, but steam curled up from it, looking like smoke. His consciousness tugged at him; wasn't he supposed to be doing something? Heading somewhere? Moving in a daze, all he wanted to do was slip beneath those comforting waters and sleep. He would only take a minute.

Each step he took, the clarity of the room sharpened. He ripped off his shirt, pain flaring from the movement. The broken ends of the arrows dug deeper into his flesh, and he reached behind his head, gripping the end. *One.* He sucked in a breath. *Two.* His blood had coated his entire upper back. He could feel it trickling slowly down his skin. *Three.* Ripping the arrow from his body, his vision blurred as pain overtook his senses. Steeling his nerves, Brokk repeated the action three more times.

By the time he was done, a cold sweat coated his body, a sense of gravity pulling him down. Running, he discarded any article of clothing that was left and plunged his body into the water. Warm water filled his mouth, nostrils, and ears. Kicking his feet, breaking through the surface, he gasped. The water had turned pink from his blood, and blinking hard, he relaxed, tension melting from his core, his muscles.

It was unchanged.

A deep tugging pulled at his gut, and a shiver ran through him. *Leave.* He was suspended, the water cradling his weight. His heart hammered, and dread coursed through him, screaming at him. He groaned as he relaxed, his eyes fluttering closed. Didn't he deserve to rest? Didn't he deserve a second to catch up, a second just to exist, not as a soldier but as a man? He didn't even know what it meant to be Brokk Foster anymore.

Closing his eyes, he gave himself up to the water cradling him, and that's when he heard the voices. They were cold and drawn out, like nails scraping over rock, sparks flying from every syllable.

"*Brokk Foster. Won't you join us?*" Eyes flashing open, his heart lodged in his throat. "*Brokk.*" The scene flickered, the edges blurring. Lightning streaked across the sky, the grey concrete walls dissolving. "*Foster.*"

A drop of rain splattered across his face as he looked down only to see the water turning inky black around him. A scream ripped from his throat, and the room fell away as he was slammed back into his reality. Thunder rolled across the sky, as he lay on his back, collapsed in the mud. Rain poured down from the sky, cold and relentless. Four sets of eyes glowed around him in the greyness, their yellow eyes predatory. Thin limbs and elongated torsos made them look like the towering trees around him. They had ripped at his clothing, their inky talons clicking as they saw his widened gaze take them in.

"Brokk Foster, come and join us. The water is nice and welcoming." The whispers froze him as he tried to find the source.

He couldn't breathe as he regained some sense of himself. The creatures were grappling at his legs and arms as they tried to tow him to the roaring river behind them. Rapids crashed against the rocks, his perception of a calm stream nowhere to be found.

"Do you think the poison has settled in enough?"

Snapping to attention, Brokk caught the snippet the closest creature had muttered under its breath. It had been a trap. Internally groaning, he calmed his pounding heart and willed his limbs in compliance. The creature's hands latched on to his ankles and wrists, dragging him through the mud. Lightning flashed, streaking across the sky, and they started singing softly in their eerie voices, as they worked, dragging him toward what they thought was his impending doom.

"*Hidden in the reeds, and streaked in the mud, we wait. Until the day comes. Raiders strike, with their might, and the Reaper will come. And so, we wait, until the day comes, we will turn you into one of us.*"

His blood turned cold as he listened to their sick, overlapping melodies. The wind picked up, wailing through the forest like a lost beast. They were about twenty steps away from the river, heading down a sloping hill. Their backs arched against the storm, their leathery skin repellent to the elements. Everything about their features suggested a hint of human qualities, only to be warped and wiped away with a tilt of their head or flash of sharpened teeth.

Brokk had heard myths about ghouls and goblins of the night. His old history teacher at the Academy used to start their lessons with folklore to scare them, of how their world used to be seen. Lurking and waiting until their prey would come along and they would sacrifice them to be turned into fey. It would seem more myths were being turned into reality than he would like to admit.

The goblins chuckled, gripping his flesh tighter as if they couldn't wait to tear into it. Clenching his jaw, the dull ache spread throughout his entire head from the pressure.

"Don't you want to return to the dream? This world is harsh and unkind. We will help you, Brokk Foster. We will set you free."

Goosebumps prickled his fevered skin as he clenched his eyes shut. No one could set him free.

They leveled out on even ground once more, and he didn't hesitate. Twisting his body violently, Brokk shifted all his weight to the right, making the goblins hiss and stumble. In a crack of bones, he shifted back, his golden fur plastered down from the rain. The goblins bared their teeth at him, balking at his new form.

"You cannot fight. The poison will take you from your wounds. The raiders always ensure it. Submit to us."

Brokk's hackles rose, saliva dripping from his giant maws. Thunder cracked through the world like a whip, and he launched himself. They collided with a shriek of claws ripping, teeth snarling. Goblin and wolf blended into one as they rolled in the mud. Brokk felt them digging their talons into his back, digging their sharpened edges into his already existing wounds. He howled, charging and throwing himself into the nearest tree, wedging the creatures between his weight. He had a moment of reprieve as two shrieked with a sickening crunch. Lightning streaked in jagged, violent lines above as Brokk propelled himself forward, rolling his body in a somersault. The two goblins sank their claws further into his back, and he desperately twisted, trying to throw their balance off. His fear made the world move in slow motion, filled with the shrill shrieking of the wind, the rain, the goblins triumphant call for his blood.

I'm going to die. The thought cut through everything else, and he threw together a desperate plan. He didn't stop to think about it, to weigh his odds. Changing his course, he galloped toward the river, his ears pinned back. The goblins' cries were the last thing he processed before his haunches pushed off from the muddy ground.

And he was flying before crashing down into the turmoil of the river: His body was instantly pushed down, scraping against the rocky bottom before being flung forward, carried by the current. The goblins bucked, trying to keep their grip, but the water was too strong. Within seconds, they were mercifully separated. Cutting his paws through the water, he fought with its force, trying to break the surface. He saw the echo of lightning from below the water before he was twisted sideways and sucked away with the bend of the river. His body slammed against boulders, dots dancing in his vision as his lungs burned. He needed air. Now.

His weak limbs futilely fought, his claws searching for anything to cling to, but the rush of water, wild from the storm, sucked him further beneath its depths. His ribs cracked and pain sung, igniting every nerve in his body before the silky darkness overtook him entirely, drowning him in its icy depths.

CHAPTER NINE
Memphis

The first thing Memphis realized was that he wasn't alone. The cold, damp air sank into his bones, chilling him to his core. He groaned as his heavy eyelids flickered, taking in his surroundings. Internally cringing, he deduced he was in another *cell*. Everything was fuzzy, from the grey bars that locked him in to Alby's flaming hair in the cell beside him. A small, barred window across the room filtered in receding daylight.

His body felt drained, like he had been swimming against the current and desperately trying to catch his breath. *How had he gotten here? What was the last thing he remembered?* His mind was foggy; he knew Azarius had brought them to see Morgan, the leader of Pentharrow. There had been a small room, a locked door, and Morgan's greedy eyes as she had taken them in like a prize. Then darkness.

"Memphis?" Alby wheezed through the bars as he slowly tilted his head toward him in response. "What's happening? I feel...weird..." Alby's words pulled at his consciousness, and he wanted to respond, but he was spiraling inward. There was no resurfacing from what he was feeling.

Emory—the memories of her billowed around him; she was cruel and above all calculating. After all these years, she was the only one who had a chance of stopping Adair, and he was the only one she wanted to go to, to *join*. *He had loved her.* He had always loved her. Even when he shouldn't have. To hold on to a ghost of a girl, to warp her memories to ensure he would always be in her favor. To still have this not be enough. He was a *fool*. He was even more of a fool for just realizing this now.

Nyx had given him years of unconditional love and support, and he loved her brokenly and dishonestly. He didn't even know if she was alive. He didn't even know if he would survive *this*. He already hated himself enough on her behalf. If he had only let Emory go, would Nyx not have betrayed them?

Thoughts and distant voices sagged heavily in his mind, his pasty mouth cracking from the dryness. He felt so heavy, and it was just so easy to keep falling until he was sure there was nothing left of him to catch. *Nyx betrayed you and Black Dawn. My family is gone.*

The jingle of keys and clicking of locks made him stir. If he could only focus more. Blurred dark brunette hair came into view, and he was distantly aware she was standing outside his cell, glowering at him, tapping her foot in a steady rhythm: Morgan. From her calculated looks and savageness, every fiber screamed at him to run and get far, *far* away. For the life of him, Memphis could barely blink.

"Well, hasn't you two showing up been a very interesting turn of events?" More foot tapping ensued as Memphis bit the inside of his cheek. Her voice was smooth, but an icy edge to it made him bite back a scream. "I do apologize about the accommodations, but I had to diffuse this situation very fast. Your brother—" she jabbed a finger at Alby "—has exceeded himself again. He is resilient to have survived such a suicide mission. For that matter, since you both won't be alive in a couple of hours, I will be honest with you. Your brother, Alby, has survived every torture and deadly mission I have thrown at him. But I know exactly where his weakness lies now."

Her smirk spilt wider across her face, as they both groggily tried to absorb what she was saying.

"When Azarius brought you to me, pleading a trial for you both, it was too good to pass up. You see, I have been around a long time, seen a lot of things, as we all have. I have knowledge that you wouldn't even begin to comprehend. This world is about to be ripped open by its seams, and I will not tolerate an annoyingly gifted rebel group getting in my way." She was murmuring to herself now rather than talking to them.

Morgan shook her head, coming back to the present. Baring her teeth, she drawled, "The evergollian won't take much longer to stop your hearts. It is very conveniently timed to not arouse any suspicion. I do like this poison. Very rare. It slowly shuts down all your major organs, one by one. Leaving the best for last." She retreated into the shadows, and he heard a door click shut in the distance.

A heavy silence pressed down on him, the roar of his own blood sluggishly pumping his final moments through his veins. The world was spinning violently.

Evergollian.

Poison.

He felt his body move toward the bars, jerkily, so desperately trying to reach out. If he could just brush up against Nyx's consciousness, they might have a chance. He had to reach someone. Darkness threatened to overtake him, and Memphis willed his mouth to form words, to call for help. He could barely move his lips before he passed out.

CHAPTER TEN

Brokk

Brokk felt the gentle swaying, as a harsh coldness settled into the marrow of his bones. He knew he should move, open his eyes, but it was here, in the clutches between life and death, that he heard them.

"*Brokk, move.*" Jaxson's voice was quiet, a gentle brush against his heart. Since his friend had fallen with the Academy, Brokk, in his delusion, wanted to let go, to join them and allow the river to take him fully.

"*Save her. Save them. Save yourself.*" The voices of his friends coursed through him, leading him back. "*It's not your time, Brokk. Save her and forgive yourself. So that you can understand. Will understand.*"

His breath came in a gasp, his eyes flying open. The murkiness of the world greeted him. The water was calm around him, the river now moving lazily, carrying him with it. Any rage he had previously felt vanished within the waters.

He willed himself to move, shifting his weight and slowly cutting through the water, toward the grassy edge. The water splashed on his face, making him blink and sputter as he willed his body to listen to his demands and not drag him beneath the river once more, to be at its mercy.

Every movement felt like a knife shredding his skin, *slowly*. He was caked in dried blood that was now painting his tan skin with slashes of ruby red. He knew, even for being a shapeshifter, he had undergone intensive injury. That he was lucky. He knew he should feel grateful, having walked away from the goblins that yearned for his flesh—that had wanted him to become a changeling. Goblins that were supposed to be of myth, not living, breathing nightmares.

His fingers gripped the edge of the riverbank as he hauled himself onto the grass.

All he could comprehend was that he was drained. The damp and comforting scent of the grass washed over him, and he drank in the air, lying back down, his sopping body shaking. *Memphis. Alby.* The names clambered back to him, nudging him, *willing* him to get up. To carry on. Groaning, it took every bit of his energy to sit up and take in his surroundings.

The forest was still dense, the storm having passed, leaving everything glistening with fresh dew drops. He was alone, and his mind felt like it was battering against an iron wall, suffocating him and making every reaction drawn out and slow.

Poison, you were poisoned. The thought reverberated through him with such force he paused, his hands searching his body for any wound still open. The last remains of his clothes were tatters. And where the arrows had been, the skin was taut and itchy but *healed.*

Brokk looked to the rolling skies that he could glimpse through the treetops. Standing slowly, his senses kicked into overdrive, his mind smoothly instructing him with a soldier's command.

Move. Breathe. Your friends are dead. The Rebellion broken. But you are still here. Move. Memphis needs you. Alby needs you.

Gritting his teeth, he shifted, his wolf form sagging with the effort. Shakily, he padded on, his sodden fur slicked to his body. Scents overwhelmed him once more, his body slowly sorting through them, his thoughts sluggishly connecting the story together once more. The river had cut a lot of scents, except one. That same male scent that had led Emory to Adair *covered* this part of the forest. A deep growl ripped through his chest, and he turned, following his nose.

And came face-to-face with a cumasach.

He froze, his ears pinning flush to his head. Blinking hard, he thought the poison was playing tricks on his mind. The fey before him was stunning, her delicate features taking him in, her pale grey eyes full of intelligence. She was petite, no taller than his shoulder, her silver hair plaited back. She wore intricate armor, the metal shimmering with an entrancing glow.

The cumasach was a myth of old, one that he had grown up with, that the world had grown up with. The *gifted*; she was practically a demi-god to him. It was said that they roamed Kiero, their magic making the forests wild and the seas untamed, that it was their magic that made up the fierceness of a warrior's heart, and centuries ago, when the world no longer needed their protection, their magic made abilities.

It had been rumored that Emory's dad, Roque Fae, had been naithe, blessed by their magic, leading the world with a true heart. Brokk had never believed that to be true.

With a hammering pulse, he bowed his giant head, his muzzle grazing the damp ground. He couldn't move. Couldn't remember how to breathe. Her laughter was like the chiming of bells, sweetly tolling their melodies.

"Brokk Foster, it is I that should be bowing to you."

He was completely and utterly frozen. Strong and gentle hands brushed under his maw, and she lifted his head, so that they were face-to-face.

"How do you still prevail, when I can see that darkness in your heart? You are shattered, and yet you still fight against the dark forces moving against you."

Shifting back to his human form, he dropped to his knees, whispering, "Would you rather I give up? Is my fight already lost?"

Moving her grasp to his shaking hands, she whispered fiercely, "Nothing is lost. You, Brokk Foster, are shielding your world and keeping the shadows at bay. I have been following you since you appeared in these woods. To see if the whispers of the forest were true." Her touch was cool, and the aura of magic rippled around them as her grey eyes held his. "It is time you know the truth."

There was a surge of light, starting first from her skin, and Brokk watched as it seeped into him, a pleasant warmth rushing through his core. The bruises peppering his body started to fade, the blood crumbling off his skin. The sluggish weight from the poison was lifted, his strength shooting back into his muscles like an electric current. The cumasach grinned with a lethal sharpness as she brushed her fingers against his skin once more, leaving three shimmering stars in its wake.

"Do you wish to find it?"

With a current of fresh breeze and fracturing of light, the forest began to shift, the dullness and murkiness of their world changing. The leaves turned silver before his eyes, bowing to make an archway before them. She raised her eyebrows at him, motioning to him.

Hoarsely, he whispered, "Is this real?"

"That will be up to you to decide." Behind her, light rippled like a warm wind licking at his skin, calling him. Soft voices circled around him. He squinted, and peerless buildings came into focus. Eyes widening in shock, he took in the city swirling and forming before him. His dreams became his reality, and he drank it in, entranced.

The lost city of Nehmai was just as much a myth as the woman who brought him here. It was legend that abilities had been born by the magic sowed in the earth by the hidden city and the cumasachs. Spreading through Kiero, it had touched the residents, their magic the core to everyone's power.

In his shock, he took in the wide courtyards and bubbling fountains, the smooth marble, peerless. Crystals formed as the water droplets touched the pool underneath it. Wide cobblestone streets wove deeper past the towering houses. Outside every window, large blooming flowers hung, their silver and gold petals glinting like jewels. Everywhere Brokk looked, lush greenery ignited the world that stretched beyond the buildings.

It was ancient and surreal. He stepped tentatively, as if it would all disappear once more. The cumasach walked into the portal, and he followed at her heels, leaving Kiero behind.

"The city of Nehmai," he said.

She beamed. "Yes."

Nehmai was a city nestled in the Warriors' forest, where magic budded first, and the fey protected it from the darkness that eventually split their world in two. It was the birthplace of magic. And he walked into it, wordlessly. Passing underneath the arch, the splintering of wood sounded behind them as gravity disappeared.

His scream caught in his throat as the city vanished, and they fell through time and space. Constellations erupted around him, stars glistening, hanging in the velvety sky, purple hues swimming through the midnight black. He dropped faster, the stars blurring into shots of silver light as wind stung his face, cold and intoxicating.

Whispers erupted around him, enticing, alluring: "*The prince has returned. He has returned.*"

The night was washed away, and he was plunged into icy, silver water; his body dragged down by unseen currents as his lungs burned for air.

Returned. Returned. Returned.

A thousand lights ignited around him as clear orbs circled the water, quizzical golden eyes shining and assessing him. He screamed, water filling his lungs, choking him. The orbs spun faster, their edges making the water shimmer as he was sucked down. Black dots danced in the edges of his vision before he broke through, cool air rushing up to meet him. Landing on a smooth cave floor Brokk gasped, bewildered as the water dissipated.

Dropping to his knees, water spewed out from his lungs and nostrils. The orbs around him broke apart in a second, each one growing and encompassing until the room around him was filled with hundreds of shimmering mirrors. The silvery light from the water speckled the floor as he looked up in awe. Far above him, above the expanse of water, the city reflected down at him.

"Brokk Foster." A mysterious voice rang out around them.

Snapping to attention, Brokk stood, the cumasach already beside him, the petite fey having composed her face in a neutral mask.

"Who's there?" Brokk asked.

"It's not me you should be wondering about."

He snarled, "What then?"

The air shimmered, that warm wind circling around him, drying the droplets of water off his skin as the voice rumbled, "We have long awaited you, Brokk."

The cumasach flinched as she leveled her eyes with his.

Wringing his hands, he asked, "What does this have to do with me? Why am I here?"

A wind sprung around him, and a whisper of a silhouette formed in front of him. The edges were dull, no features coming into focus as the voice reverberated around him. "Let me show you."

The room disappeared as images assaulted his soul, piercing through him. His world completely crumbled and Brokk was submerged.

The night was clear, honeysuckle floating on the evening air, filling their room with its sweetness. The window was propped ajar, as Kavan rolled, the silhouette of his wife carved out by the moon. He sighed, listening to the steady rhythm of Meera's soft inhales and exhales. Beside her, his son's breath was a tiny flicker in his crib, and his heart filled with every second that passed.

For so long, he had been terrified of this path, of what it meant for Nehmai. Groaning, he propped his hand behind his head, looking out to the cloudless sky, trying to find the answers laid out in the constellations. Of course, gratitude filled his heart. Of course, he could see no other way that his life could have gone. Yet, when the night swept in, that small part of himself wondered if he had made the right decision. Not for him, but for his son: What life would he lead as the Prince of Nehmai? Lord over Warriors, over magic? He smiled in the night—he supposed it would look a lot like this.

QUEEN TO ASHES

Kavan Falkov sighed, begging for his mind to settle, to allow himself to catch a few hours of sleep. The city far below him was sprinkled in fireflies drifting lazily amongst the night. Beyond that, the sad, haunting songs of the mer-people resonated from the surrounding lakes, weaving and forming a spell over anyone who was lucky to hear them.

Rolling over, his eyelids slowly became heavy, and he yawned. Meera's fingers found his, pulling him close in her sleep, and his lips pulled up. As his eyes closed, light flared, and Kavan shot up, focusing in on the flaming arrow crackling, imbedding in their wall. Bits of wood fell off, rippling embers on their floor. He turned to Meera, and her silver eyes were wide in horror.

Far below them, the city was wrenched from its slumber, screams building and toppling over one another. Stealing a look at Meera, her features obscured in the shadows-and then he was flying. Roaring, he unsheathed his long twin blades.

"Meera, take Brokk and GO!"

Another half a second passed, and Kavan saw the wall the volley of fiery arrows slicing through the air with cruel precision. Lunging, he was in front of his wife and son as the energy exploded from his chest. The arrows slammed to a halt and were turned to dust. Kavan locked on to a figure, hood pulled back, the stranger's dark, gleaming eyes flaring as he nocked another arrow. Kavan was born from the shadows, and he materialized in front of the attacker, his voice harsh and cold, his hands clenching around his throat. "Who are you? Why are you here?"

The stranger smiled, saying nothing.

Lunging, his steel cut through bone and muscle, a fine mist of blood covering him. Kavan turned, freezing as he took in the horror around him. Flashes of silver and gold erupted like lights being snuffed out in a flash of teeth, in a ripple of fur, in a crescendo of screams. And beyond, a man ran in the shadows.

Narrowing his eyes, Kavan was sprinting, his magic devouring everything, protecting his people, webbing out, creating a shield. Kavan veered left, as the man scaled the courtyard wall with ease, steel knives protruding from his leather boots as they dug into the marble. He followed and flickering, slammed his fist into the man's jaw as he materialized in front of him. Blood ran freely from his split lip as the man laughed, his dark eyes lighting up in excitement.

"Kavan. I was wondering when you would show your face."

"Who are you?" Kavan asked.

The man oozed arrogance as he smirked, looking at his trembling hands, at the chaos roaring around them, of the harsh tang of magic in the air.

"You're afraid," the man said.

He circled him slowly, antagonizing him. Kavan's magic licked around him, just waiting to lash out. But the closer he looked at the stranger, his curiosity won over his viciousness.

"You, King of Nehmai, aren't stupid. You know exactly why we are here."

Kavan's hands shook, and the man smiled. Far above them, a scream sounded in the night, and everything seemed to move in slow motion.

Kavan turned.

Far above, the marble tower seemed to pierce the clouds as he drank in the scene. The woman had wild hair, her gaze locking onto him as she clutched Brokk. His heart dropped into his stomach as he took in the lifeless body at her feet on the balcony.

"MEERA!" He twisted, the shock wave of his energy blasting from him, flattening the man on his back. Stalking up to him, a flash of silver caught his eye. The orb was small and pristine before it smashed against the ground. Gas seeped out, floating like a fog, then the ground shifted, and he gasped, dropping his twin blades. It was a flicker of energy, like the pull of the undertow before the wave crashed down. His breath caught, and he dropped to one knee and then another, winded, as every drop of magic left him.

The stranger mused, "Now we are short on time, but this city, this world, I don't want it to survive anymore. My wife and I have come to ensure that. There is another couple like you—The Faes. They think they can change everything, can make sure the magic is upheld. Yet, it is a wild thing. Shouldn't we treat it as such?"

Tears ran down Kavan's face, as he looked up; the man was illuminated by the flames roaring around him as he came face-to-face with him.

"Your son will never know this world. He will never know you or your wife. He will never know where he came from. But he will know your power. And he will define Kiero with it."

The blade appeared from nowhere, and Kavan watched it slide neatly between his ribs. He gasped as it was thrust up. His vision twisted as the fire blurred into streaks, the stranger's face swimming against it. He had no sense of gravity, as he dropped, his last gurgling breaths his reminder that time was slipping away.

The man's breath was hot against his face. "Your son will know nothing but what we tell him. He will be nothing more than a pawn—that much I can promise."

A strangled moan escaped Kavan, as he welcomed the void.

The stranger stood, grinning against the carnage he had created and the dead king that lay at his feet.

Brokk was snapped out of the memory, tears streaming down his face. The cumasach shifted uncomfortably, her silver eyes never wavering as the voice uttered, "Brokk."

He couldn't breathe. His mind scrambled, the dots connecting faster than he could digest. His heart pounded wildly as bile burned his throat. He was frozen, the blatant truth pinning him in place.

His eyes narrowed as he hissed to the empty space. "You're lying."

The voice chuckled. "The time for accusations rests not with us but with *them.*"

Shivering sweat collected at the base of his neck. He looked to the fey in front of him, addressing her. "You're telling me what exactly?"

She walked to him, her silver gaze flaring but her voice steady. "That you, Brokk Falkov, have defied all odds. When the city crumbled, your parents' magic died, most of the fey along with them. That's when the myths became reality. The Warriors no longer protected and harnessed the magic. The balance was thrown. You were stolen, meant to be used for evil. Your power to be used to ensure darkness—" she exhaled, jutting her chin out "—yet here you are. The Prince of Nehmai, a prince I would happily serve until the end of immortal existence."

He choked on his laugh. "You've *got* to be kidding me."

But looking at her, the clarity of the situation slammed into Brokk. Heat flared up along the back of his neck, into his cheeks. Pacing, he struggled to keep his reality in check as the walls closed in.

The Oilean had lied, making Brokk believe Roque was his father, to keep his rightful title hidden away with Nehmai. To keep the knowledge of his family hidden away.

In a mere second, Brokk Foster seemed like a crumbling façade, peeling back what he was always supposed to know. His parents had loved him in a kingdom carved from magic.

That his life of being Brokk Falkov had been stripped away from him—just as Adair had stripped away his shot at a peaceful existence.

She moved in a flash, and he felt the cold steel of a blade settle against his throat.

"None of this is a matter to joke about. Our people were slaughtered. I can see it. You know the truth makes sense. But I will spell it out for you anyways. Damien Foster and Morgan Foster stole you. Why, you might ask? Well, they were power hungry, to start. They were thieves and fearmongers, and amongst the fey, children are rare. An heir even rarer. They harnessed your power with the help of that witch, Peyton. Using dark magic, they stole the essence of your abilities, leaving you for dead."

"And Nei and Roque found me?"

She grinned, tapping the blade against his skin. "You're catching on. Damien died when the Oliean infiltrated Kiero, but I tracked Morgan down. She has been ruling over a town of refugees—Pentharrow. But she is not our focus, young prince."

"Of course it isn't. And what about the Oilean? Everything they showed me, the memories were all lies?"

"Yes. There is one thing you need to know about the Oilean: They are manipulators. They hit you where they knew it would hurt. What's worse than a father who you knew your whole life, never telling you the truth? The Oilean made you believe that you were a weapon, Brokk. They ripped out your humanity by making you feel isolated, by telling you that you and Emory were nothing more than pawns in a prophecy.

"There is nothing more dangerous than believing in your heart that you have no other option than destruction. But your true family was lost to you, until now. Your truth was lost until now."

His voice was raw. "This means Emory and I aren't siblings? That was a lie as well?" His eyes locked with hers and her grin widened, her eyes sparkling mischievously as she nodded.

"Exactly. You are of two royal, but very separate, families."

Swallowing hard, he was at a loss for words, his pulse roaring in his ears.

Pulling the blade away from his throat, Brokk swallowed, wary of the cumasach and her social skills.

"What more do you need to believe? Haven't you ever wondered why you are different? It's not because you were given a potion that changed your DNA. Your parents loved you fiercely, and we are all that's left. In the battle of the Academy, I was the one who helped you. You have never been alone—will never be alone," she whispered; her voice cracking.

His gaze flicked down to his shaking hands and the liquid silver marking on them. *Naithe warrior. Chosen. Marked.* The air around them churned as the cumasach twirled her blade between her fingers.

"Now, are you ready to go to war?"

Shaking his head, Brokk spat, "My friends need me. Even if what you say is true, I need to know that they are safe."

She stalled. "Your friends are on their own path. They do need you—to stop the Oilean. You are playing into exactly what they wanted, to be reactionary, to shy away from the truth. What happens if you go to them now?

"Emory is with Adair, and if the Oilean get their hands on the Book of Old, our world as we know it will end. You think Adair has caused pain and ruin over these last six years? Imagine what Kiero will look like with the Book of Old in the hands of it masters who know how to wield all its dark magic. If you leave to find the rest of your friends, then the Oilean will have won. Because you and Emory are the only people who can stop them."

His laugh was harsh. "Right. The demons who tortured and almost killed me need to fear me? Besides, they are dead."

QUEEN TO ASHES

The blade flew from her grip, soaring past his ear as he snapped his focus back to her.

"If you ever give yourself a chance, then yes. Your magic and my magic are like an army of ten thousand against them. And they are very much alive," the cumasach stated.

Brokk's chest heaved as he started to pace. "If this is true, then I have already failed."

She was back before him, her voice soft. "If that's true, then how are you here? Talking to me, and seeing that your world needs you? You are in a lost city, born and cleaved from magic, and you think you have already failed?" She grasped his arm fiercely. "You have just begun."

Warmth spread through his limbs, and he cleared his throat.

"This is insane." He shook his head.

She flickered behind him, retrieving her blade from the wall. "All the best things are."

A dull ringing thrummed in his ears, as he weighed his options. He sighed, running a hand absentmindedly over his scars. "If I agree, do you at least have a plan?"

The voice chuckled around them. "She has had a lifetime to plan."

Brokk scoffed. "Okay, seriously, who is the voice?"

She rolled her shoulders. "It's an imprint of magic. Let's just say it's been my advisor. And my company." Sheathing the blade, she locked eyes with him. "Now, should we go pay Adair a visit? We have a lot to cover on the road."

He looked at the shimmering water above him, and he sucked in another deep breath. Bringing his gaze back down, he did what he had always done, would always do: He trusted his gut and followed his heart.

Sending up a silent plea to any force that might be listening, Brokk nodded. "Let's pay Adair a visit."

Her lips pulled up over her pointed canines as he clenched and unclenched his hands, one thought running through his mind, uncaged and uncontained. He was going to Emory. A bitter taste filled his mouth as he digested this, the weight of what state he may find her in settling over him. His anger roiled as Brokk steeled his heart and prepared for the worst. His hands shook. He was going not as her brother, but just as…him. No matter what state he would find her in, Brokk would save her from Adair.

Or die trying.

CHAPTER ELEVEN
Nyx

The day had passed too quickly. Once their plan was formed, Azarius went to find Morgan and went about his normal duties while Lana went into town to warn as many people as she could.

Nyx had rested more, and now, staring in the mirror of Lana's small bathroom with residual steam from her bath curling around her, she gritted her teeth. The clean bandages bit into her bruised, swollen skin, and dots flickered around the edges of her eyesight, threatening to take over. *Get a grip.* Her shaking hands finished the job binding her wound. Lana had done a great job taking care of the initial cleaning and stitches, but it *hurt*.

Pulling on a clean black shirt, she groaned in pain as the stiches pulled. She would get through this. She was dying for a good fight, a distraction. From her thoughts, her choices. Her demons. Which, thanks to the pain medicine, she had too much time with them as of late. Staring at her pale reflection, her vibrant, purple hair framed her hollow eyes. *Was it worth it?* Frowning, she turned. Nyx would not let herself go there now. She was a soldier, and she would think like one.

Bringing her hair up into a bun, tying it tight, she put on her midnight-black pants and boots. Walking out of the washroom, she glanced at the kitchen bathed in gold, the fading daylight marking how close it was for them to begin. To fight for a new future. On the round table in front of her were two sheathed blades of beautiful make. Stepping closer, she unsheathed the steel and sighed as the pale silver curved into half-moons. Nothing took her breath away like a deadly, beautiful creation. She lit up inside at the sight of their wickedness.

Stepping from the shadows, Lana appraised her. "They are blades from my home, Langther. I thought you would need them just as much as I do mine. They are feather light, perfectly balanced, and will slice through any armor, enchanted or not."

How long had she been there watching? Eying her cautiously, the healer that she had met was gone, and in her place, Lana was every ounce the warrior Nyx dreamed she would become. She was immortal and emitted, in every movement, the true predator she was. Hair plaited back, she mimicked Nyx's wardrobe, twin blades strapped across her back.

Nyx asked, "Why are you being so nice to me?" She had always been horrible at navigating her feelings, expressing them even more so.

Lana closed the space between them, gripping her forearms. "Because, Nyx Astire, I see the potential in you, even if you refuse to see it yourself. The moment we step outside that door, everything will change, and we both will be prepared. We are strong, even though we both hold wounds close to our heart that can never be healed. But the fact that we are still willing to fight for ourselves and our loved ones makes us unbreakable."

Nyx's eyes burned, and her chest was tight as she appraised Lana. The windwalker grinned wolfishly at her stunned expression, and all she could see in the other woman was *hope*. Lana passed her the blades, and she strapped them across her back.

It was time.

Wordlessly, Lana motioned her to follow, and Nyx rolled her neck, bouncing on her heels as she followed. Her healing wounds groaned in protest: Adrenaline kicking in, her heart pounded, sweat collected on her palms, and her ability raced through her veins, all her senses on overdrive. A calm resolve washed over her as they stepped out on the nearly empty streets. By now, Lana had unwoven the spell that was on the gates, so they were sitting in the open for the world to see. *Perfect.*

They quickly ducked behind the house as Lana swung gracefully, catching the eaves trough and pulling herself onto the roof. Following suit, Nyx ignored Lana's extended hand even though her shoulder screamed in protest and her stitches threatened to rip. The shingles were smooth underneath her soft leather feet, and Lana winked at her.

"Let's go for a run, shall we?"

Taking off like lightning, Nyx followed, pumping her arms and focusing on her breath. They flew from roof to roof, scaling the jumps with ease. It was what they both had been trained for—stealth and killing, retribution and death. It was what she was best at. They were shadows moving with the light, the world oblivious to them. Like whispers on the wind, they moved faster.

It could have been minutes, hours, or seconds, but Lana motioned for her to go down, and they dropped. Slowing her breath, Nyx peeked over the edge. People had started to gather around a small podium in the center.

Morgan stood outside the house they were laying on, talking gruffly to Azarius. Their voices floated up to them.

"It is time, *soldier*, and your personal involvement in this better not override your duties or loyalty."

She disappeared and Lana stiffened beside her. Nyx closed her eyes, trying to still her heart. *Focus.* Their timing had to be impeccable. The door swung open; Morgan and another soldier dragging Memphis and Alby out-she dared another look and froze, her heart plummeting into her stomach. Both men staggered, Memphis's head lolling from side-to-side, his hair hanging wildly. His pale skin was gaunt, his bones poking out at sharp angles. He was practically a walking skeleton. Reaching out to him, she tried to brush against his mind. She battered against that wall to no avail.

With her breath hitching, she whispered, "Something is wrong. I can't reach him. That only happens when…" Nyx couldn't finish that sentence.

Lana's eyebrows knitted together, and she peeked over, trying to find Azarius. Lana took in Nyx and whispered, "We have to at least wait until they are up there, otherwise it won't work. I will signal to Azarius as soon as that happens."

Nyx knew Lana was right and went back to her deep breathing. If she lost Memphis after *everything…* Stopping herself there, she filled herself with her dark intentions, harnessing her rage. Quietly shifting, she unsheathed her blades from her back, crossing them over her heart in a silent promise. It felt like a century before a gently pulsing light flew from Lana's palms, shooting up into the sky like a star.

Lana squeezed Nyx's leg and whispered, "Now."

Eyes flying open, Nyx flung herself up and rocketed off the roof like a demon springing from hell. Lana followed, a battle cry tearing from her lips, rippling across the town. They flew, landing on the ground with a sharp thud. She locked eyes on her targets: Nyx gave in to the only thing that made sense to her. Running, her spirit and her anguish acted as wings as she unleashed her lethal dance.

Screams erupted around her. Her blade sang and sparked as steel met steel in a beautiful, deadly caress that she was all too familiar with. Her dark heart thrived in this constant state of turmoil. The guards were trained, and that made it even more enjoyable. A mad cackle erupted from her lips, and she ducked from her opponent's attack, the guard cursing colorfully.

"What happened to them?" she demanded. The guard's gaze flickered between her and Memphis and Alby. He answered by swinging his blade clumsily. Responding, Nyx's blade blocked his attack and she threw her weight behind her punch. Her knuckles cracked viciously against his jaw, and she snarled.

"I'll ask again. What. Happened. To. Them?"

He surged forward, and furrowing her brows, she dove into the well of power just waiting to be tapped into. The guard stopped mid-stride, looking confused as blood started to pour slowly from his nostrils. Her blood pounded and roared as she narrowed her eyes in concentration. Fear flicked in his features, the guard dying in her abilities' grasp. Heat radiated off her as the man crumpled.

"Wrong answer," she whispered before racing on.

Moving swiftly, Nyx turned and ducked just as the second guard's attack rained down on her from behind.

In one motion, she had both crescent moon blades grasped in each hand. Five guards now circled her, their arrogance oozing in their steps. Nyx paused for one second as she smirked, malice bleeding into her features. The previous guard should have *really* told her what Morgan had done to her friends.

Blocking her attacker's blade, both of her arms were raised in an *x* formation. She was face-to-face with the guard who paled. She smirked wickedly before throwing all her weight in and cutting downward. His blood dripped from her blades as she ducked and rolled, slicing at the other guards.

Recovering, she stood, roaring as her ability exploded from her, trapping the guards' minds under her sharp claws. Their pleas, their fears, their regrets shivered down her hold, filling her soul as they all stood before her, trembling. Using her ability, she snuffed out their lives: One by one by one.

Nyx didn't look back as she stalked through the chaos and death. She felt disconnected from her body. She wasn't Nyx Astire any more as the thrilling kiss of death and vengeance wrapped around her, becoming her. She spotted Lana about a hundred yards away, fighting through the crowds toward the stage where Morgan watched with pure malice in her gaze. The civilians were fleeing the square, racing away from harm's way, from the tyrants now before them. *Good.*

"Morgan!" Lana's scream tore through her heart, and Nyx kept on moving, her swords flashing in front of her as she fought her way to the podium. To Memphis.

Everything was a blur of red, the only sound that consumed her was the roaring in her veins and her ragged breath. A flash of silver and another body dropped. She ducked, rolled, parried, and slashed. The wind picked up, scattering dust and debris. Azarius was playing his part well, and Nyx gave herself one second to look at the scene that was splayed before her: Lana shoved her sword through Morgan's guard as she stalked toward the leader with frightening grace.

QUEEN TO ASHES

A giant silver wolf was snapping and growling, caught in her own personal cyclone, unable to move, thrashing around with bloodlust. Azarius stared at the wolf, Morgan, with such intensity Nyx could see years of hatred and pain in them.

Memphis and Alby had collapsed, unmoving at Azarius's feet. *No, you need to move!* Running, Nyx wove through the crowd, shoving people out of her way. Just at that moment, a guard launched himself at her with such determination and speed, she twirled to a defensive stance, returning his blows with equal ferocity. Sparks flew from their blades and she laughed. Shoving a knee into his groin, she didn't hesitate to land the killing blow. *Amateur.*

Leaving the bloodied scene, she knew she was almost there. Only a few more seconds...

Her scream ripped from her, "Lana, now!"

Lana found her in the crowd before she nodded to Azarius. The wind stopped, particles of debris standing still in the air, and Morgan growled and leapt, slashing at Lana's throat: Lana did not hesitate. With a skilled hand, she arced her blade down and, with immortal strength, cut through Morgan's neck with ease.

A heavy silence followed as Morgan collapsed.

"This is for my mother," Lana said to the broken body, and fire shot from her palms, burning everything Morgan was to ash.

Relief clawed through Nyx as she sprinted toward them. In a fluid motion, she dropped to her knees, desperately feeling for Memphis's pulse.

"No, no, no, no!" His skin was cold, no flicker of movement, of breath, of *life*. Lana and Azarius were beside her as she choked out a panicked scream. "Help them!"

Lana moved her out of the way, placing a hand on each man's chest. Closing her eyes, she started chanting softly, a harsh, beautiful language Nyx had never heard before. Azarius stood back from her, his face darkening as he took in Alby's lifeless body. She wondered how much more he could lose before he broke. Swearing, she started to pace, shaking.

Dragging his eyes over to her, Azarius whispered, "They will be okay."

"Trying to convince yourself?" Nyx asked.

He didn't answer, and she didn't want him to. As always, her words were fueled by her anger, masking just how scared she was.

A soft light flared from underneath the windwalker's palm, and Nyx watched inky tattoos pool onto her hands, her arms. The light grew until small droplets of blackened blood oozed from their skin. The droplets of blood were caught in the light until Lana opened her eyes, breathing a word lost to her, and the blood turned to dust.

Memphis's eyes fluttered open first, Alby's next, and she cried her relief. Nyx was there, beside Memphis, finding his hand in a second. She didn't care about the spectators; she didn't care about the gore that covered her body. Memphis blearily found her face, and she gave him a lopsided smile.

"Will you ever stop getting yourself in stupid situations?"

Coughing, he grimaced as he wheezed, "I could say the same about you, you know."

Her laugh broke into a half sob as she leaned in, whispering only for him to hear, "I'm so sorry."

"I'm the one who's sorry."

Azarius gripped her shoulder, and she jumped. "I know we are sorry, and it's all very touching, but we need to get them inside. Now."

Wrenching her gaze away, she looked around at the bloodstained ground, the gaping looks. The people of Pentharrow's thoughts drowned her.

"Monsters. How did I trust them?"

"We need to get our kids out, but to where?"

"They protected us. Finally, we are free."

"How could Azarius never tell me that his girlfriend could fight like that?"

Blinking, Nyx swallowed hard, looking at the empty faces and thin lines around her. Azarius tilted his head but helped Memphis, snapping at her, "Help Lana. We will meet back at the cottage."

"You need to diffuse the situation. Now." Her voice sounded hoarse.

Azarius looked at the people of Pentharrow, and to her surprise, he sighed. "You're right."

Nyx's body responded, her arm wrapping around Memphis's lower back as she whispered, "Can you walk?"

He frowned, saying nothing as he hobbled a step forward, his pallor draining of any color.

"Now there's the sensitive commander I know."

"Not now, Nyx."

She smirked. "What, a little bitter about things, Memph? Come now, you can talk to me." Her voice was a whip of reaction, and her stomach twisted. Her sarcasm was as sharp as a knife.

They hobbled through the carnage as she waited, her guilt building with every second.

Just tell him. Tell him that there isn't any physical act in the world that will make up for what I've done. That I just wanted him to be mine. But he never was or will be. And I couldn't see past my jealousy. And now, within a moment, I've lost everything.

Chewing the inside of her cheek, Nyx looked around. The world was constructed into splintered shards: A domino effect of decisions, of mistakes, of success, of heartbreak, of loneliness, of fear. Memphis hobbled, falling into heavy silence, and she let it go.

As they navigated their way back to the cottage with Azarius's pleas and reassuring murmurs drifting through the air, she steeled her heart. Her wounds oozed, blood running down her side, as she looked at the shaken town. She had been acting like a child, throwing a deadly tantrum.

A heavy weight settled on her shoulders as twilight set over them. The sweeping stars far above starting to come into focus took her breath away. Walking past a blur of homes, her feet led her back to Lana's cottage. Her mind was racing a thousand miles away.

Nyx had misjudged Emory. The girl, who she had preyed on, who she viewed as weak...a girl who had accomplished something Nyx couldn't understand until now. Emory must have been afraid; she was waltzing with her death, all for a cause she wasn't a part of, for a past she didn't remember. And yet, she had protected them all, granting them an impossible advantage. Time. That selfless action that Nyx was just beginning to understand was worth it a thousand times over.

The cool wind brushed over her, goosebumps prickling her arms. The small, quaint cottage came into sight as she steered the brooding commander toward it. Sighing, Nyx desperately hoped that the only Fae was still alive. That, if the fates crossed their paths again, she could try to make things right with Emory. To, at least, try to explain.

Shifting her weight, she threw open the door. Still Memphis didn't say a word when he lunged forward, barely holding himself up as he wandered down the hallway.

"The other spare room is on the left," she whispered. The slamming of the door was his only response. Her world tilted, the pain and exhaustion catching up to her. Stalling, she was caught between moving forward and looking back.

But as the tinges of night chased the sunset, Nyx took a steadying breath, her mind racing with how she could start to live her life putting one person first—herself. No more depending on other people or chasing her heart into those empty voids because she was scared to be alone. No more lowering her priorities, no more rash decisions. No more last resorts. No more acting out of fear.

The door closed behind her, and she stood taller. Breathing deeply, she made her way to her bed.

CHAPTER TWELVE

Emory

Ainthe was too heavy in her grip. The steel glinted like liquid silver, hints of embers flickering faintly like a pulse that was alive and encompassing. Emory shifted her fingers, gripping the hilt, her knuckles turning white as she took in the throne room. Running her dry tongue over her teeth, she tried to still her heart, her sweaty palms, the nervous quake in her limbs.

She should be thinking of a thousand different things, but the one thought that imprinted in her mind was, for a second, that she wanted the simplicity of earth: Of going to the movies, of dating, of the day-to-day desires and quirks that made up humans. That had made *her* up. Instead, she was a lost princess. An acting warrior. An executor. A traitor. And she had fragmented memories of her parents who had wanted more for her. But she had no idea how to get back to that little girl, filled with hope and power, who trusted in this world.

"Emory?" Adair sat behind her, taking away her ability to focus and breathe. Her chest plate constricted as she stilled, feeling the shift of needles against her skin. *What choice is there?* Her tight-fitting leather pants felt suffocating along with her knee-high boots and button-down jacket. All black. The urge to rip off each article piece by piece and scrub her skin until it was raw was a very appealing option. The magically enhanced plate tightened around her chest and upper back in response. Swallowing, Emory was constantly reminded of Adair's control over her actions and choices.

Adair's throne room was vast. Black marble made up most of the space, the windowless walls climbing to the top, where there was no ceiling, opening to the skies. She felt his stare boring into her back, and the guards flanked the walls, too still, too emotionless.

"You were brought here today to answer for your actions. How do you plead?" Emory's voice broke, crackling into nothingness as she stared at the man in front of her.

His clear blue eyes filled with fear, his ashen hair streaked with sweat, mixing with dirt and filth. He had spent weeks down in the cell, in the darkness, alone. "I-I didn't mean to! I was hungry. I didn't want to do it anymore."

"Do what exactly?"

Tears streaked down his face. "Kill. I didn't want to kill anymore."

"You realize you ignored your duties as a soldier of your king's army? Your direct instructions?" She didn't recognize her voice anymore.

He sputtered, "If I hadn't been aware, we wouldn't be here."

Save him. Save him. Save him. "Your refusal and stealing have been reported as direct defiance against King Adair. Do you plead ignorance?" *Say yes. Please, say yes. I can't do this. I can't do this.*

He jutted his chin out. "I plead guilty. If that's even what you can call this. I'm not a mindless machine. I am not killing anyone, direct order or no. These were civilians. *Our* people. Ability or not, I won't be a mindless murderer."

She choked out Adair's words, her despair clutching her fiercely in its claws. "If you plead guilty, your sentence will be…"

Stalling, her hands shook violently, and the scene before her changed. The man was washed away, blue eyes to gold. Chiselled features, alluring lips, broad shoulders. His golden hair sweeping in his eyes. A face that was a thousand things to her. Breath picking up, she wanted to reach out to him, to find warmth and safety. Brokk would never let her fall astray.

Through all the lies, scheming, and betrayal, Brokk had never changed. It was her. She had let *him* down. Emory remembered the swish of the steel, the connection as the blade bit in, and what it had felt like. Chills snaked down her spine as his blood seeped, and his breath stopped. His lifeless body was branded into her soul, haunting her. *Not real. It hadn't been him. Not real, not real.*

Blinking, Brokk washed away with the memory. The uncertainty of whether he was still alive gnawed at her, but if it hadn't been him, whose blood stained her hands? Who did she kill? The room spun, the cold sweat clinging to her brow, her lips dry.

Swallowing, she choked out, "Your sentence is death."

The man drained of color, his mouth hanging open as he searched her face, looking for a flicker of doubt, of humanity. Adair stood behind her as she glanced over her shoulder. His eyes glinted as a slow smile tugged at his lips.

The man pleaded, "This is insane. My King, please. Have mercy." She felt the needles against her skin. The plate hummed against her chest, warming her. Ripping her gaze away, she clenched the sword in her grip. The man's pleas bled away, and she couldn't look into his eyes.

Adair spoke coolly from behind her. "I have no mercy for liars and thieves."

Muscles screaming in protest, her sword sliced through clothes, muscle, bone, and sinew. His breath left him as he gaped at the blade stuck through him. Those eyes never left hers as they dimmed, the light fading into the abyss, and the man collapsed. Wrenching the blade back, the crimson blood dripped from the metal, pooling around him. The guards jumped to life, dragging the body away without a flicker of remorse.

Adair stood beside her as she stared at the stain, feeling it creep into her skin, something she would never be able to wash away. Tears burned as the world tipped, the walls swaying and bending.

"Well done."

His voice was a murmur in the sea of her anger. White hot and pulsing, it filled her cracking heart. Bile seared her throat, and panic rooted her in place, the marble walls closing in. *You just killed an innocent man.* Sweat trickled down the back of her neck, Adair's approval branding her, and she swallowed down her disgust. How far did she think she would have to go to win her kingdom back? To claim her title as Queen? She was a traitor, a liar, and now a murderer.

Her sanity crumbled as she locked eyes with Adair.

"Thank you, My King." The words were like tar in her mouth, and it took every ounce of self-control not to throw up, break down, or give up. Weakness wouldn't win this war. Love wouldn't fuel the revolution. She always knew it would come down to him and her. She forced her lips into a smug smirk and quelled her hands into compliance. Wiping the blade clean against her pants, she sheathed it.

"Now, I do believe it's time for us to resume our lessons. This was just a taste of court and our day-to-day obligations. I love my people, Emory, but liars breed doubt and defiance. My kingdom will never be tainted by it. I ensure it."

"Understood."

He stretched, shoulders popping, and then raised an eyebrow. "Let's go."

Dread flooded her thoughts, her bruised body shying away from their last lesson. But she straightened, her voice steady. "Lead the way."

He stretched his hand to her, and her bloodstained fingers interlocked through his. There was a whoosh of cool air as gravity left her, and the smoke clouded her senses as they flew, soaring away from his bloodied court.

Emory snarled against the edge of his blade. Chuckling, Adair dropped his sword, staring at the red mark against her pale throat.

"How do you figure you will prove useful to me if you cannot fight?"

Standing and coughing, she spit out blood. "Well, you know around these parts my family name means something."

Eyes narrowing, he said, "Status will not keep you alive. It will feed your ego and your arrogance, but it will do nothing against an opponent who wants you in the ground. Now, again."

They had been at it for hours. Every lunge, every trick she thought she knew had been obliterated, until there was nothing left but a dull hollow ache in her chest.

"I need to rest."

"And will you need planned rest breaks in battle? Again, *Princess*."

Biting back her frustration, Emory exhaled, and with shaking arms, she raised her blade as he roared, his attack relentless. Her body bowed, her feet keeping up with the pace for the moment. Emory parried. Once. Twice. And again. And again. Tripping, her body crashed to the ground, lights flashing in her sight.

"Pathetic."

Tapping his blade against her throat for the millionth time, annoyance etched into the crevices in Adair's features. Prowling around her, he seethed, "Again."

Narrowing her eyes at him, she shoved the blade away, the sharp edge slicing into her palms. The blood was warm, trickling down her forearms and mixing with her sweat. The pain ignited her, tended to her ire, flaming it to life, pushing her tiredness aside.

The forest seemed to dim, the lush purple leaves of the Noctis woods glowing with the filtered sunlight. The forest floor was soft, and dirt mixed with lush moss cushioned their footfalls.

All she could see were the dead man's eyes. How the blue had flamed before it bled away, dimming. He had been young, and she had taken everything away from him. She was nothing but Adair's *puppet*. Flicking her gaze up to him, Adair paused, sensing the change of energy as she gripped her sword, the embers flaming to life in the metal, sparking and cackling. *You did this.*

The bile seared up her throat, burning as she clamped her lips shut—attacking. She forgot everything Memphis had taught her.

Be better. Stronger. Time swayed them: The rebellion held her to their clock, where they had no time left, and their desperation rode their decisions. But where did that leave her now?

Emory slammed her blade down, meeting thin air as it lodged itself in the forest floor.

"Your rage masks your logic."

Panting, Emory turned, as he smirked.

"Blindly trying will get you killed. What's your plan, Emory?"

Sprinting, she left her sword behind as Adair flicked his eyebrow up. Her knuckles slammed into his jaw, his head snapping back from the force.

Biting back her string of curses, she spat, "You will train me in a way that works or not at all."

His eyes flashed, turning almost black as he took her in, his split skin raw and swollen. "And exactly what do you suggest?"

He didn't move, both of their chests heaving. She didn't care that she had crossed a line. She didn't *care*.

"Build my strength up. You have shown me that you are an impossible opponent. Allow me the chance to become your equal." Her voice cracked as she waited.

He ran a hand through his hair. Shadows danced in his eyes, his muscles feathering along his jaw. "Fine. But next time you attempt anything like what you just did—" he breathed in her face, bringing his hand up to hold her chin "—you will regret it."

"Understood, My *King*."

Rolling his shoulders, he uttered, "Let's begin. Try to keep up." He sheathed his sword, and she jogged back, mimicking the action. Shooting her a sideways glance, he said, "You haven't changed much, you know."

Sweat trickled down her back, as she stalled. That voice, she *knew*. It wasn't one of a deranged king; it wasn't the man that had just been present. It was an echo of the boy that she once had known. Tilting her head, she swallowed hard as memories tugged at her gut. He sighed before turning, taking off at a jog. She didn't think, simply responded. Her breath hitched as she followed, her surroundings blurring, her heartbeat pounding in her ears as they lost themselves to the depths the forest kept secret.

The prisoner today had a life. *Murderer.*

A home. Ambitions. Love. Secrets. A family. *Killer.*

And she had taken it all away in a moment.

Leaping over a decaying tree, her heart pounded, sweat lathering every inch of her skin, the sword strapped across her back a dead weight. Her skin prickled as a chill snaked down her spin, her muscles burning, but the cool wind cutting through the trees snapped her to awareness.

Her ragged wheezes cut through the silence, but on Adair pushed, leading her deeper into the enchanting woods. Enchanting but dangerous. Whispers chased behind her, breaths soft and alluring.

The Queen has come. She has come. She has come.

And as she ran, she lost herself in those soft voices and the flicker of life resonating in the woods. In the unseen eyes of the residents, the blackened bark of the trees, the jewel-like leaves. Each color was unlike anything she had ever seen before. Purples, blues, reds. Casting their world into fantasy, reality bleeding away along with logic and reason. She pushed harder, her shaking limbs burning, but the pain reminded her, centered her. And she repeated to herself: *You are more than what he knows. What he thinks and sees.*

She gnashed her teeth together as he picked up the pace, the slight incline of the forest floor igniting her lungs into flames.

Gasping, she slipped, her palms slicking with dirt and blood. She lurched up, ignoring his look. *You lived your entire life feeling like half of you was missing. Fight for the missing part. Fight for this.*

And she fought. Every breath, every second, she fought for that girl who was now dead. The girl who dreamed of another world, of having a family, of a home. Of a prince waiting for her. Who was never satisfied and had always wanted more than her job, than her friends. She had been displaced, like oil in water. But now. The woman had emerged, alone. She was questioning but regal. Clumsy but deadly. She was lost in a kingdom filled with snakes. Filled with lies not answers. A woman who could kill. A woman with the weight of a revolution on her shoulders. The promise of a better life. One where she might belong.

Her stomach reeled, threatening to empty its contents as her hands trembled. She numbly ran until Adair stopped at the top of a rolling hill, the trees towering above them. The crisp air carried the trace of salt, conjuring up memories of the ocean side. Stopping, she tried to catch her breath.

"Do you remember a man named Marquis Maher?" His voice was like silk. Straightening, she begged her body to stay standing. She looked onto the horizon, seeing snippets of light between the thick trees.

"No." *Lies.*

"Well, in a few weeks, we have a meeting arranged." *We?* Dread filled her core, but she held her tongue. "Marquis is the King of the Shattered Isles. He is the reason my kingdom is well fed with a healthy supply of the finer foods and wines. As we enter the war with the rebels, we will need reinforcements. It's time my old friend leaves his island."

Panic clutched her throat. "Surely you will be able to destroy them alone?"

"I will be the first to admit, I have already underestimated my old school colleagues."

Could he sense her fear? Her raging thoughts?

Her nails bit into her bloodied palms as she tried to keep her voice steady. "And what about my training?"

Turning, the wind caught tufts of black hair that weren't coated in sweat. His gaze flicked down to her for a moment before taking in the forest around them.

"I will ensure you are more than ready."

She devoured the scene in front of her as her mind scrambled. Guaranteeing Adair left Kiero would mean the Rebellion would be safe from his clutches for a time. Emory's mind spun. If she could get word to Memphis or to Azarius, they could infiltrate and take over the Draken Mountains with Adair gone. Take away his entire kingdom, his army. His allegiances. The plan was sloppy, but it formed all the same. It was her only one, and she was running out of alternatives.

A tight smile. "Of course, My King." That warmth spread over her skin, and she tried not to scream, had to stop herself from ripping that blasted plate off her skin in one motion.

He dipped his head. "There is much to learn. Their world is not like this one." Another nod. Those sweeping dark eyes took her in, and she tried not to shiver. "There isn't a moment to lose then."

Turning, he fell into a steady run once more. Sucking in a deep breath, she took one more look to where her heart knew the sea raged beyond the tree line. *Marquis Maher.* The name rolled around in her mind.

Following Adair, her body screamed in defiance at the movement. It would be a miracle if she could even move tomorrow. Forcing herself into that well of perseverance, she ignored her tingling palms and the whispers cutting through the trees.

She was lost in the fogginess of the memory as she ran, of a girl and a prince. That name, slicing through her core, resonating one thing. At one point in her life, she had trusted him, the prince from across the sea. Chewing on her inner cheek, she wondered if she still could. Adair's pace was relentless, but she said nothing, allowing her exhaustion and frustration to carry her back, trying to leave her ghosts behind her but to no avail.

They reached the mountain range as night was sweeping in. Purple hues danced across the sky, igniting the stars hidden behind the sparse clouds. With her hands on her hips, she stared up, her skin burning, her sweat having ceased hours ago. Warning bells went off in her mind as she swayed. Adair looked like they had gone for a pleasant stroll. She was dehydrated, her pulse racing too fast, her tongue thick, and her mind foggy.

"I expect you at the same time tomorrow." It wasn't a request, and she bowed her head as internally she screamed. "Should I see you to your room?"

Trying to keep her voice steady, she said, "That won't be necessary. Besides, I haven't seen much of our kingdom. The market we passed earlier looked exquisite."

Adair tilted his head, more predator than man as he weighed her request. The challenge and the danger in it.

Please, please, please, please.

"Very well, but a guard will accompany you. Not everyone is thrilled about the mysterious heir returning."

Relief washed through her, as he stepped forward to the stone face. The dagger was small as he grasped it from his pockets, slicing the edge across his palm swiftly. Crimson blood welled, and not flinching, he placed it on the rock. The stone face melted like wax, forming a smooth entryway: Low lanterns were flush to the walls, blue flames dancing merrily within the opal bowls. It bathed the walkway in a pleasant light, the decorative flooring swirling beneath them in lush colors. They both stepped in, and instantly, the rock behind them shifted and groaned, sealing them into the heart of the mountain.

Adair led the way, and Emory was speechless as she followed. His kingdom was breathtaking. Unlike the courtroom, the tunnel widened, the mouth opening to the tiered walls, the chatter of people's homes soaring down to them. Fires burned in the hearths, a thousand flickering lights, and stairs climbed to the different levels, soaring up toward that beautifully constructed opening that she realized was in every room, exposing the blinking stars.

The complexity of it, the *normalcy*, left her winded. They walked in silence, as they crossed the room leading into a bigger cavern. She froze as the smells and sounds assaulted her.

The market was in full swing, but the vendors had changed since the morning. Gone were the bright clothes and delicious foods. Lavender, citrus, and smoke drifted on the air as a roaring fire burned in a well-sealed pit, the flames a rippling green and purple. Men and women twisted around it.

Emory tried to keep up with the graceful arcs of the people as they followed the aching melody. Off to the side, the musicians stood, their bodies moving with their instruments. Fingers flew on strings, arms a blur as they commanded their bows. Drums pounded, and it was a different kind of war, one of creation and creativity.

Her cheeks flushed as she took in the dancers in more detail, their silks midnight-black and shimmering, leaving nothing to the imagination. Clearing her throat, she drank in the vendors next. One vendor sold smoky meats premade for the audience, their savoury scents drifting toward her causing her stomach to rumble. Beside them, beautifully crafted instruments hung and were propped up against a vendor, the young woman watching the crowds with a hawk-like accuracy. Beside her, the vendors continued: Crystals flashing, reflecting off the crackling flames. Books and orbs cluttered the space, silks stacked alongside them. Ale poured freely, and the carefree atmosphere was contagious.

She forgot her hair was matted and slicked with dirt. That her hands and clothes were bloodied, that she was dressed for battle. Her mouth must have been hanging open as a dark chuckle resonated from her side.

"I will leave you in the hands of my captain now."

She recognized the guard from her cell instantly, and Emory flashed him a chiding smirk.

Dipping his chin, Adair murmured, "Enjoy it. The night market is renowned, and we all take great pride in it. But always, remember yourself and who you are."

Like she needed a reminder.

Following his cryptic words, Adair vanished in a plume of smoke, every eye in the room watching the fleeting king. Throwing a dirty look to the guard, she melted into the crowd. Each pull of harmony, each pounding of the drum, she unfurled, each layer of tension shedding. She felt the guard's eyes burning into her back, as she first cut her way through to the delicious smell of garlic and chives. The woman and her husband worked

QUEEN TO ASHES

in a blur, each anticipating each other's movements. Sweat glistened on their skin, their loose clothing and worn aprons twirling as they loaded plates, talking happily to each customer. The sliced meat melted off the bones beneath the knives, each garnished with a healthy amount of what looked like golden chips.

With a watering mouth, she got in line, allowing herself a moment to get her bearings. This life, from the outside looking in, was not the group of blood-thirsty people she had seen in the Pit. Gone were the judgements. Gone were the defining titles of soldiers. In their place were husbands taking a moment to dance with their wives, their children nestled back in their homes: In the darkness, they blushed at soft spoken words just for each other and echoing laughter bounced off the walls, the crowds oblivious to those beautiful stolen moments.

Moving with the line, her heart wrenched as she took it all in. This world was bred from the darkest of hearts, and yet...it was not all it seemed to be.

"Miss?" She started at the voice, shaking herself back into reality. The woman stared at her with wide eyes, holding a magnificent plate in front of her nose. Smiling tentatively, the woman ushered the plate into her hands.

"Thank you. I'm afraid I don't have any payment."

"Dear, no one pays at the night market. Our king ensures we are graciously compensated." Her shock was evident as the corners of the woman's eyes crinkled, softening. "Enjoy the night."

The guard was her shadow as she drifted to a clear spot in between vendors, a small bench freed as the night became later. Two small wooden spears were tucked neatly beside the food, and assuming they were utensils, Emory dug in. Perching, she ignored the brooding man stationing himself beside her as she devoured the delicious food. The flavors danced over her senses, and she groaned in pleasure, not having such luxuries since being here. *The king across the sea has one thing in order.*

Finishing her meal, Emory quelled the urge to lick her fingers.

"Emory Fae." Jumping at her name, she recognized the young woman from the instrument vendor standing in front of her. Her blond hair shimmered in the dusky light, reaching just above her shoulders. Her pale hazel eyes cut into hers. It was a calculated movement, how she held her body, her voice, everything.

"Sorry. I'm afraid we haven't had the pleasure of being acquainted yet." Her words were careful, as she tried to keep the edge out of her voice. The woman took in the guard, before saying, "I was wondering if you cared for a drink? It's not every day you meet a legend in the flesh."

Dipping her head, Emory tried to be gracious. "It would be my pleasure."

Following her, Emory clamped her teeth together as she noticed her guard tailing her, quiet and ominous as a shadow. The woman made it to the vendor first, smiling wolfishly.

"Wren, two of your finest please."

The man took Emory in, stalling slightly. If her cheeks were flushed, they were a deep crimson now. A whisper of a smirk danced over Wren's lips as he quickly poured the ale, the foam luscious as it settled thinly over the deep oak color.

"Riona, you haven't introduced me to your companion here."

Flicking a piece of her blond hair over her shoulder, she mused, "I doubt you need it. Emory, this is Wren."

Emory nodded toward him before taking a seat with Riona, sipping the ale generously. Deep notes of honey and hops rolled over her tongue, wiping her palate of the lingering spices. Riona followed suit, her gaze constantly lingering over Emory's bodyguard, as her head bobbed along with the music.

Emory's curiosity nipped at her, but trying to smooth her hair out, she leaned forward. "You run the instrument vendor, right? Your craftsmanship is beautiful. I have never seen any instruments like them."

Riona flashed her teeth. "Yes, I do, and thank you. It has been my life's passion, along with being a smithy." Her admiration must have shown, as Riona leaned forward. "The best in Kiero. Though my people would beg to differ." She smirked, as Emory's mind spun.

She treaded carefully. "And where did you learn such skill?"

"It would seem, *Princess*, that I also find myself serving two kings, of two lands."

Wren averted his gaze, and ice ran through Emory's veins at the implication, at the knowledge that tugged distantly at her past.

Finishing her drink, Emory coolly stated, "I'm not sure what you're getting at. I am here to serve my one true king."

Dipping her head, she mused, "Of course. No insult intended. Though, I have noticed that your blade needs tending to. My shop is open tomorrow, and I would like to see to it." Finishing her drink, Riona's eyes danced mischievously as Emory's heart pounded. *Friend or foe?*

Emory inclined her head, allowing herself the time and chance to decide for herself. "It would be my pleasure. I will come after my training." *And my trials.*

Placing the glass on the counter, she stood. The crowd had become thinner, the flames crackling down to embers, and exhaustion pulled at her mind. With a full belly of food and drink, the drowsiness made her feel clumsy, and turning, she whispered to the guard she knew was there, "Please take me back to my room."

He nodded as he stepped in front of her, and she followed. The music became a faint pulse, and she looked up, the expanse of the sky swirling far above them. The stars twinkled, nestled in the curtains of shadows as her imagination pulled at her.

Riona's cryptic words made her pulse hammer. Was it possible she could find an ally hidden within Adair's people? Time was harshly slipping from her grasp. Maybe Riona would help her get word to the Rebellion, to this Marquis Maher, if she could be trusted. Emory's plan sharpened and honed, the foggy threads becoming clearer.

The survival of Black Dawn, and her own life was banked on her what ifs. Banked on her hopes. But she would make the world listen. And she would learn exactly what it meant to become a ruler of this wild country.

It was a series of twists and turns before they reached her rooms. Shooting the guard a glare, she left him behind. The quiet of her room greeted her as she sighed. Ripping her clothes off and unbuckling her sword, she ran to the baths. The water couldn't fill the tub fast enough as she paced. Had it only been this morning that she held her sword? That she had sealed that young man's fate? Deja vu swept over her, and she screamed, biting into her knuckles to muffle the sound.

What was she doing? Blindly dancing in the lethal game of kings and queens like her parents did?

Looking in the mirror behind her, her bruises and wounds contrasted harshly against her pale skin. Her green eyes sparked as she whispered, "What would both of you have done differently?"

Sighing, Emory limped to the steaming tub and submerged herself into the steam. She scrubbed herself raw, trying to free herself of the stains that weren't visible.

She drained the porcelain a few moments later and wrapped herself in a downy towel. Her mind roared at her as she shifted through her drawers, through the layers and layers of inky-black clothing. She opted for a loose-fitting shift and, donning it, flopped on the bed.

Where were the rebels? Alive? Back in hiding? How long would they take until their next move? Azarius wasn't the patient type. Worry ate away at her, and as the wistful grasps of sleep took her, she knew the tides of the world were changing. Where would she stand when the time came? Alone or with allies?

CHAPTER THIRTEEN
Brokk

The crescent moon hung high above them, nestled amongst the stars. Nothing stirred in the night, as if Kiero itself was holding its breath. The moonlight washed over the forest, illuminating their path in its silver wash.

Staring ahead, Brokk's silence turned into brooding, his brooding then into rage. Each step he took seemed to hammer into his heart as he tried to digest what had happened.

Prince. Prince. Prince.

He looked at Kiana. It had taken him hours, but he finally got a name out of her, instead of addressing her as cumasach. Sighing, he looked to her sword strapped to her back as she led the way, admiring the tiny details, a work of art, on both the blade and sheath. Her silver hair shimmered in the night, and he still couldn't get over the living, breathing myth in front of him. His guide. His *ally*.

"So, are we still at this silent stand off?" Kiana's words were soft, but a challenge.

He bared his teeth at her back. "Forgive me if I'm skeptical."

QUEEN TO ASHES

She shrugged. "You have questions." Again, that soft understanding voice.

He was beginning to think that the fey were annoying. "No, I just found out I'm a prince, that my family was murdered by thieves who pretended that they were my parents, only to steal my abilities. That this *whole* time you have been keeping tabs on me, watching our world get torn apart. Watching *me* get torn apart. And did nothing but sit in your blissful, lost city." A sharp ringing filled his ears as his blood thrummed. "My friends *died* for a rebellion that is broken. Died because of some of my choices. And now..."

"If you think for a minute that you should have died alongside them, you're wrong."

"You don't get to tell me what and who is worth dying for."

Stopping, she turned, eyes narrowed. "Don't stand there acting like I have known no loss. That I haven't suffered just as much as you have. But this war is much bigger than both of us."

She glared at him before turning around again.

The woods were thick, and Brokk wondered what borders they were crossing. On foot, the journey would take twice the time as it would in his wolf form. His mind churned, weighing his trust for Kiana. He barely had opened his emotions to Memphis who had known him most of his life. How could he explain to a stranger what was coursing through him? The grief that ripped through his heart after seeing he once had loving parents he would never get to know. The fear of trying to overcome the Oilean, the overwhelming impossibility of the task.

Resentment reared up and burned, pooling within his gut at the acclaimed title. *Prince.* He was Brokk Foster, rebel, not some pompous king that would lead them to greatness. He didn't want it. Emory was his hope in that she was strong enough to lead them out of the darkness. To lead him out of *his* darkness, if he could just explain how he felt to her. Swallowing hard, he almost didn't hear her at first.

"Nehmai was once a great city. Our people, under your parents' rule, flourished. The Warriors were an esteemed guard. Our training and ability was unparalleled to anyone else. And we were tucked away, the fey only having knowledge of where the city lay, magic protecting us.

"Centuries ago, the world was a dark place, split into two as your legends tell you now. Dark magic was unharnessed, breeding nightmares and unleashing them. We fought it, trying to quell it. And eventually, we did, by feeding our magic into the world. Into people."

"So, it's true then, that people of ability are gifted with fey magic?"

Chewing her bottom lip, she nodded. "In a manner. Nehmai was built to harness and nurture the magic of our world. And we were the protectors of it. When the dark ages ended, the fey lived in peace for a long time. The Warriors keeping to the city, the threats of the world having been pushed back. They were my family. And I...their captain."

His eyebrows rose.

"That night... I cannot even put into words the horror. We are immortal, a kingdom built on magic, our leaders producing a miracle. Fey children were practically unheard of. And you defied the odds. But even immortals can be killed. And conquered."

A chill snaked down his spine, settling into his core.

"We weren't prepared to face an enemy of old, but that night we did. Peyton had harnessed the dark magic that had once split Kiero. An essence of something we had fought before. I watched my friends fall; my leaders get killed. That magic... I recognized it. And I fled."

She took a shuddering breath. "I'm not proud of what I did. But I can't take back the past. I returned the next day to a city ridden with death. My family, gone. I was a coward. That was the day I left my title of captain behind. I vowed to myself I would find a way to right my wrongs. To avenge my friends.

"Centuries ago, the Oilean didn't have a form but an essence, trying to deplete the magic and us. But we won that war, and that dark magic was banished from this world. We had lived in a time where the Warriors fled the borders, the city was free of fear, and our existence bled out of reality and into legend."

"Until that night," Brokk said.

She stopped, sorrow flooding those ancient eyes. "I have lived a lifetime watching the sinister hearts of this world thrive and conquer. Have watched old enemies return by means of witches and portals. I have watched and waited to find *you*. To bring you back to your bloodline. I'm not asking for your sympathy. I'm not asking for you to accept your title. I'm asking for your help to destroy the forces that have taken away everything I held close. My life. My dignity. And to make sure the same doesn't happen to you."

Emory. Memphis. Alby.

Fear drowned out every other emotion as he imagined his life without his friends—his *family*—in it. He would fight for them until his last breath, and steeling his heart, Brokk set his intention. There were so many things he still didn't understand, but this was war. Had always *been* a war.

He nodded, and the shadows that danced across her face lessened slightly into a grim smile. Kiana continued into the heart of the forest, picking up her pace.

"We have to make sure the Oilean don't get to the Book of Old. Once, I didn't believe that such dark magic could exist, but I was proven wrong. Even in Nehmai, the Book was a story that always ended in death."

Brokk cursed under his breath.

"My thoughts exactly. Now, let's talk about lighter things, for the time being. How many ways do you know how to fight? I'm sure I can fill you in on some secrets in that department," Kiana said.

And so, he started to fill her in, Kiana only interrupting to show him new techniques or how her people were trained. *His* people: He pushed the thought aside, locking it away.

They walked deeper into the heart of the forest, Brokk swearing he could hear whispers on the wind, calling them back.

Dawn broke over the horizon, painting the world in soft golden strokes, just as Brokk stalked lower, making himself flush to the ground. Pinning his ears back, he became very still. In his wolf form, life was simpler. No fey princes or the politics of war. Just the predator and the hunted.

The beast he watched was magnificent, its towering antlers curling toward the sky. Its kind brown eyes roaming lazily at its surroundings, dipping its head down to graze the sparse blades of grass covered in fresh dew. To Brokk, the fia had always been innocent, gentle creatures.

He dug his nails into the moist ground and exploded from his hiding spot. He was a golden streak across the terrain, the fia not having time to react before his sharp teeth found their mark. It was fast and clean. He wished no pain would befall the creature as the light faded from its eyes. Instinct took over as he dragged it to where Kiana sat. The rhythmic *hiss* of the whetstone flowed over her blade as she flicked her gaze up.

They had talked all night. Brokk had soaked up every word, every motion she explained, and the feys' war tactics. It was a beautiful strange language, that of swordsmanship, but one they found common ground on. One that helped him avoid addressing how he felt about the current situation.

On a constant replay, he said their names until it was as constant as his breath, as his heartbeat. *Emory. Memphis. Alby.*

Shifting back in one motion, he had the broad knife in his hands and started separating fur from flesh, preparing the meat.

"You know I could have done that much faster with magic," Kiana said.

Stalling, his hands shook slightly as he replied, "I know."

With arched eyebrows, she sighed and continued sharpening her blade in silence.

He worked with intention, separating and weighing. Fatigued, he walked to their makeshift pit, and his annoyance flickered to life at the sudden crackling of flames crackling. The smoke curled toward the sunlight and he growled. "I was just about to start the fire."

Kiana said nothing, her luminous hair glowing in the light. He swore from the corner of his eye he saw her smirk. *Arrogant warrior.*

He had agreed to help, but he was drained. Yearning for sleep, his body ached: Instead he skewered the meat on his blade, rotating it through the slow cook, portion by portion. It wasn't fancy, but it would nourish them, and he was *starving*. Never in a million lifetimes did he envision himself cooking breakfast with an immortal. That he would be tied to them. That the answers he had craved his *entire* life had been answered swiftly in a radiant city and then explained in the shadows of the night. His lips turned down at the thought, as Kiana silently maneuvered over to him.

Settling in, she grabbed a few cooked chunks of meat. "Thank you. What will you do with the rest?"

"The other predators of the forest can enjoy it and leave our trail alone."

Nodding, Kiana smiled softly, but from behind them, a twigged cracked. Stalling and having no reason to, dread ran up along Brokk's spine as Kiana stiffened—as the feeling overwhelmed him that they were being followed.

Resuming chewing contently, Kiana kept her features in that cool mask. Whether human or not, they couldn't stop, not with the risks so high, even with Kiana. She had said herself, the fey may be immortal but they could be killed.

And they were the last.

Quickly having their fill, Kiana stood, glaring at the fire, and it ceased to be, the pit vanishing.

"Do fey usually have the same...gifts with their magic?" he asked.

"No, not usually. Like abilities, it's a wide spectrum, the magic binding with the person and feeding into their soul. Our power comes out in our personality, each unique to the person."

"And what is yours?" Brokk asked.

"Well..." Stopping mid-sentence, her eyebrows pinched together.

Suddenly, there was a snap of branches, and he was reeling, blade in hand. Kiana was right there, a phantom to have gotten beside him so fast. The hairs on his neck stood on end as the world stilled. He didn't dare look at her as he stepped forward, his human senses trying to catch anything amiss.

Another snap; a flash of light.

He was thrown back, his limbs colliding and breaking, healing and re-healing as he shattered through tree after tree.

Move, Kiana. Move.

His thoughts were disjointed as he felt the slow trickle of blood run down his nose, his breath quick. Blinking, the world swirled, colors becoming a grey mass as they blended. Staggering to his feet, he snarled before falling. The moss was damp underneath his shaking hands, and he panted, lurching forward, panic clutching at his heart, ice running through his veins. The tinkling laugh was as clear as tolling bells.

"Tuca, *you sly old bas–*"

The ability to move had completely departed as he watched Kiana swirl and spin in a sea of blossoming petals, their golds and silvers painting her skin with their shimmering elegance. Everywhere she touched turned to that beautiful will, her words dying as they turned to laughter. She locked eyes with him, and her smile was brighter than any star, any *light*.

Shock rippled through Brokk as beside her a stocky man stood, his elated features enhancing his angular face, his low hat shadowing his eyes. Two curled fangs dipped over his lower lip, and his weathered skin was covered in patches of black fur, his inky hair following suit.

"Who exactly are you?" Tuca's voice was clipped.

Those magical leaves disappeared in an instant. "I could ask the same," Brokk snapped.

Kiana stepped in between them. "Brokk, this is Tuca, an old friend of mine."

The man chuckled. "Old friend? More like your smuggler contact." Tuca assessed him now, his yellow eyes narrowing in mistrust. "I am the guardian of these borders, of what used to be a quiet town of Meer. Though like most, I have been in hiding, but this doesn't mean I don't keep an eye on things in these woods."

"Why follow us then?" Kiana asked.

"Because I wanted to make sure I wasn't being deceived. It's been some time since fey have decided to drift so far." Tuca flinched at that, and Kiana cleared her throat.

"We have other business."

He winked. "Kiana, darling, you know how I feel about your secrets. But, this time, spare me the torture. I thought you to be dead."

"Tuca, we both know I can't go into the details of that. Now get to the point. What do you want?" The lightness from the moments before disappeared, an edge filling her voice: Kind and dangerous. A warning.

He bristled. "Kiana, you know me too well. We are survivors. It has been hard these past years. The magic...has changed."

"Obviously."

Tuca growled, stepping toward her. In a cracking of bone and blood, Brokk shifted and was snarling in his face, Kiana standing beside him. His golden fur was raised, as he snapped his jaws again, the warning clear.

Tuca whispered, "Kiana, what have you done?"

Her blades were flashing-Brokk barely had time to register what was happening. Tuca bowed, charging at her, teeth elongating. Brokk lunged, trying to get in front of Kiana. His mind went numb as his gut screamed to trust Kiana. He had no other choice.

QUEEN TO ASHES

Hearing about the fey's fighting tactics was one thing...seeing it completely floored Brokk. Kiana was a blur—one second unsheathing her blades and then disappearing in a blinding light. Kiana reappeared behind Tuca, slicing behind his knees as he fell to them. Brokk bayed just as Tuca looked up to him and smiled. He felt the blow rip through him, throwing him backwards.

Get up. Up. Up. Blood filled his mouth, the fire roaring in his body, but Brokk made himself move, despite the fact he could barely feel his limbs. Rolling over, Kiana screamed as Tuca's boot connected with her shoulder; a sickening popping sounded at the impact. She rolled, baring her teeth, pointed ears slipping through her silver hair. Charging, her knives were extensions of her arms.

Rolling, Brokk dug his paws into the earth as the smuggler roared, Kiana's knife sliding in between his shoulder blades, only to quickly pull back, black blood dripping from its point. A flicker, that's all it was, his pain, his confusion and adrenaline rolling into one.

Kiana was slammed back, Tuca's hand wrapping around her slender throat. "Give it to me, and I may let you live." Kiana spit in Tuca's face which only made him press harder. Brokk was almost there, and he wove around the tree trunks. Tuca leaned over. "The magic, it's *mine*."

Brokk leapt, wind howling through his senses before he slammed to the ground, his mammoth maws grabbing the man's back, and he tore down. Kiana dropped, gasping, and all Brokk could taste was death. Rotting flesh filled his mouth as he let go, wrinkling his nose.

Tuca laughed as he turned slowly. "I will start with you." It was that voice, cold and eerily thrilling that froze him. Flashes of knives in the dimly lit room. The water on the walls. And always their giggles in the night. Hidden in the shadows.

The man tilted his head slowly, whispering, "Is there something you would like to say?"

Whoever Tuca had been, he was gone. This empty shell, this puppet, was the Oilean's dark magic. Fear immobilized him, snaking into his spine, clutching his heart. Even now, their grip was deep, and he felt like he was once again strapped on to that table, blood draining from him as they watched and waited. Feeding him lie after lie after *lie*.

Tuca's lips curled over his teeth, and Brokk watched in horror as the man's skin shed off his body. Black smoke poured from his skeletal nostrils and empty eye sockets as the remaining image of Tuca was devoured by the smoke. What emerged was far from human, but a monster Brokk was familiar with: *The dabarnes.*

When the Academy fell all those years ago, they had raged around him. Brokk remembered the blood and the broken screams of his friends as one-by-one they were slaughtered.

Blinking, he dug his claws into the earth as the dabarne stalked toward him, its grey bald skin stretched too tight over its lanky serpentine body. Its yellow eyes shifted between Kiana and Brokk as if deciding who to attack first. Growling low, the dabarne bared its teeth, salvia dripping thickly from its maws. Brokk tensed as the monster lunged at him, but he was a fraction too slow.

Kiana charged when she saw the massive maws close around Brokk's midriff.

He heard cracking; his howl cut through his mind, and there was pressure again and snapping as he felt his ribs shatter, puncturing his lungs. His body tried to heal itself, but there was something wrong; his ability was faltering. Warmth spread through his side as pain made his vision tip. He couldn't breathe or move.

Brokk's body was flipped, and he stared into those yellow eyes just as his paw connected with the dabarne's chest, his nails shredding through the paper skin. Pain erupted through Brokk's entire core, but he closed his eyes against the sudden silver light blinding him. The pressure left, and he heard Kiana's voice float around him.

"Hold on. Please, hold on."

Brokk's breath caught, and then he passed out.

CHAPTER FOURTEEN

Emory

Staring at the door for a solid minute—throat tightening, palms sweating, and heart pounding—Emory wondered if it was the right decision coming here. Ainthe was sheathed across her back, the leather digging into her bruises, her chest plate suffocating her. Her hands clenched and unclenched. Inhaling, she breathed in the traces of smoke and burning metal. But before she could turn around, Emory raised her chin and knocked.

A deep echo boomed as the steady beat on the anvil against metal stopped. Swallowing, she nervously glanced across the cavernous room. Adair permitted her to see Riona alone, but after this morning, she had earned it.

After a minute, the door swung inward, revealing a sweaty but smiling Riona. Her blond hair was streaked with inky traces, smoke and sweat clinging to her.

Emory's black uniform and red sash made her want to scream. To rage and to consume. To break away. The chest plate heated, as if sensing her thoughts, and she tried to calm her pulse. She needed to put that mask on her face, to stand straight, as she tried to figure out who her allies were and who was trying to kill her.

"Well, do come in, Princess. I'm glad you came. I wasn't sure if you would."

Emory's lips tugged up. "Well, you did need to look at this blade of mine."

Lies. Every second, all of it.

Entering, Emory unbuckled the leather straps, as she took in the forge. A huge fire crackled hungrily, and the smoke tugged up in a cyclone of air that constantly churned, the invisible suction leaving the air hot but clean. Tools hung from a belt, hammers leaned against the walls, and chisels, angle bits, and mandrels scattered the ground.

"So, should I tell the truth, or should you?" Riona asked it so causally as she took Anithe from Emory's grasp.

"Excuse me?"

Riona smirked as she unsheathed Anithe, taking in the deep red steel. "This is one of the most unusual blades I have ever seen. Almost as unusual as a princess returning from the dead. Almost as unusual as the rumors being whispered. So, why are you *here*?"

Swallowing hard, Emory didn't waver under her pinned gaze. "Why did you bring me here when there is obviously nothing wrong? What do you *want*?"

A bark of laugh echoed around her. "I don't believe for a second that you are here for anything other than to benefit yourself. Not for a second. You were with the rebels; they trusted you, and then suddenly, you turn your back? For what? A dream of grandeur, of fine living? Of royalty?" The aggression in Riona's voice bled out. "You had *hope*, right there in front of you. You turned your back. But now..."

Riona sheathed the sword, prowling around Emory.

"The rebels are done. I have come to serve King Adair," Emory said.

Tilting her head slowly, the shadows of the room deepened in Riona's features. "Then you are deeper in your denial than I thought."

Her pulse jumped, racing, as ice thundered through her veins. *There was no choice. No. Choice.* Lips pressing into a thin line, Emory didn't look away. One second passed and then another in uncomfortable silence.

Sighing, Riona said, "Your sword has a hairline fracture. Bring it back tomorrow." A dangerous invitation, but behind Riona's flaring eyes was a kindled curiosity.

Without saying another word, Emory turned and left, no promise of tomorrow on her lips. But Emory knew she would go. And while she didn't look back, with each step, her frown deepened. How did Riona know? How *could* she know what her moment of freedom cost her?

The door slammed behind her, and she heard the steady rhythm return. Grinding her teeth, Emory cut through the market, the bustle of the day in full swing, the clatters and cries of life around her.

Keeping her eyes down, she walked with purpose as her mind churned. Flashes from this morning's trial flowed nonstop, how she had ended another man's life, and she wanted to cry, to scream, to *give up*.

Picking up speed, her nails bit into her palms, and she felt the warmth trickle down her wrists. She was just one woman. A savior? A lost princess? No. Any essence of who she was had been stripped away by Memphis when he took away her memories. Any hope of who she could be had been was only now being pieced together by her instincts and actions, but all Emory could see was the mess she was in.

Her cheeks burned thinking about Memphis as her resentment built. *Foolish.* Turning down the hallway, leaving the cavernous room behind, she thought, *you were manipulated. Used.* Her eyes welled and a tear escaped from the corner of her eye. *Because of you. Of your family.*

Emory stalled, looking down the hallway, recognition slamming into her suddenly. When she and Azarius infiltrated Adair's kingdom, this was where she forced the guard down to the dungeons to find Memphis and Nyx.

Part of her now clung to that time when she had just been a girl blindly chasing a hope. She could have never imagined what it would mean to make Adair believe that she had truly come to join him. She wished that her sacrifice had ensured the rebels' safety.

Sitting down on the first step, ghosts of memories began swirling around her-her hands shaking violently in her lap. All those days with that caving helplessness inside of her. Suspended in her daydreams, filled with magic. With hope. With *life*. Her hope had bled away with her actions since coming to Adair's kingdom. Now she didn't recognize herself.

A chilling numbness filled Emory as she sat, dread and defeat demanding her attention, and it was a void she couldn't navigate alone. Her muscles cramped, and she stood after a group of soldiers passed her on the steps.

Her ability was a spark, flickering, trying to push through and keep her going. To keep the girl alive that believed that this world was worth fighting for.

"The Winter Yule is the most celebrated season in my kingdom. An exquisite night and a dinner to die for, to celebrate the change in the world around us."

Emory panted, sweat clinging to every ounce of her body, as she ran; her muscles quivered and burned. There was pain, but Emory noticed the hardening muscles as her body grew stronger. She had requested more sessions, and thankfully Adair had agreed.

The sun sank lower in the sky, yet she relished being outside so she was not sitting in Adair's kingdom, thinking about what was coming.

Though, being with the king wasn't much better if she was being honest. Looking at his back, his black shirt hugging his body, the muscles feathering underneath them, she saw how strong he was... She would just have to be stronger.

Pushing harder, the forest glowed in the twilight, and those whispers again, chased her, called to her, egged her on, and challenged her. Emory tried to clear her mind, but all she could think about was what had happened that morning. The girl had been brought in, like all the rest, begging for mercy, claiming the king was a madman. Her brown eyes had flared, like molten, as Emory brought her sword down. *Bringing justice for Adair's kingdom.*

All she could see was Adair's smirk; him looking at her like a prized trophy. And the blood.

She cursed now between breaths. Sweat trickled down her spine, and she turned, trying to clear her mind once again. Making herself focus, so that the blood that stained her hands wasn't for nothing. That she *would* make a difference. That she wasn't a mindless killer, a monster. That all of *this* was for a purpose.

Adair murmured, "You will do beautifully that night." With a lurching heart, the world twisted. "No one will doubt your allegiance to them, to *me*. In one week, the world will shudder, and the rebels will be forgotten."

The king stopped and faced her. The blade materialized in front of him from smoke and ash, and she ducked, scrambling for Ainthe. The blade was secure in her hand as she stumbled, trying to remember the steps.

In the dying light, she seethed, trying to get the upper hand, to be that powerful weapon that her destiny called her here for. And bathed in the last traces of light, she failed.

And failed.

And failed.

Materializing in front of her room, her clothes stuck to her, bruises and dried blood covering her. Adair stepped back, and shadows were casted across his features as he looked over her, devouring every detail, and she wanted to shrink back, to disappear under his intense gaze.

Stalling, Emory clenched her teeth, the slow panic burning through her body. It had occurred to her, when Adair was beating her into a senseless pulp, that she hadn't worn her mother's pendant since after the first day in this kingdom. There was a comfort knowing that she had something of her mother with her, when her world was now dictated by violence.

Adair's lips turned up slowly as he whispered, "Goodnight, Emory, and good work today."

Smiling weakly, Emory fumbled with the door handle until finally, the door shut behind her firmly. Sighing, Emory tried to forget that whisper of a smile on Adair's face. So what if there were flickers of normalcy between them? Nothing would ever change the fact he killed her parents, nor would it change her intention of being here. Pushing down her thoughts about the Mad King, Emory set about her task.

Drawers were thrown open: She sifted through the sea of black clothing, and a cry broke through her lips when she didn't find it. Running to the washroom, she scoured the counter, throwing the cabinet doors open, and sitting on the clear shelf, the amethyst glinted back at her. Tears slid down her face as she shakily picked up the chain and fastened it around her neck.

She stared at her reflection, her pale skin, her matted hair, the blood red ends. The coolness of the gem washed over her, and a tingling sensation ran down her nerve endings. Emory's mind raced with the possibility that maybe her mother knew something she did not. Maybe there was more to this gem...

She could hear the traces of the Night Market flickering to life below her room and wrenching herself away from the washroom she began to pace.

She would make Adair pay. For killing her parents, their dreams, and Kiero. She would make him bleed. Without mercy, without any more hesitation. For too long, she had pretended to be the innocent, naïve girl who was grateful to be there, to be reunited with him. All the while her ability waited in the shadows for the perfect time to sink her claws into him and destroy every dream and fantasy he had about her.

He would regret the day he had made their world bow, shackling it in fear. Shackling her.

Storming back into the washroom, she ripped her clothes off and climbed into the tub. The golden chest plate shimmered, having to constantly stay on her, which constricted uncomfortably in the water. It was a reminder of Adair's power over her and her decisions. She would *not* kill any more innocent people. She would *not*. Starting the water, hot steam began to curl around her.

Flickers of memories, of a shadow of who she used to be assaulted her, fueled by her rage, by her heartbreak. Dunking her head underneath the filling water and resurfacing, she grabbed the bar of soap off the ledge, scrubbing her skin raw as the water turned pink around her.

Quickly she got out of the bath, wrapping the towel around her as she prowled into the bedroom. Grabbing a loose, black shirt, fitted pants, and her button-down jacket, she got dressed with a new-found purpose, strapping Ainthe across her back and securing the buckle. Tugging her boots on, she tied the laces.

Looking around the room, she braided her hair back and took in a deep breath. Then turning, she crossed the empty space and opened the door.

The guard raised his eyebrows in surprise. "Going somewhere, Princess?" All it took was a moment. To be brave. Or weak. To be selfless. Or fueled by greed.

She calmly responded, "King Adair called on me. I wish you to take me to his chambers."

A tilt of his head. A pause. He turned and started to lead her away.

Following, her pulse hammered viciously against her ribs. The distant echoes of song called to her, and she tried not to think of Wren or Riona down in the market. Or the possible alliance she could have cultivated with them. Swallowing hard, she kept her chin up, making her body respond: One foot in front of the other.

The hallways curved, and the staircases loomed in front of her as she paused, the hairs on her arms rippling in goosebumps, when she first heard the voice.

"*Emmmorrrry.*"

The chilling call stopped Emory in her tracks as the crisp high notes of the whisper shivered down her spine. The guard continued, the flickering lights dancing along the wall. Her breath caught as the temperature suddenly dropped in the hallway. One-by-one behind them, Emory watched the lights snuff out, plunging them into shadows. Turning, unsheathing Anithe in front of her in one motion, Emory squinted into the semi-darkness: The hallway was empty.

Her ability surged down her arms and pooled in her palms as the blade ignited, responding to her fear. Swirling embers trailed off it, flickering in the shadows. She was utterly frozen, adrenaline making every noise too loud, every shadow tricking her eyes. The guard must have stopped, his footsteps ceasing behind her. Another light was doused until only one was left.

"*Emmooooory.*"

Clenching her jaw, she yelled, "Show yourself!"

Emory caught a glimpse of the guard, his face taut with fear, before he turned and ran away, leaving her alone.

Her breath caught.

There at the end of the hallway in the shadows stood a woman, her long, stringy, black hair framing her pale face. She wore a simple, white dress that was unstained. Ice ran through Emory's body as the figure slowly looked up at her, lips pinned back from her pointed teeth. Her empty eye sockets, macabre.

Slowly, she tilted her head, her bony limbs lengthening and cracking before Emory's eyes.

The last light ceased to be, and Emory was plunged into complete darkness.

Screams clawed at her throat as she heard the thud of flesh against stone, and the creature charged at her, hidden by the shadows. *Run.* The air rushed by her, her footfalls like thunder as she raced blindly. Giggles sounded from behind her, as below, the screams climbed up towards her.

Pumping her arms, she concentrated on her breath as she flew, her feet connecting with the floor. She swore as she narrowly missed slamming into a wall when she sharply cut left. Sweat clung to her skin, and she pushed harder, trying to not look behind her, trying not to imagine why these creatures had come, *who* they were.

Run. Run. *Run.*

The thought seared into her mind, and she felt the solidness of the floor beneath her. And then she was greeted with air as she fell. Screaming, Emory plummeted down. The air howled around her as she slammed into the concrete, tasting blood in her mouth, the pain lacing around her ribs. There must have been a staircase. Cursing, she pushed through the pain making her body move. At the base of her neck, hot blood trickled down her skin. Looking ahead, the stairs slowly came into form as her eyes adjusted; a light flared at the mouth of the entrance about a hundred feet away. Her body lurched as cold hands gripped her arms, pulling her back.

"*Emorrry*, we have waited a long time for this."

She saw saliva dripping off the creature's teeth, coating her cheeks as she thrashed.

"You will pay for what you have done. For what you have destroyed."

Wrenching her arm down, she slammed her boot in the creature's chest, buying her a moment. It hissed as she scrambled up, slipping on the cold stones, crying.

"You are only delaying your death. It is time we finally spill Fae blood."

No, no, no!

Her palms found the hilt of Anithe, and she gripped it, slashing it as she poured every ounce of her ability down the handle, into the metal, into the lingering magic she knew was there. Flames erupted between them, sending the creature rolling back from the golden inferno. Her chest heaved as she now looked at not one but four women baring their teeth at her, trying to press forward to rip and tear at her. To end her.

Running again, she soared down the steps, the trail of fire searing behind her. Smoke choked her as she wheezed, coughing up blood, and pain overtook her thoughts.

Charging through the entranceway, Emory stopped, looking at where the Night Market was usually in full swing, the beauty of the night sky blinking down at them, to where she had entered a nightmare. Dabarnes roared around her, their long bodies flexing, revealing the muscle underneath as they crashed into the vendors, roaring. Their yellow eyes too familiar, their hooked teeth and grey bald skin transporting her to a different time, when the Academy had fallen. Adair had said the monsters that made up his army had lived in the Noctis woods as his *allies*.

A green gas bathed the cavernous floor, wafting between the creatures and clawing into people's mouths, into their eyes and ears. Emory watched in horror as their eyes turned dim and empty, their pupils gone, until all that remained was an inky emptiness. Screams overlapped one another, piling and piling and *piling*. But it was one scream—Riona's scream—that slammed her back into reality as she spotted the blacksmith wielding a hammer—one edge flat, the other sharpened into a deadly hook—swinging it with fierce precision toward Adair. The Mad King laughed amongst the chaos. Amongst the monsters and death, he *laughed*. She felt her body respond, charging through the gas.

The last six years bled away from Emory. She felt that ghost of a boy get whisked away as she allowed herself to remember that he had once been her friend. That she had once cared for him. Trusted him. But he had chosen this path; he had chosen to kill and to segregate. He had killed her parents, and he had bred fear in their world. Bred a fear in her, shackling her to the darkness. To a life of pain. And she could never forgive him for what he had done.

Her roar was all consuming as the flames grew, and her ability raised its head as Adair turned.

Confusion flickered across his face for a split second before she was met with a wall of ice. Slamming her sword down, it cracked through the ice, and their blows met with equal ferocity.

"RUN!" she screamed at Riona, blood and spittle flying. She willed her body into compliance, into remembering their deadly dance: Adair was relentless, and she ducked, as his blade missed her by inches.

"You cannot win this." It was a quiet whisper.

She bowed her body, slashing at his chest as he turned to smoke, appearing behind her.

Turning, she said, "I can try."

He arched an eyebrow. "Oh, the truth comes out now. Very much like our visitors tonight, you have come to take what you have lost."

"Yes." She was blasted back, her head slamming against the floor as he stalked up to her.

"Then take it." The floor shook beneath her as she staggered back up to stand, blood dribbling down her chin. Her breaths came in short, wet-filled bursts as she ran up, screaming. The flames from Anithe's blade roared, forming a protective shield before Emory as Adair's dark magic slammed into her.

She felt that prick of needle against her skin. *No.* And then a hundred followed the first. It was like falling through ice, the adrenaline turning into shock. Each moment was captured with a serene clarity. The poison surged through her just as she erupted through the flames, her mother's pendant burning against her flesh, as her free hand closed against Adair's wrist.

Her world exploded.

She gasped as his energy drained into her body, his ability racing through her veins. Looking into his wide eyes, fear filled them. Pressing harder, each second slipped her closer to her death, but she pushed the monstrous creatures from her peripheral. All except one.

"Emory, please," Adair pled

It was one last desperate attempt. To manipulate, to play her for a pawn. She would *never* break. And she would never bow to him.

Lowering her lips against his ear, she rasped, "I tried to believe in you."

Adair stilled, the inferno of chaos rattling around them, splitting their world. His breath was hot against her cheek. *Gods above.* There was pain everywhere. Erupting, splintering pain.

All she saw was his eyes when she said, "But you underestimated me."

The end of her sword drove upward, right into his heart. Her world was filled with screaming as she watched black blood pour from his wound, from his mouth, racing up her sword, she tried to pull away, to fight against it. But she was so tired. She just wanted to lie down. Just for a moment.

Adair's blackened blood raced up to her as she fell backwards, everything blurring together, the fire and ash, her guilt and rage. All greeting her one last time, intertwining around her heart. In the distance, a silver light brightened, calling her name, softly as if it had always been waiting for her. Always knowing it would come to this. *Her end.* She smiled as she met it, hand outstretched, leaving the pain behind.

CHAPTER FIFTEEN
Brokk

Ice cold water slammed onto his face, and Brokk lurched up, sputtering. He saw the hand blur as Kiana slapped him hard, his head snapping back from the force. Her silver eyes came into focus, along with her scowl.

"Took you long enough."

Blinking, he took in the gentle swaying of the leaves, the warmth of the sunlight against his skin, and the blue sky above him. There was no trace of the dabarne as he rasped, "Water."

It was a second before a cup was before him, her ancient eyes roaming his own. "You took a beating with that thing. It's been a day, but you have healed." Groaning, he sat up, drinking deeply. "You have seen something like it before?"

Sighing, he nodded. "Not one that had inhabited a body... But yes. A long time ago."

Darkness filled her face as she whispered, "We have to go. There has been a...shift in the magic. I'm afraid time is working against us."

Pausing, he closed his eyes. Around him, the calmness of the forest serenaded him, luring him into that peacefulness. But on the edge of it...silence—a harrowing emptiness that settled right into his gut. The hair on the back of his neck stood on end, and he breathed into the fact this was his fate. He thought he knew what fear felt like, but nothing compared to the realization he was finally going into Adair's kingdom, into the heart of evil itself.

Dark thoughts pulled at the edges of his mind. Was he too late to save Emory? Brokk could feel there was a greater evil in this world—bigger than kings or queens—and it was time to face it no matter the outcome.

His eyes flew opened. "How far away are we?"

"A few hours. We must leave. Now."

He stood, stretching, and she snapped her fingers. The camp they had set up disappeared.

"Handy trick."

She smirked. "I had to be comfortable while I worried over your dying body."

Rolling his eyes, he grumbled, "I hope you have a plan."

Her lips pressed into a hard line, and she nodded. He had seen that look before. He had accepted that sinking feeling many times himself.

Without another word, he shifted and ran, assuming Kiana could keep up. If not, he couldn't stop. Wouldn't stop. If Emory was about to face...to face an ounce of what he had experienced with the Oilean... He couldn't bring himself to think about it. Couldn't accept that reality.

They flew, weaving in between the trees, and leaving his past behind. His paws shredded the earth, and he steeled his heart.

The hours bled away as the tinges of night swept in. The Ruined City encompassed them, and Brokk shifted back, looking for scouts, for soldiers...for anyone. Kiana leaned against the dusty, crumbling wall, her scowl deepening with every minute.

"Just get it off your chest now, Kiana."

Her eyes glowed in the dying light; her face unreadable. "I should have known that Tuca was already gone."

His heart turned to stone as he whispered, "That's what the Oilean *do*. Blend reality and nightmare. Truth and lie. What happened to Tuca was just a taste of what is waiting for us. We can't prepare for the impossible, Kiana."

Kiana unsheathed her sword, following his gaze. "I have lived a thousand days, century after century, waiting for the time that our world would settle into some sort of resolution."

"How about we focus on not dying for the next couple of hours, okay?"

A ghost of a smile. "No promises, My *Prince*, but I will certainly try my best." Her wicked grin made him swear colorfully under his breath.

Wrenching his gaze back toward the mountain range, he stalled, his heart hammering. "Ready?"

Emory. Time suspended in the clutches of the thrill. The anticipation. Brokk was terrified of what he would find nestled in the heart of the mountain. The soldier he had been trying to escape his entire life overtook every nerve, every fiber in his body.

Kiana replied, "Yes. Now, how we have to enter Adair's kingdom... Well, I just want to warn you, you probably won't like it."

"What are you thinking?"

Kiana smirked, "For your nerves its best just to trust me on this one."

Brokk shrugged, trying to settle his hammering pulse. "Let's go."

Shifting back, he snapped his teeth. Kiana nodded, placing a hand on his colossal shoulder. At her touch, coolness settled in his muscles, and he arched his head, watching her magic weave into leather across his back, the straps secured- holding beautiful lethal knives.

"You can never have too many blades."

Rolling his eyes, he charged, jumping over rubble, dust clogging his senses as he heard the soft footfalls of Kiana racing beside him. Faster and faster, they pushed until they were blurs of gold and silver, the destroyed remnants of the capital encompassing him.

Don't think. Don't think. Panic wasn't an option, not when he was so close to helping end Adair, even if it meant facing the Oilean again.

Kiana made a sharp left, cutting in front of him as she sprinted farther into the Ruined City, Brokk following her. At the end of roadway they were following lay huge chunks of rubble piled against one another. Brokk thought it built a disjointed looking stairs, and suddenly, Kiana propelled herself forward, grappling with the stone, pulling herself up. Following with ease, Brokk scaled the rubble, and they both climbed higher and higher. Wondering exactly where she was headed, Kiana turned, as if reading his thoughts and smiled softly at him. It was a snap of energy, of light and sound as one moment he was scaling the debris and the next he felt pressure.

And then, the wind was howling as gravity left him. Shifting back to his human form, a steady stream of curse words flew from his mouth as the Ruined City became smaller and smaller until it was just bones scattered across the land.

Then they were flying.

Kiana grinned down at him, a cyclone of light circling around them as they sliced through the sky with ease. The Draken Mountain range grew closer, the mammoth's jagged edges severe. He didn't understand it, her magic, or how every story he was told as a child had become his life. But the landscape below him was nothing more than veins mapping the story their world told and the energy he felt.

And Emory was somewhere down below him, fighting a battle alone or having accepted her fate was lost. But it never was or had been. Or would be.

His cheeks burned, the air grew thinner, but Brokk tried not to look down. Kiana flew beside him, her magic propelling them at unearthly speeds. Through squinted eyes, he could see the top of the peak. It had been cleared off, revealing a massive space.

It was like a window to the stars, and Kiana yelled, "It took me years to find out that Adair had done this. Naturally with a little help. Hold on. He has wards up."

The air howled around them when they shot down. Kiana screamed as sparks flew from around them, and he felt it, the ripping at his mind, at his soul as the magic devoured them. Her inhuman hold on him tightened as they spiraled faster toward that brilliant expanse, the glass sheen coming into focus. They gained too much speed and he yelled, bracing for the impact.

Flickers of yellow and red flared far below like those long nights when Adair would bomb them, and he could feel nothing but the bone-rattling shudders through the ground. He always imagined, above them, that the explosions of light, of destruction, of *fire* were breathtaking, just as much as it was lethal.

"SHIFT!" Her roar brought him slamming back to reality as Kiana dropped him.

Brokk's heart dropped into his stomach, as gravity sunk its claws into him.

And he fell.

The wind sounded like screams as his body flailed, and he caught snippets of the world: Fading of light, the night sweeping in. The glass that separated him from the war that awaited him. And *Emory*. There were a thousand things he had always wanted to say to her. That he was sorry for betraying her. For choosing to stay behind when he should've gone. For not standing up to Memphis.

His scream tore through him, and if he lived, he would *try* to put into words how the gaping hole in him had never healed since that day in the woods six years ago.

Shifting, his screams turned into growls. The sunset reflected off the pane as the sharp tang of magic filled his mouth when he crashed through it. There was a crack like thunder, and shards buried themselves deep, tearing and flaying his skin effortlessly. His howls echoed around the cavernous room as the world seemed to hold its breath. But he only gained speed, and the floor rushed up to meet him. His body desperately tried to back pedal, but he couldn't think, couldn't breathe. Finally, he slowed, Kiana's magic making sure they both landed safely, as his paws touched the ground.

The air was hot, and all he could smell was blood, and *that scent*- the smell of rotting flesh, smoky and acidic. Terror shredded through him just as he felt her grip around him, her magic radiating like a shield.

A wild look sparked in Kiana's eyes. "Let's go get your girl, shall we?" He couldn't even form the words that Emory was *not* his girl.

Pure undulated bedlam met them. Kiana roared, two swords in both of her hands. Her eyes seemed to glow, and the magic exploded from her like a dying star. In waves, it battered against what surrounded them. It shredded through bodies so fast, he couldn't even recognize human from beast. Beast from monster. His body healed rapidly, and blinking, he tried to take in the surroundings. The room was *massive*, and, homes nestled on the side of the walls, echoing of a life. Of everything Adair had taken.

A deep emerald gas floated everywhere, the men and women and children walking through it like ghosts, their eyes pitch-black. The white light flared and rippled, parts of it dying as it collided with the gas.

Brokkkk. He dove as a blade slashed at him, his growls growing as he soared, the attacker smiling down at him. The woman, her hair hanging limply, her eyes holding no flicker of humanity. Of life.

Brokkk Fosterrr. Chills snaked down his spine. Those voices, they haunted him every night. Every day.

The blade slashed toward his belly again, and he jumped, teeth meeting blood and bone. Shaking, his mind reeled, the blackened blood covering everything. Behind him, Kiana was yelling, but all he could feel, could smell, was the Oilean's voices. Their essence. Brokk tried to find them, but the fog thickened, blotting out the people until it was just Kiana's light guiding them as they were transported from the warzone into a space of nothingness.

"Can you track them?" Kiana asked.

He shook his massive head. There were too many scents, and the Oilean were everywhere—*in everyone*: The air they breathed. The ground, soaking into their nerves, their flesh, their blood. Cursing, Kiana kept her hand on his shoulder, squinting into the emptiness. *Find her, find her, find her.* Growling, he stalked further into the oblivion, his heart hammering, and he was met with monotone laughter. The fog cleared slightly. Stalling, he tried to make out the shadow coming toward them.

"Brokk. Foster." Each word was a promise. Each breath a secret, and Brokk stopped at the sound of the Mad King's voice.

Adair came into their view, and it was like he was back at the Academy, that burning hatred for the man in front of him raging until he was reduced to only his emotions. Until it was only them. Bruised skin rimmed beneath his eyes, his hair tousled, his button-down jacket torn and blood-soaked. Amongst the carnage, Brokk took him in, his jet-black eyes flaring ravenously.

"It's been a long time, and I must admit, I'm surprised you're alive. I saw Emory kill you. Right in front of me."

Brokk shifted back to his human form in one motion, his body ten steps ahead of him. His hand unsheathed the blade, charging. Brokk's screams turned into bellows, his rage into obsession.

Adair ducked too fast, and the edge met empty air. Contorting his body, Brokk slammed his boot down, hoping to meet flesh. The Mad King smiled at Brokk's horror-filled gaze as his flesh turned to smoke, and he materialized behind him.

"You know there wasn't a day that passed where I didn't hope for this moment with you. That I could look you in the eye and watch everything you hold close dissolve into *nothing*."

Brokk charged. He wouldn't fall into this verbal battle. Mid-step, his bones cracked as his shapeshifted, launching his powerful muscles over Adair; and his maws latched onto his shoulder. Snapping his teeth down, he expected the screams, the gore. The advantage. Landing hard, Brokk pinned his ears back, and Adair laughed. There wasn't a mark on him.

"I expected you to have more questions. But, *why*, Adair, did you do it? Why kill the Faes? Why did I think you were dead? Why, why, why?" He circled him slowly. Calculating. "I killed for *power*. The Faes were hiding something that wasn't theirs to keep. But it saw my heart and knew that I wasn't different. It accepted me, my darkness and my broken edges. And never asked for anything more than what I am."

Brokk's chest was heaving as he saw in Adair's exposed skin that his veins were inky. Dread pooled into his gut.

"And you, I have learned are so, *so*, *talented*, Foster. These rumors that have trickled down to me are most intriguing." Giggles rippled around them.

Brokk whipped around, and Kiana was gone.

Adair circled him, murmuring, "We all have our secrets. Yours running deeper than others, it would seem. The Oilean were eager to have the Prince of Nehmai deceived. You were so concerned with your precious rebellion that you gave them the time to spin their lie. To allow me, for a second, to believe Emory. For you to think she had betrayed you. They were even more exhilarated to come finish me off. But it would seem we have come to an agreement under the circumstances." A slow smile split his lips, his white teeth flashing, coldness settling over his features. "You see, someone beat you to it."

Shifting back to his human form, Brokk's heart pounded. Quickly, he unsheathed one of the blades from his pack. The steel shook from the tremors in his hands, as he rasped, "Beat me to what?"

The King stalked him, and Brokk couldn't move. "You cannot kill someone who is already dead. No more lies. No more hiding. I will remake this world. And, I will break it."

He stood there and watched the man he hated burst into a thousand shards like glass. Ducking, his forearm flew up, protecting his face. He was thrown back from the impact, and the room came back into focus, the fog ebbing, and he realized he was surrounded. The blank stares, the vacant bodies...

An entire kingdom under the rule of the Oilean.

Ice shot through his veins as he ran, pushing past the grappling hands, the bodies, the whispers of *"Brookkk Fosterr."* Blood ran down his arm, and his body was slammed to the ground. He choked as dots danced in front of his vision, and he was dragged backward. Adair stood behind him, his invisible claws locking into his heart, his body.

"You're leaving before the best part. Aren't you wondering who stole that privilege away from you?"

No, no, no, no. A broken sob raked through him. Rising and falling.

"You see, this body, the man who used to have it, thought he could win. Every second of every day, they have been planning for this moment. Emory was nothing more than a confused woman manipulated by the friends she loved, not understanding what she was fighting for, who she was fighting for. An heir of a family lost. A princess to what? To become queen to whom? There is nothing left of her life here but the ashes that remain."

The tears spilled fast and hard.

"She buried her sword in my heart, knowing I would kill her." Adair stood on his chest, pressing down. "And all this time, we were playing into my beautiful chaos. Every second of every day, I have us all exactly where I want us now."

Bones cracked, and Brokk was paralyzed. He couldn't shift; he couldn't breathe.

Adair sighed. "You know, I will relish tearing you apart. Bit by bit, until you are begging."

The world exploded into light. Peerless, untouchable, blinding *light.* Lying there, Brokk was stunned, watching Adair stagger back. Watching the *kingdom* stagger back.

A deafening roar echoed out as a fierce woman ran into his view, a mad glint sparking in her hazel eyes as she yelled, "Brokk Foster, come with me. Kiana has Emory." She held the most fearsome and exquisite piece of weaponry he had ever seen in his life. The hammer was massive, her toned muscles flexing as she held it with ease. "Move, NOW!"

Taking in this strange fearsome woman, Brokk couldn't move. Couldn't think. All he could hear was a sharp ringing and Adair's words wrenching through him. *She's. Dead. Dead. Gone.*

Cursing, the woman grabbed his shoulder, shoving him forward and taking his hand to drag him behind her. It was all he could do not to throw up. "Look, Prince, if you *do* want her to live, you have to move. But you need to hear what I am saying. Emory is with Kiana. She needs help, but we must *move. Now.*"

Looking behind him, Adair brandished a massive broadsword, black smoke gathering around his feet like a cyclone, the promise of death in his gaze as he rushed toward them.

Not needing to be told twice, Brokk gripped the stranger's hand just as the floor beneath them began to shudder. He shifted and the woman stopped, her mouth hanging open, taking in his wolf form. Snarling once, he tried to say, *I believe you.* A maddening grin split her face and she jumped, nestling onto his back, hammer in hand. And then, they were galloping.

The mountain was trembling, but Brokk didn't look back. The woman's yells mixed in with the cracking of stone. He could feel the ground beneath him, the air rushing past him as he became the creature he was born to be: The man, his breaking heart and fears bleeding into instinct; bleeding into this.

Huge chunks of stone crashed in front of them as she screamed, "To the left!"

He responded, feeling the shards of stone against his body, just of out of reach. At the mouth of the hallway, a staircase met them, which he scaled with ease. He heard the screams climbing, their reprieve vanishing with every step. A roar sliced through everything else, and Brokk tried not to falter. Adair screamed his name behind them. *Do not stop. Emory tried to kill Adair.* Images of her lifeless body fractured through him.

Brokk pushed harder, the woman screaming at him from his back. But all that mattered was that he went further than he had ever granted himself to go. Past lies and thieves. Past rebels and soldiers. Past his fear and expectations. Past princes and kings. Because a second of this life where Emory wasn't safe would end everything he had strived to become in a man.

The sickening blow of metal against flesh brought him shattering back to what he was doing. Recognizing the twisted body of the dabarne, the woman on his back said, "You need to head up these stairs, *now,* or you will get us both killed."

He didn't need to be told twice. The concrete underneath his paws was anchoring. Focusing on his breath, his muscles burned with each propelling motion up the second flight of stairs. The whispers, the screams, the carnage, and the loss bayed at them, their personal serenade, but the woman kept yelling, swinging her hammer unmercifully, and it kept them going. Kept *him* going.

Skidding to a halt, the top of the stairs twisting into a darkened hallway, their breath misted in front of them, the chills of winter snaking down his spine. "What the—"

Brokk felt her get ripped from his back. He shifted in one motion, ripping one of many blades from the sheath and sprinting into the darkness, following her screams. Cursing, he raced into the night. He couldn't breathe, horror snaking underneath his skin, embedding there, as he stopped. A shadowy figure stood at the end of the hallway, holding a gleaming knife against his companion's pale throat.

The shadows were thick, as he growled, "Let. Her. Go."

A giggle floated down the hallway, high and chilling. He felt his mouth go slack. His hands started to shake, his breath catching. All he could focus on was his growing panic as he watched the Oilean.

"*Brrrrrroookkkkk.*" The Oilean's neck rolled, cracking as her chilling voice rooted him in place. "I miss the sounds of your screams. The way you looked before we tore you-inch by inch by inch. I miss the way you would beg. The way you looked when you had given up." The knife moved. "It will be fun to play again, Prince of Nehmai."

He was running. The fear a wild thing in his blood, pushing him toward the shadow, the knife, that *voice*. The shadows exploded, and they surrounded him, his companion they had at knifepoint forgotten. Their pale bodies reached for him, their giggles wrapping around his mind. Brokk roared as he plunged, slashing, his body responding to his will as he shifted back. Blindly, he unsheathed a longer broadsword, the steel hissing as it cut into the air, as he panted, the cold sweat trickling down his neck.

A cool breath tickled his ear, as the high voice cooed, "*Now, you know you have to do better than that.*"

Brokk's cry broke as he swiveled, and he was transported to that damp basement again. The Oilean held a flickering green flame in her palm, casting the hallway in its sickly glow. They were face-to-face, and ice ran through him, freezing him. The Oileans' bodies cracked, their limbs extending, turning them into the monsters that had haunted him ever since he was caged under the ground.

"Come with us, Brokkkk."

"Come and play. We want to thank you. What you have allowed us to dooo."

Roaring, he forced his body to fight, to react. Their laughs echoed in the darkness as the flames went out. Long, bony fingers wrapped around his wrists, gripping too hard. More fingers grasped around his ankles. A hand was clasped around his neck.

Screaming, he shifted into his wolf form as he saw them swivel in the darkness, everything sharpening into focus. He saw their pointed teeth, drool trickling down their chins. They ripped at his fur, at his limbs, pulling and dragging. They were too strong.

He plunged. Gravity slipped from beneath him, and his body folded in on itself, as he was yanked backward. That simple movement and despair welled in his heart. How would he survive the Oilean again? The thought paralyzed him, tunneling down into his thoughts, the darkness waiting for him. It always had been.

The grittiness of the stone below him dug into his skin, even as Brokk contorted his body, flipping onto his back and shifting. He had lost one sword, but the knife strapped onto him dug into his side, secure. Panting, his hands searched, but he only found empty space. And then he was falling. His screams tore from his chest, his body shifting between man and beast as terror took hold.

He couldn't see anything as he dropped.

Faster.

Faster.

Faster.

The illusion of Adair's kingdom bled away, slamming onto the slab of concrete, every bone in his body shattering. His vision spun, wheezing as blood bubbled onto his lips. *Slap.* The sound of flesh on stone echoed around him as he bowed his head, his hands shakily trying to support his body weight, as bone, marrow, and sinew healed at an expedited rate. A long, pale finger pulled his chin up, the cry on his lips dying as she breathed in his face.

"You have a fire in your heart. Just like your parents, or so we were told."

The cavernous room ignited, revealing a huge pool in the middle of the room, the water as smooth as glass. Mammoth, purple amethysts clustered at the bottom, casting the room in their rippling light. The Oilean tilted their heads, their sharpened teeth bared, those lips peeled away.

"Our newly acquired army would have relished in killing you. The king even more. But after this world, where could we travel, when you can direct us with ease. World after world, we will drain *everything of life*. Of power. All for our true king."

Giggles floated around him. Black dots danced in front of Brokk, blinking furiously as tears streaked down his face, over his scars.

"But what will be more pleasurable, and don't you agree, sistersss, is making the prince watch us kill the rebels, ripping and t-tearing them apart." She shivered in pleasure, her tongue flickering out over her teeth. "Only when you are truly broken, will death be a mercy."

They came closer and closer, his heaving breaths coming faster, until they were nearly holding him down again.

"But that doesn't mean, Prince—"

"I am *no* prince." Brokk seethed through his tears, through the blood and split skin. Forcing his face into a scowl, he said, "I am a man who is a soldier, but also a dreamer. Who has deep hunger for a better world than *this*. My best friends have lied to me, manipulated me, and I have blindly followed. I am no longer what anybody *claims* that I am."

His growls turned into yells, as he dipped into his ability, neither caring which one flowed through his veins but allowing all the power to shudder, singing in his blood. "My name—" he rose, claws sprouting from his knuckles, as a pure light ignited around him "—is Brokk Foster. And I'm going to kill you."

The shadows erupted around him as he was torn apart. Screams echoed, his own the most prominent. In slow motion, he watched his skin fracture, lines splintering through him. A burning clawed up his throat; light fissured through his body as the Oilean hissed. Shadows met light as he shifted, snapping his massive jaws.

And then he evolved.

He ran, but it was more than just moving. He felt it in his blood, in his heart, his *soul*. It was a steady whisper against the destruction, against his pain, and it was everywhere: In the air, in the stone, in the mountain. And it told him not to be afraid. He felt that familiar pull in his gut as he lunged toward the creatures from his nightmare.

Time started to fall away, the calls of distant lands beckoning to him, before Kiana's voice broke through to him. "BROKK!"

A cold, snapping wind slammed into him, as the Oilean whipped their heads, the emerald gas growing around them. Landing, Brokk reined his ability in as Kiana stood behind them. Brandishing her blades, she whispered intensely under her breath, and the mountain trembled, the water churned, and the air sparked as it filled with her rage.

"Sisters of Old, you are *not* welcome in this world."

They hissed, ripping their attention to the new threat.

Kiana sneered. "Do not make the same mistakes as in the past."

They hissed again, whispering, "We will kill you first, Warrior."

Kiana smiled.

Move. Move. Move. Huge chunks of stone started falling all around them, gouging out huge crevices, dust and magic clogging his senses. Kiana was running, her screams calling to him, but he could only take *her* in. The woman with the sledgehammer bowed her head as she held his best friend cradled in her arms. How she had gotten out and found Kiana was beyond him.

The woman they had brought back was gone. Emory's hair framed her face, bloodied and matted, fiery-red ends tangled. Her body, which had *never* been *weak*, had more definition. But her chest was caved in, hundreds of needles imbedded into her body. She was drained of color, utterly *lifeless*. It suffocated him, his mistakes, his grief, destroying him.

A body slammed into him, and Kiana grabbed his scruff. "Move, Brokk, Move!"

The Oilean were screaming, as mountain and water surged toward them. It was an indestructible wave of elements, buying them time. Another shudder as emerald light flared. He shifted, grabbing Kiana's hand as they turned and ran. He shivered against her power, feeling it seep into his skin. They were going too fast, running toward no exit.

"What plan do you have to get out of this?" They ran faster, as the woman holding Emory followed, her face paling.

"I always have a plan, Brokk." She winked and his stomach dropped.

The mountainside loomed in front of them, the rock grey and impregnable. That was when he heard it. *Boom. Boom. BOOM.* They skidded to a halt as he looked behind them. The Oileans' bodies were swept up in Kiana's ability, drowning in the water, rocks pelting them. Fear sliced through him as he saw one pale hand shooting out from the rubble. And then another. And another. Below them, a roar vibrated through the stone.

"One." Kiana's voice was low and urgent. "Two." The woman beside him sheathed her hammer, gripping Emory's body, and quickly nodded her head, determination sparking in her hazel eyes, as Kiana said, "Three."

The ground exploded from beneath them, and Brokk balked in horror. Five monstrous beasts bellowed at them, blinking furiously, saliva dripping from their maws. Their muscular bodies were scarred and tough, their long snouts flaring, their ears pinned back. Three of the five locked their eyes on them as Kiana bellowed a war cry, elation brimming into her features. The beasts shivered, an ancient acknowledgment sparking in their eyes as they bowed their front legs, offering their backs.

A madness of survival had taken over them all.

Kiana swung around, her energy blasting from her as it demolished the side of the mountain. And beautiful, crisp air howled at them. Confusion clawed at him, but there was no time. The Oilean had created the illusion of falling when they were nearly at the peak. They were so high, the world sprawling below the mountain range was nothing but lines. In the night, Brokk could barely make out the forests, and farther along, the horizon the Black Sea. His body was tugged, and he responded. *Breathe.*

Kiana leapt at the beast, grinning madly, holding her hand out to him. *Trust.* If he lived his life without friends, where would that lead him in this war? Kiana was barking mad, but he would be dead without her. He wouldn't be in Adair's kingdom without her.

Clasping her hand fiercely, he was pulled up. He twisted his body, trying to see Emory, as Kiana said, "Riona has her, Brokk. Trust me. The blacksmith won't harm her. But right now, I need you to hold on."

Wrapping his hands around her waist, gravity left them. The beast barrelled forward, roaring, running full tilt-right at the opening. The mountain shuddered, and the last thing he heard was the Oilean screeching, the sound making his hair stand on end: It was a call for blood.

And then they were falling. The beast had leapt without faltering, without fear. He glimpsed the night sky, the wondrous deep blue hues, purple lining the clouds, and above them stars embedded in the sky like crystals.

Then everything was a blur. They raced toward the ground at a dangerous speed. His scream was lodged in his throat, adrenaline roaring in his ears—everything was a mass of grey. It sounded like thunder as the beast dug its claws into the side of the mountain, sparks flying in the night from the force. And then in a controlled arc, they were swung upward, freefalling once more. His scream dislodged from his throat, and it carried through the air as the monster repeated the powerful motion again. He realized they were *using* the mountain to travel down to the ground.

Gagging, Brokk choked down bile. Clenching his eyes shut, he tried to block out the screams lacing the night, becoming more unearthly with each passing moment. He tried not to think about what had happened. That part of himself and the history that was tied to it. *Prince.*

It was just a title. Just a claim that two people he never got to meet made. Earned. Prying his eyes open, they were dropping again, the shadowy forest rushing up to meet them too fast. Sparks flew in front of his eyes as the beast swung its weight, almost crashing into the rock face, only at the last minute to fling itself forward. Finally, they crashed onto the earth, dirt and grass flying from the impact. Kiana leapt off with a lithe grace, a string of filthy curses flying from her as she stared at the mountains. The blacksmith, Riona, by miracle, slid off, Emory cradled in her arms. He saw red.

"Are you *insane?* Kiana, what are these things? You could have gotten us killed!" Brokk shouted. He hurriedly got off the restless beast, eyeing them carefully.

Lifting her eyebrow, she shrugged. "And you would have died without them. You almost did. You played your part beautifully though. I was banking on the fact that you and Adair would be...preoccupied."

"*Preoccupied?*"

Riona stepped in between them. "You two are forgetting yourselves. What do we do?" The ground shuddered, and Brokk looked up, the moon illuminating the silhouette of where they came from. A pulsing, green light was growing and growing, and he ripped his gaze from it.

"We don't have much time." Kiana shook her head, turning as she looked past him. She bowed her head and whispered soft words to the monstrous creatures that had saved them. With bared teeth and vicious growls, they turned, disappearing into the shadows.

Goosebumps rippled across Brokk's skin as he stepped closer. "How did you even know about these beasts?"

Those silver eyes locked on him. "Those *beasts* you are referring to were once wild creatures of these forests. They were free, fierce, and answered to no *one*. That was the treasure in our world, all the power and secrets it held at its core, and all the creatures that found their home.

"That monster of a man enslaved them and drove them into madness. They were tortured. Had everything stripped from them. Were shown brutality, and they forgot who they *were*." Kiana's chest heaved as she set her jaw. Swallowing, she wiped angrily at her eyes. "I had heard rumors. Unfortunately, they proved true. Riona, put her down now."

Sizing up the other woman, he said, "Do I even want to know how you two know each other?"

Gingerly laying Emory down, Riona smiled. "*Some* people don't like talking about it."

Kiana scowled, the vulgar gesture flying before she sighed. "Brokk, may I introduce my sister."

He blinked. *Sister.*

"Who against my better judgement purposefully went and joined Adair, posing as…just another person with an ability. It was beyond *reckless*."

"She really means intuitive and helpful."

"She could have gotten killed."

"Don't talk over me. I didn't get killed and our plan beyond worked. Now, *Emory.*"

Kiana shot her sister a glare so vicious, Brokk wanted to laugh. He had forgotten what quick banter was like. What family was like.

"It's nice to meet you. And thank you for watching over her."

Kiana knelt, placing her hands over Emory's chest, the needles digging in further. Light flared from her palms and Riona stepped back.

"Don't thank me yet, lover boy. I had no idea what Adair would do. What he put her through…" Shadows formed in her eyes, as Riona's words died midsentence. His pulse picked up, and she sighed. "She won't be the same person if she comes back."

"She has a choice?"

The Warrior nodded. "I like to believe she does."

He was fixated, as a light grew, pulsing like a heartbeat. The world bled away, the mountains and the quaking of the earth about to be split in two: Bloodied and worn, barren and without an escape of the impending war. Tears burned in his eyes, and his breath hitched.

Brokk. Ice shot into his veins as Emory's voice resonated within his mind. *Help me.* Everything started to spin, and he was filled with Emory. Panicked, he looked at Kiana, her silver hair framing her face before a roaring washed over him. The world became fuzzy as he was pulled into his ability and was ripped from the sisters.

The wind howled as he fell, his screams tearing from his chest. *What's happening?* Squinting, Brokk tried to control his breathing, tried to focus. All around him were echoes of sounds, playing tricks on his ears. The gentle gurgle of water, smoothing and alluring, and then transforming into screams. The scents of hundreds of places: earthy, fresh, damp, and musty. Every time he had traveled the channels, he had a clear intention in view. But now? The colors around him churned, ribbons of silver and gold swirling around him, around his legs, his arms, his neck.

Brokk. It was only a whisper, but he dove toward it, abandoning everything. He filled his entire body with the sound of Emory's voice, honing his ability to it. There was a hush on the wind, an explosion of light, and everything went quiet. Shakily, he looked at the floor, his eyes trailing along the bookcase, the all too familiar bookcases and maps. His exhale was hoarse, as he stepped forward.

"Emory."

She was seated away from him, stiff-backed, and slowly, she turned. Her delicate brows pinched together, her ebony hair cascading past her shoulders, the red-stained ends out of place in the neutral tones of the study. Her eyes met his, and he stilled as he watched that flicker burning in them.

"I knew you would be here. That you would come." Standing, her cheeks flushed. "So, I really did die then?" A pause. "Brokk, I am so, *so* sorry. I thought it wasn't you that I killed. I thought I understood what I was doing better."

Tilting his head, his voice was gentle as he replied, "Em, you're not dead."

She stilled, shaking her head. "Then how are you here? I *killed you.*" A dark chuckle erupted from her. "I tried, and I failed."

Clenching his fists, he took another step closer. "The Oilean. Em, it was dark magic. It wasn't me but a doppelganger. An illusion." She paled, her lips moving wordlessly. Panic bled into her features.

"I don't understand this either. But I am here with you. I traveled to... Where exactly are we? I was just with you, and Em..." The words tumbled out of him.

She stood, closing the space between them. "I was dead. I *am* dead."

He choked on the words he couldn't say, on everything, and just stared at her.

Emory murmured, "I remember this study. Vaguely, but things have been getting clearer. This is my parents' office. Which is impossible, with the Academy being nothing but ash."

Emory started to pace, her agitation rolling off in waves. "We are...what...on the brink of the afterlife?"

Gods above, it ripped everything out of him not to hold her face, run his thumb over her lips, her cheek. He had so many things he wanted to try to explain, but the looming danger of what Kiana and Riona may be dealing with clouded his thoughts. They were running out of time. "I have friends trying to help you."

Emory locked her gaze back on him, and it was there. Subtle, but he saw *her*. The essence, of who she was, had been, and had become.

"And what if I don't want help?" She frowned and sat down. "I could just drift away. Everything that was banked on me was wrong. You were wrong." The glint died in her eyes as she soaked in the room; the details. "Their memories are like ghosts. Translucent, and yet, I know they had been here. That I had been *here*. I had a life, hopes, and dreams. Had a purpose." She played with the necklace around her neck, Brokk focusing on the amethyst, his eyes narrowing.

"I accepted everything Memphis said without a doubt. That I must have glimpsed flickers of my past life in my dreams. That I had been in *love*. That I had been chosen." She scoffed as she dug her fingernails into her palms. "I have been so *wrong*. I have done wrong by you." Locking her burning eyes on him, she said, "All this time, you have been the only one who has truly looked out for me. Not for your own benefit, not because you wanted to attain something. Brokk, I—"

"Enough." The words snapped out of him brusquely.

"No. I need to say this." Emory jumped to her feet, shoved the chair back, pacing again. "I remember that day. In the woods. The war and the Academy was lost. My parents dead. I remember making the decision to leave. I remember what it felt like hoping to any god you would come with me. And Memphis took *everything* away. My judgement, my choice, my memories. As he did for years." Her chin wobbled. "I never questioned it. I believed that story he spun in my mind. That you couldn't be trusted. I walked right back into his arms, and all of it was a lie. I am *so* sorry. For not seeing through him until it was too late. To me, Memphis was safe. I wanted to believe that he was my path. But I wasn't right."

Brokk couldn't breathe as Emory continued. "I had *hoped* that maybe through all of this, Adair was still in there, fighting. That I could find out why he killed my parents."

"You can't reason with a madman."

She stilled, and he saw the echoes of grief flooding her eyes as she whispered, "I know."

"Emory, you did what you had to," Brokk said, closing the space between them.

She blinked, looking past him. "Maybe I don't have a choice, Brokk. Not anymore. That person who came to Kiero is dead. I have done terrible things that I can't forgive myself for. I bowed to Adair's will. All for what? To be a pawn for a more dangerous force to take over? For the Oilean to win? For Kiero to end?"

A cool wind brushed up against his skin, sending shivers down his spine. His body responded, and he didn't think. Not anymore. Not when he was so close to losing her.

In two strides, he gently cupped her hands, his fingers curling around her frigid hands. His fingers shakily stroked her skin, his breath hitching. "You always have a choice, Em. I understand, about before. You weren't the only one to be strayed by Memphis. To put all your trust in him." Slowly, Brokk lifted his eyes to meet hers. "Whatever you choose to do, I am behind you no matter what. But choose what you want to fight for. What is *worth* fighting for. For you and no one else."

A thousand words flared on his tongue, a thousand things he wanted to say. *I've missed you.* A ragged breath loosened from his chest. *I want to go back to those simpler days.* Squeezing his hand, tears brimmed in her eyes. *I wish it were different. I wish you hadn't believed he was still in there.* Emory was shaking. *I wish you had believed in me. I am in love with you. I never stopped loving you.*

His gaze lingered on every shadow, every bruise, every haunted look flashing behind those emerald eyes, and he wanted to help. Wanted to ease her pain. But all he could do was wait. Heat flooded through his palm as she shuddered, stepping back.

"Thank you." Shakily she wiped the tears from her eyes, looking around. "You know, it was easier living a lie before. I was safe. But now, knowing the truth of who I am, knowing what is at stake, I want to fill my very *bones* with my rage. With my grief. My vengeance." Pausing, she whispered, "But I am also not enough. And this darkness in me, Brokk, *consumes me.* It's all I see. All I feel within myself. I don't see a way through it." Cringing, he watched her fold in on herself and crumble.

The room was a blur. His arms were around her, and he swallowed through the tightness in his throat, as he whispered into her hair, "Emory Reia Fae, there hasn't been a day that has passed that I haven't thought of you." Her body stilled against his rampaging heart. "Em, I want you to *fight* for *you*. You are enough. You have always been enough. We can work through anything together. Don't give up on that, please. Don't give up on us."

He pressed his eyes shut, murmuring, "Without darkness, we wouldn't be able to see the stars. The flames when fire burns. We all change over time. It's what you choose to do with the darkness you feel within you. Are you going to be blindly led by it, or is it time for you to use what has hurt you to make you stronger?"

She shivered. "But to go back? To what?"

Brokk broke away, lifting an eyebrow. "Are you saying you are coming with me?"

Sighing, Emory looked around the room. "You are persistent, you know? For someone I killed and all." Hiccupping, the tears rolled down her cheeks as she searched his face. "I thought I would never see you again. I tried to convince myself that it couldn't be true, but all I can see is my blade and the blood—"

Grabbing her hands, he squeezed them gently. "You believed a flesh and blood lie. Don't tear yourself apart for not seeing it."

"I couldn't live with myself. I can't forget."

Her eyes blazed, as he leaned in close. "I'm not asking you to forget. But to learn from it."

Her mouth twisted and she paused, scouring his face. In that moment of stretched silence, he caught a flicker. A pulse of shimmering light. The necklace around her neck started to burn like a star itself. Pinching his eyebrows together, he *felt* her fear, like a cloud surrounding them. Pulling her in close, her body tensed.

"It's time, Em."

With salt-crusted lips, her breathing wobbled. "Let's go see what kind of queen I will become."

Then his ability crashed into hers. His breath was swept from his lungs, ice filling them as fire ignited in his veins. It was a crack of light, an explosion of space and matter, energy and expansion. Of give and take—it was all Brokk knew as he squeezed her hand tighter.

They were falling; he felt the pull in his gut, the power thrumming in his veins. Most importantly, he felt *her*. He was screaming, the fractured light fading until darkness swept in around them. And he heard the voices.

"Emory, darling."

"Em, we are so proud of you."

"Darling, come home. To us."

There was a flash of silver, and he saw their decaying hands tearing at them, just out of reach. The pale hair, broken and dull, Nei Fae's face contorted. Another arm shot out toward them, the jacket torn and draping, the grey flesh underneath ripped and exposing bone. The empty eye sockets stared at them, and they were falling but also suspended in this moment. The crown was flawless: the curled iron, the thorn vines, and the roses.

"Emory, darling, it's time. Come with us. You're ready."

She leaned forward, her hair floating around her face, as if they were underwater. She whispered, "Mom? Dad?" It was the slow tilt of their necks, at her voice, that gave them away.

"Em, NO!" Contorting his body, the shadows exploded, revealing their true intention.

"We see youuuuu, Prince and Princess. Our king is coming, and he will tear your heart out. Will tear your kingdom's heart out. We see you..."

Somehow finding Emory's hand, they plunged away from the Oilean, and sucking in deep breaths, he concentrated, mentally yelling, "KIANA! RIONA!"

A moment passed. And then another. They freefell, picking up speed in the channel between life and death. Giggles chased at their heels as he swore, allowing that intoxicating power to fill him, as he roared, "KIANA!" once again.

Below them, a silver light ignited. It twisted, bending and churning, shooting up to them. Sweat slicked his entire body, and Brokk dove straight toward it, just as Emory screamed. The inky shadows clawed at their ankles, drawing blood, and the voices attacked relentlessly.

"You will die if you go back. Give yourself to us. We know your heart. How the innocents you killed begged for mercy. How you would kill the rebels to win his heart. To save a man that had died years ago. How far will you go, Emory Fae, to win this war?"

Her blood-curdling scream sliced through Brokk's core, but he couldn't stop. Stretching out his hand to the light, roaring, he then collided with it. Slamming onto his back, he could smell nothing but smoke.

"Thank the stars! Brokk? BROKK!" Kiana exclaimed.

The ground was trembling. The smell of wet grass and leaves floated in his senses, and for a moment, he wasn't sure if he had made it back, if this was reality or just another pocket of magic, one he could access and travel. His eyes fluttered open, and he soaked in the stars high above, nestled in the sky.

Kiana's face came into focus, as she said, "You did it. Whatever you did. But you must move. Come on, we need a plan, Prince."

Prince. Snarling, he leaned up and she grinned. "I knew that would get a rise out of you. And you know, it was a team effort after all."

His anger dissipated slightly. "You helped me back. I can't thank you enough for that." Dipping her chin, Kiana helped him up as Riona came up to them, supporting Emory whose eyes were blinking too fast, her skin drained of all color: The blacksmith had ripped out most of the needles.

All his words died on his tongue when he took her in.

Smirking, Kiana looked between them. Sucking in deep breaths, he steadied himself, looking toward the towering mountain range instead.

The arrow missed him by a hair's breadth, and as it hit the tree behind him, it exploded into green smoke. Behind Kiana, the Oilean stood, their bows sleek, their arrows aimed at their hearts. Their pale shifts stood out like bone.

As they giggled, one voice cut through the others, "Sisters, you did not disappoint with this world." Adair came into view or at least his body did. His eyes were completely black and merciless. Shifting, Brokk growled, low and guttural, to which Adair lifted the corner of his lips-he charged, shifting from flesh to smoke.

Riona jumped on Brokk's back, Emory in tow, and Kiana was already yards in front of them, running into the heart of the forest. Following Kiana's trail, he didn't look back, as a volley of arrows thudded behind them, each explosion closer than the last.

CHAPTER SIXTEEN

Adair

He had always imagined dying would be painful, filled with gut-wrenching agony. That maybe his demons would be waiting beyond the veils. But as he felt that blade slide in between his ribs, there was only a wash of pain before he watched the light behind Emory's eyes fade as well. Adair wasn't aware of gravity, of the war raging around them. All he saw was her-then nothing.

He knew, deep down, that he was drifting. He recognized the soft voices around him: his mother, his father, the Faes. Memories from another life, another man that had been long forgotten until now.

Blinking slowly, Adair took in the soft light, the weightlessness of the water carrying him. For the first time in *years*, he could think clearly. Running a hand through his hair, his muscles relaxed, and he allowed the current to gently pull him forward but stay true to their course. Beyond, he felt the shudder as his eyes flew open. His hair stood on end when he heard *his own voice*. Except it was far away, words falling into soft hushes by the time they reached him.

Clenching his jaw, he felt the magic of the thousand realities, the thousand courses his life could have taken him. He never thought it would have taken him here. Another shudder, and he looked to the horizon. The river twisted, the water a deep blue, and everywhere around him *was light*. There was no definition, no ending or beginning. Only the journey in between.

The whispers built, layering over another, calling out to him. Blinking, Adair laid back down, closing his eyes and submitting himself to the waters. No more questions. No more wondering. In the end, he knew he would pay for his actions.

A shiver ran down his spine as he sighed, opening his eyes. Far above him, the light was waning, the pull of the water settling.

"*Adair.*"

The shivers grew, rumbling along his bones, soaking into his core. Sitting up, he turned around, not an article of his clothing getting wet as the river suspended him. The voice was gentle. A softness he hadn't earned. Not after years of killing and madness. Years of destroying and breeding fear. A bitter taste filled his mouth. How did *he* deserve peace?

His pulse picked up with his panic. A cracking-like thunder rang out in the space, echoing for miles as he watched the light disappear, replaced by a roaring darkness looming on the horizon, flashes of emerald lightning slashing against the backdrop. He couldn't move as a hundred yards away an inky droplet rippled in the water, disappearing for a moment. His breath caught as he squinted against the rolling thunder. A moment passed and then another.

Lightning shot down, exploding as it contacted the water. The darkness spread like a disease, Adair watching as the water around him turned black, and he was immobilized. Lightning streaked across the sky again just as he looked down, only to see a smiling face of one of the Oilean. She was floating underneath the water, grappling at him, wordlessly, all sharpened teeth and empty eyes.

After all these years and the battles, the Oilean had finally come for him.

As if sensing his hesitation, her pale hand shot forward, wrapping around his wrist in a single motion. His scream died in his throat as they hissed around him, those voices and unseen bodies that had owned his soul for the last six years.

"*You are ours, Adair Stratton. Never forget that.*"

Kicking, Adair tried to swim faster, to get out of their grasp, to allow himself to reach the end. The Oilean dragged him down, as they fell faster, faster, *faster*. He could taste the electric current in the air, pulsing as if it was trying to resuscitate him, calling him back. Her grip tightened, and they plunged fully into nothingness.

"You thought you could drift away *now*? After years of grooming you, poisoning your body for our King. Ensuring it would hold when the time came? No, Adair Stratton. War is beckoning us, and we only answer to one call."

She giggled, as her face blurred, the surroundings becoming suffocating, like a box. His eyes bulged as he clawed at his throat, at his face, at his body.

"This world only ever needed one king. And he has returned."

Pain peppered his body, making his vision tunnel.

The light broke through as the scene focused, the kingdom burning around him too familiar. The Oilean everywhere—bodies and smoke, magic and mist—and he knew he was lying on the floor bleeding out. The fluttering of his pulse as he was slammed between the edge of life and death shocked him. His heavy eyes shut, and he felt the dampness, felt the life being leeched out of him, and all he could hear was the call for more *death.*

The stranger's voice was thick with disappointment. *"This boy is the body you wish for me to inhabit?"*

Wrenching his eyes back open, he scoured the scene before him. Blood and bone riddled the cavernous walls, and all around him, an army was bred, one that he could have never achieved.

"This is all you have?"

Someone screamed in the distance as a broken sob escaped him, and he fell back, his eyes rolling into the back of his head.

"I expected more from you."

Caving into himself, Adair felt it. A small pressure at first, a tingling through his chest, running down his arms, torso, and legs. Filling his lungs, coursing through his blood, becoming an insistent presence to be known.

"Open your eyes. Look at me."

Turning toward that deep command, Adair opened his eyes, blinking. The world had bled away as he lay on his back, the enormous figure hovering over him. It was just them.

His adrenaline pumped viciously, begging him to fight, as he realized the Oilean were right. Everything he had done led to this exact moment: The figure's hand pressed against his chest, and he drank in the pale skin, black eyes, ravenous hunger burning in his features. And all around them was smoke.

He tried to cough, to breathe, to break away, but all he could feel was the pressure building and *building.*

The man leaned closer, the smoke closing in, seeping into his blackened blood, and he couldn't stop watching it soak into his pores, snaking into his mouth, parting his lips on a sigh. The stranger stopped just below Adair's chin and slowly took in a deep breath. Shivers snaked down Adair's spine when the stranger closed his eyes, as if savoring his scent.

Ice filled Adair's veins as empty golden eyes landed on his own. A glimpse of sandy hair, a hooked nose, and a strong jaw was all Adair caught, the rest was darkness.

"You will have to do."

Adair felt the crack then-the bend of magic, the hush of death. He felt it in every fiber of his being as the man dissipated, crashing into him, consuming him. Being slammed back, he screamed, a broken cry, as one-by-one the fleeting memories came to him.

"Adair." Her voice was smooth, her excitement ringing in every word. He cringed, sweat collecting on his brow. He turned slowly, clearing his throat, trying to not look at the students around them.

"You must be Emory Fae."

She tilted her head, amusement flickering across her face. "Something like that."

He nervously stuck out his hand, shaking her hand awkwardly. The smile blossomed across her face, lighting up her features as she rolled her eyes.

"Come on, Stratton, just because it's the first day of the Academy doesn't mean you have to pretend we are strangers. Let people talk." Looping her arm through his, she had swept him off his feet. And had continued to ever since.

Adair was reeling when he saw her face with such a burning clarity, and then in a moment, it was swept away. It was as if his chest had a hole punched through it, and the pain, the fading of memories, the guilt, the loneliness, and madness consumed him.

Emory Fae had never existed to him.

He wheezed as the shadow man snarled in pleasure, the sound vibrating through his mind. And little by little, everything he once was, had been, and had become was ripped apart, destroyed, and lost.

The Dark King, known as Declan, stood slowly, getting used to his new flesh. The boy had been weak and dying, but his ability was still strong. Declan marvelled in its potent *energy* as he flexed his blood-stained fingers, admiring the feeling of having a *physical* body, of walking on a world that hummed with raw magic. Grinning, he looked to his assassins, the Oilean, who bowed their heads to him.

"We have work to do."

After years of being left alone on Daer, a husk of a world, waiting for the day they opened the channels, it had finally come: Declan thirsted for blood.

The Oilean giggled, and then they were racing toward the scents of the prince and princess that had destroyed *so much* for him. Snapping his fingers, he felt the consciousness of the hundreds of dabarnes awaiting his command. He sent the same order through their consciousness. *"Kill the prince and princess."*

Licking his chapped lips, he relished in how they would taste as he drained them of life. This world would break from his reckoning, and it all started with them.

Part Two

LAND OF STARLIGHT AND IRON

CHAPTER SEVENTEEN
Emory

The first thing Emory heard as she came to consciousness was the steady stream of curses coming from behind her. Blinking, she took in that first ragged breath, tears brimming in her eyes from the pain blooming in her chest.

"Easy there, Princess," a familiar female voice said from behind her.

Strong arms held her waist, and she recognized the golden fur, the mammoth size of the wolf underneath them, and the voice soothingly whispering in her ear as they galloped through the woods that had haunted her for the last month.

"Riona?" she rasped.

"The one and only. Let's concentrate on staying alive before we go through the tedious social obligations though, okay?"

What had happened?

Shutting her eyes, Emory concentrated on taking steady breaths, her panic clawing at her mind as the last twenty-four hours flashed before her: Adair planning on taking her to the King across the Black Sea, to Marquis Maher. His plans to end the rebellion. Planning for the Winter Yule. And the needles plunging into her heart as she had...

The panic attack crashed down on her, ice running through her blood, and she couldn't move. She had *died*.

Brokk lunged to the left, as an explosion of bark flew from their right. Twisting around, she squinted in the darkness, her heart thudding. Appearing from the shadows, the Oilean were too close, closing in on them, flanking their sides. Her heart raced as Adair found her eyes and snarled, nothing human left in him. Behind them, Emory caught hundreds of yellow eyes igniting in the shadows, the army of dabarnes trailing them. *Shit.*

"*Emoryyy.*" The Oileans' voices echoed within the night, as Riona yelled, "EMORY!"

She felt Riona's grip around her waist tighten, as the blacksmith unsheathed her hammer in the other hand, swinging it as it crashed with a burning emerald light, exploding like a thousand stars upon impact. Brokk yelped, and Emory found her hands searching, feeling the softness of the fur under her skin, and the tears fell, all at once, her body shuddering against the whispers curling around her mind.

"*Emoryy.*"

The Oileans' call jolted through her as her tears fell across her skin, her sobs turning into hiccups. Her grip tightened as the innocent faces of the men and women Emory had killed raced across her mind, one-by-one. Their pleas for mercy. All she had taken and all she had lost. And it stirred within her. Stirred her broken heart with her pain and resentment, confusion and griefigniting her intention.

Heat surged through her as she looked down to her necklace; the once deep purple gem was now an inky black. Swallowing, she twisted, locking eyes with Riona, and the blade buckled on her back. "Anithe?"

"Like I would leave that piece of artistry behind," Riona said.

With that confirmation, Emory lunged, slamming her body into Riona's, knocking the blacksmith down. Landing on the forest floor, they rolled, her scream cutting through the chaos. Brokk skidded, digging his claws into the ground, the sound a sickening crunch.

"The sword. Now." Riona looked behind them, the army racing toward them. "NOW!" Emory repeated.

The blacksmith moved with grace, and shoving the hilt in her grasp, she shakily clasped it.

"Make for the docks. Adair was preparing our ship. We sail for the Shattered Isles. I will meet you there." Emory urged. The air dropped several degrees, their breath coming in quick pockets of mist. Riona stalled as Emory said, "Trust me."

Plunging into her ability, Emory shuddered against it. *Something was different.* Anithe surged to life, black flames running up the steel. *Run, run, run.* The thought screamed against her instinct, and she breathed, just as frost started covering the ground.

"I admit, I imagined more of a chase in my mind." Adair appeared, his inky eyes lazily moving up and down the length of her body. Behind him, the Oilean hissed, their bodies cracking and moving in angles that defied having a bone mass.

"Well, we can't always have what we want. I presume you have a name other than *King.*"

Adair is gone. He is gone.

His chuckle bounced around the forest; he watched her, weighing her words. "You are very right, Princess. May I formally introduce myself? Declan, the ruler of Daer. And my faithful servants, the Oilean. It's a shame that we are born enemies of each other. I quite enjoy your...spirit."

"Well, claiming war on our world—that's hard to move past from."

The wind picked up as he circled her, the Oilean giggling behind him. "I'm not the one who ignited this war. Adair had already done my bidding; he just didn't understand it. He thought he was climbing to power." He smiled. "Adair Stratton was weak. And now his fate awaits all of you. To be wiped from the face of Kiero."

Jutting her chin out, Emory stilled her raging heartbeat, reining in the power that was begging to release from her and kept this verbal sparring going. "He was my friend, once. I like to remember Adair as he had been. Not as the *monster* you bent him to be."

Assessing her, Declan's cruel smile grew. "You truly believe that you can make a difference? That you aren't just as weak and insignificant as everyone before you that has claimed to rise as a ruler? Come now, Emory." He tutted, like he was scolding a child, and she gritted her teeth, her body quaking.

"I may not know exactly who I am yet. I am weathered and broken from this world. But not even death can stop me from trying to save it from *you*. And that is something worth fighting for." The back flames grew more from Anithe, and she couldn't hold on. Seething, she said, "Let's see exactly who will turn the tables of this war."

His face darkened, and a hush fell over the forest, the Oilean watching her, their bodies too still, the hundreds of dabarnes now awaiting Declan's order. Roaring, Emory buried her blade in the half-frozen ground: The world exploded in flames. The wall of fire grew and consumed, the sheer force of the heat making them stagger back.

Swearing, she wrenched the blade from the now melting ice and ran. The wall remained, sweat trickling down her spine as she pushed her energy into it, making it circle them, holding them off for a moment. She didn't understand it, but suspended between the threads of life and death, something had happened. An exchange of energy within her ability where she had absorbed Adair's magic, but instead of fading, it had *stayed*.

Stumbling, Emory fell, skin tearing from her knees. Pushing off the ground, she stood back up and stilled. One of the Oilean stood in front of her, pale skin, slowly tilting her head to a sickly angle.

"You and Adair are so similar. The power flowing in your veins is intoxicating."

Emory didn't wait as she charged. Her sword was sturdier in her grip than she had suspected. With protesting muscles, and gaining momentum, she swung Anithe toward the Oilean's throat. The creature dodged Emory with ease, and as Emory watched in horror, her sharpened teeth grew and elongated along with razor-sharp nails. Panting, her arm shook, and the creature surged, emerald light shooting forward.

For me. She screamed as she ran, flames around her roaring, jumping to life from the steel. *For my family.* They collided, and she felt the claws dig into her skin, throwing her down to the ground. Scrambling up, Emory wheezed, lashing out with a small push dagger she had sheathed in her boot. Gravity spun as she felt the ripping sensation-she was torn from her body, her claws sinking into the mind of the Oilean. Commanding her ability, Emory bowed against the force of the power running through her veins.

"Do you think you can touch me with your little tricks, girl?"

Emory felt the fist connect with her jaw, as she was slammed back into her body, landing on her back completely winded. All she could see was the night, the leaves in the Noctis woods illuminated, as if they contained their own moonlight. The stars winked down from the velvet sky as embers fell around her. She tasted blood, trickling slowly into the back of her mouth and the world spun.

The Oilean burst from the shadows, teeth snapping, bones cracking, pinning Emory down when she went to get up. Saliva dripped from her peeled back lips, dripping on to Emory's cheek. Screaming, Emory tried to push the Oilean off her as all around her giggles erupted-her heart dropped into her stomach.

A slow clapping sounded as Declan emerged from the shadows, the dabarnes snarling at his heels, looking at her with burning hunger. Those familiar features cut through her like a knife. His dark hair. Brooding features. His stance, his jacket.

"Emory. Emory. Emory. What were you hoping to achieve? I applaud your valor," Declan cooed as he crouched down beside her, and the Oilean pressed down harder on her chest when she squirmed. Emory felt tears slip from the corner of her eyes.

"I wish I could promise this is going to be painless. And fast." He licked his dry lips, his anticipation bleeding into his voice. "But it's going to be neither." Panic flared within her, but instead of debilitating her, Emory felt a spark of something stronger: The feeling first within her core, her ability intertwining with Adair's. It spread fast, into her arms and legs, that familiar tingling building within her palms and spirit. It felt like a breath of fresh air, as the veil within her mind was pulled back and what Emory found there was power.

QUEEN TO ASHES

A streak of gold flew from the night, his howl earth-splitting as he locked his massive teeth around Declan's midriff, throwing him halfway across the clearing. Brokk shifted, pulling two elegant twin blades from their sheaths strapped across his back. Locking eyes with the Oilean, pure hatred flashed in his eyes.

"You." That one word Brokk spoke completely shattered her. The pain laced his words, as he became nothing but pure and undiluted power.

Shoving hard, Emory's knee jammed into the creature's stomach as she rolled, finding her feet as the Oilean's hisses surrounded them in a sick harmony. Brokk was shifting between wolf and man, using each strength to his advantage, and she was stunned as she watched him. He wielded the swords with mastery as he cut and slashed so fast that he was a blur. The Oilean circled him, lunging and clawing, for the moment completely forgetting her.

Suddenly a hand wrapped around her matted hair, pulling her across the forest floor, her screams escalating.

"You both are becoming an annoying problem, *Princess*."

She felt Declan's magic start to trickle into her veins, and screamed, "No!" She slammed every ounce of her ability upwards to meet the king: The ground beneath them shuddered. Declan paused, narrowing his eyes before their world erupted in shadows.

She flew straight for him, slamming her fist into his jaw, snapping his head back. Her ability was *strong*, but Adair's had always been stronger. And now Emory realized the two were intertwined, coursing in her soul, making her blood sing with lethal power. A wall of ice erupted in between them, the expanse of it circling around the king. He rushed up to the ice wall, both of their chests heaving as their reflections shone off the peerless surface.

"It seems that I have acquired a few new *tricks*," Emory said.

With a flick of her wrist, the world changed again. Tree roots shot from the ground, the gnarled edges surging toward him. Locking her eyes with Declan's, she stalked forward. The wind started howling, ice and rain, whipping around him, the rolling thunder rolling in the cover of the night. The ground rumbled louder, this time splitting as bones of animals long forgotten floated up. She blanched at the dark magic, but the skeletons appeared, skulls turning in her direction.

Emory whispered, "Help me." In a flash of lightning, the bones reconnected as they circled the king, and she stood taller. "This is my kingdom. *Mine*. And you will never take that away from us."

The creatures attacked as she slammed back in to her reality, rushing to pick up Ainthe as the flames jumped to life, dividing the Oilean and Brokk. Brokk locked eyes with her, the flames dancing in his wide eyes. Charging up to him, he shifted as Emory clamored on his back, yelling, "RUN!"

Galloping through the night, Emory hunched low, gripping his fur. She couldn't look back and shut her eyes. "I'm so sorry. I will explain the best that I can. Go to the docks, and we'll sail for the Shattered Isles to get to Marquis. I think that's the only way, Brokk, that we can save the rebellion. We need help."

Brokk's muscles tensed as they wove deeper into the forest. A roar erupted behind them—emerald arrows exploding into the tree next to them. Pushing faster, the forest blurred as the wind roared in her ears, Brokk's pounding paws against the earth her personal metronome. Panting, she held on, her energy having expended too much. Once again, Brokk was her only hope.

QUEEN TO ASHES

Snow appeared suddenly, fast and blinding, and ice cracked behind them, consuming the trees, covering the forest floor, racing up to meet them. Breaking through the tree line, salty air whipped around them as waves crashed, wild seafoam rushing up to meet the shore. Brokk's head whipped to the north, as they spotted the tall ship and the two women screaming at them from it. Not breaking stride, his paws beat against the ground, and she felt the tug of energy, the cutting edge of the ice.

"BROKK FOSTER!"

Twisting, she saw Declan emerge, his sword dripping with ashes as if it was just incinerated. The Oilean came up beside him, the woods shimmering behind them, but they paused, the dabarnes filing into a line, watching them escape. Narrowing her eyes, Emory locked eyes with the Dark King as he smirked dangerously.

"I will start with them!" he shouted.

Her blood ran cold, but Brokk didn't stop. Rushing onto the dock, they flew, the wood bending under their weight; growling, he jumped, scaling onto the vast ship's side.

Rolling, the wind was knocked out of her as she landed. "Riona, now!" Emory barked.

The blacksmith jumped at her voice, cutting ropes as the ship groaned, bending toward the will of the ocean.

"Get the anchor up! And the sails!" Kiana yelled.

Brokk shifted, crossing the space as he loosened the sails. Kiana snapped her fingers, and with a crack, the anchor flew on board from the sea. They caught wind as the three of them ran, securing knots. The ship lurched, waves crashing all around them. Staggering, Emory wobbled to the edge, looking out to her country, the five figures slowly becoming distant shadows until they disappeared, completely lost on the horizon.

The waves swelled around her, but she still heard Brokk softly clearing his voice behind her.

"Em?" Her heart rammed unevenly against her chest at Brokk's voice as her shame rushed up to meet her. "Em, *please*."

Her muscles quaked as the horizon bled into the night, and they were left at the mercy of sea. Its untamedness. Its unpredictability.

Slowly, she turned. His shirt was bloodied and plastered to his skin, the sea spray and vicious bucking of the waters beneath them making it impossible to stay dry. Her gaze traveled up to his arms, his neck, the scars roping thickly across it.

Swallowing, she found his burning eyes, flashing like embers. "We did it. We escaped them," Emory breathed.

A sad smile tugged at his lips as he nodded. "For now, anyway."

Emory and Brook looked at the fierce women staring at them openly, both beaming as they steered the ship into the wrath and freedom beyond. Brokk cocked an eyebrow shaking his head. "These two don't know the art of being subtle."

"Are they from the Shattered Isles?" she asked.

"I wish. Truly, it would make things simpler." Looking at her quaking body, Brokk's voice was soft, unsure, as he continued, "Kiana and Riona don't need help sailing. They are...talented. We can't do any more for right now. Let's try and get some sleep."

She tilted her head, taking him in. Exhaling hard, she nodded. "Okay. Okay." And Brokk was there, reaching for her hand. His skin was warm, despite having the freezing water soak them to the bone, despite the fact he had defied life and death for *her*. Despite everything. Her actions. Defiance. Mistrust.

As Kiero became nothing more than a speck, a lingering knowledge that it was *there*, Emory smiled. Time and time again, he showed up at her side. Taking the first step, Brokk led her and supporting each other, they made their way down below decks. The wind was freezing, the echoes of autumn haunting at their backs.

"So, you remember Marquis, huh?" His voice was low.

Shrugging, the movement seared through her muscles. "Adair had a great interest in trying to...appease him for the war. I intend to do the same."

His golden eyes darkened, the ring of molten around the iris turning almost a deep chocolate color. "He will not take Adair's death lightly. Despite everything."

"I haven't taken his death lightly. Despite everything." It snapped out of her and a shadow crossed his face. Sighing, Emory picked up her pace. Their boots hit the wet floor with a slap as she grappled for words. "Brokk..." Her voice dropped to a whisper as she tried to find a way to begin to explain, to *cover* what had happened while she was with Adair.

The waves crashed against the ship viciously, pounding and *pounding* as if every attempt was to capsize them. Thunder rolled, slow at first and then building, until it crashed around them. *I killed innocent people.* Brokk's eyes found hers in the half-darkness, his breath catching. *How can I become queen when I feel like I am barely holding on? How can I be me?*

They stood there, suspended between exhaustion and silence. *This hunger in me...*

Her eyes burned, and she blinked hard, looking past him.

"Where are the bunks?" Emory chose to say instead.

The wind howled-their gravity bucked. Narrowing his eyes, he motioned for her to follow. With wobbly legs, she forced her body to comply, shoving the last couple of minutes behind her. Sleep was quickly chased away by her impossible task at hand,

and she bit the inside of her cheek until the thick taste of blood filled her mouth.

Flinging a door open, the hinges creaking, she watched his defined back tense. Two bunkers were neatly stacked on the right side of the room which was the size of a closet. The air was musty and damp, but a stack of blankets waited for them. She just wanted to be able to *sleep* without nightmares, without friends and family that were long lost whispering to her. Of a life that was now lost.

"If you need anything, Em, I'm just down the hall…"

"No." It was a whisper, a conviction, a plea, a hope. She had been so *wrong*. Locking onto his gaze, she murmured, "I want you to stay." Lifting her chin, the storm raged outside as they sailed on the edge of the world; she searched his face.

"I know I have let you down. I know I'm not the same person, but how can I be? Both of us, our lives have been ripped in opposite directions, and now everything is patched together, and we must figure out a way not to fall. I can't do this without you. I don't even know if I can *do this*, but I'm here. I'm fighting. Like you said, I'm fighting for me."

Brokk was frozen, his gaze flickering over her.

"I'm *terrified*, Brokk. A few months ago, I was worried about dating and starting to plan the end of summer bazaar at work, and now…" *I've defied worlds because of you.* Swallowing hard, she tried to still her shaking hands. "I doubt that I am the person the rebellion has been waiting for. That Memphis was waiting for. That *you* were waiting for."

In a second, he was there crushing her against his chest. Warmth blossomed through her aching body, and tears began streaking down her cheeks.

"Em. Em."

His hug was like walking home after a long day. Knowing that at the end, a safe space was waiting for her, no judgement, and unconditionally always there. The ship bucked as he broke away, gently grabbing her frozen fingers, leading her into the room. Shutting the door, she looked up, finding such a deep understanding waiting for her in his eyes, and she didn't know what to do or say.

"You know, after you left, I was angry for a long time. The world literally fell apart, and there wasn't a day that passed that I didn't think about what happened. What you asked. Did you make the right choice? Could we have confronted Adair then? After a long time, I realized beyond that anger and jealousy, I found something within myself," Brokk said.

"What?" she breathed, as she sat on the lowest bunker.

"Trust. That above all else, I trusted you. I always have. And I knew the day would come, and we would meet again." He paused. "Emory Fae, you are still my best friend, so don't think for a minute that you aren't the one I was waiting for."

Her cheeks burned as her mouth ran dry. Sitting next to her, he leaned back against the damp bedpost. "So, with that out of the way, what are we going to do? You believe Marquis will be willing to hear us out when he has been absent this entire war?"

"Has he known that you were even alive?" she countered, as she leaned back, hyper aware of the little space between them. "Besides, if Adair had his eye on him, don't you think we should see why?"

Running a hand over his mouth, he murmured, "And what about the Rebellion? Memphis, Nyx, and Alby?"

"They are with another group. You weren't the only ones to survive. Alby's twin brother, Azarius, got them out. Or so I hope."

Recognition lit in his eyes. "So that's the other scent I tracked then. He saved you?"

"Yes," Emory said before launching in to her side of what happened. At first, the words felt awkward and dry, and again, she was a ghost, living a second life. One that had died in her innocence, in the trust she had placed in strangers.

Time slipped away as she finished, leaving Brokk gawking. "Alby has a twin brother? All this time, and he never thought to mention that?"

"Seriously? That's what you're stuck on?"

His lopsided grin lit up his face as he shrugged, then he fell quiet,shaking his head. "That night...everything changed. For all of us."

Shut in the dingy room of the ship, she looked at him. The world started to feel far away as she nodded. "But not as much as it changed when two strangers showed up in my apartment living room."

Rolling his eyes, Brokk stared at the ceiling. "Well, you know, I was tired of waiting for you. The world needed the Fae name back."

"And what makes you think I wasn't equally waiting for all of you? This world? My story?"

"Even a bloodied one?" he asked.

"If it was the truth, then yes. It's better than living a lie."

He sighed, rubbing at his eyes. "Then I should tell you who those two talented women are up above and why they can sail a ship by themselves."

The storm raged all around them as his tale dipped into the darkest corners of her heart, one of witches and torture. One of dark forces beyond her comprehension, of the magic that had manipulated them all to this moment. Of a lost city, of myths and a stolen prince.

The hours slipped by, and she gaped, at a complete loss for words once again when he finished. Meekly, Brokk searched her face. "When the Oilean were torturing me, they mentioned a prophecy that I believe held a sliver of truth. But not of us as siblings. And not that we would destroy the world. It was of us born from two crowns; having the ability to stop their war. They knew exactly why they were coming to our world. They just tried to ensure we wouldn't find out the truth."

The ship bucked violently, thunder reverberating outside. The world spun and she swore, holding her head in her hands. Sucking in deep breaths, Emory tried to digest it all. Panic clutched her heart.

"One step at a time, Em. Like trying to get some rest from coming back from the dead?" His tone was soft, his concern hanging in the air.

Blinking tiredly, she ran a hand through her tangled hair, whispering, "We should check in with Kiana."

"Em."

"I'm fine." The lie was blatant, but Emory couldn't begin to address her emotions.

Narrowing his eyes, he nodded, standing; bones popped causing him to groan. "I will go. Just try and get some rest okay?"

Sighing, she gave in. Emory watched him step out of the room, then her gaze landed on her necklace, the ebony reflecting against her pale skin. The door shut with a click. She swore again, grabbing a blanket and moving to lay on her back. Her stomach rolled viciously as she pressed her eyes shut.

The sea crashed around her as she whispered to the empty space, "I'm fine." She couldn't move. She couldn't pry her eyes open. She gave in to the numbness waiting for her as Brokk's expressions were branded into her mind: His fear. His anger. His conviction.

As they sailed to the edge of the world, she allowed herself to feel every sharpened edge of her pain, and she knew that in the process of claiming her throne, she had lost herself. How much more was she willing to lose in the process?

Grabbing the stale, musty pillow, she covered her face, allowing the screams to claw out of her throat, and the waves and thunder to drown her anguish.

CHAPTER EIGHTEEN
Brokk

Endlessness surrounded them. The sea and the horizon blended as the traces of dawn ignited in the sky. Flecks of midnight-blue and silver lingered, the turmoil from the storm long over, but as always, the trace remained.

"Are you trying to be brooding, Foster?" Riona was at his side, the sea salt caking her skin, hair unbound, a sly smile hiding in the corner of her lips.

"No."

Riona looked up to her sister, the light illuminating her. With wide eyes, Riona constantly searched for something more than the crashing of the inky sea all around them. Something more than what they had all left behind.

To be honest, it put him on edge. Turning to look at Kiana, Brokk said sarcastically, "So, it must be hard being good at everything you try, isn't it?" She flashed a rude gesture down at him, and a snort escaped through his lips.

"In all seriousness though, are we safe for the moment from the Oilean and the Dark King?"

Pausing, Kiana furrowed her brows. "Nothing is for certain; our fates change like the push and pull of the tide. Now, we wait and see where our decisions lead us. Do I hope that we are safe? Of course. Can I be sure? Absolutely not."

"Are you always this cryptic in the morning?"

"A war is exploding behind us, Brokk. I'm just focusing on making it to the Shattered Isles alive. There are worse things than Marquis Maher within these waters."

Curiosity piquing, Brokk was moving. The deck was soaked from the raging storm, but he was sure-footed as he climbed the crooked steps.

Kiana manned the ship's wheel; she said between pursed lips, "Are you ready?"

"For Marquis? Do you know him as well?" Brokk asked.

"Of him. And we are on a dangerous path. How else do you think he has survived Adair untouched? Because he has played the game, Brokk, and he has played it *well*."

He ran a hand over his chapped lips, his mind spinning. Naturally, their world had made them all adept to survive in whatever manner they could. Them in resistance. And Marquis...?

"We have to make him listen, Kiana." His voice cracked.

She finally locked her ancient eyes on him, the depth of her stare pinning him. "I have lived through a lot of dark times. I have lived through thinking I lost you, the sole person I swore my king and queen I would protect. I have lived through losing my Warriors and our magic. Our world whittling down to nothing more than shadows and myths.

"Prepare yourself, Foster, because this time is different. I can feel it quaking the world. Whatever those demons are after, your princess has it, has defied *death* for it. We all have a reckoning falling on us."

Looking out to the horizon, he allowed the words to sink in as he watched the sun crest above the waters, shimmering like a fine jewel.

Clearing his throat, he murmured, "Don't you need to sleep?"

"You're sweet, but no. Being an immortal and a Warrior does have some perks." Riona smiled.

Shaking his head in awe, he turned. "Well, I'm glad you have this under control. I need some rest though. Not all of us are *naithe,* Kiana."

"You make fun, but just give us some time, *Prince.* You will see."

Sighing, his bones popped as he stretched. "Do we have food and water on this forsaken vessel?"

Her grin widened. "Why, not a fan of open water?"

"No, it's fine. But your mood swings are giving me some trouble."

Her laugh chased him down the steps as she decided not to answer him. Brushing past Riona, Brokk tried not to think about the king across the sea. Digesting his own past had his mind reeling. Or that Emory had *died.* And last night...

Sucking in a deep breath, he leaned against the stairwell wall. Fear burned deep within him as he still tried to digest everything Emory had told him. A growing doubt pitted in his mind. How could they conquer the Oilean after both needing time to heal? Adair had broken her in the deepest way—making her become a nightmare, blood staining her hands. And himself, in the quiet of the night, he could still hear the Oilean whispering to him, wanting his blood, and he would wake from the nightmares, prepared to still be captured deep beneath the earth.

Yet, there was no time to allow the pain to overcome him. They were broken—lives constructed from love, pain, loss, and hope, and for the moment, he would have to hold on, instead of wanting to fall into that oblivion. Groaning, he silently prayed to any force looking over them to keep the resistance alive and his friends safe.

"You look well rested."

Snapping his head up at Emory's voice, he pushed himself off the wall. She dug her hands deep into her tattered pockets, her hair catching in the salty breeze. The obsidian gem rested on her chest, the patch of skin showing from underneath her collar looking as if it had been burned. But those emerald eyes blazed, clear and focused.

"Brokk?"

He had always been terrible at small talk. "And you too, Em." Both clearly lies. She smirked, her hands fidgeting. He climbed down the rest of the stairs, his voice even. "Want to help me find something to eat?"

Her face cleared at the normalcy of his question. "Absolutely."

The air was musty below decks, the constant moisture clinging to the boards. Goosebumps raced along his skin, as he frowned, trying to remember the crisp air of the forest, the ground beneath his paws, his safe space.

"So..."

"So?" A thousand possibilities coursed through him.

"After we find food, maybe we can sit down with the others. After what happened yesterday..."

"You don't need to say anything more. I agree. We also need to plan. Do you have an idea of what Adair was after? Other than Marquis himself?"

"No. I mean, Adair was after his allegiance. We can't win against the Oilean without the numbers. It was a risk, but we were lucky that it wasn't worse."

"Wasn't worse? Em, you died." Gone was their second of peace as the ice cut through him again.

"I was *almost* dead. A key point, but it would have been worse without you. Also, it bought us more time."

"What do you mean?" Brokk asked.

"I think my mom... Somehow, she left me this necklace knowing that I might be in this position with Adair, harnessing this dark magic. You know how I was telling you that I am...changed? But this necklace, Brokk, I think is somehow containing what was *in* Adair."

The world stopped. Turning, he stared at the blackened gem, his mind racing. "You're saying you think the Oileans' magic from the Book of Old is in your necklace?"

"I know it sounds crazy, but with my ability, I can sense it. I can *feel* it."

Exhaling hard, he ran a hand through his hair. "Em, if that's true, they will be hunting you. They want that magic, and then they want to kill us. All of us."

"Well, I guess we better find some food and then put our heads together. I have no intention of dying again anytime soon." Brushing past him, he gawked but followed, dread pooling in his stomach.

The jerky and stale bread was disgusting. Gripping his cup, he washed it down, the water cleansing his palate as Brokk watched the dark rolling waves. They had been at it for hours, sitting around the wheel as Kiana steered them toward the Isles. She was constantly smelling the winds and looking to the skies as they bantered. Swearing, Riona polished her hammer with vengeance, not looking up.

"Do you think Emory is right?" Riona asked.

Sighing, he said, "Without a doubt."

She stood, and Kiana whispered, "Riona, don't."

The hammer swung from her grip, to which she pointed at her sister's chest. "No. You two are blindly following her calls? How can we trust her?"

"And how can *I* trust you?" Emory stared her down.

Riona smirked. "I sacrificed my entire life to be a spy! I watched how you were with Adair for months, all the while the Rebels scattered, and now, I can guarantee you they will all die. All for what? So, we can go visit a man that wants nothing to do with this war."

"You're not the only one who has sacrificed their life." Emory scoffed.

"From what I gathered from Kiana, it's more like you ran away from *your life*," Riona sneered.

Standing, Brokk downed the rest of his water. "And continuing to argue isn't going to get us anywhere. Riona, Kiana, once we reach the Isles, if you want to head back, then go. I stand by Em."

"And you know I stand by you, Brokk, until the end." Kiana's voice was soft, but her conviction rang true.

"Well, that's great. Because I'm not leaving my sister to get herself killed." Riona shot a glare at Emory but, sighing, said, "I guess time will tell. Do we all agree then that our priority is to keep the resistance alive?" They all nodded, and the blacksmith relaxed, sitting back down. "Okay. Well, we best sail fast, sister, courting a king takes time, as some here know."

Emory's face darkened, but Riona grinned.

Stepping in, Kiana ordered, "Emory, Brokk, until we reach the Isles, train. Riona will gladly show you what Nehmai holds as a standard. We reach Marquis in five days." Kiana turned her back, as Emory locked eyes with him. Nodding, she looked at the blacksmith, both sizing the other up.

"Well, let's begin." Brokk's voice was gravelly, as he looked behind them, at the rolling inky waters, the crisp afternoon air swirling around them. His heart wrenched, and he hoped wherever the Black Dawn rebellion was, they were preparing too.

CHAPTER NINETEEN
Memphis

The light stung his eyes as blinking rapidly, Memphis was thoroughly confused about how he wasn't dead. The room was small, and the bed he lay on was neatly tucked in the corner. His body felt as if he had been pulled apart muscle by muscle and put back together again. Sitting up fast, nearly smacking his head against the wall, his vision dipped, pulling him under. Groaning, he cupped his head, breathing deeply. Snippets of blurred memories tugged at him. A room, the bars...and *Morgan*. If he was here, she must have been stopped. If she had been stopped... Memphis's thoughts churned, not quite connecting.

"It's about time you came around." Jumping, he looked up to see a very alive Nyx. Her purple hair was braided, and she wore leather boots, pants, and a loose grey shirt. And of course, she was armed to the teeth. Her eyes glinted as Memphis stared at her open-mouthed. She was *alive*. Jumping out of bed, he didn't care that every move felt like knives stabbing him. He wrapped her in a bear-gripping hug, nearly crying. She was *alive*.

QUEEN TO ASHES

Shoving him back, her lips curled up. "Memph, get off me. I'm not nearly as happy to see you. Though, I'm glad you're not dead."

All he could do was stand there, mouth gaping. Nyx threw clothes at him. "Get dressed and get ready. A lot of things have changed."

Nyx left the room as Memphis ran a hand over his mouth, hastily putting on the fresh clothes and fitted leather shoes. Pulling his long hair back with a leather band, he sat on the bed for a moment. Coughing, he straightened, staring at the back of the door and what might be waiting for him behind it: The Rebellion broken and split, dancing with death, a world in turmoil.

A thousand whispers hurled themselves at his mind, making the room spin slightly as he tried to take even breaths. *Stay in control.* Taking a step, his lungs ignited into flame. Another, and his bones felt like they were grinding into dust. And another, his gut felt like it was being wrenched out of him. Through the lacing pain, he made it to the door and, with shaking hands, pulled it open.

They were in a small cottage, the pungent smell of herbs filling the air as voices overlapped one another down the hallway. Dappling light came in through the windows as he passed them, stalking into reality in a dreamlike state. The kitchen was small and cramped, cupboards and shelves toppling with books, utensils, plates, and well-worn cups. Nyx stood off to the farthest corner, arms crossed, shadows cutting across her sharp features. Grief flickered to anger as she took him in. The conversation died as he cleared his throat, looking at the group.

Azarius stood first, Alby behind him. "Memphis, how are you feeling?"

"Truthfully?" He scoffed.

Alby smirked. "I can imagine just as youthful and jubilant as I am feeling."

"Sit, please. You will need your strength." Azarius motioned for him to sit down.

Memphis complied. Groaning, his senses were filled with velvety steam as he looked down to the cup that was placed before him.

Lana smiled kindly, trying to break the tension in the room. "You will feel better, trust me. Drink it."

Stiffly, Memphis clutched the cup, the warmth searing his skin. The others took their seats, watching as he sipped; his taste buds exploded with citrus and hints of lavender.

Azarius seemed to assess the dark bruises while he sized him up before sighing. "What do you remember?"

"It's all very choppy. After Nyx was brought here, I remember going to Morgan. After that..." Memphis trailed off, lost in the darkness of the bars enclosed around his mind as his body relived the dragging moments of desperation.

"You were poisoned. You are lucky to be here, if I'm being honest with you. You should thank both of these talented ladies for that," Azarius stated drily.

Looking around the room, Memphis tried to voice his gratitude for being saved. But seeing Nyx so comfortable amongst these strangers, his resentment seared within him, until the harsh words burst from his mouth.

"So, you have warmed up to joining the rebellion I have seen? Despite what Nyx did?" The darkest corners of his heart roaring at Nyx's betrayal. In all their betrayal.

Nyx pushed herself off the wall. "You want to do this now, Memphis? *Fine.*" Nyx stalked toward him, everyone else frozen in their seats. "I did go to Adair. I did *try* to trade the lovely princess for our freedom. Because I have navigated my life based on waiting. Waiting for a plan that would drag us out of this nightmare, for a miracle.

"And I took a blade for you because I will always have that blood on my hands, and there is nothing that will ever take that back. That will make it better. That will bring them back. And I am not asking for your forgiveness. But right now, you need to put what happened between you and me aside and listen to what Azarius and Lana have to say."

Swallowing hard, he looked to Lana, and she leaned forward. "You will want to drink your tea for this."

And she began. This woman laid bare the truth he had been seeking his entire life. Of hidden worlds, lying monarchs, hiding the one thing that poisoned their world. Slowly draining his tea, his mind became clear as Memphis tried to grapple with it. Once she stopped, his mouth was dry, his head pounding. The walls seemed to close in as he slammed his fist against the table, making everyone jump.

"All this time. *All this time.*" He fumed, pushing his chair back.

"Memphis, listen to me." Nyx was there, trying to navigate through his anger. "This is our shot. This is it. We have to trust them."

"Or what? Brokk is our only hope to have a fighting chance? What about finding him? I don't even know if he is *alive.*"

"We kill Adair, and the Book of Old will die with him." Azarius's voice cracked. "I have a hard time wrapping my head around this, but we cannot fall into the lies and mistakes of those who are long gone. We can't find the answers there. The answers are within us now. We are our future—this group here."

"So, what's this *grand plan?*" The sarcasm dripped thickly off Memphis's words.

Lana looked at them all fiercely. "I have been waiting my whole immortal life to liberate this world along with my own, Langther. The Faes' reign is long over, and we all must prepare that in this life, rebuilding the foundation will mean lives lost, and all our hands will be covered in the blood of our friends and family. It will mean the ultimate sacrifice and not letting our emotions rule our actions." Her gaze burned into his.

Alby laughed. "Well, by fire and flame. So, we are the start of what Lana said, The Original Six? A group of rebels to tip the scales of good versus evil. This is historical."

Lana shook her head. "No, we are the start of our freedom. No titles. Just us."

It was all too much. Memphis felt a hole being punched through his heart as he grieved for his family slaughtered at the Academy, but the wheels of war were only spinning faster.

He couldn't help himself as he asked, "And we truly believe that Emory betrayed us for Adair?"

Azarius snarled. "She could be sitting here right now if she had chosen to. She betrayed us. Now we must move forward, understanding she is the enemy."

Narrowing his eyes, Memphis's mind churned. It would appear Azarius was right. He had been there, hearing her scream tear through the stadium. Her conviction. Memphis wanted to let her go, but gods above, deep down, he knew he couldn't. Not until he had a chance to talk to her, to separate his nightmares from reality.

Lana stirred her tea slowly. "We must scour this land for every living soul that will join our cause to unite against Adair. If we are all in agreement, we start after today. Memphis and Nyx, you will leave to find survivors and bring them back safely. Azarius and Alby, you will man Pentharrow and make all the preparations needed. I will find Brokk, and once we have our army, we march on Adair."

Memphis was a recruiter now, his leadership whisked away on a memory. He was a pawn in war, and he didn't call the shots anymore: Chaos awaited him.

Nyx paced over to the windwalker. "We head north?"

Lana smiled slyly, as she rolled up her sleeves. Memphis couldn't move, yet numbness spread through him. Azarius searched him, trying to gauge his reaction from across the room. His emotions were still, his face a mask. He would not let the disarray he felt inside bleed through, letting them know just how unhinged he was.

Lana twirled around, which was a feat in such a small space. "You will have today to prepare and celebrate our gains. Tomorrow, we begin. But before that, Memphis and Nyx, come here."

Spreading her hands over the table's surface, an inky map bled onto it. "We are here in Pentharrow. You need to travel north to the Risco Desert and Arken mountains. It is unmarked territory, with the stretch of the Forgotten Bogs."

"That will take months. Adair could show his hand by then. He could *kill us* by then. We don't have the luxury of time," Memphis stated.

Lana chuckled darkly. "On foot, it would take months. How you two are traveling, it will take a matter of days. Luckily for you, I have been preparing for this ever since I arrived in Kiero." Lana motioned then for them to follow her.

Everyone, equally confused, filed out of the cottage following Lana down the cobble road.

Inhaling deeply, the fresh air was a slap to his face. Alby walked beside him, his hair looking aflame in the sunlight. Casting a sideways look to his friend, Memphis asked, "How are you holding up?"

Alby shrugged. "Azarius is still pissed with me, and why shouldn't he be? We are all each other had, and I abandoned him here to go to the Academy. Now, we're all one big happy family, preparing for war. It will take time for those wounds to heal, and as you pointed out, we don't have a lot of that these days."

An unsettled silence came between them, neither saying what they were thinking. Looking around, Memphis couldn't believe this fractured piece of normalcy had been protected. Had been saved. It was everything he wanted, and everything he couldn't do.

Jealousy burned in his gut when he thought about the town around them bustling with life. No one in this world was free or without pain, but these people didn't have to hide in the earth with a target always on their backs. His guilt laid heavy on him, making him feel constantly shadowed. Memphis knew he hadn't done enough, and now, he couldn't take back the consequences. His fear and his selfishness had ruled his life. And his heart.

Stopping, Lana beamed at them all, motioning below her at a small carved statue beside a rotting, abandoned cottage. The marble was flawless; at the base, roots entangled one another, curling up to a broad chest with strange markings he didn't recognize etched upon it: Towering antlers curled toward the sky, sweeping and cutting. The artistic design swept his breath away, the angles and dips capturing the light, creating shadows and depth. The group stopped before it, everyone thoroughly confused.

QUEEN TO ASHES

It was Nyx who spoke up first. "You do know it's a rock, right?"

The healer looked at her friend, gleefully whispering, "Watch."

Bending down, she brushed her hand along the statue, gently like a caress. The tattoos bled onto her forearms at once, blurring beautiful scenes of monsters of old, of warriors and battles. Of a beautiful, fierce world Memphis didn't recognize, filled with magnificent beasts taking to the skies.

The crack shuddered through the statue, and they seemingly held their breath. Another pause and chunks of the carving were bouncing off the ground. The wind picked up, and all at once, the broken carving exploded, the chunks of rock practically humming with magic.

Lana watched, bouncing on her feet as the pieces started to rise off the ground, spinning so fast it was all just a blur. There was a crack like thunder, and the ground shuddered beneath their feet. Blinking, he gawked at where the statue had once been, completely at a loss for words.

The creature was easily the size of the houses around them, its muscles rippling as its hooves pawed the ground, dust flying from the incinerated marble. With the body of a stag, its peerless white fur seemed blinding. Huge wings tucked neatly on its sides, feathers reflecting every color of the rainbow in the sunlight. Its intelligent eyes assessed them, massive antlers curling up toward the peerless sky.

"What, by fire and flame, is this?" Memphis asked.

Stroking the beast's fur affectionately, Lana beamed. "May I introduce Aella. She is a native animal from my world, Langther, that windwalkers are paired with from birth. They are called perytons, a herd animal, and none more loyal. I brought her with me but, for obvious reasons, kept her hidden with magic until the day I needed her. She can cover distances with a speed very few people have experienced. Also, as windwalkers are, she has been trained for war since she was old enough to fly. She is my partner and comrade."

Nyx choked out, "Her antlers..."

Lana curled her lips even wider. "Are pure iron. Sharp as any blade. It has been far too long since she has been able to put them to use."

Nyx raised her eyebrow, admiration crossing her features as Aella trotted forward, taking deep whiffs of them.

"She is getting your individual scents in her memory," Lana explained.

Reaching Memphis, she stopped short, meeting his gaze head on. Outstretching his hand, Aella slowly brought her muzzle up to meet him. Her fur was thick and soft as he shakily petted her. She was magnificent, born out of a myth. It was so light at first he almost wasn't sure it had even happened. But there it was again, a light brush up against his consciousness, and Aella stared intently at him.

Nyx walked over to them. "I felt that as well. She is trying to communicate with us telepathically."

Lana said, "You two are the first telekinetic's she has met. What is she like?"

Nyx whispered, her eyes never leaving the beast, "Beautiful."

Clucking her tongue, Aella walked beside Lana, the group following behind them.

Townspeople stopped to stare at the sight of the fearsome group they were. Whispers chased at their heels, but Memphis threw his iron walls up, pushing them out. Turning the corner, a pasture came into view and Lana jogged ahead, fetching a massive water jug.

Squaring her shoulders, Lana watched as Aella drank deeply, rumbling contently. "We need to make an announcement. This is no longer just a town. This is a haven for the Rebellion and refugees. We're no longer hiding in fear."

Alby cut in, "We don't want to draw Adair's attention to us. Not yet."

Lana nodded. "But that doesn't mean we can't keep him busy."

She winked, grabbing Azarius and towing him with her to the town square. Azarius shot them all a look that could wither any living thing and, again, not leaving them room for choice but to follow him. Alby sighed, taking the first step. Begrudgingly, Memphis followed; Nyx on his heels.

The town was bursting at its seams, thousands of voices and thoughts littering his senses. Memphis *tried* to hold on, but they slipped through the cracks and dragged him down.

Nyx, Alby, Azarius, and Lana reached the heart of Pentharrow first. Shadows danced at the corners of his vision as he melted into the crowd, just another face amongst them. Reaching the marred podium, Lana clapped her hands, and in a dramatic splay of her arms, sparks danced from her fingertips. A wave of Lana's magic rolled across the courtyard, silencing the crowds murmur immediately. Not for the first time today, Memphis felt like he was drowning.

"People of Pentharrow, you know me as Lana, your local healer. As the events of the last couple of days have unfolded, we all know this to be a lie. I have lived beside you all, suffered with you, suffocated under Morgan's reign. One tyrant is enough for this world.

"Azarius has completed another successful mission, freeing Adair's hostages, including survivors from the Academy. We have never had this much strength, and we must act now.

"What you don't know is that this world is the center of a web, tendrils of energy and space attaching other worlds with us. We have a plan, but we need your help. United, we will bring Adair down into the flames he has ignited within this land. I promise you, after we are through with him, his kingdom will be nothing more than ash."

The roar of the crowd was deafening and all consuming.

"Tonight, we celebrate as free people who refuse to live in fear any longer!" Azarius yelled, pumping his fist beside Lana.

Memphis was sure the world was about to split open from the excitement and unrest. It was like watching an electric current run through the crowd. People cheered, bustling around the square, and no one besides him noticed the dried, cracked blood that still painted the stones. Nyx stood proudly with Lana, and hope was tangible in the air; shouldn't he be happy about that? Lana and Azarius had achieved something he failed to do in six years.

He jumped a little when Alby snuck up on him again, asking, "Memph, are you okay?"

"No. But who is? We're born into a world bred on betrayal and blood being spilt. When does it stop?"

Alby grasped his arm tightly. "I don't know. But I do know we have to fight for a better future than the one we were given. This is our chance to set things right. To no longer hide."

He curtly nodded, his throat becoming thick. He *needed* to make amends with his mistakes from his past to be able to fight for his future. This was his chance, and he needed to ignore the fact that his heart was pulling him in the opposite direction. He needed to let Emory go; she had made her choice.

It was time he made his.

QUEEN TO ASHES

The chinks of glasses and hearty conversations drifted on the night wind as ale and food ran freely, the twinkle lights encircling every building, transforming the town in a dazzling display. Sitting in the corner, taking in the celebration, his stomach churned. Lana had truly outdone herself. The windwalker spun in an array of sparks and whispers with Azarius.

At a table to the left of the cleared dance floor, Nyx and Alby clunked their glasses together and drank deeply. Laughter and song filled the night as families and children were dancing in the heart of Pentharrow alongside the Rebellion. The carefree and celebratory grins on every face Memphis took in left a bitter taste in his mouth. How could everyone for one night live in a reality of oblivion when all Memphis could obsess over was the truth?

Nyx had betrayed him, half their people had been killed, and within the same breath, Emory took the first opportunity to flee into Adair's kingdom. The question that hovered along his lips and in his heart was whether he truly believed Emory *could* do that.

The silent battle within himself just darkened his mood further as seemingly no on else truly cared what happened to Emory Fae.

His mind wandered back to the beginning of the afternoon which had consisted of packing food and weapons for their journey to the Risco desert. At dawn, they would go their separate ways. At dawn, everything would change—again.

Memphis took a deep swig of his ale, welcoming the numbness that was overtaking him. He wanted to wash away the bitter taste that filled his mouth.

The ground shook from the feet that stomped on the dirt like beating drums as bodies twirled through the air. Lights flashed;

yells echoed through the night. Pentharrow was creating their own personal storm, relishing in the fact that they had a shot, a chance of being free. Truthfully, he couldn't stand another second of it. Clanking his empty glass down harder than he had intended, Memphis stood, slipping around the edges, trying not to draw more attention to himself.

"And where do you think you are slinking off to?" Nyx tailed him, her violet eyes glowing in the night.

He ignored her and kept walking.

"Memph. Memphis!!!" Nyx ran ahead and cut him off, saying, "Just because this isn't how you envisioned your path to be, doesn't mean you can't be open to it. We both made mistakes, and I won't even touch on our romantic relationship.

"But that's a part of life, Memphis, to *make* mistakes. I never thought another option would open to help rid Kiero of Adair. I went to the Mad King as a stupid last resort, and now, I am going to confront my demons. You have to do the same." She stepped on thin ice-his heart shattered.

The alcohol made his tongue loose as he snapped, "I'm not ready: To forgive you or to forgive myself. The ghosts of our friends visit me in my nightmares. Their deaths are constant bleeding wounds that will never heal. Then you..." He choked. "I did every wrong by you. I thought I would never get another chance to say I'm sorry. I thought I had lost you. I have been selfish, and I can't go back and make it right. I don't know how to *make* it right."

Her lips turned down as she stepped toward him. "Memph, we all have our ghosts. And sometimes we can't right our wrongs. We just have to learn how to live with them."

"I'm scared to move on. What of the Rebellion?"

The moon reflected in her glossy eyes. "And you think that I'm not? We are all scared, but we use that fear to remind us that we are still alive, and that we are fighting for our friends we lost and for *us*. We can't stop now until this is finished. If we are fighting, then that's *something*."

Her hand brushed his heart. He let loose a ragged breath, realizing his hands were shaking. Nyx reached out, interlocking their hands. It wasn't a tender gesture but a steadying one. *As friends.*

Nyx smiled sadly. "I know we can never forgive each other, but we can continue to fight each day. Come on."

Gently leading him away from the crowd, the world around them was a kaleidoscope of color and sound, of light and dark. It pierced through Memphis, registering in that moment more than ever before how unbalanced their lives were. How unfair.

Soon enough, the pulse of life was behind, and quiet empty houses surrounded them. Wind gently shifted around them, and the night was cool and clear—the air of promise. Turning the corner, he realized that Nyx was leading him back to Aella's pasture, and in that exact moment, she came into view, bathed in moonlight.

Aella snorted sleepily at them in greeting, taking them in curiously. Sliding down beside her, Nyx sighed. They rested their backs against her side, as a content humming filled his senses. He relaxed, feeling his attachment growing for their steed.

Tension slowly started to uncoil from him as he quietly asked, "What was he like?"

Nyx twisted her braid between her fingers.

After a few silent minutes, she said, "Adair was entrancing. He was...not as twisted as I had made him out to be in my mind. And he was much more human than I thought. He was fascinated about us of course. But beneath his calm, I could sense the chaotic storm of his anger, and that's what scared me most. To be honest, he reminded me of Emory, their strength and unpredictability is a lethal combination."

He turned, looking deeply into Nyx's eyes. "And you truly believe that Emory's decision was to play us all along? To join Adair?"

She twisted her braid more frantically, not answering right away, as she looked to the stars. He knew the signs when Nyx got nervous about something.

"Nyx, answer the question," Memphis quietly said.

Nyx met his gaze, pleading. "When I saw her in the cells, she seemed determined to save you, but there was a flicker of something...more. I can't say for sure what, but as much as I haven't liked Emory, I feel in my heart that there is more to her story than just to walk into Adair's arms. I truly believe that Memphis."

Time and space were frozen before he jumped to his feet. "We have to go to find out the truth. Now."

"And let everyone else think we have betrayed them as well? We move forward with our orders."

"And leave Emory a prisoner to Adair? Nyx, when have you ever followed orders? I need to know the truth!"

She stood, meeting him face-to-face. "All Adair knows is that his long-lost love has returned home to him. Memphis, she has returned to him as *Queen*. We have to trust that Adair won't harm a hair on her head unless he finds hard evidence that she is still tied to the Black Dawn Rebellion. Us showing up at Adair's door will be hard evidence, Memphis. Think this through.

"We have Adair for the first time in years not focused on sorting through who is left in Kiero. We have time to help build our strength and our army. We have a legitimate chance to end him for good.

"I am begging you to stand with us, to see this through, and then, as one, we plan a way to reach Emory. As your friend, I am begging you, don't run to her now. Doing that will get you killed, and then everything will be for nothing."

Memphis clenched and unclenched his hands. Nyx spoke some truths, but she also had found her place within their new hybrid Rebellion. Her path and allegiance were true. He, on the other hand, wasn't so sure where his place was anymore. By suffocating Black Dawn, he had doomed them by not taking risks. He had suffocated himself by not taking risks.

"Memphis, please. Don't go."

Sighing, he had never seen her as clearly as he did in that moment. Her stern mouth frowning, panic making her hands shake, dark bags marring her eyes. Memphis closed his eyes, overwhelmed by the consequences of his decisions.

Adair was Emory's enemy but was also a man who had always loved her. She had chosen to let the Rebellion go to take that burden on her own. *She had chosen to put you through that much pain to make her actions believable.* If he loved Emory, he would have to trust her.

A small dark whisper ran through his mind: *But what version of her do you love?*

Sighing, Memphis rubbed his temples. "After we gather the troops, we go to get her out. No matter what, and no matter what they say."

Nyx's expression shadowed. "Only if we are still alive."

"Always the vision of optimism, Nyx. I'll see you in the morning."

He left feeling the newfound truth steeling into anger, licking at his heart. He headed back to Lana's house, wanting nothing more than silence and to be alone.

The party was an ember in the distance, pulsing soft light and music crooning to the stars. Only he sought out the darkness.

CHAPTER TWENTY

Nyx

Nyx waited in the town square, her breath coming in misty puffs. The new light of dawn peaked over the cottage roofs, washing Pentharrow in brilliant light. It was surprisingly cold this morning, and Nyx tried to stay warm by bouncing on the balls of her feet. Her mouth felt dry and cottony, her headache pounding as she fought her hangover. It had been a lifetime ago since she had reason to celebrate anything.

Nyx looked at their group: Memphis, Alby, Azarius, Lana and Aella. The rest of Pentharrow was asleep, unaware that the fates of five people were about to irrevocably change. Each one was donned in soft leathers and armed to the teeth.

It was time. After years of hiding, years of living in fear, it was time to start the beat of their war drum.

Peeking up at Memphis, her once commander and friend, he looked ashen and taut as he palmed the hilt of his sword. His hair was braided back, his severe features illuminated, but there was a hollowness in his eyes that echoed throughout him, rippling out to her. She wanted to say a thousand things to him, to tell him that no matter what, she would always love him fiercely, that they would be okay. That he would see Emory again, that they would survive this. That she didn't mean to make such a bad decision.

Her words clogged her throat, and all she could manage was a breathless whisper, "Ready?"

Lana looked to her first as Nyx mentally crooned, "*Find Brokk, and find him fast, windwalker.*"

Lana gave her a small nod before she looked to them all, dipping her head and touching her brow. "The winds will have your back and may the moon's light guide you home." She paused and looked at the dawn of the new day. "You have two minutes before you must depart."

Nyx nodded to Lana and winked at Azarius before coming to Alby. "Take care of them, Alb, and keep them in line for me."

Amusement sparked in his eyes, clouding the worry that lingered on his features. Standing beside Memphis, Azarius and Alby talked quietly amongst themselves.

"Ready?" Nyx asked.

"Not even close," Memphis replied curtly.

Her mouth ran dry, and she clamped her teeth down hard, allowing the strangled mass of grief to be pushed down.

Looking once more at where the group stood, she silently said goodbye, and with her head held high, she turned to Lana, softly saying, "We will see you in a couple of weeks."

"By which time we will have built an army that will shake this world," Lana said confidently.

They clasped hands, and she broke away first, stalking toward the pastures with Memphis at her heels. He said nothing, just a lingering look before he turned, his complexion paling with every step.

QUEEN TO ASHES

Weaving in between the quiet houses, the occupants of Pentharrow were still asleep, recovering from the late night's celebration. Taking two calculated deep breaths and silencing her churning emotions, Nyx focused on their mission ahead: Sweep the Risco Desert. Find allies there and within the Arken Mountains. Survive the Forgotten Bogs. Return within two weeks.

Then - war.

Reaching Aella, the peryton raised her majestic head, her iron antlers glinting in the sunlight. Their mount was dressed in fearsome black leather to match their own, her saddle nestled in between her wings. Attaching her supply bag, Nyx softly whispered to the beast, "We won't lead you astray if you do the same for us."

She softly patted her head before climbing up into the saddle, strapping her legs in. Memphis finished tying his bags and then swiftly climbed up behind her, making sure he was secure as well. Her breath came out in quick puffs, adrenaline and fear making her body practically buzz with anticipation.

The sun crested, rising into the endless sky, and she dug her heels into the beast's side and hoarsely said, "To the desert first then."

Aella roared her reply, spread her impressive wings out, and rose up. Without missing a beat, she started to gallop, the rhythm of her hooves beating into Nyx's skull. The houses were a blur of colors, the wind screaming around her until all it took was two powerful beats of the wings, and gravity, as she knew it, was abandoned. Memphis clutched her waist tightly as they tipped, climbing higher into the clouds. All around her was an untouched world of mist and light as they left the town behind.

They broke through the clouds, and her breath was stolen away. Aella circled to steer her course right, and they soared; leaving Nyx entranced by the beauty around her: Pale blue sky kissed the cloud banks, a clash of color erupting as the light hit each crevice. It was untouched and peaceful.

Nyx loosened a whooping cry which trilled in the endless space. Her blood debts would be paid, her family avenged. The promise of war made her heart pound. Aella, sensing her delight, dove deeply, twirling and swooping through the clouds, making Memphis clutch her tighter. She wolfishly laughed as they surged forward. She was lost in the wind, the light, and the vastness that only the sky could promise.

Memphis flicked the match aggressively, snapping it in half *again*. Perching across their makeshift camp, Nyx watched his struggle, trying not to laugh. He, of course, refused any help, so Aella and she watched with luminous eyes as darkness was trying to take hold. Having flown for hours, the speckled landscape churned and changed beneath them. They had long ago crossed the Academy's border and were perched on the brink of the Forgotten Bogs. The steamy, humid air clung to their fighting leathers and even Aella snorted heavily, agitated from the climate.

Sweat rolled off Nyx, and she stood, sighing. "By fire and flame, Memphis, let me *help you*."

His eyes narrowed, and she could already hear his response. Stalking over, she grabbed the match from his shaking hands and swiped surely. The tiny flame sparked to life, dancing between them. Tucking it in the tinder they had gathered, the flames caught, cracking hungrily. Memphis grumbled and seated himself opposite of Aella, watching the fire grow.

The events of the last few weeks had caught up as Nyx settled in the silence. Pulling out a dried chunk of meat to chew on, she took in the bramble and bushes around them: Rolling hills in the distance were bathed with the fading light, looking like ocean swells from here. She had learned about The Forgotten Bogs as a child, about the story of the woodland people who were legend to be protecting their sacred waters—seers of the Bog, she recalled. It was foretold that the water reflected the future of whoever was daring enough to look through and cunning enough to survive the wrath of the lands. It was myth that the Bogs were ghost lands. Spirits lingering here who were caught in the veil unable to cross over to their final rest.

A chill rippled through Nyx, and she returned her gaze to the flames. They were just myths. Fables. Ones that had died long ago. Flicking her long braid over her shoulder, she absentmindedly stroked Aella's soft fur. The land here was strange and harsh, thickets of bramble twisting and churning along the mossy ground. In the distance, a low humming of insects sang softly. It created a white noise, and along with the cackling flames, she felt like a sitting target, wide open, begging someone to find them.

"We should take cover, douse the flames," she said in between bites of meat.

Memphis cocked an eye at her, and his voice reverberated through her mind. "No." Anger flared within her at the curtness in his tone.

Huffing, she stood, throwing her arms out. "Memphis, what do you want me to say? I'm sorry you're here with me? I'm sorry we are part of a Rebellion that has a chance now. That things have changed, and you are out of control? What do you want?"

Aella flattened her ears back as Nyx's voice rose. The commander looked like a statue carved out of stone before he flicked his gaze to meet hers. The flames reflected in his eyes. Standing slowly, each movement was sure and emphasized.

"I want to *hear* that you're sorry, and you mean it. That you know that your actions have consequences. That you're under the delusion that while you're playing warrior our rightful *queen* is falling further and further away. Emory could get *killed* being with Adair. She could be lost to us. She probably already is." His voice broke as he deflated.

She looked at him, an echo of the man she knew. Recognizing every emotion that flickered across his face and every curve of his body.

"I *am* sorry. You have my word that after this is done, we will find her and rescue her," Nyx replied.

He glowered. "Don't lie through your teeth at me. Why would *you* want to help bring her back? You hate her and always will."

His words collided with her, each blow marking: Her blood ran cold as she marched past the flames and up to him. "You listen to me, Memphis Carter, and you listen closely. I hated her because I was jealous that you loved her. But for better or worse, Emory has made her own decisions, and we can do the same. We have a chance to make things right for Black Dawn, Memphis, if you can move past what haunts you. I faced my demons. I know what I did is something that will always stain my soul. Can you say the same?"

Before Memphis could put in another word, she stalked past him, twisting through the low brambles and twigs. She needed a breather and to leave him to digest her words. Disappearing into the night, she took in a deep breath of the damp air, sweat rolling down her neck and making her agitation grow.

Who was he to grow angrier and angrier with each passing day? To blame her? Yes, she knew the weight of her actions with Adair, and that had carved a deep gouge within him that could never be healed. His hands were stained with blood just as much as hers.

The firelight died behind her as the night swooped in. The open sky was sprawled overhead in beautiful constellations twinkling down at her. It was moments like this, when the night was quiet and the whispers of the world faded, that Nyx could dream. Dream of a land untouched by the desires of man, of a land that was wild and untamed, one not scorched and beaten.

Onward, she walked, hoping to outrun her thoughts. The thick air clung to her, and the smell of stale water and dust hung throughout it. The insects' hum had quieted, and out of habit, she slid her knife free from her belt. The night was peaceful and undisturbed, but by fire and flame, she wasn't going to trust the cover of it. Anyone could be watching her.

The land twisted and curved, her path widening slightly to come to a forked road. The paths here were more distinct, the bramble and trees more spread out and less overpowering. Stopping, Nyx looked behind her to be met with nothing but shadows. There was no trace of the flames in the night; it was as if the camp had been whisked away. *You should head back.* She hadn't realized she had come so far, her anger and thoughts propelling her.

Reaching out to Memphis mentally, Nyx hoped to hear his worried whispers from here, yet she was met with silence. Her brows furrowed in silent concentration. The wind picked up slightly, loosening some stubborn hairs from her braid-they tickled her face. The nape of her neck crawled, her hair standing on end as she slowly turned; her blood roared in her ears as she saw nothing. The two paths stood before her, empty and beckoning, yet she stalled. Something didn't feel right. She took a step back toward camp when a twig snapped, breaking the silence.

"Who's there?" Her voice was hoarse, sounding small even to her. The night had fallen unearthly silent as a figure stepped out onto the road in front of her. Dressed in a thick cloak, she couldn't make out if it was a man or woman.

Steeling her nerves, Nyx whispered, "Show yourself."

The figure slowly started to wring its hands, clutching some sort of fabric tightly. It twitched back and forth as a small steady *drip, drip, drip* sounded, landing thickly in front of her. Nyx's hand shook slightly as she repeated herself, "Show yourself!"

The figure stopped, and its head slowly rose. Two large luminous eyes stared back at her. Fear held her entranced, even though her senses roared at her to *run*. The creature started wringing the fabric in its hands again, the rhythm of the dripping acting like the rhythm of a drum. It took a slow step toward her, its cloak billowing in the night.

A crackling, wheezing sound started as it opened its mouth, singing in a harsh whisper, "Beennighe, beennighe, what have you done? I bring misfortune to all that have come. Beennighe, beennighe, what do you see? I see someone who is about to die in front of me. Beennighe, beennighe, what can you do? I can allow her the chance through. Beennighe, beenighe, why do you cry? I cannot change the day that this world dies."

Nyx hands were shaking so violently, she dropped the knife. The beennighe had stalked up to her as she stared into the nothingness of its face. It slowly raised a slender hand to her cheek, and she flinched. Its hand was stained in fresh blood. The creature dropped the fabric at her feet-its breath now warming her cheek.

"Walk forward to see your future. I grant you a safe passage, but take my warning, Nyx Astire, that as the seasons change and the ice takes over this land, you and I will meet again. Tonight is my gift to you. The spirits slumber, and the night will rest. Your test is to come."

The beennighe cupped her face, blood slicking her skin, those luminous eyes filled with ancient sorrow. The wind picked up once more as the creature turned and dissipated in a plume of smoke as if it had never been there.

Dropping to her knees, Nyx tried to breathe. *Focus. Focus. Focus.* Her entire body quivered as she dug her nails into the dirt. She needed to inhale. Her blood had turned to ice, a cold sweat having broken out on her skin. The beennighe. A myth as old as these lands, and one she truly wished she didn't know.

Nyx quickly glanced up to the fabric in front of her and froze. Despite being coated in blood, the black fabric emblazed with a fiery red sash was all too familiar: It was Adair's sigil. Kneeling, Nyx picked it up, standing slowly. She choked on her breath and clutched the fabric desperately. The chunk of shirt dissolved to ash in front of her, fear rooting her in place.

It had been always rumored that the Forgotten Bogs harbored a slumbering magic. One ancient and unrelenting. That the oracles and spirits that roamed these lands could grant great insights or great misfortunes.

The beennighe was a tale most children shared to frighten each other. A tale of a woman that had been wronged, ripped away from her life too early. She roamed the night bringing her presence to the mortal land of those who were ready to cross over-to join her in the everlasting night. It was always told to Nyx that the beennighe had been a witch who had been betrayed by her children, killed for the powers her body possessed for the price of gold. Her spirit was unhinged and tied to her lands, never resting. And so she forever roamed, choosing her victims to grant either a warning or to steal their lives.

Nyx lowered her head, closing her eyes as she went into shock. Her world tilted as the iron tang of magic filled her mouth. Myths becoming legends, legends becoming reality. Her stomach rolled viciously as she panted, trying to make sense of it all. The beennighe was the deliverer of death, her presence before her promising that. She was warning her. About Adair? About something that was already happening? *Then why was it Adair's sigil?*

Her mind worked swiftly, repeating what the spirit had said. That they would see each other again, yes, but it was no mistake to grant her the option to glimpse into the oracles, nor was it a mistake that it was Adair's sigil that was presented to her. Her skin crawled as her heart pounded. The wind had begun to stir again, the orchestra of the night coming back to life.

Glancing up, she looked to the forked path, the curving way to her left illuminated with lazy fireflies. They swooped and danced before her in a hypnotic way, beckoning her onward. *You could know what will happen. If this cause is doomed or if there is a promise of a future. If it is all for nothing.* It was a great weight, the power of knowledge.

Gripping the pommel of her knife, she stood on shaking legs. Her chest heaved as she centered herself, trying desperately to push the presence of the Beennighe out of her mind. Nyx would deal with that later and figure out the omen's cryptic message. For now, though, her decision awaited her.

Glancing nervously over her shoulder, she spotted the soft glow of the fire behind her. *This place is playing tricks with you.* The camp lay behind and forward...forward could grant great pain or great solace. Either way, it would be answers. Her blood hummed with pleasure as she took a step, the wind seemingly whispering for her to continue.

As if in a trance, she walked forward, the heavy blanket of magic surrounding her, shielding her. Picking up her pace, fireflies circled her—guiding her. It was a darkly beautiful place, and she was enthralled by it, wanting to learn its secrets. At first, it was the distant sound of heavy wings, but then in a flurry of movement, Aella landed brusquely in front of her with Memphis perched on her back, frowning disapprovingly. The peryton pawed at the ground, nervously huffing at Nyx while bowing her iron antlers toward her chest.

Jumping off, Memphis rushed to her. "Are you all right?"

Nyx stopped, taking him in. Worry pinched his features while his skin was slick with sweat.

"Nyx! What happened? This one over here was raising alarm at the camp." He jabbed his thumb at Aella who was poised, stopping her from moving an inch forward. It was a standoff, and one she was not going to win. She clenched her fists once, twice. Both of her companions wore equal expressions of worry as she said nothing. The clamber of magic in the air and in *her* was slowly ebbing away. Along with the access the oracles, to answers.

Memphis hissed pointedly, "*Nyx.*"

It took every fiber in her body, every ounce of her strength to clear her face of any stress and breathe. "Nothing happened. I thought I saw something."

Her core quaked, and the night seemed to exhale: this *place* was acknowledging her dismissal. She would take the spirit's warning, but nothing could compel her to look in those pools. Even though that dark part inside of her crooned to know. Would kill to know.

With shaking hands, she picked up her weapon, Aella following her every movement with her doe eyes. Stiffly, she turned her back, leaving her companions to follow. Their stares burned into her back, and she knew in a second that she hadn't convinced them. The faster they maneuvered through this place, the better. Even now, her pulse thrummed with the need to cave into the ancient magic.

As their camp, at last, came into view, she swiftly strode to her tent, not granting Memphis a goodnight. Not wanting either man or beast to catch the flicker of fear in her eyes. Collapsing onto the ground, closing herself in darkness, the beennighe's promises cast her heart in an iron cage. They would all meet their end; she wasn't naïve. But even her warrior heart faltered at the knowledge that she was on borrowed time already. They all were.

She would follow through with her instructions. They would rally their soldiers. They would win over the raiders' clans. Then, she would bring Memphis to Emory. To save or to condemn, Nyx wasn't sure.

Unsheathing her blade once more, gripping the hilt hard, the cold metal bit through her clothes reassuringly. She would never go down without fighting. *Never*. The knife reassuringly in her grip, sleep found her fast and true, and as she entered the world of dreams, reality slipped away.

CHAPTER TWENTY-ONE

Emory

Riona's chuckle was dark, echoing around Emory as her face slammed onto the slippery deck. Riona trilled next, practically skipping around her, "Again."

Blood filled Emory's mouth, the bruise already starting to flower. Shakily, she stood up, her gaze naturally drifting over to *him*, Brokk's shadowed eyes lingering on her.

It had been three days of crossing the Black Sea, and her schedule had a regimented sense to it: Sleep. Wake up. Train. And then she was left alone with her thoughts, her theories, and fears. Brokk was her shadow, distant, she could feel the tension building between them.

Clenching her jaw, she ran, lunging, swinging Ainthe powerfully down, jumping as Riona sliced at her legs. Smiling, they danced, their bodies bending to speed and reaction. The afternoon was surprisingly hot; sweat dripped down her nose as she ducked, Riona swearing colorfully. Emory's hope surged as embers sparked at the end of her blade, causing a second of distraction, as the blacksmith took in the flare of ancient magic.

Tapping the back of her calf lightly, she made a fake slicing motion. Emory said, "Got you." Bowing low, she caught the flicker of challenge in the woman's eyes.

"Next step, with abilities." Riona looked away, "Foster, you're going first."

Stepping back, Emory sheathed her sword in one motion. Months ago, she would have balked. Would have called them crazy. Months ago, Emory would have never imagined her body slowly toning to the weight of the blade, becoming stronger as she pieced the truth together, her story becoming clearer. She would have never imagined how much of herself she would have to sacrifice. How much of herself she had given up, had allowed to become broken.

Taking a deep breath, she passed Brokk. The energy crackled between them as she caught his eyes, a question in them.

Pressing her lips into a thin line, she leaned against the rail, looking up to a smiling Kiana at the wheel. Steadying herself as the planks shuddered, Emory turned and took in the massive golden wolf before her. His lustrous fur shimmered in the light, inky claws clinking across the panels as he circled Riona. Riona smiled, deep and true, and not for the first time, Emory was lost in the wondrous power these immortals had.

Swiftly, Riona picked up her hammer that was resting behind her, swinging surely as the metal started to morph, the particles breaking in the after light, elongating and becoming spears before her eyes. Brokk balked, looking at the sharpened points, growling deeply.

"Annnnd, you're dead," Riona said again, triumphantly.

Shifting back, he asked, "That's a fair fight?"

The particles soared back, reforming the hammer, her voice carrying on the wind. "Every enemy from here on out will never fight fair. We are going up against these Oilean and their king. Possibly this Marquis Maher. It's time to dig deeper, Foster. Again."

Tensing, Emory watched him chew over Riona's words. Again, the metal broke away, cutting through the air, and he unsheathed his curved swords, lunging. No wolf. No talons. Just. *Him.*

Emory's body reacted before her mind could catch up with her intention. Running, closing the space between them, her blood pounding, her breath stalling as she felt that molten rush through her. And black streaked down her arms, tracing her veins. All Emory could think of was to shield him, *protect* him. Palms searing, the energy expanded from her, this power she had stolen as ice exploded between them. Riona was wide-eyed on the other side as Emory stood, heaving, beside Brokk.

The spears that formed from Riona's hammer soared through, dissolving to nothing more than dust as they shattered through her wall, the particles catching on the wind.

"Now *that's* what I'm talking about. Never forget that we are more powerful united, that our abilities, together, will conquer them."

Emory reached out with the power, the ice immediately turning to water, sloshing against the deck. Riona's gaze lingered on Emory's skin, eyes flicking between Emory and her necklace. Emory guessed Riona was piecing it together, slowly, what haunted her every waking moment.

Turning, Emory stated, "I'm done for today." Staring out to the endless sea, she started to feel the adrenaline slow, the darkness recede. Paranoia clutched her that the immortal could see through her with ease, somehow sensing that Adair's dark ability was at her disposal, trapped within her amethyst necklace.

"That was good, Princess. But I'm interested how you pulled it off. No one is that fast of a learner," Riona called to her skeptically.

More footsteps sounded behind her.

"Lay off, Riona. That's enough for today. We can't achieve anything half dead. Let's rest, okay? We are almost there."

Brokk's voice was soft, and annoyance flickered in Emory at his neutrality. Racing to the bow, the crisp sea salt spraying her face. The clouds rolled lazily above them, their creamy edges casting a comforting shield over the world and the inky waters. Strands of her hair tugged loose, tickling her cheeks and her neck, and she craved normalcy for a second.

She wanted to be back on Earth where she didn't have to worry about being a princess. Where she wasn't fighting for her throne or acceptance. But her reality was that here in this moment, she was just a girl on the edge of an adventure, craving the wildness in her soul, trying to understand her heritage, to know her past. To truly know who *she* was.

"Em."

Her eyelids pressed together. *Breathe.* Her pulse thudded, and opening her eyes, Emory became lost in his golden gaze—lost within him.

She looked away, a small smile dancing on her lips. "Brokk. Fascinating training session." Even to her, her voice sounded forced and on edge.

Shimmying closer, he stretched his arms out, staring at the sea. "You know I hate the open water. Scares the hell out of me."

He caught her off guard. "Really? It doesn't show."

His scars stretched as he pretended to shiver. "When we were younger, I was fascinated with the ocean. Of wanting to see it, to cross it. My curiosity slowly turned into anxiety, my anxiety into fear as I got older. I'm not a strong swimmer. Fear of the ocean was too immense, and that itself turned it into a monster.

"I remind myself to not allow that single thing to rule me, though. It sounds like a small thing, but it's not. It's crushing to me. It took a long time to figure out that it's okay to feel this. To own it. With more things than just the open water."

Pursing her lips, she let loose a shaky breath. "Even when you feel suffocated?"

"Especially then. Em, *please*, let me in. Let me be there for you. I can't begin to understand what you went through, but don't shut me out. Don't shut down."

Her throat burned, as she looked to him, his willingness. His honesty. "I have done unforgiveable things..."

"You've made mistakes. We all have. But what matters is *now*. Not the paths we shouldn't have gone down in our past. Not how things panned out in the Rebellion. We are *here*, and I can see your pain. I can see your heaviness. Let me share some of that weight, Em. We can't win this war separated."

Chewing on the inside of her lip, she stared at the rolling waves, her knees shaky from the days at sea.

"Sometimes, I feel like this is a beautiful dream. Distorted and foggy, but some people and places bring me slamming down into a memory. Into a feeling. Into a point of time that was obscure. But now, the thing I have been searching for my entire life has been turned into a nightmare.

"I have let the people closest to me down. I'm learning and harboring this ability, this *power*, and there are moments I am completely high on it. And it's in those moments I see how you can get dragged under, get obliterated by the obsession to become more. And that terrifies me. But I swore to myself I would end him. No matter the cost. No matter what happened."

Tears burned her eyes. "This world isn't broken into a war of dark and light. Of weakness and power. It's broken into obscurities, into perspectives of what must be demanded, and what is craved. What kind of queen am I, if I can't navigate that in myself?"

His eyes were pure *molten*. Particles of sea salt stuck in his golden hair, strands of it having grown since last time she had seen him.

His lips pulled into a sly smile. "And what does your *heart* demand?"

Blankly staring at him like a fool, heat flushed deeply in her cheeks.

Chuckling, he shook his head, tilting his head toward the sun, soaking in the light. "Go rest, Em. And try not to forget that this will take time. But I'm behind you every step of the way—until the end, and then some." His smirk transformed into a beaming grin as he walked away.

Her gaze trailed behind him, her mind running in circles. Sighing, Emory turned back to the Black Sea. "Is this what you felt, abandoning everything you knew?" The wind carried her whispers, envisioning her mother making the same journey a lifetime ago. Playing with her necklace, she frowned at the crashing of waves. Eventually, she made her way to her bunker, sending a silent plea out to any unseen forces that she would get some sleep.

Staring at the bottom of the bunker, Emory knew she was losing her mind. Her stomach clenched, growling fiercely, letting her know that the minutes had blurred into hours. Sleep eluded her, her skin stretching too tight as she felt the swelling and bruising there. Sitting up, her tongue felt thick, her joints sore, cursing Riona and her so-called training. Truly, she had questioned how much was therapeutic for the blacksmith to beat them senseless time after time. The thought turned sour as she stretched.

Anithe was propped beside her bed, her clothes still covered in sweat and blood, her own stench becoming unbearable. Swearing, she strapped the blade onto her back, turning to find Brokk, when she heard it: Like nails against a chalkboard, the screech was like being doused with cold water.

Her hair standing on end, Emory threw the door open, running to the stairs. Again, the wail pierced through the normal lulling of the ocean as she cleared the stairs two at a time. The noise had sounded from *underneath* the ship.

Flinging herself onto the deck, unsheathing Anithe in one motion, Emory looked up to see the sisters talking in hushed tones at the wheel, Brokk beside them. Kiana's eyes found her in the dying rays of sunlight, and she brought her finger up to her lip, silencing her.

Ice ran through her veins, her adrenaline thundering behind her fear as a third time the screech tore around them. The sunset blazed on the horizon like a flaring beacon, the spatters of midnight-blue streaking through the clouds. The full moon nestled high above them in clear brilliance as the inky waters were doused in the masterful colors of the fading light.

A break in the wave had her pivoting just in time to see the ripples in the wave as the ship rose and lowered. The world fell quiet like fresh snowfall blanketing a forest or when someone held their breath. Sparks flew from her blade's end as her ability rushed through her body, the ancient magic churning inside of her as she prowled to the edge of the ship, trying to get a better look.

The stern of the ship was thrown to one side. Gravity left her, her scream slicing through the air, forehead cracking against the railing. Warm blood trickled down her skin. Again, that wail racked through her as she tried to stand. Dots blurred her vision as, again, the ship was thrown to the opposite side, wood splintering, making choked sobs tear through her. *Get up. Get up. Get up.*

There was the sound of crashing water. Of splintering wood. Screams surrounded her, and she was transported. Back to those marble rooms. To the blood-spattered floors. And Adair, always his eyes, his voice, his presence, weighing her. Watching her.

Dropping to her knees, Emory heaved, trying to find breath, to push down the clawing panic. Hands lifted her up, warmth spreading through her, his ability, his touch becoming more familiar.

"Em." The words sounded so far away, like echoing down a tunnel.

Behind Brokk, Kiana and Riona were yelling, a shimmering force field building between the two sisters like glass. It grew, rising to meet the gurgling water. Her heart dropped into her stomach as a colossal shadow was cast over the ship, and she took in the source of the wails: Its scales were metallic; the silver and black looked sheen as droplets of water fell on them like rain.

Brokk grabbed her hand as the creature towered over them. It was easily the size of her old three-story walk-up. Sneering, its green teeth curled over its lip, its ice-blue eyes drinking in the sight of them. The ship tipped, a terrible wrenching sound shuddering through it, a flash of claws sinking into the side, as it raised its entirety out of the water.

Breaking free from Brokk's hold, she was running, Brokk yelling after her.

The creature craned its head down, its nostrils flaring as its voice rumbled like thunder. "It has been a long time since anyone dared sail these waters."

Those icy eyes locked on her as she grabbed onto the side of the rail, Brokk running behind her. Soon she and the monster were eye-to-eye as she yelled, "We mean you no harm!"

A thundering chuckle exploded around them as it lowered its snout, its mammoth eye flicking as it blinked, voice rumbling. "I highly doubt that."

More boards splintered, sweat coating her palms; her grip slipped.

The beast boomed, "I have guarded these waters for centuries, casting misfortune for the souls who dare cross my territory. I take their ship and their riches in exchange. And those souls who know of my presence come bearing offerings."

Her mind immediately soared to her teens, curled in her favorite chair, first discovering *The Hobbit*. Being a fantasy book lover had educated her dreams with endless possibilities; they now bled into her reality. Dragons and Sea Dragons? Both had an infinity and obsession for treasure.

Biting her lip, hoping her gut was right, she yelled, "And if we could offer you something for safe passage?"

Its sides billowed out, a gale of air rushing past them as it exhaled hard, its eyes narrowing into slits. The ship shook, more splinters flying as it curled its talons.

"And what could mere mortals offer *me*?"

Everything around her was becoming white noise. She refused to die as one. Diving into that well, her world completely ruptured. Vividly, she painted the scene as she felt that familiar molten feeling sear through her—her acquired magic from Adair, the ability that was magnified and twisted. The power she had stolen. It was a bottomless well of possibility. In her heart, the darkness roared.

The sea salt burned her senses, the crashing waves the immediate threat. Her mind spun and spun the tapestry of every conceivable type of riches. Rubies, sapphires, gold, silver. She could feel them, the coolness and their sharp edges. Like a gale of wind, she felt that energy expand, and opening her eyes, the monstrous beast craned its neck toward the clouds. The jewels were falling stars in the darkness, the shards of light hitting their deep colors before sinking into the waters. Exhaling, the beast roared, dropping the boat and, snout first, dove toward them.

Screaming, Emory grappled for anything to hold on to as gravity completely left her, and they were all thrown into the air. She caught Brokk's eyes for a split second before everything was a blur.

Her adrenaline morphed into shock, as the wind screamed around her; water crashed into her like a wall. All her breath was pushed out of her lungs, her clothes dragging her down. Her lungs burned as water flooded her nostrils, her mouth, filling her lungs. Kicking hard, she clawed, craning her neck toward the last dying light, only to see huge portions of their ship broken, sinking to the depths. Ice cut through her veins as she panicked, kicking too fast, searching for anything. *Anyone.*

Violently, a current gripped her and pulled as oxygen slowly ran out, the seawater completely flooding her. A deep emerald jewel sank down beside her, and Emory followed its path, into the darkness of the ocean, into infinity. Her muscles shuddered, her ability fading in the shock as she thought of what it might feel like just to let go. Her fears and doubts were bred into viable monsters, but as she stared at that sinking jewel, all she could think about was him. That Brokk had defied all the odds, all the obstacles, all his fears, to find his way back to her. She realized, as spots danced in her vision that she wanted to do the same. That this time, he needed *her*.

Screaming, bubbles flew from her mouth, just as she caught a flash of white, miles below her. The monstrous dragon sliced through the water, its body moving fluidly. She kicked her feet desperately. It raced straight toward her, victory shining in its eyes as she pieced together that, like many things in this world, it had been playing them. In the end, they were its payment.

Sinking deeper, Emory fought against her heavy clothes, trying to swim back toward the surface. Flaring pain raced up her left side, her lungs burning, begging for oxygen. Far above her, the moonlight cut through the inky sea, taunting her. *Keep going.*

The water pulled her back, the beast creating its own suction as her body lurched. Flinching, Emory couldn't hold her breath anymore, and water rushed through her parted lips, filling her lungs. Weakly, she kicked just as the arrow punctured the water, missing her by a hairsbreadth. Up close, the feathers were tinged with the faintest green hue. The roar behind her was colossal as she dug deep, swimming past the arrow. Black dots speckled her vision, and she desperately looked around her for any sign of Brokk. *Find him. Find him.*

Ten more arrows followed the first as her world was illuminated in chaos. Oranges and deep red hues danced above her, and screaming, she did a broad stroke, breaking the surface and spewing water. The waves rolled, threatening to push her under once more. Bile seared her throat as she choked, taking in the scene before her. Everything was consumed in flame. It rippled on the inky water so fast and unnatural, she barely saw the enormous ship breaking through it. Its sails were illuminating the crew against the night sky as the ship raced toward her.

"BROKK!" Her voice broke, as she swam, screaming, "BROKK!" A thousand possibilities cut through her pain, cut through her heart as she dug deep. The water started to churn, and she screamed again, "BROKK!"

The world disappeared as a wave pushed her under. Eyes wide, she tried to claw her way back, but the water spun and spun and spun, and slowly, she felt gravity shift. Stilling, she raked her gaze around, trying to spot the monstrous beast, but it had vanished. The water lurched up violently, still spinning around her, faster, *faster, faster.* Thunderous heartbeats reverberated through her as her pulse picked up, racing, her mind scrambling to find her bearings.

Breaking through the surface, still spinning in an orb of seawater and despite all odds, Emory rose up, cutting through smoke and flame straight toward the towering ship. Trying to make out the silhouettes below, the orb of water that contained her stilled, dropping her onto the ship's deck.

Emory screamed as the deck rushed up to meet her but not before a gust of warm wind caught her body, drying her, and slowing her fall until gingerly her knees touched wood, and she collapsed on all fours. Emptying the contents of her stomach, she heaved, tears brimming her eyes.

Tap. Tap. Tap. Squinting, the boot came into focus. Polished leather. Knee-high, lace-up. Recognition hit her like a wall as she took in the lush red jacket, the black leather pants, the billowing shirt. The short, emerald hair stuck up at every angle, the spatter of freckles making his emerald eyes look luminous, his pale skin bathed in firelight.

A sly smile crept onto his lips; unsheathing his sword, he tapped it under her chin. "You *do* know you almost threw up on my boots."

"Excuse me?"

Arching an eyebrow, he repeated, "My boots. They are new, and you almost made quite the impression on them."

The steel pressed harder against her throat, as Emory slowly stood. "You do know you almost drowned me?"

He paused, tilting his head. "And how could you possibly think that?"

She held his gaze, unflinchingly. "Where are my friends?"

He dropped his sword to pace, his crew tightening around him with every second. Emory scowled deeper.

"You know, when most people meet me, they are near death already or desperately hoping I'll spare their lives."

The water churned around the ship, as she caught a glint of silver scales, sending shivers running down her spine.

"I'm not here to flatter you. Now, where are my friends?"

Another tilt of his head. "My, you are something, aren't you?"

"You listen and listen closely, *Marquis Maher*. It will not take our ship sinking, or almost dying, or being captured by you, to stop me from getting the truth. I am not going to ask you again."

His eyes flashed. "So, it's true then. The rumors?" Her finger trembled against his chest as they stared face-to-face, memories flickering alive. Snapping his fingers, his crew lowered their weapons, and he exhaled. "Come with me."

Emory stared, not sure if she had heard him correctly. His crew jumped to action, a layer of yells and commands being thrown about. Turning, Marquis stared at the burning water, whistling sharply. Freezing, Emory saw that massive head rise, hungry eyes turning to her. He barked down at the creature, "They are mine."

It snarled but nothing more, and it sank back into the inky depths. Not wasting a second, she raced to him, her mind connecting the dots. "It's no coincidence that you are here, is it?"

Shrugging, he quipped, "I could say the same to you."

"The dragon? Yours too?"

Whipping around, he snarled, "You mean the cianes? Yes, we are under agreement to protect the Black Sea and the Shattered Isles. Anyone who sails this far either dies at their hand or mine."

Hurriedly, he went below decks, and she followed, her ability churning. The sea roared once more, the sounds of wreckage falling behind them as the sails caught the wind. Her heart pumped double-time as they rounded the corner to a dimly lit room. A light hung limply from the ceiling, swinging from side-to-side as her breath was knocked from her chest.

Brokk's head hung lowly. The binds around his ankles and hands were tied with silver rope, and water dripped steadily onto the floor. His chest rose and fell softly, the only signs of life. Behind him, Kiana and Riona were in the same state.

Tensing, she was slammed back but not before she felt his palm pushing her, and she stumbled. Emory saw the sheen wall catching the light. Passing through it, the effect was immediate. Wheezing, her pulse slowed, her ability retreating into nothingness. Her necklace turned cold, the usual thrumming disintegrating like dust. She wobbled, turning to the king wordlessly.

Marquis sketched a bow, his voice dangerous and low. "You think that I would allow you and your company to pass through my borders without taking my own precautions. *Tsk, Tsk,* Princess. You should learn quicker than this."

QUEEN TO ASHES

The room spun, and she felt her knees hit the boards. Colors blurred into a mass, as she felt binds clasping around her wrists and ankles. She hissed when they cut into her skin, her breath a whisper on her lips before her body dropped, and she entered a peaceful nothingness.

CHAPTER TWENTY-TWO

Azarius

The whetstone sang over the blade in even strokes as Azarius pushed it harder. The small cabin was quiet, as Azarius took in the traces of early morning bleeding into the sky. Sweat dripped off his brow, and flipping sides, Azarius went through the meditative motions. He had been sitting here for hours, trying to quiet his mind and heart.

Lana was immortal. And him? Lost in between worlds. The war in his heart raged, breaking him. The promise of forever, that's what Lana was to him now. She had lived through a lot. What was another war to her when the price of surviving it would be their freedom? The thought left a bitter taste in his mouth. Azarius finally stood, stretching, joints popping loudly.

Lana had left a few days ago, on her way to the Ruined City where, in her words, she could, "Make Adair sweat a little bit," while searching for the man who could turn the tables.

There was no word from Memphis and Nyx on their travels through the Forgotten Bogs. No word from Lana. So, he was left there waiting, going crazy as he and Alby kept calm throughout Pentharrow while sending out pleas to the unseen forces that his friends would return safely to him. That Lana would.

A cold wind stirred around him, his ability like a loose cannon under all the pressure. Running a hand through his unkempt hair, he headed for the door, buckling his blade onto his back. The morning air met him with a crisp vitality that sank into his bones. The roads were quiet as people still slept, but his gaze went to the small sentry post about a mile away, his brother's flaming hair blazing in the new light.

Lana had put the blanket of magic over the town again but, this time, allowing them to see the land around them instead of being sealed in the darkness. Azarius's boots crunched as he made his way over to the post, knowing Alby could hear him and that he wouldn't turn around.

So much had changed all at once for them both, yet the days went on while their friends risked their lives, and they just sat there. Day by day by day. Calming the storm brewing in him, Azarius squared his shoulders. In time, all wounds would heal, especially between him and Alby.

He had never understood why his twin had left all those years ago, left his *family*, to go a place where he thought the Faes were just building an army. He had been wrong. When he had seen the bonds between them, he had realized that while the Academy had fallen with the Faes and was now burnt down to rubble, that the family of the Black Dawn Rebellion had not and would never fall. Despite the betrayal, despite the war, despite the change.

His jealousy was a raw and encompassing thing as the ugly thought clung to his heart; why hadn't he followed Alby? Instead, he had decided to harbor his anger and judgements that his brother had abandoned him. The question now was how to bring his brother back to him. To mend their own bonds was an entirely different problem.

Azarius awkwardly coughed. "Any sign?"

Alby flicked his tired eyes toward him for only a second, whispering, "Nothing. Not a stir."

He couldn't stop the wind that engulfed them as he said, "They will come back. You have to believe that."

Alby narrowed his eyes. "And while they risk their necks, I'm stuck here with you. Not out there being useful." The words found their mark as Alby knew they would, cutting deep.

"You're doing your part, Alby. Now go get some rest. I will take it from here."

Alby's face pinched, and he didn't say another word as he slipped away and started walking back haughtily. Hauling himself up with easy grace, Azarius sat, his heart sinking.

In time. They would be okay in time.

The morning brought harsh golds and pinks swirling on the horizon as the sun rose. From Pentharrow, the plains of the land were flat, bathing their world in the brilliance of colors. It took his breath away. To the east lay Lana, and he found his stare never left that escarpment of horizon, willing her back home. Back to him.

Rolling his shoulders, Azarius would stay for a few hours and then find another sentry. His afternoons were filled with Alby and him training the townspeople, man or woman, in the ability of combat. He loved it, seeing with each passing day what gains were made. What hope grew among them all. What hope grew in him. He breathed deeply, clinging to that scent of damp grass and deep earth as he settled in for another quiet morning.

QUEEN TO ASHES

The hours blended, the sun now resting at its peak in the sky. Azarius had to peel off the lined jacket from earlier that morning. Blinking hard at the now constant bustle of the town behind him, the clang of swords and wafts of delicious smells drifted toward him. Azarius knew he should go and start his afternoon, but this was the hardest part of his day, peeling away and accepting that tomorrow might prove different, or that he might not be the one to spot Lana first. His stomach growled viciously, and he sighed, resigning himself.

Standing, he gripped the wood and lowered himself to the ground and paused. On the wind, a bitter smell filled his senses, making his skin crawl.

Azarius's head snapped to attention, glaring out to the landscape. Nothing stirred, not yet. The hairs on his arms stood up, his ears ringing. Something was wrong. Looking behind him, seeing if he could spot Alby in the distance, his brother was nowhere to be seen. Looking again to the east, he almost fell over at the scene materializing before him. A dark speck of a figure pushed forward, soaring across the grass faster than any human could run. Behind it, fires raged, and four more figures appeared from them. He didn't hesitate when he brought his fingers up to his lips and loosened a whistle so sharp it made his skull ache.

"Prepare the wall!"

The people of Pentharrow stopped and, with drawn faces, looked at him if they heard wrong. But as they took in the flames and the ash, chaos broke out. Swords unsheathed in a unison of metal singing.

He cried out again, "Now! MOVE!"

The citizens of Pentharrow were a blur as they ran up to him. He squinted as the smoke curled and funneled up to the sky, blocking out the sun. He was under strict orders from Lana that under no circumstance was anyone to go outside of her protective barrier; it would weaken the magic significantly and risk exposing them all.

Alby pushed past the crowd with rudeness to slide up beside him, panting. "What is it?"

"It's Lana," Azarius breathed.

A sickening crack sounded as the earth itself seemed to buckle and cave in the field. Right where she was running. The four figures followed effortlessly, the flames spewing from them, demolishing all that was in sight, focusing on their prey in front of them. He had no idea who they were, but his resolution cracked. "With me. Now." Azarius barked to Alby. Rage and adrenaline clouded his senses as he yelled to the citizens of Pentharrow, "Do not break your formation!"

Grabbing Alby's arm, the brothers ran through the magical wall, feeling as if they had been squeezed through a small tube to be met with the raging fight in front of them. Allowing himself one second to look behind him, he saw nothing. Smiling roguishly, he grabbed his sword, looking to his twin. "Ready?"

Alby was pale but determined as he mimicked his movements, nodding. "Ready."

Azarius felt the familiar pull and crack of the electricity in his veins as his ability roared to life from its slumber. He didn't hesitate as he sprinted forward, pumping his arms and racing toward his world, knowing that Alby was close on his heels, visible or not. That familiar bitter tang bit into his skin.

The flames behind Lana turned a sickish green hue, and a crack echoed across space and time. Snarling figures were born from the ash and embers, glowing red eyes and hungry fangs as *hundreds* charged toward Lana and them.

QUEEN TO ASHES

Smoke billowed from their muscles as their gray flesh materialized before Azarius. With pointed ears and strange elongated limbs, the monsters came into focus. Howls and cries overlapped, and he heard Alby curse behind him, faltering at the sight.

Skidding to a stop, Azarius stabbed his sword into the dirt and grass in front of him. His muscles tensed as he exhaled, rubbing his palms together. Azarius's world went silent except for the pounding of his blood through his veins and his ragged breath. He dipped low into that well of power, and in one exhale, it tore through him. The wind screamed around the brothers, flattening the grass flush to the earth as the force echoed out from him in catastrophic ripples. Lana had the sense to fall to the ground as the wind charged the darkness. When they collided, it was nails screeching against glass, the monsters' screams and hissing of fire swelling into one.

Azarius's brows furrowed as he shouted to Alby, "Get her out of here now. I will keep them at bay." His brother took off running, avoiding the dips and cracks in the earth. Clapping his hands together, another sonic wave boomed from his body, pushing Alby faster and the demons snarling and fighting against his winds. He was only warming up.

The darkness grew as the four figures emerged from behind their army, rushing at Lana and him. Azarius took in their grotesque figures, their faces in grimaces as, in unison, they raised their pale hands, pointing at him. Then, all chaos broke out. His wind hardly pushed back as the creatures raced toward the two people Azarius loved most in the world. Their claws were outstretched, their snapping teeth razor sharp as they ran like wildfire. He would never reach Alby and Lana in time.

Bellowing his pain and anger, he plummeted into a space he had rarely been. One of raw power, of not knowing where he started and the wind ended. Gritting his teeth, space and time cracked as six funnel clouds tore down from the sky, screaming as they touched down and barreled toward the demons, creating a shield for his brother. Alby reached Lana and, with an outstretched palm, grabbed the windwalker's hand, and they both disappeared into thin air. Their disappearance was answered with roars and screeches of anger as the army of ash and smoke barreled into one mass, the creatures changing, shapeshifting before his eyes.

The figures' giggles sounded from far away as Azarius ripped his sword from the earth, screaming at Lana and Alby to run. A wall consisting of embers and pieces of the earth that reached almost to the clouds roared toward his tornadoes, surpassing them in strength and size. Azarius cringed as his storms dissolved in the crackling and hungry mass. His skull rattled with the force, and for a second, he was frozen, watching as the unnatural storm front towered over him, readily eager to swallow him whole within it.

"Azarius!" Lana and Alby appeared in front of him with grappling hands, forcing him to run. Fear tore at his limbs as he obliged, the three of them running for the hidden barrier.

Lana seethed. "It's the Oilean."

Shit. Pushing harder, Azarius urged his legs to move *faster*. His military mind flickered from scenario to scenario as he asked, "Will the barrier hold them?"

Lana nodded. "For a time."

They couldn't look back, not when Azarius knew their world was being ravaged by dark forces they couldn't even begin to understand. Or defeat.

Sweat poured off his limbs, and pain laced through his chest. They were maybe five yards away from Pentharrow. Screams encased his mind. Four yards. Lana bellowed at him and Alby to keep going as he stumbled and fell. Three yards. Heat licked up his back, burning his clothes. Two yards. Smoke stung his eyes, making them water. One yard. Lana grabbed his hand fiercely as they avoided the spilt earth, jumping over crevices. Alby cursed fluently under his breath. The three of them pushed off, soaring through the air as he felt the compression of the barrier, and they slammed into the wall of people in Pentharrow.

Bones cracked as he hit the ground hard, spots filling his vision. The collision of the tidal wave made the magic groan and bend as he looked up, panting, to see the destruction that had been left in their wake. The army dissipated once more, breaking into hundreds of smoking tendrils, flaring out and surrounding the dome that was under Lana's protection. Azarius shot up and stalked toward that thin wall, gaping at the four figures that walked up to their shield, not able to see him staring back. *The Oilean.*

They cocked their heads in surprised amusement as they came to the wall, hands lightly caressing it. Their voices were ancient and hungry as they murmured, "Lana Steethea, we smell you behind this veil. We will wait to taste your blood, windwalker. For old times' sake."

Dark swirls of green oozed from their palms. His hands shook as the army of humanoid creatures materialized from the smoke once more, licking their putrid tongues over their fangs, eyes glowing as they all sat back on their haunches. They were surrounded and outnumbered. By the hundreds. Dread filled every orifice of his soul as he slowly turned to Lana.

"What happened at the Ruined City?" Silence had fallen amongst the townspeople as they cringed away from the hungry stares before them. He snapped, "Lana!"

She brought herself up to her full height as she said, "I made a mistake. A lethal one. I didn't realize the Oilean were in the area, let alone had caught whiff of my scent, until it was too late. I was trying to infiltrate Adair's mines when I ran into a barrier much like ours. His kingdom is sealed in."

"You have brought an entire army to our doorstep!" he bellowed.

Lana strode up to him, her features darkening. "Azarius, you and Alby should come with me. Now." Licking his cracked lips, he followed her gaze, their friends and neighbors quaking with the fear men knew when their death was near. Silent tears ran down drawn faces, and nobody uttered a single word. Deflating, he recognized this wasn't the place to have this conversation.

Looking to his brother, Alby gave a slight nod, and he said, in the steadiest voice he could muster, "Go back to your homes. Stay behind closed doors until notified otherwise."

Everyone dissipated with an efficiency that made his heart swell. Gripping his sword, he looked once more to the army of decay and demons, their claws trying to rip through Lana's magic, their maws snapping and thick saliva dripping from them. The Oilean stood calmly amongst their army, sickening grins never changing as they waited and watched. As if the Oilean could sense they were all on borrowed time now.

"Azarius." Lana's voice was quiet but strong. Hadn't she always been his anchor in the churning mass of the storms that have been their lives? Leveling his gaze with hers, taking the time to study every inch of her skin, her features, how her hair caught the light, how her full lips turned up in mock amusement. He knew what she would suggest. And it shattered him to his very core.

Numbly, he forced himself to walk, Alby following and Lana leading them back to their cabin. His breaths came in panicked gulps as the distant screams and roars of their fate beckoned to them. Azarius was trying to clutch to time as it slipped through his fingers, moments feeling like snippets, cut up and choppy. They walked in silence down the abandoned road.

The door to the cabin creaked familiarly as they all entered. In two strides, she sat down, cupping her head in her hands. He had never seen her crumple like this. Alby stayed back, standing in the half light, arms crossed, face solemn. The tides in the world shifted, and he swallowed past the lump in his throat.

Walking up to her, holding her cold hands in his, he whispered, "Lana."

Her caramel eyes found his, her dismay and determination shining in them. His love. His world. She reached toward his cheek, and her fingers cupped his face. Leaning into the gesture, he closed his eyes.

Her words tumbled out in a breathless rush. "The Oilean are relentless. Now being unleashed on our lands, this is only a taste of what is to come. The barrier won't hold more than a couple of hours against them. Their magic is ancient and cruel; even though I have lived a hundred centuries, I have never encountered anything like it. The town of Pentharrow cannot fall. *You* cannot fall. Not when this war is just beginning, and as fates will have it, you will have to battle two enemies now. The people cannot lose you."

His eyes snapped open as he bared his teeth. "*I cannot lose you,* Lana."

Lana's hands trembled as she gripped his hand, hard. "I have lived a hundred lifetimes and not one can compare to this one with you. To the brightness you have brought into it, to the life you have restored in me. I love you, Azarius, and the moons and winds as my witness, that is something that will never die.

"Not even when this world is cast into darkness and our souls become ignited in the fires of war. We cannot lose sight of all the years of happiness we have had. We cannot lose hope or fall into the darkness our enemies are trying to cast upon us. We hold on to our love for our future, and that alone is a weapon creatures like the Oilean cannot defeat."

Hot salty tears burned his skin as they spilled without control. She lowered herself to him, whispering her promise on his lips. "Even then, when my body is nothing but ash in the wind and our story is long forgotten by this land, I will burn for you. In the stars, in the whisper of the wind, in the sigh of the trees. By my blood and spirit, I have sworn my immortal soul to you, and we will never truly lose each other."

Their foreheads were pressed together, his eyes closed tight, breathing in the scent of her and allowing her words to sink in. Allowing the fact that she was saying goodbye to sink in.

"Isn't there any other way?" Alby's voice was a soft hush, and it broke their trance.

Lana broke away first, gripping the edges of the table hard. "My barrier will not last. I can't kill the Oilean, but I can lead them away long enough that you and Azarius can lead the people of Pentharrow to safety. It is written in the fates already that this war will happen. We will all die if I don't do this. It's not a matter of question or even of options. This is the only way."

Alby's features pinched as he mulled this over.

QUEEN TO ASHES

Azarius looked between the two. "No." He looked to Lana now, venom filling each word. "Are you so willing to throw away the potential life we would have had together? To know what losing you will do to me? Lana, I am begging you, *don't* do this." His chest felt like it was caving in on itself, each second getting harder to breathe, to see clearly.

Lana's expression was a stony neutral as she stood, appraising the two brothers. "It does not do well, Azarius, to dwell on what could be. As soldiers, I am pleading with you to see that this is the only way."

Her eyes softened as she walked toward him, and she wrapped her arms around his neck, lowering her lips to his ear. "You are the star of each night, and the brightness to every morning. Never forget that. But I will not allow everyone to die. Not now."

Her body was warm against his own, radiating to his core. Her lips roamed beneath his ear, leading along his neck and jawline. Finally, just when he thought he was about to combust from the agony, Lana's lips found his, and Azarius was lost in the fierceness of the kiss. Flames licked at his skin, making his body shake, desperate for it not to end.

Breaking away, he breathlessly whispered, "I love you. But promise me you will let me do this. For your future and the one of Kiero." He exhaled, his blood running cold, his heart cracking as he said, "I can't let you go."

Lana murmured, tears welling in her eyes, "I don't expect you to." Breaking away, she left him.

He was shivering, unable to look away, each loss crashing into him: Of losing his home, his family. By thinking Alby had been lost to him. By being familiar with the cracking whip biting and breaking into his raw skin. Of the feeling of his flayed flesh swollen and his blood running freely. He knew what it felt like to be hopeless. His freedom and will broken and chained by Morgan and her manipulative plans. But nothing compared to him watching Lana turn her back, accepting her fate and death. *Nothing.*

She loosened her belt and cloak, leaving her in fighting leathers and her crescent moon blade strapped to her thigh. She walked with calmness to Alby, clutching his hands and whispering too low for Azarius to hear. Alby flicked his gaze to Azarius and nodded. Seemingly satisfied, his love turned to him, looking completely feral and not quite human.

"Once I walk outside the barrier, you will have one hour to evacuate everyone. Head north toward the Risco Desert and find Memphis and Nyx. Once the Oilean have had their fun with me, they will come back looking for you all. But especially you, Azarius. They have seen your ability-you saved me. They will realize that we are together." His hands shook violently as Lana continued. "Start to prepare everyone. Pack light, weapons and food only. We will meet here in half an hour." Turning, she exited the cabin, leaving them in a tense silence.

His world was slowly shattering as Alby came up behind him. "Azarius, we have to move. Now."

It was as if he was jolted, and he snarled at his twin. "I know what needs to be done."

They both left the cabin to be greeted by the thrumming of roars and cries from the army beyond their shield. Azarius looked to the darkened sky and the mass of bodies, and he felt every human inch of himself slip away. Throwing up his iron barricade, he processed only one thought, and that was he and Alby would not let her down. They would protect Pentharrow and their Rebellion. There was no sight of Lana, and Azarius

QUEEN TO ASHES

twisted toward Alby, saying, "You start with the north houses, and I will start with the south. We will meet back here."

Not waiting for a reply, Azarius started running. The colors of the passing houses, the smells and noises all blurred together as he gulped for air. He found the first house and pounded his fist so loud he thought the wood would shatter. A tall man slowly opened the door, peeking out at him with wide eyes.

Azarius barked, "Henry, it's me. Get your family ready. We are evacuating and doing it now."

House after house, he peeled through, saying the same gruff words, sweat trickling down his body as time disappeared in his flurry of movements.

Time slipped too fast as he ran down the streets again, people in a panic as he spotted Alby once more amongst the throng. His brother thrust a small leather bag toward him and two more swords. He buckled them swiftly and then, before he could think about it more, caught Alby in a crushing hug. He couldn't say anything, but he didn't have to as Alby relaxed and hugged him back, hard. For a second, they stood there amongst the sobs and frantic words of families trying to find their own reprieve.

In the distance, a slow, earth-shattering crack sounded. The brothers broke apart and Azarius's heart dropped into his stomach as he saw Lana walking toward the sentry post and the demons. A low humming sounded, and as crack after crack followed, he realized in horror the army was creating the beat, a tempo like a war drum as they sensed a change in the air. It was a crack of energy from the Oilean, like electricity rippling through the air as green flames erupted around them. The fire billowed, roaring toward the skies, burning fiercely.

The Oilean took in Lana like hunters stalking their prey. Behind them, the town of Pentharrow collected, watching in horror as Lana loosened her crescent moon blade in a fluid motion. She gripped it in her left hand because in her right hand, black flames danced and licked her skin, dying her arms in black ink. Her chestnut hair was loose, catching in the wind as she turned around once, meeting his gaze. Her eyes blazed, and he nodded his head slightly, even though that one last movement, last acknowledgement, broke him in the deepest way he knew.

Lana loosened a slight smirk as she turned her back to him. Her black flames danced and flared, encircling her in an inferno that matched her enemies', her power making the wind howl, echoing his roar as Lana squared her shoulders and loosened a war cry that shook the boundaries of this realm. Her flames surged forward, and they clashed with the barrier, molding to their shape, the force of the collision sending Azarius staggering back.

Lana ran to greet the hungry maws of their enemy, her flames pushing forward with her and with a force of power that was ancient and lost upon them all. Azarius watched as the old shield disintegrated, falling like ash around Lana as the beasts roared, taking in their opponent. Alby had already started the evacuation of the townspeople, leaving Azarius to watch alone as green flames, claws, and teeth descended upon the love of his life. Lana pushed her power and flames out to meet them, and they collided in a clash of screaming fire, swords, and claws, the rage and inferno threatening to take over them all.

CHAPTER TWENTY-THREE

Memphis

The first thing he noticed was the steady rhythm of Nyx's breath softly inhaling and exhaling. Memphis rolled over carefully, looking over to see, her violet hair spilling around her, her dark lashes resting against her skin. Swallowing hard, he tried to push past the assault of emotions that were demanding his attention. Sitting up, he was quiet as he left the tent. Aella slept close by outside, and she lifted a bleary eye, assessing him.

He had begun sharing a tent with Nyx a couple of nights ago when they got caught in a very unnatural wind storm in the Bogs, and in their haste of trying to put out their fire, the embers had blown and caught Nyx's, disintegrating it to the ground.

Now, left with only one tent, Memphis had insisted that he sleep outside with the peryton. He had quickly been tackled, knife to his throat, and Nyx hissed at him not to be ridiculous or she would make the journey alone.

So, the days had passed in a heavy tension as they established a routine, navigating the Bogs and falling into an exhausted sleep every night, side by side. Stretching, his joints popped, and muscles screamed in stiffness. The new morning greeted them in heavy humidity and grey clouds, making the surrounding landscape seem more ominous than it already was. He looked over to Aella, who by this point was looking at him as if saying to get a move on.

Tying his long, tangled hair back in one motion, he murmured, "I know, I know."

He walked to the edge of their camp, maneuvering through the low brambles and slick mud. The Bog seemed never-ending and full of malice. Ever since four nights ago when Nyx wandered off, she hadn't been quite the same. Black and purple bruising underlined her eyes as if at night she was haunted just as much as she was during the day.

Not that you care. He reminded himself viciously that he was not allowing Nyx to have an inch of his heart again. It had been shattered and hastily put back together, but he was tired of the lies and deceit. He was lost about how to reach Emory again, if what Nyx claimed was true: That she sacrificed herself to grant the Rebellion time and distraction they needed from Adair. But at what cost?

Stopping, Memphis stared out to the never-ending moss and water pools. How were his friends faring? In gathering forces both in this world and in others? Was it a good thing the land had been quiet with no whispers of despair? That Adair had also been quiet in his kingdom of rock and darkness? A deep tugging in his gut pulled at him, constantly reminding him they were running out of time for their mission. There had been no sign of terrain change, and each day proved to be as humid and dreary as the last.

Looking down to his well-worn fighting leathers, the black straps empty from the usual occupants of his swords and knives. Sweat had already soaked through the light fabric, making him feel more irritable than he already was. Exhaling, he turned to meet the peryton pawing nervously at the mud, her large eyes seeming luminous in the weak daylight. He huffed as she watched him cross back toward their tent and practically roar at Nyx. "It's time to get up. We can't waste daylight."

He barely looked at her as he grabbed his pile of weapons near the foot of their rolls as she opened her eyes. Now, he did growl. "Now, Nyx." He let the tent flap close shut, not quite catching her flow of curses flung at him.

Efficiently adorning his weapons, he was about to pry Nyx off the tent's floor when she appeared, hair braided and blades in hand. Nodding, he quickly unlatched the hooks and poles propping their tent up and stuffed it in their pack. Walking over to Aella, he attached it to her side while digging through a smaller bag to reach their dried meat portions. Having a hound's senses, she was right beside him and already grappling for her portion. Memphis handed it over to her in silence while chewing on the dry, salted meat.

"We should hit the Risco Desert today," Nyx stated.

He stopped chewing. "How do you know that?"

After finishing her breakfast, she replied, "The slight changes around us, less moss, more of a dry heat, less insects. If you weren't so distracted, you would notice them as well."

His patience was on a short leash, but he resorted to gruffly saying, "A dry heat? You've got to be insane. But let's get on with it then."

Climbing on Aella, the peryton was unusually strung, pawing the ground anxiously. He strapped his legs in, Nyx scaling her side gracefully behind him. Once they were settled, the peryton shook once and then propelled her body forward with such force that they were thrown back as her massive wings stretched out, then they were climbing toward the sky.

He settled into the usual feeling of the wind screaming around them and accepted the wet condensation collecting on his skin as they gained altitude. For miles, all he could see was the same sprawling flat greenery of the Forgotten Bogs, no movement whatsoever. To the north, to what looked like a tiny speck on the horizon, he could barely make out the splay of golden sands. Nyx had been right. The Risco Desert, though still hours away, was attainable. Which meant they would soon be meeting with the Dust Clans, trying to convince the raiders to join their war.

Gritting his teeth, Aella broke through the clouds, her wings pumping hard. She dove dramatically, making Memphis lurch to grab anything to hold on to. Memphis could hear Nyx's whooping cry as they were one with the winds, leaving the old magic of the Bogs behind them.

Memphis's legs screamed in protest as Aella landed hard, bowing her head against the headwinds and billowing sand around them. Both he and Nyx jumped off their steed with equal enthusiasm, their cramped muscles seizing as they staggered to an upright position.

Nyx playfully jabbed him in the side. "I told you we would make it."

Petting Aella's side absentmindedly, he took in the world around them.

The heavy humidity of the Bogs had passed hours ago as the clear, warm air of the Risco Desert beckoned to them. The land below them changed from twisted paths to barren ground, sloping dramatically to the golden sands beyond them. They had flown for hours, his agitation turning to a hard fear as they landed. *It was time.* Time to convince the clans to join them, to ignore their warning. To try to make things right.

Looking over at Nyx, her violet hair was piled high atop her head, and her crescent blade was out in front of her as she twirled it. It was about midday, but he felt as if they had entered a pit of fire itself. Heat scorched the land, and he could see the shimmering waves of the sand in the distance, making it seem as if the whole world was flickering in and out of perspective. Aella flattened her ears on her head and pawed the sand nervously, making low clicking sounds.

Looking to Nyx, he murmured, "We need to rest and water ourselves before moving on."

"Not eager to get this over with?"

Memphis ignored the question, knowing Nyx knew him too well to sense that something was wrong. He *knew* what seeking out the clans would mean. The Dust Clan leader's warning tolled in his mind from when they last met outside of the Academy. But it was the only way. The Rebellion needed more numbers and so he resigned himself to the fact he would make the clans listen. Or die trying.

Sighing, he turned to pull out their water skins. Passing one to Nyx, which she gulped down eagerly, he reached further down into the bag. He pulled out a thinly stretched leather skin, and he held all the corners while Nyx stood up and poured the rest of her water for Aella. The peryton dipped her muzzle down appreciatively and drank deeply. Once she was done, he grabbed another skin and closed his eyes as the cool water surged down his throat and filled his belly.

Once they had all refreshed themselves, Nyx picked up her blade and, looking pointedly at him, asked, "What now? I have a feeling the clans are not waiting for us out in the open."

Neither did Memphis. Slowly chewing the inside of his lip, he went over what he knew about the clans. Vile, proud men that wanted nothing to do with the happenings of the monarchy but instead built their own judicial system and way of life. They *hated* outsiders, but there was one thing they prized above all else.

His lips tugged slowly, lifting as he appraised Nyx. "I know how to get their attention, but you're not going to like it."

She crossed her arms as he unfolded his plan.

Night had fallen fast, the coolness kissing their skin in blissful washes as the wind danced around them. Closing his eyes for a second, gathering his bearings before opening them once more, he spotted Nyx's fire speckling far below him from his view on Aella's back. They had taken to the skies once dusk had fallen and flown in lazy circles high enough not to be spotted but not high enough to lose sight of her. Gritting his teeth, hours had passed with no sign, but Memphis knew the raiders would come. That they had already been watching. He patted the peryton's soft fur, murmuring, "You know what to do. Stay hidden. Stay safe."

She snorted as they dipped again, repeating their loop.

QUEEN TO ASHES

Leaning back, he scoured the horizon once more. Deep purple clouds tinged the horizon, diamond stars imbedded within them. His gaze trailed the rolling sands, scouring for any sign of life. Minutes turned into hours until finally... There. Squinting, his body tensed as he looked to the darkness that was rippling around Nyx. He watched as she stood, baring her blades and squaring her shoulders. Sweat trickled down his neck as her consciousness brushed up against his before disappearing. He knew she was reaching out to every raider that surrounded her now.

There was one thing that the raiders found more appealing than protecting their lands, and that was a blatant challenge. He squeezed his thighs on Aella's side as ten men materialized from the sands, weapons in hand, surrounding her. She gently laid her blades down, and he watched as she gestured with her hands, pleading their cause. They wouldn't have listened to him if the clan had spotted him first, not with a price on his head.

Minutes passed tensely, but finally, Nyx let out a low whistle. That was his cue that the clan knew he was here, but they wouldn't kill him on sight.

"Aella, now," he whispered as she dove, wings tucked tightly into her side until she was low enough that he could jump without hurting himself. Pushing himself off the leather saddle, gravity took hold of him as he plummeted through the air, and tucking his limbs in, he met the rolling sands, his body being thrown forward from the impact. Rolling, he gruffly got up, knowing by now Aella was gone, seeking refuge in the skies. The peryton was too rare and too important to be gambled right now.

Finding his feet, Memphis stalked toward the fire and Nyx while taking in the shadowed raiders in front of him. Severe brows framed their brooding eyes, and they were clad nearly head to toe in midnight-blue, being able to blend in with the cover of darkness. A slow clap resonated through the silence, and Nyx took a second to turn toward him, her features clouded with worry.

The tallest man closest to them stepped forward, lowering his hood. "Memphis Carter of Black Dawn, it would seem we meet again. Though, I am surprised you sought us out after my warning."

"I am pleading for you to listen."

The leader of the Dust Clans stepped up. "Your *lovely* friend here already went over it. The Academy burnt to the ground by her mistake, and your queen is in the hands of your enemy. Things have turned dire for you over the months, it would seem, since we have been apart."

Nyx had taken a step back now, and he could feel her consciousness quietly start to expand toward him. The Dust Clan leader noticed the movement and barked in the tense silence, "I would take advice from your friend here, *Commander*. Leave now, and we won't have to end this in blood."

With narrowed eyes, Memphis studied the man; he was tall with a strong build, his features alit with malice.

Memphis stalked up to the man so that they were face-to-face and said, "We will not leave unless the clans are united in our Rebellion. Do you think that once Adair is through with us, he won't target the raiders? Until you either bow to him or die?"

The leader thundered, "You are as foolish as you look. Adair has not tried to invade our lands in years. This is not our war."

Memphis clenched his fists, his nails biting into his flesh as he whispered, "You're right. Adair hasn't tried to take on the clans because he has been happily destroying our world, and you have joined in with him. But what happens when there are no towns or people left to create havoc with and all that remains in this desolate world is you and Adair? I promise you; he will turn his attention on you then, and it will be your war. Adair was my friend; I know his lust for power and, above all, to rule. For the first time in six years, we have a chance, and I am begging you to help us."

By now, the remaining nine raiders had drawn ragged swords, and their leader laughed, nearly doubling over. Nyx threw him a blazing look, her fingers clenched and her knuckles turning white. Gasping for breath, the raider straightened and sneered at him, jabbing him in the chest. "Let that day come; for now, we are more than happy to watch you tear each other apart. Now leave."

Nyx stiffened as Memphis said, "No. There is no turning back now for us. There are no second chances." *No fear, just forward now.* Memphis's breath came to him in deep gulps as the tension rolled off everyone in waves.

Lifting his gaze to the clan and, in a steady voice, he said, "If you refuse to see reason, then I challenge you for your position as Clan Leader." It was like dropping a rock into still water. Surprise shone in all the raiders' eyes as murmurs rippled and broke out amongst them.

The closest man behind their leader gripped his arm hard. "Zander, end them. Now."

Memphis didn't back down as he pushed on. "A fair trial, just you and me. If I win, you step down as Clan Leader, and I will uphold the position, and you will join us in the war. If not, then kill me, but let Nyx go."

Zander arched an eyebrow at him, while Nyx's consciousness barrelled into him like a roaring wave. *"Memphis, what are you doing?"*

He slammed an iron wall up and focused on Zander, whose face had darkened even in the shadows. His entire life, he had thought he had been making the right decision by protecting the Rebellion, by protecting Emory. Shutting out his friends and the people he loved most for the bigger picture. He was selfish and scared to lose what he held closest to his heart: Not anymore. Not when that suffocating urge to prove himself battered against him so violently, he had to let go and give in.

Zander flicked a long thin blade from his wrist and stalked up to him. From his powerful strides to his gaze burning with pure vengeance, Memphis knew that he had him hooked.

The Dust Clan leader breathed onto his face, the overwhelming stench of ale and meat colliding with his senses. "I accept your conditions. Except for a slight minor change on my end, Commander. The trial will be upheld by the traditions of the clan, and we will decide exactly how your worth will be weighed. As for *her*–" his eyes ravished every inch of Nyx, and in response, she flashed him a very vulgar gesture "–if you fail, Memphis Carter, she will die right beside you."

He chuckled, still looking bemused by Nyx, though the withering look on her face would send most men running. Ice ran through his body, and time seemed to twist and turn, flashes from the past and dreams of the future creating a kaleidoscope of memories that encased him and, in turn, helped him find his courage.

He didn't break Zander's gaze as he said, "I accept."

The movement was so fast that he almost didn't catch it; the thin blade sliced Memphis's cheek in a fluid arc, hot blood rushing up and seeping out of the wound. Zander's long finger brushed the cut, smearing Memphis's cheek in blood. Zander mimicked the mark on his own skin, booming, "Then it is sealed.

QUEEN TO ASHES

By the sands and the sun as my witness, Memphis Carter, you are now our prisoner until the trial. As for your friend..." Zander trailed off and low chuckles spread throughout his men as their leader sauntered over to Nyx, whispering, "Such a waste to also put you in the dungeons..."

Lunging forward, Nyx loosened a growl and arced her crescent moon blade toward him. "Let's get acquainted then." The raiders were like wildfire as they fanned out, two pushing him into the sands and two shoving Nyx onto her knees as Zander squatted down in front of her, brushing a loose strand of hair from her face.

Memphis's muscles burned as he struggled to get to her, which just resulted in a sharp crack as the raider who restrained him stepped down hard onto his shin, bone breaking under the man's boot. Red-hot pain laced through him, his cry making Nyx scream against the raiders restraining her. Zander lashed out, his fist colliding with her gut, cutting her off and leaving her panting, trying to find her breath. His world spun and spun as he gripped hard onto his consciousness. His stomach heaved and churned, begging for release as sweat slicked every inch of his skin. *Do not look at your leg; do not look.*

Zander gently lifted Nyx's chin, forcing her to look at him. He whispered, "I'm sure I can find a special place for you." Jeers and hoots broke out as Nyx spat in his face, and he growled, standing up. "Let's go and bring these prisoners back to camp, shall we?"

The roars of his nine men seemed to shake the very core of the earth as Memphis was shoved forward but collapsed quickly, the pain from his leg making him throw up. The bitter taste of bile burned through his throat and mouth, leaving him gasping in the sand. Rough hands pulled at the collar of his shirt, trying to heave him up. He couldn't move, couldn't breathe. Sluggishly,

Zander came into focus, his dark eyes looking like empty pits; he was lost in them.

"You won't last ten seconds in the trial. You have doomed yourself, Commander."

Doomed. The word danced around his mind, licking at his heart, trying to feed the small spark of spirit in there, caged and dying. Memphis laughed, and the world of ghost and sands tilted and sifted as white-hot light raced into his vision. He could have sworn the sand beneath him solidified and rose, racing through the night across the land, carrying him. The dimmed yells of their travelling companions were honed into white noise as he focused on the stars high above him, glinting like lost gems, begging for someone to find them.

CHAPTER TWENTY-FOUR

Emory

She dreamt of great and terrible things. Of a world inspired by magic. Then a world abandoned, becoming isolated. All the while, Emory wandered, searching through the rubble of a life that once had been, walking down the street, sweat seeping through her pale blue dress. A lifetime ago, it had been one of her favorites. The straps hung loosely, hugging her shoulders, the downy fabric floating from her waist down past her knees. Mist blew in front of her as she exhaled, but she felt no cold. Onward, her feet carried her, her heart lost, but a path set out before her, the empty buildings cracked and deteriorating. She lurched forward as if being reeled in. The wind stirred, and she froze.

"Emory."

A small whimper escaped through her lips. "Mom?"

Nei Fae's arms opened, welcoming her. "Come here, my darling."

She was running. The world splintered and changed but this... This was what Emory's heart yearned for. *Her family.* They collided, Nei's golden hair framed her face as Emory hugged her fiercely, tucking her face into her mother's shoulder.

"Mom, what are you doing here?" Emory asked.

Breaking away, Nei smiled sadly. "Don't you know when to stop?"

The wind stirred again, Emory felt with every passing second, the sharpness to it, the shivers snaking up her spine.

"What do you mean? I'm trying to make things better. To be better. I'm lost, Mom." Her mother's grin twisted, as she stepped back, tilting her head. At the end, her golden hair turned grey, her skin started to crack, her body shuddering.

"Don't you know when to stop killing? To stop fighting?" Nei took a step, her skin flaking off to ash, dissolving into nothingness. "Learn from my mistakes." The wind picked up, and Emory watched her whisked away, nothing more than a memory. Just like her past. Her present. Tears streamed down her face as she fell to her knees and was doused in icy water.

Cursing, her head swung wildly as she slammed back into reality. Sputtering, Emory blinked, and her surroundings came into focus. The room was different, a small desk tucked in the corner, a half-empty brandy bottle atop it. The lamp casted the room in a pleasant glow as she focused on those boots again.

He was seated across from her, a glass clutched between his long fingers, the amber liquid swirling. Marquis smiled, those freckles stretching across his features, his green hair glinting. "Now, should we talk like civilized people?"

"Where are my friends?" Emory countered.

QUEEN TO ASHES

Marquis took a deep swig, mulling over her question. "In this scenario, it would seem, since you are bound and my captive, you're not quite in the position to do the asking."

"Then what's the point of talking civilly, when in your mind, I'm already your prisoner?"

Setting the drink down carefully, he leaned forward. "How is it, exactly, that you have returned from the dead?"

She spat, meeting his stubbornness head on. "My friends, are they alive?"

His eyes ignited, as he chuckled darkly. "You really haven't changed much, have you?"

"On the contrary, I'm hoping I have changed completely."

He raised an eyebrow. "Oh?"

"So, you haven't changed at all over the last six years?" Emory retorted.

"I find it extremely overrated, for the most part, self-growth." She shook her head, lost in his impossible dance, in his sarcasm. He looked back to his drink, and he picked it back up, casually drawling, "The Isles are only hours away. I have pulled you from the shield to give you a chance, for your side of the story before I decide what exactly to do with you all."

Her breath came in fast gulps. "I come to you as Queen of Kiero, pleading for you and your peoples' help."

He paused. "Queen? What happened to our deranged king from across the sea, or have you forgotten about him?"

The question slammed into her, and all that resonated was the dripping of water off her clothes. The ship rocked, and the catcalls of the crew above drifted down to them. An entire world away.

"You tell me if my friends are okay, and I will tell you why I killed Adair."

Marquis froze, a muscle feathering along his jaw. Those green eyes cut into her, a tremor running along his hand as he set down the glass a little too hard.

Emory back pedalled. "Years ago, when I saw you last, you swore to me that I would always find refuge amongst the Isles. With *you*."

Leaning closer, a darkness crossed his features. "And I also told you not to fall into the same mistakes as our parents."

"I did give him *every* chance," Emory whispered.

"Oh, I can imagine, especially seeing how eagerly you are using his death as leverage to get what you want from me." He was pacing now. Back and forth. Back and forth. Scoffing, Marquis shook his head. "Your companions are safe."

It was like a taught line being cut as the relief flooded through her. Slumping back, Marquis raised an eyebrow at her, waiting.

"You know I cared for Adair," Emory sputtered, "and he was my...my..." Her words died as Emory tried to find where to begin.

Marquis sat down, filling his cup, as Emory told him from the beginning of her story what had happened. What she had done. Had asked of Brokk. Where she had been. Earth. The Rebellion. Adair's Kingdom, all but a distant echo now.

The cup had been refilled and was half-gone as he sat in silence, his face unreadable. Her body was completely numb as she said, "In the end, we both destroyed one another. I completely shattered myself to give back something to the resistance. Something that wasn't manipulated, something that *I chose* to give. I have made mistakes. But I am asking you to help me not make the same mistakes as our parents."

"You're asking me to just believe you and give over everything I have built. That I have protected."

Her heart sank at his tone, but his gaze was fixated on her necklace. A thousand emotions flashed in his eyes, all of them unreadable to her. A shudder jarred through the entire ship, and Marquis ran a hand through his emerald hair, strands shooting every which way as he pressed his eyes together. Another shudder and he cursed fluently.

In two strides, he crossed the space between them, squatting so that they were face-to-face. "I need time."

"Kiero is burning. The fate of our world is suspended between us."

"And as I said, I need time. You will enter the Isles, as my prisoner. All of you will."

Emory's thread of hope broke, as she stared at Marquis. Pressing his lips into a thin line, he whispered, "Our lands are nothing alike. It is not just my decision, Princess, to choose to die for your cause."

Snapping his fingers, warmth spun around her, the wind evaporating and lifting away all the moisture. His body arched over hers when he sliced through the binds around her wrists. Leaning back, his mouth paused by her ear, "I would not tell anyone what you said to me here. Watch and learn, Princess, what it means to rule."

Groaning, she shakily stood, and he flashed her a dark smirk, grabbing her hand. Tensing, she clenched her jaw, waiting for the familiar rise of ability, rushing to devour.

"Forgotten, have you?" Marquis asked.

"What, that you're not only annoying but immune to my talents?"

"For a prisoner, you're pretty snarky, you know that?"

She stretched, joints popping. "I highly doubt you're going to throw us in the dungeons to rot."

A flash of teeth. "First lesson—I wouldn't assume anything." Opening the door, the chatter hit them like a wall as the crew bustled around the ship.

Squaring her shoulders, Emory whispered to his back, "We both loved him. I won't stop trying to make things right."

Marquis didn't turn, but she could hear him whisper back, "I hope so."

Following, she took each step one at a time, feeling the rush of crisp air whipping around her and the crashing of waves. The light was blinding, and she blinked, her eyes adjusting.

All around her, men and women jumped into action, knotting ropes, shouting orders, moving in a chaotic harmony. The morning light was jarring, noting just how much time they spent in oblivion. Sighing, she followed Marquis, trying not to stare at the piercings, at the swirling tattoos, at the expressions of clothing: Bright jackets, bright pants, shirts, boots. Intricately braided hair bobbed by her, smiling as she took in the diversity.

Keeping an eye on his emerald hair, they walked toward the bow of the ship, the rolling black waters endlessly surrounding them. Stopping, she gripped the rails. "Marquis?"

"You know how we survived Adair's reign?"

She tensed, grinding her teeth together. "By ignoring the rest of the world?"

He chuckled. "No. By having something he wanted. Something he needed."

Looking at the rolling inky waves, she whispered, "And what will you do now when you have the choice to help people this time?"

"I will always do what's best for my people; that's my promise as king. But, from what you've told me, you have something that our enemies *want*. And need." Her stomach dropped, the pit in her heart growing deeper. She stared at the fracturing light, not wanting to accept what had happened. Not ready to confront it. The exchange of powers, what she now possessed. That the thing she feared most was becoming a part of her.

"I told you what happened, hoping it would sway your mind. To help us. Not to use us."

Arching an eyebrow, his smile held the promise of danger, of excitement, and above all else, trouble. "You're not the one who gets to decide that, Princess. Trust me, it's nothing personal."

The ship lurched as he leaned over, grabbing her hand too hard. There was an explosion of energy as she watched in shock as the shield flew up like a peerless glass dome over the ship. There was a grinding noise, so loud it reverberated through her entire body, Emory watching in awe as the masts lowered, the sails jumping to life on their own accord, wrapping themselves around the oak. A woman with golden hair locked eyes with her and waved as she stalked around the ship, black jacket flaring around her.

"My second, Diedre, has some specific talents, as you can see, when it comes to entering the Isles."

Her words lodged in her throat, as the *entire* ship jumped forward, diving beneath the waters, and the world was transformed. They cut swiftly, diving at a speed that made her heart drop into her stomach, strands of filtered daylight streaming down, igniting the sea. Schools of fish darted away from them like comets streaking through a night sky, their scales brilliant reds, golds, and oranges.

Deeper they plunged, maneuvering around reefs, their ivory shimmering like a beacon in the night. To her left, she caught movement, and her mouth hung open as she saw a trident, a flash of scales. Their haunting looks, staring as they passed, bore into her.

Marquis's breath was hot on her neck, as he leaned in too close. "Obviously not your first mer-people encounter?"

Shaking her head, Emory watched as they passed underneath what looked to be a form of jellyfish, their bodies a flush pink. A deep *whine* echoed out in the water then as a huge body swam into view, its blue skin shimmering like a gem. Its intelligent eyes locked onto them, gnarled fangs hooking over its lip. Propelling its huge fins, it dipped and cooed, the song echoing in the lonely expanse of ocean.

The ship dipped below, coming up to a carved archway. Like a magnet being pulled, they darted underneath, and she cringed against the assault of magic. Breathing heavily, her eyes widened as she looked down. The water had transformed before Emory, magic being the only explanation as she took in constellations being mapped out: They glided on the map of the night sky. The stars glinted like diamonds, the moon reflecting up at her. She tried to pull away from Marquis, but up the ship soared through the waters, the dark and mysterious creatures being left behind. Leaving the dimension of stars and moonlight as they broke through the waters, sunlight basked them again. Her knees shook from the speed, and she tried to find her center.

"Emory Fae, welcome to the Shattered Isles."

Emory gaped, taking in her mother's birthplace.

Breathing deeply, the salty air clung to her, droplets of water raining down on them as the shield lowered, but she couldn't look away. Two massive land masses curved in toward one another, one magnificent cliff face to another. A fleet of at least fifty ships were docked at port, but it was the lush deep green landscape that held her attention. The baying of gulls in the distance. The flashes of silver rock face, the wildness that made her blood pound. Her skin pricked in anticipation as her soul lifted its head in recognition. This forgotten part of her, her heritage, her blood, all began here. Her mother began *here*.

The tears burned her eyes, and she swallowed. Drinking it in, looking back to the King from across the Sea, only to find sorrow flooding his green eyes as he said, "Second, never trust a pirate. Sorry, Princess."

Emory saw him lunge. Heart pounding, she tried to get out of Marquis's range, but the hilt of the sword slammed into her temple, blood filling her mouth. They were now prisoners and hostages; the last image of their freedom burned in her.

"Em. *Em*." Like always, Brokk's voice pulled her back. Fluttering her eyes open, the world tilted as she groaned. Focusing, Brokk came into view across from her, shackles around his wrists and ankles. Looking up, the cell was small, a tiny crack between the bricks allowing her to lean over, spotting flickers of the ocean and the deadly drop below.

Swearing, Emory leaned back, her own binds cutting into her wrists. "He really did put us in a dungeon."

Brokk shrugged, obviously relaxing. "I'm not surprised. Marquis has always had a flair for the dramatics." The cold air clung around them, the hint of winter on the air.

She groaned. Her head throbbed as she asked, "Kiana and Riona?"

He frowned. "He has them." Her heart dropped, and she closed her eyes, exhaustion clinging to her. She was so *tired*. "Em. One step at a time, okay? We will win him over."

"How?" she asked.

"By playing by his rules. And earning their trust. Their respect. The Shattered Isles is your heritage. They are your roots, your people, just as much as his. We can do this."

Brokk's eyes turned molten again, and her breath caught in her throat. She paused, the energy in the air changing. His full lips pulled up in a timid smile, unsure but warm. His muscles flexed as he pulled against the iron, the quiver of nervousness making his words shake.

"You know, all my life, I always thought there would be moments. Moments where the timing would be perfect, that I could see the signs. But, to be honest, I'm tired of almost losing you. Of dancing with death too closely." His breath was ragged. "But you need to answer one question."

Her pulse raced, heat climbing up her neck. How could she have been so blind? So reckless? So afraid? Emory shivered, her body arching, yearning to be closer to him. His voice was hoarse.

"Who does your heart want?"

The clarity she felt radiated through her entire being when a tiny frown formed on Brokk's lips as he waited. Looking into his golden eyes, they seemed to glow in the dismal setting of the cell, but her voice rang true, her heart bursting with every word.

"I want you, Brokk Foster. Now until the ends of Kiero."

A blush stained his cheeks; Brokk looked to the chains murmuring, "Damn these cuffs."

In one motion, Brokk lurched forward, veins growing visible in his neck as he pulled against the iron. The chain links, attached to the brick behind him, started to wobble. Then the chain let go, taking chunks of the brick with it, freeing Brokk enough so that he emerged before her on his knees, tentative.

QUEEN TO ASHES

With sea salt on her lips, she lowered them, and Brokk was there, waiting. Her lips parted as he exhaled, and he moaned out of pleasure. Their lips met, metal biting into her wrists as she pressed forward, her hands wanting to roam, to search the valleys and crevices of his body. His tongue parted her lips, a soft growl escaping from him.

They slowly explored one another, and she was fractured and put back together.

Parting, he hoarsely murmured, "I was hoping you would say that."

Flushing, her heart drummed against her ribcage, warmth spilling through her entire core. Emory wanted more. To explore, to devour. Brokk beamed, absolutely radiating, and she knew: It had always been him waiting for her to catch up and see him. He was her sun, and she gravitated toward him, needing him. He had always been there, and *now...*

Emory was not ready to stop kissing Brokk when the door creaked open. Two men looked at them, both clad in black. Their faces gave nothing away when they looked to Brokk, who was mostly free from his restraints. Walking to him, they wrenched him up, his protests drowned out against her screams. Brokk shot her a reassuring glance before the door shut behind them, leaving her. Screaming, Emory dove into her ability, finding nothing. *The chains.*

"BROKK!"

There was no inclination of what was happening. Of what would happen. The heat drained from her, replaced by an iron cold. She fought, blood running along her wrists, screaming at the door. In a matter of seconds, she had lost him. Time slipped away, as her voice broke and became hoarse, pain lacing through her body. She whispered his name repeatedly, her pleas turning into promises. Her promises turning into rage. Her rage turning into resilience.

As the sun slipped low, casting her into darkness, Emory sat in the cell, waiting. He wanted to play the game; she would play.

And so, she waited, readying herself for Marquis Maher.

CHAPTER TWENTY-FIVE

Nyx

The steel caught its opponents, sparks igniting between them. In that moment, Nyx hated Memphis Carter more than words could express. The sun baked into her skin, stinging as she rolled, the sword slicing the air *way* too close to her throat. Nyx realized Memphis had known the Dust Clans terms and yet had insisted on them addressing the matter. And where had that landed them? Memphis locked in a secret cell, beaten and broken, and her in the middle of this fighting ring.

The jeers of the onlookers drowned her, as Nyx caught snippets of the insults that were being yelled at her. Bruises peppered her skin, and her muscles screamed as she kicked her leg out, her opponent grunting from the contact. Standing, allowing herself one second to flick her gaze toward the stands, she found *Zander* leaning casually over the rails, his gaze fixated on her.

He had the nerve to wink down at her before she had to duck and slash at her attacker's belly, swearing with the effort. Oh, she was going to make him pay for this. Sweat stung her eyes as she blinked rapidly. The harsh sun made her fine skin blister and peel from the hours spent down here already. They had arrived three days ago to a world filled with billowing tents and intricate buildings, and she hadn't seen Memphis since. She rarely saw the Dust Clan leader for that matter; in between fights, she was chained in an iron cage to be leered and jabbed at like an animal.

Their swords caught again, and she rammed her knee in the man's groin, making him double over in pain. *He wanted a show; he would get one.* Flicking her braid over her shoulder and flashing the Dust Clan leader a most brilliant smile, her sword point found its mark, fast and true. The man crumpled to the ground. This was the tenth today she had killed.

Curses and insults were flung at her, but jutting her chin out, she watched the clan leader like a hawk, waiting for him to send the next raider in. If he wanted a display of strength and resilience, he would get one. Nyx would not roll over and wait to die. It would be on her terms, with her sword swinging until her last breath. Always.

Zander started to clap, lazy and slow, and the crowd quieted, watching their leader. His muscles flexed in the golden light, his inky blue tattoos covering almost every inch of skin, the intricate and beautiful line work curling around his limbs and neck. His dark eyes shone with amusement, and they assessed her as they always did. Day after day. Fight after fight. Nyx knew he was toying with her, just waiting until the second he released Memphis to take him up on his challenge. Allowing his broken leg to fester with infection and his defiance to wane.

Zander wanted her to know that each second of each passing day, their chances of living were disappearing. Like he wanted her spirit to. In response, she twirled her bloodied sword and waggled her eyebrows, daring him to make his move. She wasn't afraid of dying. She was afraid of him making her feel—or to even think—she was weak or what she was fighting for wasn't worth it: It was.

The Dust Clan leader spat on the ground and gazed at the clan around him. "Bring in the laghairts."

This time, his sharpened gaze held her for a second longer, and she saw it in his eyes. Whatever was coming was bad.

Dusty iron portcullises groaned open as she brandished her blade in front of her, squinting in the shadows of the mouth's wall. Laughter and cheers filled the pit as her gaze widened. Three monstrous creatures stalked in, their scales a deep golden brown, shimmering like gold in the sun. Their huge bulking muscles made the colors blaze in brilliance with every movement. Intelligent black eyes met hers, their razor-sharp teeth salivating as their huge nostrils flared.

By fire and flame, they were *smelling* her. Inky black talons shifted through the sands, and for a moment, the creatures stopped, licking their maws and flicking their huge, powerful, spiked tails.

Then, all chaos broke loose.

They charged her, roaring so loud her eardrums swelled from the onslaught and pain coursed through her body. She did the only thing she could think of in that moment. She ran.

Pumping her arms hard, the earth shook from the force behind her. She heard the crowd yelling insults, and she could feel Zander's gaze burning into her back. He was pushing her, putting her into a corner so she would have only one option to truly make a display.

Urging her legs to move faster, she ran the perimeter of the forsaken pit. Zander was smart, she would hand him that. This had been a test to try and break her but to also learn what her ability was made of, what he had to be wary of. Her heart rammed against her chest as she suddenly changed directions, so that she was now running at the savage beasts.

The clan seemed to still around her, and she could feel the pit hold its collective breath. She was maybe fifty yards away from the charging beasts; their snarling and hungry looks were as if they thought their prey had made their fight easy. That she had submitted.

Smiling wickedly, she threw her sword down and skittered to a stop, throwing up her hands and allowing her ability to shoot through her, dipping into everything she had. It was like every single one of her bones cracked at the same moment, every nerve singing, every sense heightened.

Nyx was infinite as she projected one thought, *Freeze*. And that's exactly what all three creatures did.

One moment, they were charging, the next frozen in time, their roars of protest shaking the stadium as the raiders' unease started to spread. Swaggering toward them, she took a minute to glare up at Zander, who had gone red in his golden face with anger. *Good*. She wanted him to understand just who he was dealing with. That's when she brought her fierce gaze back to the raging beasts, suspended in her firm holds, and pressed harder.

Her pulse roared, the world tilting, but she held on. Pristine black droplets of the creatures' blood started to ooze from their skin and glisten around them like crystals. Her ability dipped and spun, and as the creatures' eyes widened: She drained them of all life until they crashed around her, and she released them of her hold. The reptilian bodies collided with the sandy pit, making dust clouds erupt. Boldly looking to Zander, her smirk was as sharp as swords. It was his move now. Cries of protest rippled amongst the clans as he raised a dark eyebrow and dropped his façade all in one motion.

Gripping the railing, he swung his toned body over the edge, landing hard, several feet below. Ripping his blade from his belt, he ran, loosening such a war cry it split through the protest. He slammed her hard onto the dirt floor, black spots erupting in her vision as he pinned her, the cool edge of the knife against her throat. Thrashing, her numb muscles tried desperately to throw him off.

A low baritone chuckle sounded as he lowered himself close to her ear. "Don't fight, unless you want to meet your end now."

She knew he wasn't toeing that line anymore. Making her body still, she gazed up, staring at the Dust Clan leader, who in turn was grinning down at her.

His voice was still low as he murmured, "Now, either you agree to my terms, or I will ensure I spill your blood until the last drop."

In response, she tried to slam her knees into his gut, and Zander pressed the blade harder into her skin. "You are truly a spectacle to behold." He pressed down just a little harder. "As clan leader, I am meant to choose a partner in this role, one who stands by my side as an equal. No one has ever defeated the laghairt other than myself. All others who have tried met their demise. So, Nyx of Black Dawn, I grant you a choice. You either agree to stand with me as my equal in the clans or refuse and die beside your commander."

Nyx's blood roared in her ears as she registered what he was proposing: To stand with him, to rule the clans. As a team. *Think of the Rebellion.* Her revulsion took hold as she snapped, "I would rather *die* than bow to you!"

Snorting, he said, "I was hoping you would say that. Because either way, you are *mine*. I hope you enjoy knowing that you had the choice to achieve what you sought for. That you could have spared your commander. I was feeling particularly lenient after that show you just put on. But now, you will see the wrath of the raiders." Bucking beneath his hold, she wanted to scream, to shatter him. He smirked in his arrogant way and murmured, "Oh, this *is* going to be fun."

As quickly as the clan leader had pinned her, he gripped her arm hard, pulling Nyx up to stand beside him. All she could taste was dust and blood as she looked to the empty, angry faces of the crowd around her.

His voice shook with the strength of iron as he addressed his clan, "Who would like to see such a force broken? This prisoner—" he spat the word "—is now my property. Anyone touches a hair on her head will pay in the only language we understand-pain." He considered the eyes of the uneasy raiders, making sure his message was clear. Flickering his attention back to Nyx, he sneered. "You, with me."

It wasn't a request.

Looking up into the blaring sun, she squared her shoulders, following him, not looking back at the bloodied pit. They walked underneath a crumbling archway, where he shoved a rusty gate open, motioning for her to follow.

Outside of the arena, she blinked hurriedly, trying to keep up with the explosion of energy around her. Raiders of all ages and their families filled the street, vendors' calling to potential traders and buyers, their carts full of merchandise, ranging from clothes to weapons to food. Homes lined the streets, golden rectangular buildings with huge bay windows giving her a peek into each individual life that resided there.

Zander barely gave her time to adjust before snapping his fingers, and the particles of sand were summoned to life underneath and all around them. The particles flew together, banding and molding in a brilliant display until the flying carpet made of sand swept underneath them, and they were flung toward the skies. The hot afternoon wind whipped around her, and she gave herself one second to let her guard down. Her shaking limbs and clenched fists were the only signs she allowed in front of the Dust Clan leader: Zander didn't miss a thing.

Seeing that wicked glint in his eye, Nyx demanded an answer, "Why are you doing this?"

He tilted his head in the most innocent way as they raced above the bustling colony and retorted, "Doing what? It was *you* who came to me. It is not my fault your friend ignored my warning or that you two cannot adjust to our laws here."

"Laws? Where is the justice of ensuing pain and death to establish your leadership and dominance? Why not press the importance of humility and empathy since you are a part of this land, as well as this world, instead of deciding to ignore the war raging around you?" It came out in a breathless rush, and her voice hitched as she swallowed her pain down.

That same smug look crossed his face as he snorted. "Then why are you here in the first place? If you already understand so much about me and the clan laws, then you should already know that I never would have said yes in the first place."

Nyx clipped back, "Doesn't everyone deserve the benefit of the doubt to change for the better? Don't you deserve more than for us to assume you will always be a prat?"

Turning away from her, he looked out to the horizon. "You talk too freely. If you didn't already realize, it will get you into more trouble than it's worth here."

She rolled her eyes. "Then you obviously don't know a thing about me. I would rather cause trouble than complacently bow. Especially if it means bowing to you."

"I would think of your commander before saying such things."

She narrowed her eyes, silently seething as the carpet dipped and rippled with the currents of the wind. They both sat in tense silence.

You must get Memphis out, get him to safety.

Chewing her lower lip in silence, her mind ran in circles. Memphis was a lot of things to her, had meant a lot of things. She had loved him and hated him, tried to forget him, to forgive him. He had been her passion, leader; her regret, her ghost. And now, they deserved to see and experience a better future. They wouldn't walk themselves to their executioner.

Her bruises and minor wounds thudded with pain, her blood sounding in her ears. It was a crisp, clear day; the heat haze made everything seem to move slower, as if they were in a daze. Her eyes streamed from the force of the wind as they dipped lower, cutting through the clouds with grace. Below them, a singular building rested, nestled in billowing, deep blue curtains and a small courtyard. Zander's house, she assumed.

They descended closer and closer to the ground until, with a start, the sands disappeared in a plume of dust, and they were dropped. Her cry caught in her throat as she hit the ground hard, and all the wind was driven from her lungs.

She lay stunned in the sands, the sun burning into her back until Zander strode past her, dusting himself off.

"You will want to follow me, unless you prefer sunstroke." His façade had slipped slightly, to become less of the roaring beast of a man and more of a brooding type.

QUEEN TO ASHES

She got up while trying to decide which was more dangerous. Keeping her head high, she greedily took in her surroundings, desperately trying to find *anything* that would hint to Memphis's whereabouts. They entered a small side door to the same identical golden building and stepped inside. He closed the door behind her with a click.

Squinting, Nyx allowed her eyes to adjust as he quickly passed through the living room, motioning for her to follow. She stalled, taking in the room. It was bathed in such rich, beautiful colors, from the walls to the furniture, to the assortment of fascinating objects that lined the various shelves. The house was empty and silent. It was forbidding and peaceful all at once, and it made her hair stand on end.

"Will you stop gawking?" His voice shook her from her spell, and she slowly stalked toward another hallway where he stood. He gestured up to a sweeping stone staircase. "You will stay upstairs, in the room on the left. Everything you need is up there."

"And if I don't?"

He smirked. "Then I promise you, it will only end with blood."

Weighing her odds against the clan leader in her state and sighing, she made her way up the stairs without a backward glance. She needed to rest before she found Memphis. She needed to ensure when she took her one shot at rescuing him, it would be with everything she had.

Reaching the top, she slowly propped the door open, its hinges creaking slightly. After she stepped inside, the door instantly slammed behind her: Locking. She hadn't expected anything else, and so, she relaxed, knowing, for the time being, she would be safe.

A luscious bed with deep crimson pillows was splayed in front of her, the headboard carved with images of blades clashing. A small, barred window faced the north, its curtains moving lazily. Maneuvering quietly until she reached an adjoining door, she peered inside, marvelling at the handsome porcelain tub and bottles of oils on a shelf beside it. Groaning, she shut the door behind her and started the tub, the noise of rushing water keeping her company. Shimmying her bloodied clothes off her aching body, she lowered herself into the steaming water, nearly crying. *You will be no use to Memphis until you're thinking clearly.* Dumping a healthy amount of what smelt like mint oil into the water, she closed her eyes. Breathing deeply, the tension unwound and exhaustion swept in.

Hours had passed until she re-emerged, her long violet hair plaited back, bloodied, dusty fighting leathers back on, and weapons adjusted to their normal places on her upper thighs and back. She rolled her shoulders as she stepped out of the bathroom, leaving the pink-tinged water behind her. Her boots hung loosely from her hands as she looked to the tiny window. The golden tones of the sunset bled into the skies, turning her room into a brilliant display.

Narrowing her eyes, she knew she had one of two options: escape through the window or confront Zander directly. Huffing, she listened to the bustle of life outside, as the clan prepared for the night and the festivities that awaited. Her skin crawled at the thought, and she knew they didn't have much time. It was at that exact moment that the door opened behind her.

He leaned against her doorframe, oozing arrogance. In his hand, he held a beautiful flowing dress, its golden fabric shimmering, the black empire waist clasp dazzling.

Lifting his dark eyebrow, he drawled, "It certainly seems you have made yourself at home. Now put this on so we can join in the festivities."

"Festivities?" Tossing the dress at her, she caught it.

"Before the fight begins."

Her stomach dropped, but her mind was already ten steps in front of her. This was good; if they were preparing, then Memphis had to be close. She looked at the fabric in between her fingers. "I'm not wearing this."

He chuckled. "Suit yourself. Tonight, is a night for celebration, wear whatever you want. I was just giving you options."

Mashing her teeth in aggravation and with tight lips, she followed Zander into the hallway. The house was just as quiet, small candles lit on every surface, illuminating their world into something beautiful, softening the edges. He was dressed in inky, leather pants and boots, with a flowing, blue, short-sleeved shirt, his tattoos dancing in the light. Nyx pushed her emotions down, resting a reassuring hand on her blade hilt. So much had changed and would still change. All she could do was be ready for her opportune moment.

Formulating a quick plan, Nyx sent silent prayers to the stars as the duo stepped into the night. They were met with an explosion of *life*. Raiders packed the streets in their best dressed clothes. Jackets and cloaks, dresses and glittering jewelry.

Torches lined the outskirts of the road, creating a walkway of flame, licking the shadows back, forcing the darkness to retreat. Billowing silks and caravans bustled past them, their inhabitants hollering at Zander, raising their glasses while the contents sloshed on their arms. He nodded at them in acknowledgement as she followed him into the street, and they became one with the beautiful chaos.

Two drinks were immediately pressed into his hands, and he passed one shining goblet to her. The deep red liquid had the brightest aroma of spices and fruit as she gently lowered her lips to the rim and drank.

He watched with appraising eyes and lifted his glass to her. "To my good health." He emptied the glass in one go as she sipped once more. *To your good health indeed.*

Bitterness filled her as they slinked through the crowd. Zander stopped to talk to his people while she watched at a safe distance behind. It was overwhelming as she tried to take everything in but act like she was seeing nothing. She followed the clan leader until they broke through the crowd and were halfway through the street when he stopped, inclining his head toward the spectacle.

A group of six men and women were beautifully dressed in midnight-blue silks, their foreheads adorned with black gems. They bowed lowly to him and then proceeded to start the most beautiful dance she had ever seen. Their bodies moved smoothly as the pairs reacted to one another's step so fast their silks flew behind them, creating the illusion of billowing sails. And the *music.* Spotting the musician, the stringed instrument was so small, yet the melody was strikingly powerful. The player moved his bow faster and faster as the dancers spun, and it was hypnotic. It was compelling. It made her heart race, the climb and crash of notes. It was magic.

Leaning closer to her, he said, "It is the dance of winds. Here throughout the clan, it is the dance of tribute, of power. It is good luck for a fighter to see such a thing before a duel. It is also a sign of the deepest respect."

She was speechless as the dancers continued to spin and arc, and it took all her will power to tear her eyes away and follow him through the crowd once more.

It seemed like an infinite amount of time as they walked through the winding streets, Zander eyeing her, trying to be inconspicuous. *You are not mine. You will never be.* She chewed on the inside of her lip and tried her best to ignore the clan leader and his roaming eyes. It made her want to show him very clearly that he was wrong.

Breathing deeply, she steadied herself. She would be compliant until the last—and right—moment. Until then, she fantasized about all the things she would like to do with the steel she possessed.

Onward they walked, and Nyx quickly realized that the crowds behind them were also moving with them, a hundred or more people, their boisterous noise clouding her thoughts. The road in front of them turned slightly, and she faltered, taking in the sight. The stadium that she had once occupied had been transformed; barbed thorns covered every inch of its walls, and roaring fires held in huge barrels were in front of every archway. He lit up with pride at the sight.

With every step closer to their fates, Nyx, with a roaring certainty, knew she would make the clan leader pay.

They passed by the fires and under the golden archway where she filed into the stadium. Zander walked into the center of the pit to await Memphis. Climbing through the rows agilely, sweat slicked her palms as she perched in the same spot he watched her from earlier. The stadium filled at a steady pace, excitement and impatience brewing amongst the clan as they looked down to their leader. They wanted their bloody show, and it made her stomach churn even more.

Finally, when all the rows were practically teeming, Zander raised his hands, and a young man stood in the stadium, nodding to him. The whole crowd fell silent as the man whispered into his palms, opening them up. Fire roared into the sky, twisting and consuming, illuminating the Risco Desert for miles around them. Cries of awe and approval were met with this, and as the fire roared, embers slowly drifted back down to the earth while deep, tribal drums sounded. The players were stationed outside the area, and each stroke, each beat trembled the night. They pounded like a heartbeat, the deep rhythm making him grin wickedly as he unsheathed his sword, waiting.

Dread pooled in her stomach as she frantically tried to form a plan to stop Zander, and sway the clans.

CHAPTER TWENTY-SIX

Memphis

The fire looked like a comet streaking across the night sky, illuminating and consuming anything in its path. *This is it*, he thought. The wind howled like banshees while the world burned. It all led up to this moment, the tip of the blade between life and death. Gritting his teeth, he opened his heart up to the darkness and stepped forward, blade in hand. The beating of the drums reverberated through his bones, each stroke electrifying his senses. Beckoning to him, calling him closer. The blade felt a thousand times heavier in his palms, and he twirled it slowly.

This moment was not just about him, and that weighed heavily on his mind.

Embers floated through the air, gently brushing up against his skin, their warmth scorching where they touched. He checked to make sure the armor was in place, weapons tucked in neatly on his back and thighs. Healers had set his broken leg in a brace, and he understood that Zander wanted him to be in pain. To struggle.

The tempo of the drums hurried, and jeers from the crowd echoed in the night. Before stepping forward, he thought of Emory. Her lips, how the light caught her hair, by flame and fire, her *laugh*. He thought of what could have been.

Suddenly, silence sounded, and gripping the hilt with white knuckles, he stepped into the arena. The brace for his leg would ensure the illusion of a fair fight. Zander had promised him that much. Each step threatened to shatter his resolve as he walked toward the clan leader, pain lancing through his body, the smell of infection overwhelming him. He stopped, breathing heavily and allowing his eyes to adjust to the burning ring of thorns that surrounded him.

Being kept in a cell deep in the stadium, he hadn't seen the outside world for days. Hadn't eaten a morsel. Only the tiniest amount of water had been permitted, just enough to keep him alive. That was also strict orders on Zander's end. The Dust Clan leader didn't utter a word to the crowd, no pleasantries of justice. No beautiful words of freedom or haunting promises of revenge. His sword glinted in the night, and Zander charged toward Memphis, embers floating down between them.

Memphis saw the promise of pain in the clan leader's eyes, and he loosened a hoarse cry, bringing his blade up to block Zander's attack. His arm nearly broke from the force. Shouts and jeers sounded from the crowd as attack after attack he parried the blows, grunting as he moved as fast as he could. The world tilted on its axis in a sickening motion as Zander threw a punch, suddenly connecting with his jaw. Blood filled his mouth. Zander laughed as he rolled, missing the raider's blade by a hairsbreadth. Scrambling up, he roared, his blade meeting the Dust Clan leader's.

Blow for blow, they continued their deadly dance. He would not yield. He. Would. *Not.*

Dots danced at the edge of his vision, sweat soaking his skin. He wondered in that second if the clan leader had purposefully ensured that Memphis was given plated armor to weigh him down and make him slower.

Jumping back, Zander swiped at his legs. Memphis swore, allowing the full force of his ability to rush out of him aimed at Zander. The sand sparked underneath their feet, particles rising. The power rippled, and the sands pelted like shooting knives.

The raider flicked his eyebrows up. "You want to play that way?" Sheathing his sword, he clapped his hands, and the sands froze a second away from cutting into his skin then dropped to his feet.

He charged, but not before Zander snapped his fingers and the sands twisted, banding together, creating a mass so large he couldn't reach him. The crowd roared, begging for the blades as he cocked his head to the side, his eyes glinted. Zander snapped his fingers again, and the sands hissed, the mass moving toward him like a giant viper slithering at him, and he saw Zander unsheathe his blade. Memphis looked to the tumbling mass rushing at him. And ran.

CHAPTER TWENTY-SEVEN

Nyx

Nyx gripped the railing, her knuckles turning white as she watched Memphis run for his life. The raiders had mended his broken leg enough to make a show of his death, the brace fluid with Memphis's movements. He was moving too slow as the monstrous, churning sand snake coiled in front of him, cutting him off. And Zander charged up on his flank to meet him.

Nyx continued to chew the inside of her cheek raw-fresh blood filled her mouth. Memphis was sheet white as Zander grinned a blood-thirsty smile. The excitement through the crowd spread like wildfire as the Dust Clan leader soared over his fabricated creature and slashed his blade down at Memphis's neck. Memphis, at the last second, brought his blade up, sparks flying between the two men. It was a dance of death, a dance of defiance.

Do something, do something, do something.

Her body and spirit willed her to act, but as soon as she did, it would break the promise of the duel, and everything would have been for nothing. They needed the raiders in this war. And so, she watched swords clash, and the roars of the crowd crashed around the stadium. Blood spurted as Memphis's blade clipped Zander's shoulder, and the raider rolled away. Memphis charged, seeing his opening, but Zander was too fast. The raider threw his elbow up into his nose, and with a sickening crack, blood started to pour. The drums had started up again outside their perimeter, their beats rolling like thunder.

She felt as Memphis poured all his energy into another mental wave toward Zander, who distracted the commander's ability and broke his concentration. Her heart dropped into her stomach as she watched Memphis block, again and again, Zander's relentless attacks. The two blades flashed in the flames like liquid silver. The Dust Clan leader was pushing Memphis into the corner of the stadium purposefully.

Her heart pounded as she watched Zander, as fast as lightning, duck from his blow and sheathe his sword. In the same motion, he loosened a leather whip from his belt and sent it flying. Her scream cut through everything else as the leather bit into Memphis's skin.

CHAPTER TWENTY-EIGHT

Memphis

"MEMPHIS!" He heard Nyx yell as he watched Zander change his weapons in one sickening motion.

The whip was black as night as it lashed out toward his right wrist, the leather biting in his skin and ripping through it. The steel dropped into the sand. Searching the crowd, Memphis found Nyx's violet eyes blazing into his. There was so much he wanted to say to her. He hoped she would forgive him for hurting her, forgive that he couldn't love her as she deserved. Memphis's pain demanded him back into the moment as Zander prowled toward him, and he dropped to his knees, scrambling for his sword. Scrambling for anything.

In that same moment, he felt the cool sands shift under his weight, and embers drifted down in front of his vision, taking focus. Tiny, burning pieces of power just waiting to be sparked to life once more. He took in the beautiful golden, fiery hues, and he found comfort even though he was afraid. Every fiber in his body begged to stay alive.

His pain crashed into him again as the whip bit into his midriff, tearing flesh and muscle. Panting, Memphis crumpled, and his blond hair spilled around him. The world spun, pain turning to numbness, his thoughts soaring: Thinking of everything that had once been beautiful in this world, he allowed it to fill every crevice of his soul.

Zander approached, his leather boots crunching against the sand, as he lifted his gaze to find that dark smile, that smooth smile, lips curling over his teeth. The shake of anticipation. The promise of his end.

Chapter Twenty-Nine

Nyx

The sword glinted up at her, mocking her, as Zander moved in lithe strokes. Nyx realized that the Dust Clan leader was *smiling*. Her blood turned to ice as the drums pounded faster. The crowd cheered, demanding the killing blow be met. And in that second, she screamed, and seeing the flash of metal, she hurtled herself over the railing, landing hard into the pit. *No, no, no, no!* Charging, her ability clambered through her body, watching Zander's blade slice into Memphis's heart.

"NO!"

Memphis's eyes widened, just ever so slightly, as the light drained out of them. Hot, salty tears ran down her cheeks as Zander pulled the blade out of his chest and took a triumphant stance. He was met with a roar of approval. That was until her energy slammed into him, making him fly and collide with the stadium's wall.

QUEEN TO ASHES

There were no words she could utter; there was only the pounding in her heart as Nyx cracked in two. And so did the world around her. Screams sounded as the golden structure around them split, fire spilling into the sands only to be extinguished. Raiders scrambled to stay away from the fissures. Zander shook his head, honing on to her as his blood poured from a gash in his forehead. Now it was *her* turn to grin wickedly.

Her voice sounded far off, like she was swimming through deep waters. "I challenge you. I will finish what Memphis started."

Her voice cracked, as she charged. She didn't allow him a second before she screamed, her throat burning from the force.

Zander froze as he watched his skin start to peel, particles of his existence breaking off. Grabbing her blades, she whipped them out of their sheaths, the metal shining in the night, the sharpened edges begging to bite into anything. Her blood roared, her muscles relishing in the burning as she dove into the darkest parts of her ability.

He was slammed back into the wall, his head cracking from the force. Her hands acted on their own accord as she sent the metal flying, and each knife found its marks in his shoulders. Each wet thud made her tears run faster, her anger flare. Pinning him in place, Nyx dissolved into the adrenaline rush of the fight. Allowing the monster to surface: A monster of magic and power. A monster trained to kill. Zander shouted at her, but she didn't hear him. She didn't hear anything except the cruel melody orchestrated by her pain. Memphis's face flashed over and over in her mind. She had done *nothing* but watch Memphis die, because of the man that stood in front of her.

"I would make you suffer slowly," her voice cracked, "but that would mean I care. And you? You are *nothing* to me." She dragged her blade along his cheek, breathing in his fear. She grinned.

"This world is meant for more than brutality. It is meant for more than to be dictated by men like *you*." Her hand shook, as her blade stopped just above his heart. Locking eyes with him, she said, "You will not break us."

The blade dug in, and she felt the warmth of blood on her hands, his exhale as the life bled out of him. And she watched, her fury, her pain, locking her in place. The Clan leader dropped, and she collected her blades. Panting, she stopped, her stomach rolling, blood and sweat mixed into her tears. It felt like a lifetime had passed as she lifted her gaze to the stadium around her and was astonished to find every single raider knelt on one knee, bowing their heads toward her.

Silence echoed throughout the stadium as she turned and collapsed, her raking cries taking over her body as she took in Memphis, spread eagle on the sands.

She gave in to her pain. She gave in to everything, and it pulled her down and drowned her.

CHAPTER THIRTY

Emory

The sun sank lower, dipping beneath the horizon as she stared at the opposing wall. The stone was weathered, chunks and cracks spattering over its surface. Green moss crawled over the bottom, eventually reaching for the top of the cell.

It had been three sunrises and three sunsets since they took Brokk. *Three. Days.* Breathing deeply, Emory clenched her jaw, her skin no longer feeling the cold, her body no longer feeling tired. Stripped bare, she found what she had been waiting for her. It had been concealed, been channeled. Her anger licked at her heart, and she smiled grimly in the fading light, knowing now, that she was ready.

The door creaked open, golden hues illuminating her bloodied wrists and the chains linked to the wall.

"Hello, Princess."

Marquis's voice was a soft drawl, Emory's body bowing, metal slicing into her skin as she lunged. Leaning against the other wall, his brows rose, and he frowned. His jacket was pitch-black, his boots polished. His loose pants and shirt were casual, but he looked *good*.

"What's the occasion?" Emory demanded.

"I see you haven't lost any of your spirit."

"Why would I? I quite enjoy your accommodations, oh *noble* King."

He tilted his head. "Why should you be treated differently than any other person that comes to the Isles? Because once upon a time we were acquainted? The princess I knew back then didn't do anything about her cage. Why would you now?"

"Because..."

"Because you think you understand this war? You're being a child."

"And you have hid from your problems." Her words landed right where she wanted them.

"Spoken like a girl who doesn't understand what she has done," Marquis snapped back.

"Or like a woman who has given up everything, unlike you."

His hand was suddenly around her neck, and he slammed her back, stars igniting in her vision.

"Don't you dare begin to think you understand what I have given up." His breath was ragged; his gaze scoured her as his hand dropped and he stepped back. "Time can only tell if what you and your party is saying is true. But you and I, Emory, need to have a general understanding of one another before we even begin to win this war."

"We don't have time," she wheezed, sliding to the ground.

He smirked. "For this, we have to make time." His slim fingers dug into his pocket. A small, silver key flashed as he crouched down, his lips in a thin line. The manacles shivered as she craned her neck to watch the metal quiver, a keyhole appearing above her head. Marquis unlocked them, and they dropped from her. Exhaling, she rolled her shoulders, rubbing her wrists, smearing her blood.

Offering her a hand, he said, "Come with me."

Her curiosity overruled her better judgement, and so, she did. Standing, her bones popped, her muscles cramping. Salt, blood, and sweat covered her tattered clothes, and she sighed, not unaware of how she smelled. Marquis turned his back as they left the cells, her heart in her throat.

He pushed the door open, and the wind was there to meet them. Stopping, she breathed in the crisp air, the crashing of waves an orchestra, the sounds of the Isle still so new to her. Shivering, she looked to the ocean, the moon nestled high in the blanketed night. Shimmering down, the reflection was stardust, turning this wild land into one of magic and mystery. The cliff face was jagged, and following the edge, it was an endless amount of grasses, of slated rocks, until she found what she was looking for. There wasn't a city or *kingdom* in sight.

Instead, a crowd of women and men were gathered, their faces illuminated by the line of torches. Their eyes glowed, the smears of coal along their jawlines and cheeks, their images haunting her. Stalking toward them, ice shot through her body as she straightened.

Throwing a cheeky grin over his shoulder, Marquis whispered, "Do you still wish our allegiance?"

"Your allegiance and your sworn promise that you won't hurt any of my company." *If you do, I will end you.*

"*Tsk, tsk.* Princess, I'm not a monster."

They moved closer to the group, Marquis's jacket flapping in the night. Fate had always been a fickle, taunting dream to her. Like anyone else, she wanted her stars to align, to lead her in the path that she was meant to go. Doubt rose in her. Was it the right decision to come to the Isles for help? Or would she just become another prisoner to a king's madness?

Walking up to that group of strangers, their severe edges, their pointed looks, and sharpened weapons, she wondered, if maybe, being lost meant she would find everything she had ever yearned for.

"Emory Fae." Her eyes snapped to Marquis who now stood at the front of the group, the waves crashing behind him viciously. Magic tinged the air, and as she met his gaze, that familiar pull of electric current filled her soul. Looking down, her necklace flickered, the storm within it stirring too. Her ability returned to her, and it was revitalizing as she dug her nails into her palms.

"You come here demanding we help you in the war against Adair's kingdom. To help you liberate this land. To fight alongside a stranger."

Chuckles sounded all around her as she took a step, Marquis's eyes flashing in the firelight, shadows dancing along his skin.

"We have heard your company's story. Of the maybe truths. And maybe lies. But here, we do decide what is best for our kingdom. It is not just my decision to let you dictate what the Shattered Isles will do." He paused a moment before continuing. "It has been decided that we will first learn what the acclaimed queen has to offer us. How dangerous you are as an enemy. And how important you are as an ally."

Marquis stepped forward, and all the air left her lungs as the crowd started a slow stomping beat. A tremor shivered along the earth as she turned, blanching.

His wrists were bound, the same smooth metal interlocking them. Brokk's golden eyes brightened as he drank her in, the gag tied over his mouth tight. His shirt has been ripped, and he stumbled over the terrain. A strangled choking broke from her lips as Brokk was shoved to Marquis, who shook his head at her.

Marquis moved lithely. The crowd around her had turned feral, their catcalls and insults floating on the wind around her, egging on Marquis to act. Marquis ran, ripping the first torch from the earth and throwing it over the cliff face, and it streaked, flaring as it plummeted toward the ocean. Cries of joy, of anger, of fear circled her, her pulse thundering to the beat of the ocean, to the beat of the footsteps as the men and women gathered and mimicked their leader's actions. Twenty more torches were thrown into the night, a burst of life against a blank slate. Her mouth ran dry as she locked eyes with Brokk.

Imagining his lips meeting hers. What they could explore, if only given the time to learn. Not as strangers and not being afraid anymore. But as broken parts finally becoming whole. Of two lost souls finding their way after a lifetime of mistakes.

Her cry tore through her lips as she watched Marquis's hands collide with Brokk's broad chest. As Brokk stumbled, his eyes widened, shock and fear igniting in them. A sharp roaring filled her mind as the world churned, and he dropped over the cliff's edge.

Falling into the treacherous sea.

"NO!" she screamed; her cry echoing in the night.

Time slipped. The ground lurched as she scrambled, pumping her arms, forgetting about the flames and the Isles. Forgetting about everything but him. It had always been him. Shooting forward, she gulped down air, pushing faceless bodies out of her way. She would not lose him.

A flash of green was the last thing she took in of Marquis before she threw herself off the side of the cliff, and gravity disappeared. Screaming, the inky depths rushed up to greet her, the wind howling, the cold slicing through her body. Biting down hard, blood filled her mouth. Swearing, she flipped her body, bringing her arms together, just in time before she sliced into the water.

Her limbs flailed as she dropped from the dive and instantly got pulled into the tide. The cold knocked her breath from her chest as everything became compressed. She couldn't think. Couldn't *breathe*. The sea commanded her, dragging her deeper, spinning her, and she went limp. Ice clutched her muscles, pounding into her chest, into her mind.

Brokk. Her eyes snapped open, and she screamed his name, bubbles flying in front of her. The sea churned, and she couldn't see anything as it heaved. A pulsing ripple shivered around her as she looked down. Her necklace was suspended in front of her, the gem blackened yet somehow glowed dully. The light was weak, but it was something. *Think*. Her lungs felt like they were about to burst, a ragged burn spreading too fast.

Clenching her fists, she closed her eyes and dove into that depth within herself: That blackness, that darkness. If the price was bearing it now, then so *be* it. If the cost of using it was to save him, she would do it a thousand times over.

The energy exploded from her, the shockwave sending her spiraling. But there—she gulped down the delicious air, as she snapped her eyes open. The bubble encased her face like she had seen Memphis do. The blissful oxygen flowed freely as she choked, trying to steady her breath. It felt like a lifetime ago when she dove into those rose-gold waters; blindly following and trusting Memphis.

She whipped her head around, searching for a flicker of anything. The waves pushed and pulled as she stroked with her arms, swimming as fast as she could. In the half-light, she saw patches of her pale skin traced with black lines, exactly where her veins would be. *Don't think about it.* Fighting against her tiredness and defeat, she kept going.

Her pulse thudded dully in her ears. Marquis dictated a monstrous kingdom, the people of the Isles thriving off violence. Swimming faster, Emory pushed down her anger—she would deal with Marquis after.

Fighting against the pull of the ocean, Emory's ability protected her. Her gaze scrounged the underwater world, nothing but shadowed reefs for miles, the flicker of movement sending shivers up her spine. She swam faster as the feeling she was being watched overwhelmed her. Kicking her feet faster, she dove, and it was the flash of gold that froze her. There on the reef, he hung suspended, the manacles flashing against the light.

"BROKK!"

Her screams did nothing as the knife flashed from behind him, the assailant hidden in the inky cover of the sea, as the weapon dove toward his throat.

"NO!" she screamed, but that's when she felt her necklace slam against her chest.

She gasped when heat blazed through her. Her necklace slammed against her skin again, and she tore at her own throat as the gem ripped through flesh, blood washing into the seawater. The knife paused right above Brokk's flesh as her back bowed, her screams climbing as the pain ravaged her. She watched in horror as the chain dropped, complete and utter agony demanding her compliance.

The gem dissolved, and she gasped—unharnessed raw magic shuddered through her. Bubbled flesh rose, as she felt the magic expand into her, no longer just harnessing it within her necklace. No longer borrowing it or keeping it safe. It *was* her.

Looking down at her arms, all Emory could see was her blackened veins grow and bulge: Watching in horror as the dark magic ravaged her body, her vision dipped, and all she could process was the screams echoing. Her own, or was it Adair's? *No, he is dead. You killed him.* Convulsing, her eyes rolled into the back of her head, and the last thing she saw was the knife drop, sinking to the bottom of the ocean, being swallowed whole.

CHAPTER THIRTY-ONE

Azarius

The blood poured from his nose, gushing through his fingers as he tried to stem it. Whipping around, Azarius faltered in his sprint. Alby ran behind him, his sword bloodied, his black eye swollen, his left eye filled with fear. Their group, which started out as one hundred refugees from Pentharrow, was now down to thirty. *Thirty.* A wretched noise broke through his lips, and he couldn't think. He pushed down his aching heart as he roared, "MOVE!"

A flicker of a shadow was the only warning they gave them. Shooting past Alby, he rolled as the monster dove at his brother. His blade arced up, slicing the underbelly of decaying flesh, black blood washing over him, and all he could smell was death. Sputtering, he found his feet and stood. The cover of night had done *nothing*. Running had done *nothing*. Yellow eyes found his, as it snapped its maws, rotting teeth breaking from the force.

"Come get me then." Azarius smiled, crazed.

It roared, charging, as he shot forward. He could hear the cries, sending a silent plea that Alby was protecting them. That they would make it out of this. The monster lunged, and his fist connected with grey flesh. Its head snapped back from the force, and its claws viciously swiped at his belly. Lunging back, he laughed, his blades edge slicing clean through the creature's arm. It landed with a sickening thud. Snarling, it narrowed its eyes when the black blood sprayed. Gods above, the *smell*.

The wind picked up as Azarius said, "You cannot have us."

The trees around them bowed, branches cracking, and he couldn't hold on. He didn't want to hold on. The fissures cracked as he let go, and the gale picked up the howling creature.

"Azarius, NO!" Alby was there pushing at his chest.

He cackled. "They are not going to pick us off one by one, Alb." They ducked as the funnel cloud ate up the ground, the trees in its path snapping.

"Azarius, STOP!"

He panted as he squinted down at the wreckage from the winds picking up. It was intoxicating, and Azarius grinned.

Then a fist slammed into his jaw.

Dots filled his vision, blood filling his mouth. He looked at Alby. "What was that for?"

"You can't lose it now. What about using no abilities, so they can't pinpoint us easier? What about trying to stay hidden?"

Laughing, he swept his arms out wide. "Like that did us any good. Look at us. I used my abilities, and if they come, then so be it."

"Is that what Lana would have wanted?"

He froze. Just her name ripped open his body, leaving him stunned. He looked back at Pentharrow where nothing waited for them except for the ashes of their lives. Azarius had given up his life protecting that town, and now, all of it was gone. Surrounded by a world that had fallen into destruction, he had taken his personal punishment for his people. But now, they had liberated themselves and, in the same breath, shackled themselves to this war in one motion.

Stomping up to his brother, he grabbed fistfuls of his shirt, spitting in his face, "You have no right to talk to me about *her*."

Trembling, Azarius tensed, wanting to tear apart the world inch by inch. Shoving Alby back, he looked to the surviving members of their so called *rebellion*. Pacing back and forth, he pointed his sword at them.

"Do any of you actually think that we have a chance? If we are going to be hunted, then why not use everything we have now?" Their faces blanched at his words, at his tone. The men and women around him deflated, anxious murmurs spreading through them.

"No. Stop. I know you're hurting. I know that your entire world has just been ripped away from you. That your life at this point, in your eyes, is nothing without her. But look at me!"

The tears burned in Azarius's eyes as he looked to his twin, at the cold rage he found flashing in Alby's eyes as he spoke. "You do not have the right to strip the hope from these people. From me. Even from yourself. The Rebellion is alive if we are. Our mission is to make it to Memphis and Nyx. Make it to the raiders, and we have a chance. I'm begging you not to fall into madness. I need you. We need you."

Howls in the distance made him flinch as tears streaked his cheeks.

"Decide what man you want to be, brother."

Heaving, the world tilted, but he felt a pressure on his arm. Blearily looking, he found Alby grimly smiling at him, his hand around his forearm, squeezing.

"I'm sorry I punched you. But you are not alone in this. Never forget that. If you can start to forgive me for my decisions in leaving Pentharrow and you all those years ago, I will try to forgive you for almost killing us with this stunt."

The laugh choked out of him, as the howls escalated.

Alby furrowed his brows. "We need to run now."

Azarius forced his legs to comply. It was one foot in front of the other. Sheathing his blade, he numbly looked to his brother. "Okay. Okay I will try."

Nodding, Alby yelled to the rest. "Keep together and keep moving!"

They set off, leaving behind the wreckage. Gritting his teeth together, each jarring movement was a stab of pain. Of absence. Would she have wanted him to keep going without her? Leaving her to face the eternal nightmare alone? Azarius's chest ripped open, his emotions festering, but he kept going.

Hours had passed as the silent of the deep night fell over them all. The howls had stopped for the time being, and he didn't know if that was a good thing or a warning. Sweat poured down his body, his legs feeling like glass about to shatter at any moment. Every step, every ragged breath, brought them closer to thinning treelines, and he fell to the back of the group. Every pause, he looked back, panting and discreetly slashing a bloody mark into the bark. A trail, just in case the right person may be looking for them. Or this *rebellion*.

"AZARIUS!" Ice shot through his body as he charged forward to his brother.

The group had stopped as he came up beside him. "What?"

Alby was ashen, as he whispered, "Look."

Stepping forward, the treeline finally faded, blending into an expanse of marshland for miles. His breath misted in front of him as he took in quick gulps. He felt as though the thickening fog clung to the land. Then he saw the figure his brother had spotted. The person was tall, its tattered hood hiding their face. Alby came up beside him.

"Azar, you know where we are, right?" It was the childhood nickname that sent the fear shooting up his spine as Alby trembled beside him.

"The Forgotten Bogs." The words came out in a hush as the figure slowly lifted its arm, pointing a finger straight at him.

"Gods above." Alby gasped, taking a step back.

The myths that clung to this land were ones that Azarius didn't take lightly. Staring at the figure, the wind picked up, the cool edge of autumn clinging to it, but neither of them moved. It was once again the screams that brought him slamming back down into their present situation. The back of the group scattered as, whipping around, he saw the face of Calla, the town's local stained-glass artist, before she was dragged back into the forest, arms flailing, her screaming cutting off into a sickening silence.

The ground beneath him shook as two of the monsters from the Oileans' army landed where she was, grey skin sagging; they snapped their teeth, thick saliva dripping from their maws. Behind them, three more yellow stares flickered in the night, growls circling them. Looking at Alby, time seemed to stop, and he saw the dabarne there.

The two monsters grabbed victims, and he balked, screaming, "ALBY!" His brother found him as his ability cracked through his body, funnel clouds landing every which direction, slicing through rebels and monsters: Bending trees, breaking and snapping them.

He lost himself in the chaos, not knowing where the man started, and the monster began.

"Alby, run!" The scream choked out of Azarius as his brother grabbed two people scrambling toward him, and they all disappeared into the fog.

Two creatures locked their gazes on him, snarling, charging. Scrambling back, a funnel cloud touched down, catching the two dabarnes and sent them screeching toward the sky. Tripping, he ran, the wind picking up, the gale ripping trees from the forest, and he couldn't hold on anymore. Running full tilt, the fog ate up his surroundings. Tripping in pools, water soaked through his boots, freezing him.

"Alby! Alby?" Shivering, he pulled his jacket tighter, his sack half-ripped but still full enough with supplies. Panic clutched every orifice of his body as the screams echoed further behind him, and he ran, falling and getting up repeatedly. Mud slicked his pants as he heard a gentle footfall right in front of him. Shaking, he whispered, "Alby?"

A thick dripping sounded as a strangled voice whispered back, "Azarius Walsh. You have come." It was the same hooded figure he'd seen earlier, ice blue eyes fixated on his own. Her robes were tattered, her pale skin drawn, silver hair flowing down past her shoulders.

His mouth ran dry. "How do you know me?"

A small smile tugged at her lips. "I have been waiting for this moment for a long time."

"These lands are cursed. I'm just trying to pass through with what's left of our party. And my brother."

She stepped forward, tilting her head. "But your path is so much more than that. I have seen it." She took a step closer. "Cursed lands, gifted lands. Either way, it is a land that will save your life in this moment, if you will it."

"Who are you?"

"My name is Hesen. I was once part of a war, of a city lost many years ago. Now, I have lived in these lands, watching the fates intersect and collide. Waiting for this day." Her eyes glowed in the night, as the hairs on his arms rose.

"Why?"

She stepped forward, cupping his cheek. "Because all is not lost. Do you wish to see? To venture in the Bog?"

"I can't go back. The Rebellion has to live." It was a statement or maybe a question to himself. She smiled, pointed teeth glistening.

"Azarius? Is that you?" Alby's voice rang out to the left, desperation clinging to every syllable. The woman snapped her head at his voice, and he stepped in front of her. "It's my brother."

Turning, Azarius headed toward his voice. "Alby? Are you okay? Where are you?" There was a shift in the fog, and he was there, colliding with him. He crushed his twin against his chest, relief flooding through him. "Gods above. You're okay. Alby? Alby everything is okay."

Alby's sobs raked against his body, as he held his brother, looking over his flaming hair to the two figures watching nearby. "Ren. Iri." The couple nodded at him; their pale faces tight with grief. Azarius knew their son had been traveling with them and was one of the many casualties of this living nightmare.

"Come with me." Hesen's voice was sharp, as Azarius focused back on her. She huskily addressed them all, "As you said, Black

Dawn Rebellion cannot break. Come with me, and I will help you."

Alby grabbed his arm. "Who is *that?*"

His gut churned. "I think she is our only chance right now, Alb." With raised eyebrows, he murmured, "Come on."

He followed the mysterious woman: Alby, Ren, and Iri trailing tentatively behind.

The fog grew thicker, and he could swear whispers followed him on the wind, Lana's voice hidden amongst every sigh. Further and further, they walked into the Bog. Every crack of twig making him jump.

"And how do we know those monsters aren't hunting us in here?" Azarius asked.

Hesen looked over her shoulder. "The Oileans' power only stretches so far within our lands. My powers protect these borders and the creatures who are here." Azarius frowned, looking at his twin who shrugged. Stopping, Hesen motioned to him. "Will you look into the pools? To see your fate?"

Scoffing, Azarius said, "Our future? And if it only ends in our death?"

She shook her head. "It does not, Azarius Walsh. Now come and see."

Stepping forward, the fog curled around him, and the others faded. In front of Hesen, a small clear pool was nestled in the ground, its silver waters churning as if smoke was captured beneath the surface. Crouching down, he felt as if he was in a trance, and all he could think about was Lana. He had to know if she was alive.

The coolness of the wind stirred as Hesen whispered to his back, "Yes, now look closer."

QUEEN TO ASHES

Bending down, his nose was an inch away from the surface as the water spun. Shadows started forming, coming into focus as he exhaled hard. Tears ran down his face, his nails digging into the mud as the image became clear, playing out before his eyes. Nestled in the Forgotten Bogs, it was his own screams that pierced the night as he watched.

And watched.

CHAPTER THIRTY-TWO

The Oilean

There was pain. Darkness. And hope dwindled down into nothing as the Oilean circled around the staked windwalker, her breaths coming in quick, strained wheezes. Her arms were bound tightly to either side, her ankles as well. She would not hold on for much longer. Their green, jagged gems pulsed on the floor, the energy humming and creating while also destroying. Lana's head wobbled and dropped, the crescent moon they had carved on her forehead glowed in the night-connecting to them, her blood seeping and oozing, thick and black onto the floor.

Blood was always the key; it was such a tangible and *alive* source. It was the key to magic, to abilities, to holding, to creating, and sustaining. The rocks flared as the windwalker's blood ran toward them, touching their edges. Blinding light and a resounding crack flared deep in the forest where the Oilean had taken her. They liked it here; it wasn't like a regular forest. It hid creatures like them in its inky cover of a forever night. Deep purple brush crumpled around them, and the Oilean fell quiet and waited.

"How much longer do we have to wait?" Declan snapped impatiently.

"Soon, our king." The Oilean cooed, still not used to seeing their master in his new body of the former boy-king.

In the middle of the rock circle, instead of the forest floor, the surface rippled and changed. Sleek, crystalized frost swirled like a pane of glass. Smooth and impenetrable like a polished stone, its opaque surface shone up at their marred faces. The Oilean dared not breathe as they waited. Seconds passed and a hush fell over the forest. Lana's blood ran more freely, her body jerking wildly. Then the surface shattered in an explosion, shards lodging themselves in the black tree trunks in proximity. The rocks seemed to hum, the energy and heat pouring from them as the magic built.

The Oilean cackled as the creature rose in smoky tendrils and dangerous strength. The laughter floated through the crevices of the forest, and they knew they had succeeded in connecting the channel to their world, to allow the most dangerous and ruthless army access through.

Dark body after dark body, they appeared, opening their eyes, burning silver in the night. More tendrils of darkness flew through the portal, forming cloaked creatures behind Declan. and

Their army formed before the Oileans' eyes.

And for the first time in their forsaken life, they had broken through; the hunger evident in each of their features cloaked in darkness, in every prying eye.

The reign of humans and pure magic was ending.

They would take this world, together, a broken court long reunited. It was their time. Their war would rewrite history and ensure one bathed in blood. The time for dreamers was over.

A low chuckle resonated behind them as they sank low to their knees, and their king hissed in pleasure. Looking around at his new army, he whispered, "Find them. And destroy them all. But keep the girl for me."

Hisses and whispers broke out around them all as the Oilean watched their king bend his hands, a crown of blackened thorns and roses emerging from the smoke. Lifting it, he placed it on his brow.

"The new age of this world has begun. I am depending on you not to fail this time."

The sisters bowed lower, their anger and bloodlust sparking. They would find the warriors. The queen. And the shifter. They *would* not fail their king. Not this time.

They turned their backs, disappearing into the night, to begin their hunt.

ACKNOWLEDGEMENTS

Publishing a book takes a village, and I am lucky to have such wonderful and passionate people in my life that, without them, the new editions of the Black Dawn series wouldn't have been a possibility.

First, to all my family. Thank you for your endless support and enthusiasm as I pursue my passion for writing; Mom, Nate, Dad this one is for you. Mom, Matt, and Jess a special thank you for reading all the initial versions of this series, I can't put into words how much it means to me.

Thank you to my readers for cheering me on and following Emory's story as I got the new editions out- your endless support means the world to me.

To Emerald and Rae, thank you for being THE BEST editors a girl could ask for. Your support and suggestions brought Queen to Ashes to the story it is now, and your enthusiasm for the world of Kiero literally is a dream come true.

To Jaime, thank you for only being an email away; you are an amazing publicist and confidant.

To Matt, you are my rock, and you pushed me to see the potential in myself when I refused to look. Especially this year; battling Lyme disease was my personal demon and you helped me get stronger each day. You are my best friend and an amazing husband. Writing sometimes takes an author into the over caffeinated, binge watching *The Office* non-stop, sleep deprived stage, and thanks for always taking me to Starbucks when the opportunity calls.

Lastly to Link, Leonard and Lola, thanks for being the best dachshunds in the world, and even though you can't read this, thanks for all the snuggles as I go through the many stages of drafting a novel.

ABOUT THE AUTHOR

© Tiny Islands Photography

Mallory McCartney currently lives in Sarnia, Ontario with her husband and their three dachshunds: Link, Lola, and Leonard. When she isn't working on her next novel or reading, she can be found daydreaming about fantasy worlds and hiking. Other favorite pastimes involve reorganizing perpetually overflowing bookshelves and seeking out new coffee and dessert shops.

Follow her on Instagram @authormalmccartney

CPSIA information can be obtained
at www.ICGtesting.com
Printed in the USA
LVHW010932261022
731609LV00002B/149